Foreign Exchange

SCEPTRE

Foreign Exchange

MONIQUE CHARLESWORTH

SCEPTRE

First published in Great Britain in 1995 by Hodder and Stoughton
A division of Hodder Headline PLC

A Sceptre hardback

10 9 8 7 6 5 4 3 2 1

British Library Cataloguing in Publication Data

Charlesworth, Monique
Foreign Exchange
I. Title
823.914 [F]

ISBN 0-340-61365-3

Typeset by Hewer Text Composition Services, Edinburgh
Printed and bound in Great Britain by
Mackays of Chatham Plc, Chatham, Kent

Hodder and Stoughton
A division of Hodder Headline PLC
338 Euston Road
London NW1 3BH

For Lorie Charlesworth

∫

Summer

Hilary Lennox found himself staring gloomily up at two tonsures, a double crown and one greying middle parting. The occupants of the single aisle seats were reflected in the long strip of overhead mirror which snaked down the Train Grande Vitesse that was taking him all too speedily towards the Loire.

By tilting his head right back, he was presented with a long-chinned pixie version of his own face, a fall of middling brown hair over eyes so dark they were almost black, a bumpy nose. He thought of himself as a bit on the thin side. Was he attractive? Was not knowing one of his charms?

The view on the other side was worse. In the four-seat part slouched a spotty French lad about his own age, who was hunched over his GameBoy, poke-poke-poking at the controls. Opposite him, legs firmly clamped apart, sat his dear old mum. She was a small fat person who had been knitting a pink thing ever since they left the Gare de Montparnasse. At the end of every row she did a little grimace which made the hairy wart on her cheek waggle. This was her way of propelling her large rainbow-striped glasses that crucial millimetre back up her snout to the ridge where they felt really comfy.

Because he could not stand to see her do it one more time, he looked out of the window, where the waggle and specs reappeared in spectral reflection. Spot-face kept his head down, but every now and then he'd splay his fingers and blindly feel over for the raffia bag which lay on the table and burrow in until he found a bag of corn snacks or sweets or some other spot-inducer and slowly rustle out the contents.

Meanwhile in his corner seat, Father slept on. His way of coping and very understandable too. He was a repressed little man with wire-rims falling off and sad furrows down his cheeks, his wedding ring embedded in his finger. And this tribe of pokers and clackers probably represented a typical French family. The Beauregards would be like this. Except, since they were country folk, they would be less sophisticated. Ha. Hilary was struck by the unfairness of it.

There he was, seventeen going on eighteen with exams behind him and the prospect of a year away ahead, a great biker's jacket and a personal self-improvement programme. There was no point being too specific with the whole gleaming universe of opportunities and choices right ahead, but his aims included some sketchy thoughts about tennis and a few to do with reading matter. Mostly, he was concentrating on how he would set about getting his leg over as many girls as possible.

It seemed impossible to Hilary that a day would come when he neither woke nor fell asleep thinking about sex. Age would unsex him, as it had his parents and his friends' parents. Meanwhile, it didn't even take girls to arouse him – anything, from the touch of certain fabrics to the shiny smooth polished surface of things could do the trick. Surprising, really, that he ever managed to give his attention to anything else.

So what was he doing spending two weeks with some acned Frog? His mother had pulled rank on him. Amanda had announced that he would go and had refused to be precise about why. Mostly, she had cried. Hilary couldn't refuse her anything when she cried. She did this as if it didn't count or matter at all, when the reverse was true. It was apologetic, that was the funny thing, that something could happen and be life and death stuff, enough to turn the world's least weepy woman into a running tap yet she treated it as a little ongoing embarrassment. It was so strange and potentially catastrophic that his thoughts wouldn't stick, they preferred to veer off to some safer topic.

For what his mother usually fixed up was girls. These were always truly terrible girls, the lumpen daughters of her contemporaries. Even in middle age, even though seriously bleached and caked with make-up and ultra tweaked, these women weren't dogs. How come so many of their daughters had drawn the short straw?

This time, Amanda had announced that she had fixed up 'something special' for the summer. He'd made his dubious face, wiggled his jaw.

'If it's a May ball, forget it. I've been fixed up before. You tell your girl friends I'm out of the country or dead or something.'

'Oh, darling, there's no girl involved here,' she'd said, fiddling with the coffee machine. 'It's a really wonderful opportunity. A foreign exchange for you, in France, two weeks with a really marvellous French family.'

'Bloody hell – you're kidding.'

Tight-lipped, Amanda had risen and carried the milk jug to the fridge, closed the door with that slight excess of pressure which meant real annoyance and returned bearing the coffee pot and two cups. Silently, she'd shoved one over at him.

'I don't like that language, Hilary. I'm trying to arrange something, well, rather special and I think you should listen first, hear what it's all about and then you're in a position to decide.' She'd begun to pace from the window to the door. 'Look. Here's a free, all expenses paid trip to France for two weeks, which'll do wonders for your French, darling. Then you host the return visit for this young man – well, of course I'll do most of that. And that's it, simple.'

'But I'm nearly eighteen. Kids do these foreign exchanges. I've just given up French, haven't I? So what's the point? It's just stupid.'

'I want you to do this.'

'Look, don't think I don't appreciate – look, Mum, it's just not on. I don't want to. I'm sorry, but it's no.'

She'd stood still then and stared out of the window. Then she'd drawn one of those bad-news, deep shuddering breaths.

'Mum?' No reply.

'You said I'd get a whole year off if I got into university, right, and I worked my arse – very hard, and, look, this is my year. I'm too old. Come on, you know it's a silly idea. OK?' It was his reasonable voice. He'd come up close and put his arm round her, had given her a hug.

'Huh, huh, uh, Hilary.' There'd come another of those breaths, only worse, and she'd turned her face away and she was crying. She'd shaken her head at him and motioned to him to go away and then she had remained quite still while tears flowed out and rolled down her face. He'd held onto her, waiting for her to find the words to reassure him. But she'd been unable to say anything at all. Crying, like a mad thing. What the hell was going on? There was nothing you could do. It wasn't the first time, either.

The time before, it had happened like this: Hilary had come into the sitting room and found his mother sitting on the sofa crying, quite silently, without moving a muscle, while beside her his dad turned the pages of the evening paper. Hilary had half turned to do the sensible thing, which was to push off, but then he couldn't. He had come to kneel beside her. He had fished a tissue out of his pocket. Carefully, he had tried to dry her face. That had made her cry more than ever and given her the impetus to go out of the room with his arm round her. His dad read on, had not looked up once, while he was leading his mum away. Not once, he'd not looked once.

The green clear land flowed by, a gentle seesaw of lush fields with small copses, embankments succeeded by picture-postcard farms, all nicely wooded and cultivated. The gardens of la belle France. Madame continued to knit. At the end of the compartment, the door slid open and the inspector appeared.

He progressed towards them pursuing his calling with slow dignity. 'Tickets, Messieurs, Dames.'

Hilary's multiply-perforated computer-generated slip of a ticket was appraised and returned. He was travelling in the période bleue. How appropriate. Madame put down her knitting. A killing look was flung at the inspector who forced her to pause, to plunge deep in the raffia bag and find her ticket. She fumbled and sighed and dawdled about it. It got right up the inspector's nose.

You could see that he was a careful man, it was in the way he spoke, polite and precise. No breath of impatience ruffled his calm face. His uniform was pressed, the red enamelled badge shiny on the peaked hat, a careful tiny mend in the special oversized pocket for the notebook of authority. He took his time scrutinising the ticket and its accompanying reservations bit.

Did Madame have the special rail traveller's certificate of the troisième âge which had enabled her to buy her ticket?

Voilà, Monsieur.

He looked at it with his special hot brown inspector's eyes, which had seen it all before. Madame's certificate was out of date. He would regrettably have to tear it in half – for it is no longer valable, Madame. Politely, he returned the two halves to her. Next he whipped out his book and ran his manicured inspector's finger down its index, flicking through and then taking out his pen. Not for him the chewed stub of pencil behind the ear. The inspectors of the Société Nationale des Chemins de fer Français had proper pens. He made her wait a good long time.

The inspector rolled his beautiful pen through his fingers and proceeded to fill in a form rapidly, but pleasantly enough, finally tearing it off, handing it to her and requesting the sum of two hundred and forty francs – that being the difference, Madame. Between the ticket purchased with the invalid certificate and the full price. For the three of them.

Spot-face paused in his game. Hilary thought, but no doubt he was imagining it, that Papa in his corner paused an instant in his stentorian breathing, to shut his eyes tighter still.

Madame appealed with a shrug of her hands to the denim-clad young Chinese mother whose little boy sat on her lap to be fed continually. The young mother busied herself opening another Coke. The man beyond with the mustard coloured shirt and matching socks, whose vast feet jiggled incessantly to the sound of his Walkman, heard and saw nothing. With heaving bosom, Madame appealed to the inspector in the name of reason, of sense. If she had known that the ticket was not valid, she would of course have replaced it. It had been valid on the aller journey to Paris three days ago and was not now upon the retour. Quel malheur. And so on. She would not have made the trip to Paris – no, she would not have dreamt of going to visit her sister-in-law, frail and dying though she was, had she known. She was on a mission of mercy. Her fingers meanwhile clutched the brown leather purse very tight.

Ah. There was a long pause. The inspector drew breath. Was Madame refusing to pay the sum due?

She snapped her mouth shut and the purse open and counted out the notes in various thousands and millions, as the older generation was wont to do, which aptly illustrated what, in her eyes, the cash represented. Hilary continued his inspection of the gardens of France. The inspector counted the notes and nodded and then went about his business with just the faintest air of a twinkle about him and Madame knitted on at excitable double speed and Hilary sighed for pure pleasure. So. Being young, abroad, being alive was not so rough and this little aperçu sustained him all the way onto the platform at Saint Pierre des Corps and across the platform to the waiting navette, the little silver shuttle that took a couple of minutes to run passengers over to Tours.

The train chugged to a halt in an old-fashioned arching terminus of a station with a seventies interior. He got off the train behind two brown-legged American girls in shorts with rucksacks and allowed their handsome, Identikit knees to carry him to the exit. So where was the French lad? God, that must be him, a weedy-looking boy with his mummy. Hilary walked up, extended his hand. Toujours la politesse.

'Bonjour, Madame Beauregard. I'm Hilary,' he said.

The boy made a strange face and backed off. 'Eh, alors?' he said, pulling out his lower lip into a rubbery ape face.

'OK, OK, sorry.'

So it wasn't him, the goon-faced twit of anoinkhead. Hilary looked around. There, standing under the huge archway, was one of the most gorgeous girls he had ever clapped eyes on, a beauty perhaps his own age with a long shining fall of silky hair, cut off jeans and a sexy little T-shirt. She was standing talking to someone in an old Peugeot and now turned, slipped a pair of sunglasses over blue, blue eyes and came towards him. He stared like an idiot.

The Peugeot slammed at full speed into reverse, shunted back into a parking space and stopped and a large middle-aged man got out. He was the ageing hippie type with longish hair and jeans and a pugilist's nose. Hilary's head swivelled to watch this lovely creature enter the station with him a dozen steps behind.

Her lover, uncle, father? She was Beauty to his Beast, but they had similar colouring. She was upon him – she passed, inches away. Star quality. He sniffed at something amazingly wonderful and erotic in the perfume line which trailed behind her, which was worth whatever it cost, whatever.

Hilary now understood that it wasn't just the shape which counted, no, there was the incredible texture, the brown all-over colour of the skin, the incredibly fine-textured, faintly blue-veined piece of silk from which the master tailor had cut. The planes that shaded into other ones, lines that intersected with heart-breaking accuracy, geometry worth a lifetime of study. There was a caterpillar scar on her left knee, a round injection mark on one arm, two delicious imperfections that merely underscored the heavenly rightness of the rest of her.

He turned to watch her walk onto the platform. Even the back of her head was something. She was perfect from every angle. She was, quite simply, the most beautiful girl he had ever seen, anywhere, every line of her a poem – no, a bloody ode. She was gone and he closed his eyes, to commit her to memory. For later use.

A couple of minutes later she walked out again and stood no more than a few yards from him, looking up and down the road. The line of taxi drivers in their cream vehicles drawn up outside ogled her openly. One of those saps wolf-whistled, the clown, as if a girl like this would even know blokes like that existed. And where had the hippie gone?

Feasting his eyes, Hilary smiled at her in hope. Her face was impassive behind those sunglasses. He winked. She looked at her watch. He took a step forwards, laid his hand dramatically upon his heart, gave her to understand in sign language that his heart was hers and no mistake. Not for nothing had he done his Malvolio two terms ago at school. There was a tiny movement around the mouth – aha, a twitch. He bowed dramatically and edged a fraction closer. The closer you got, the more flawless she was.

There was the hippie. Over her shoulder, Hilary saw the big man ambling into the Informations kiosk and joining a good long queue. He stood, tapping his feet behind a whole horde of tourists and a dwarf-sized old lady with a very fat pug. Hilary reckoned that he was probably going to be stuck there for ten minutes if not longer. Certainly he was good for five.

Hilary sidled up to the ravishing girl in order to explain how crucial it was that he see her again.

'Bonjour, Mademoiselle,' he said. The explanation of this great need, which all but emptied his small reservoir of French, was because she had dealt him a terrible wound. A biggie. Une grande plaie. Right here. In his heart. He took hold of her hand, just for an instant, to indicate the area of the wound but she pulled it away. It must be a wound, you see, or why would his heart flutter so? Like a thousand butterflies, all beating their little wings. Mille papillotes. He made wings of his arms.

Her lips curved up deliciously. He pressed on. In England if there was a medical or social emergency, then anybody present was expected to help. She, who had dealt the wound, was responsible. What was she going to do about it? She could not refuse help in an emergency of this sort.

'C'est la vie ou la mort,' he said.

She was studying him now over the dark glasses, the smooth brows, as gleaming as the rest of her, arched with gentle irony. She nodded her head gravely.

'Il vous faut un médécin, peut-être?'

No. Yes, anything.

If so, there would not be a problem, she would go and fetch one straightaway, to sort out this poor young man – and now, watching for his reaction, she smiled. Touché – and she laughed. It was a gurgly, real thing, this laugh, with her head thrown back to expose that kissable throat.

This was the moment when Hilary felt his heart break or melt or at any rate do something it never had before, something it never would again. It felt important and irretrievable and final. That wonderful sound.

No, he said, he thought that what he needed was a nurse. Une nourrice. Only a lovely young girl could help him. Oh, she said. When she smiled, one dimple appeared in the right cheek. Things were progressing sweetly and enjoyably and so Hilary, rummaging in his bag for a piece of paper and pen, found the name and the address where he was staying. Carefully, he copied it out. He presented it to her with a flourish. Here, he said, and

I forgot to tell you my name, Hilary Lennox. This gave him an opportunity to shake hands, or rather to capture her hand for a second.

'Hilary is a girl's name,' she said, looking at the paper.

'Girl or boy, it can be either.' He loved the way her eyebrows flew up and down as she read what he had written. Now she took off her sunglasses to inspect him closely. There was a long pause while she looked at him and he stared back, dazzled.

Oh dear, she said, what a pity. As luck would have it, she knew the place and knew the people who lived there. They were not at all nice. So she had a suggestion for him. Why didn't he come and stay at her house? Hilary's face now bore the dazed expression of a small boy, all of whose Christmases have come at once. He was by no means sure that he had understood her properly.

'Chez toi?'

'Yes,' she said, with glorious simplicity. Hilary thought for a bit.

'Me?'

'Yes. Why not?'

'Why not?' Indeed. Rapid thoughts buzzed through Hilary's already intoxicated head. 'You know,' he said, 'these people – well, actually, they're nothing special. I don't know anything about them. I mean – why not?'

She gazed at him quizzically, waiting for him to make up his mind.

The hippie approached, explaining to the world that the navette was unmissable for une personne alighting at Saint-Pierre des Corps. The guard on the platform would have directed her to it. It was, however, always possible for a person to have dozed off, not to have got out at all, since the TGV only halted its restless flight for two minutes precisely – zoom – and his hand took off along an imaginary runway.

'Papa,' the beauty interrupted, laying her hand upon the hippie's arm. 'I think you must meet this new friend of mine whom I have invited to stay. He is English. Isn't that delightful? Papa is wanting that I must speak better. You were saying again today, weren't you, how important it is for me to improve my English?'

Hilary shuffled his feet in fascinated embarrassment and

watched Papa's face, which certainly was a study as he took in this outrageous piece of news. His eyes closed in a pained expression, opened again and looked Hilary up and down in a way which suggested he was not impressed. Then the big man shrugged his shoulders as if to say, what can we do against this sort of thing? Yes, what?

He beckoned. Hilary smiled a touch nervously. Papa drew him over to one side, put his gorilla's arm round him in a slightly alarming way and leant to whisper in his ear. 'Au revoir,' he said. The centime dropped. Right, thought Hilary, fair enough and he shuffled back to his bag.

'Wait, Papa, did I not tell you? May I present to you Hilary Lennox?'

There was a long pause, during which Papa did an expressive double-take, twisting his head round and back again and then throwing it back. A great roar came out. He lunged for Hilary, who nervously tried to sidestep him, dodging only to be caught by the daughter. She held his arm. She put those luscious lips next to his ear. Her warm breath was the most delicious thing in the universe. It melted every bone in his body.

'This is my father, Dr Charles Beauregard. And I am Michèle.' Hilary looked at her. She looked at him. Papa caught up with him for a serious handshake cum hug and over his heaving shoulder, Hilary continued to stare at this remarkable girl. When she really smiled, like now, the corners of her mouth curved up in the most – the most deliciously fascinating way and she burst into peals of laughter and a second later, as the full wonder of it struck him, so did Hilary.

There was no Michel nor ever had been. Glory be, she was an only child. For some minutes they babbled Euro-semantics and gender-benders about Hilaire and Hillary and Belloc and Clintons and Michels with and without an e and Hilary explained that his mother was very bad at distinguishing between the masculine and the feminine.

'Aha,' Charles said. 'Is she? That surprises me, I would not have thought so,' and everybody laughed. Hilary was laughing like an idiot at anything anybody said – he was so high that there had to be some release. As they all got into the car, Hilary could not help noticing that the delicious Michèle did not stop looking at him. As he looked at her. He repressed the urge to bray with pleasure.

Charles drove just as Frenchmen were said to, using the stop-go method. Bursts of speed alternated with screechings of brakes, the whole accompanied with gesticulations and comments flung freely from the car. He lit the first of many Gitanes, driving with one arm hanging out of the window so it was available for the kind of Gallic insult that demanded the upraised, phallic clenched fist. He smoked continuously, eyes narrowed against the smoke.

'OK, Hilary, what did your maman say about me? Did she tell you much?'

'Hardly anything,' he said. Sitting in the back, with his gaze fixed on the back of Michèle's head, he saw against that halo the handsome façades lining the Boulevard Heurteloup which they passed with surprising speed for such an old vehicle, before hurtling up a ramp improbably signposted both 'BORDEAUX' and 'PARIS' and onto the motorway. The idea that he hadn't wanted to come was a distant dream. Mothers were always right.

'She said I'd have a wonderful time and she was right.'

'Come on, what else she say? You know, she is an extraordinary woman, yes, yes, very, very special.'

'She's great, yes,' he said, seeing in the driving mirror Charles's inquisitive eye fixed upon him when it very definitely needed to spare the odd glance at that lorry just ahead which they now pulled out to pass with inches to spare. Hilary's own gaze could not stop wandering back every couple of seconds to feast upon Michèle. Her long hair hung down to just a couple of inches above his knees, which would have been eternally and achingly grateful to be swept, just once, by that fringe. Her smooth brown shoulder, which he could have reached out and touched, shimmered just a few inches away.

'OK, OK,' said Charles. 'You can tell me after.'

When they left the motorway and drove past a large pond, the road came out in a long sinuous roll of cornfields. The ears of grain were exactly the same ripe yellow as Michèle's hair. Charles pointed out the landmarks, two ancient walled farms dating back to who-knew-when, slowing down and swerving slightly. Down that way you could just see the beginnings of the park of the local château inhabited by the Count of something or other, very spry for his age, the place was littered with his middle-aged bastards, all manfully striving to keep up the family tradition. Le tout countryside sported the worthy nobleman's distinctively pointed and cleft chin.

And this way was the house of the notaire, a pretty seventeenth-century moated house, most unusual – the poor man had had a terrible growth here, just here, and Charles pointed at his shoulder, half turning round dangerously while Michèle also turned, laughing, for Papa knew everybody for miles. Hilary saw at this funny three-quarter angle how amazingly similar they actually were, in terms of cheekbones and colouring, as similar as two people could be when one was gorgeous and the other pretty worn out – and he yelped and pointed as a tractor loomed up between the two similar heads.

Charles veered away and they stopped, just in time. Perfectly unfazed, Charles leapt out of the car, lit another fag and went to chat to the rustic perched high on the machine. They launched into a discussion about whatever incomprehensible thing it did, complicated by the equally incomprehensible thing the disease of some mutual acquaintance was doing.

Listening to the rise and fall of their voices, Hilary seized the chance to lean forwards in the gap between the front seats, thus coming within two inches of Michèle. He allowed his senses to frolic, to revel in the smell of her. That skin, that perfume. Dizzy with desire, he saw the old bloke jump down into the road. Charles was examining his machine. Now – and anyone who had spent even a few minutes in a car with Charles would have known that this could not be a good idea – he was climbing up into the seat. He sat in a commanding pose. The engine throbbed. He fiddled with levers and switches. The old bloke was bent double with laughter when the big man couldn't get it into gear, then unexpectedly drove the tractor backwards at speed. He was still guffawing as they once more drove off, swivelling his head to keep his weeny bull elephant's eye on target for an eyeful of Michèle.

The house, ten minutes further on, was a handsome manor house on top of a hill, with cornfields undulating right up to it. They bumped through the corn down a track which led off from the main road. Over to the left Hilary spotted a monument historique announcing itself. A rather impressive-looking old ruined château. There was just a glimpse of this as the Peugeot hoppety-bumped at speed over tractor ruts and then through some gates and past an orchard so it wasn't until they had actually driven round the building that Hilary saw that what he had taken for the front was the back.

The house had a formal entrance here, a big flight of steps sweeping up in wings from the long garden with its beech-shaded drive. It had been built on the crest of the hill with a commanding view of the village which lay at the bottom in a snaking cluster of red-roofed houses. The whole business was as pretty as a picture.

Standing very upright on the flight of stone steps and thus dominating the whole shebang was a beautiful woman in a white silk frock whose face, as Hilary neared, expressed an almost comic disbelief. As he shook hands with Louise Beauregard, Charles and she launched into a very rapid exchange to do with his being un garçon and Hilary wondered for one intoxicating moment whether he might have been going to share a room with Michèle and was there any hope of this substantial house being equipped with only two bedrooms, or of the other rooms being suddenly struck by rot or damp or deathwatch beetle. While the vision this offered danced through his head, he studied his beloved's mother. If you were interested in the daughter, you should always look at the mother.

There was a lot to consider. She was quite tall and had an older version of Michèle's beautiful face and a lot of dark hair which was pulled back into a chignon which exposed the nape of her neck and her small ears, all of which were very nice indeed. The rocks in those ears looked pretty substantial to Hilary. Certainly, his mother didn't have anything like that, nor the fancy enamelled pendant watch nor the three or four jangling bracelets, all of which seemed real enough. Nor, of course, had he ever seen his mother wearing what he took to be an evening dress in the day time or standing at the front door to greet people in this regal and, let's face it, pretentious fashion.

Louise paused for a moment in her discussion with Charles and stared at Hilary who now expressed his hypocritical regrets at being a boy. There was quite a lot of 'Quelle difficulté, je regrette' and a lot more of 'Pardonnez-moi, madame' before she calmed down a bit which gave Hilary time to look from Madame to Michèle and take in how brilliantly terrific it was to be a boy in this particular corner of the world. There were a good ten minutes of this while Hilary hung about the steps with his bag at his feet while Louise went into the house, came out again, stopped having a go at Charles and started instead having a go at Michèle for not being more hospitable.

'You poor boy,' Louise said, 'You must let me show you the house,' as though he'd been forcibly stopping her from doing that. She swept him in and, silk skirt swishing, rushed round the house in a voluble whirlwind tour. Hilary was encouraged to shake little fingers with a greasy-pawed Madame Moulins on her knees in the pantry. Various bottles of home-preserved fruits were pointed out to him. He was led to inspect the salon and dining room and even the surgery with carved wooden whatsits on the panelling before being led up an elaborately painted trompe-l'oeil staircase and through various bedrooms and bathrooms. Louise, always two dancing steps ahead, threw open cupboards to reveal piles of linen and towels and cloth whatsits. Hilary couldn't have cared less for the whereabouts of the sheets and bolsters and drawn-thread work antimacassars, any more than he cared about the confit de canard or the preserves. Hilary was fully occupied examining Michèle. The French girl smiled very sweetly at him and he smiled back.

Finally they reached the guest room, conveniently adjoining Michèle's, where Hilary and his bag were deposited and where the sight of various feminine items such as bowls of potpourri and cotton-wool-ball-type stuff all laid out sent Louise Beauregard off downstairs to do a reprise of the whole boy-girl thing with her husband. Hilary did wonder then as he lay on the bed and stared at the ceiling (this, like the walls and even the chest of drawers, was completely covered in flowery paper) whether Louise wasn't perhaps a teeny bit off her trolley.

Amanda Lennox would never have shown anyone round her house – people his age were expected to find their own way around without fuss. Nor did she seek approval for her kitchen stuff, though she was as keen as anyone on that department. Hilary hung his feet over the end of the bedstead which had been designed for a French midget and had a bit of a think about this whole exchange business. It was deeply unlikely that his highly organised mother could have failed to work out that the Beauregards had a daughter and not a son at all and, indeed, vice versa. He only had time to decide that it was probably Charles Beauregard who was to be blamed, or rather thanked, when a knocking on the door woke him and it was dinner time.

Various things became clear at the dinner table. Louise Beauregard was no slouch in the cooking department. One course succeeded another, not to mention one clean plate after another and a bewildering assortment of glasses, doo-dahs, knife rests and such like.

'Things are very simple here,' Louise said. 'We will have just a little pasta to start, then a little meat and a little salad and perhaps a sliver of cheese. That is it.' And she shrugged, self-deprecatingly. The pasta was homemade and meltingly delicious with olive oil and wild mushrooms and pungent scraps of rubber – these turned out to be scrapings from a simple bit of fresh truffle from the forests here. The fillet turned up, seared on the outside, tender pink inside. Cheese meant a goat's cheese, simply rolled in volcanic ash, a sheep's milk one and then of course the ordinary buffalo milk jobbie, not to mention the simple unpasteurised brie that kept rolling off its corner and oozing onto Hilary's plate.

Hilary wondered as he drained his glass for the fourth time whether they would eat (and indeed drink) like this every night. French people were very different, clearly capable of no end of good living. Then there was the way they dressed up. Louise's white silk number revealed its everyday status compared to the little black job she was now sporting. Michèle had also changed into a simple silk shift thing which didn't seem to leave much leeway for underwear anywhere. This supposition had forced him to undertake a detailed albeit surreptitious inspection.

The phone rang and it wasn't a patient as Louise feared, but Hilary's maman. He stood waiting for the phone as Louise spoke volubly of her surprise and so on and smiled at him meanwhile, to show that she was perfectly reconciled to, if not thrilled by, the whole thing. Hilary could imagine his mother in the sitting room at the other end, struggling to understand the flow of words.

'Darling,' Amanda said. 'Good grief.'

'Mum, yes, it's great, you see she's just pointing out that I'm a boy. And guess what. Michèle is an elle – is a girl.' And what a girl she was, he could see her gorgeous long legs crossing under the dining table through the double doors at this very moment. Oh, girl.

'Oh, darling, silly me. You're not disappointed, I hope, it's not going to spoil your stay? Charles found you all right, though, all the same. How is he, darling? Shall I have a quick word? Shall I? Hilary?'

He was still laughing at the idea of the disappointment he might be suffering. 'No, yes, God no, it's fabulous, Mum. Look, I don't think he can talk right now, we're eating. I don't want to be rude to Louise. Call you soon, OK, Mum. Give my love to Dad – byee.'

Back at the table, he saw that Charles was stroking Louise's hand appreciatively. All through the meal husband and wife had discussed the food and where it had been bought and how it had been cooked in immense detail. Appreciation was due, was offered and received in a way Hilary couldn't imagine at home. Also the pair of them lit up every other minute. This was equally unimaginable in the Lennox household, where Nicholas permitted himself a cigar only on such festive occasions as his birthday and Christmas.

Charles, fag in mouth, went to make the coffee and offered a Gitane to Hilary, who puffed and coughed unenthusiastically. Through a blue haze he looked from the gorgeous girl to her parents and wondered why his mother hadn't told him what they were like. How was it possible that she hadn't known about Michèle? Because the more he thought about it, the more unlike her it was and he leant forwards then and caught Charles Beauregard's eye.

'When did you arrange it, for me to come here?' he asked.

'On s'est rencontré à Pâques,' he said. 'Oh, quite by chance.'

Easter

Amanda Lennox stood at the top of the black run, facing down the steep gully. The day was overcast and chilly. Yesterday's mush had frozen. A young man skied past and she watched him begin to skid. His arms jerked up as he tried to save himself. He was halfway down before he came to a spraying halt, almost bent double with the urgency of stopping on the sheer ice before he cannoned off the edge. Slowly, he straightened up and then slid again, toppling over backwards with windmill arms. When at last he regained his footing, he stood for a long time at the edge of the piste and looked down the steep and treacherous way.

Her husband came up beside her, glancing her way and half waving. She opened her mouth to speak, but Nicholas carried on. She watched him go down in his usual manner, not so much stylish as capable. Down he went, slow and steady. At the very bottom, he stopped and looked up at her and then he beckoned. He did it again, then a third time. He put his hands to his eyes, staring up at her. Surely he knew that she was terrified.

Amanda remained where she was, the whole of her body trembling. She was tempted to break into loud, hysterical laughter, but a couple came past so she watched their careful descent instead. Their skis scraped loudly on the ice and they shouted encouragingly to each other, they waited and pointed out good places to turn. These sounds reverberated up, amplified by a funnel effect. She had come to a point where there was no option but to continue. Far away down below, Nicholas waved again. She leant on the sticks and watched them all down, safe. Again, Nicholas beckoned. No option, she said to herself. She had come to a certain point. But she could not go on. Behind her, unreachable, the chair lift swayed its way to the summit carrying its pairs of skiers, two by two, and then came floating back through the sky, empty. Away up beyond, the Matterhorn rose up to challenge the sky.

She took a deep breath and pushed off, without hope. At once her skis slithered unstoppably down the narrow path and she tried to control the urge just to sit down, to give up. Little stones in the ice, freezing air, her body refused to face forwards.

She was leaning back, the skis getting faster, out of control. She began to fall, awkwardly, full of self-loathing, arms flailing. As she fell, she screamed silently.

There would be bruises all along her thighs. Shaken, winded, only slightly hurt, she lay for a long time on the ice, invisible to those below and, more dangerously, to those above. Her teeth chattered. Her nose was runny. Eventually, after a struggle, she extricated a tissue from the recesses of the stupid salopettes. It came away black and damp from mascara and tears. What would happen if she never came down? She stared at the brownish patches where the hill was struggling to break through.

A stranger stopped. Was she OK? Kind eyes, a helping hand. Amanda smiled for him and began to get up again and there was her husband still watching, the beckoning hand angry now.

'Nichts kaputt,' she said. But it wasn't true. As she rose up, the slope seemed so terrifyingly steep that it made her heart lurch. The world wheeled about in front of her and then shuddered to a halt. A moment of pure fear. Some kind of separation from this was imperative. She was not going down. Never, he couldn't make her. In sudden exaltation she released herself from the struggle. She stepped through a door and slammed it shut and locked away all the misery behind it.

And so the whole slithering cowardly descent was carried out in tearful haste by somebody else. Nicholas's wife underwent the ignominy of a second fall, of sliding right off the path and having to scrabble, hot-faced and shivering, for a lost ski. Amanda remained standing where she had fallen and risen again. She watched the poor wife tumbling down, seeing before her, clearer than ever before, the dangerous consequences of a lack of nerve. She skied that slope in her head as she would have done if she had had the luxury of being alone. She was elegant and she was fast. Singing in her head were the words alone and free – alone and free.

By the time wife, chilled and stained, caught up with him, Nicholas was chatting to another bloke, an Englishman they'd bumped into in the restaurant at the top. 'You took your time,' he called out to her, all jovial and hail-fellow-well-met. 'Wasn't that fun?'

With a wave of the hand, unable to reply, she skied past,

digging the sticks in and spurring herself along. He turned and followed and soon caught up and passed little wife in the make-believe jolly race. Wife averted her blotchy, ugly face. When he was ahead, Amanda skied elegantly. As they went down to the valley she felt, for the first time in years, some of the joy that skiing had once given her, that sweetness of propelling yourself forwards wherever you might choose to go.

'Jourbon Ellrigab, va ça?' said Nicholas. Bonjour Gabrielle, that meant. 'Amanda taught me how to ski, you know,' he said, leaning against the little bar in the hotel and talking a little too loud as he always did after a few drinks. Twinkly-charming and ogling the handsome French barmaid. He often chatted up women in her presence, just as he always mentioned his wife in those conversations. She knew that he never looked at a woman except when with her. She knew that he didn't actually fancy other women. Unlike most men, he did like them. The barmaid had been telling them all about backwards language, which she spoke with incredible fluency and speed and which Amanda was completely unable to grasp. Nicholas, who wouldn't speak normal French, with characteristic perversity had cottoned on to this.

'He's such a quick learner,' said wife in her schoolgirl French and Gabrielle swiftly replied with some kind of barmaid's heavy double entendre that she could well believe that. The three of them laughed, Nicholas throwing back his head and roaring with his face rosy and full of pleasure. Such pretend intimacy delighted him. 'He's better than me – at skiing, I mean,' she said. Nicholas haw-hawed. Gabrielle looked at him as she turned away, looked at her too. Don't you dare judge me, she thought fiercely.

If he was in a good mood, dinner would go well and she could think her own thoughts. There was the whole evening to be got through before she could lie awake and think. She had travelled light years already, had got through the lawyers and the divorce courts and custody of the children and become a free woman just while soaking in the bath. Poor wife, a mass of bruises and bumps. Amanda was already so very distant from her. She relished her new capacity to laugh at the absurdity of it all. Her situation, as his wife, was so strange. She was tempted to go back, to touch Gabrielle's shoulder as that solid creature polished the glasses, to say, 'It's not how it seems. Really.'

The minestrone was good, better for being cooked by somebody else. Wife said as much, nicely, and buttered her roll and smiled and meanwhile Amanda thought with astonishment what an elaborately structured life had evolved over the years without her having exactly chosen any of it. She rolled it back in her head, as Gabrielle did her sentences, and found no sense in it. She had given up her career as a doctor and had children instead, and Nicholas had become the successful surgeon she had always wanted to be. Yet in return for very menial tasks, housekeeping and cooking and childcare, she was rewarded with very high pay. Unthinkable that wife might give in her notice when this barter system provided expensive holidays and good clothes and a half share in a house envied by those who did not have to clean it. There would never be cash for her to spend, without asking, and sexual intercourse was on demand for him but not for her. On the other hand, there were the two children, much loved. There were plays and outings and cultural events, but also a dull series of conventional evenings with people just like them, for whom she was expected to cook with gourmet flair. There was the occasional company of Nicholas, that solid husband, that brainbox, who had competed for her, who had been her chosen one. They spent perhaps five or six days a year alone together. For a further three weeks they might be ostensibly in the same place but never sharing it. Nicholas always ran ahead, one way or another.

He raised his glass to her across the candlelight, pleased with her. 'Are you happy, darling?' he said. 'I so much want you to enjoy this.'

'You know I am,' said his wife quickly, gulping a little, for kindness was hard to bear when it seemed genuine. Amanda wasn't having that. She swigged down some wine and let it rise to her head a little. Stupidly, she had often bemoaned the extent to which her husband lived in his head, unconscious of other people. So many nights when he sat to think and she had resented it. Wife was such a fool. And now, unable to think of a single remark she could conceivably address to him, Amanda understood the urgent necessity to be left alone with one's thoughts.

Leaving Zermatt had always been hard, but this time the journey down could not depress Amanda. The prospect of freedom made her light-hearted. Secret knowledge transformed the world. All the way to Zurich she stared at the lovely scenery and watched the snows melt away without regret.

She hated flying but even this worst part was now bearable. At the airport, wife did tend to make heavy weather of the skis, huffing and puffing and manoeuvring her trolley. Lightweight stuff, yes, but she found it tricky, like all the jobs that Nicholas allotted to this anxious soul. The skis stuck out, they stabbed at corners and threatened shoulder bags. How hilarious wife was, how absurdly her trolley plunged and heaved across the shiny concourse of Zurich Airport in Nicholas's wake. Amanda found her so easy to impersonate that she had begun to ham a little, to play up that dizzy dame. A parody of a parody, Amanda playing wife.

Nicholas always had his part by heart. He had the heavy suitcases and the money and the tickets and on he surged, all weight and frothing behind. Amanda let wife lag a little, so she wouldn't have to listen to him. His chuntering drove wife bananas, poor thing, but Amanda quite liked the way it showed Nicholas up. It was a kind of long-range extended nutter's mutter which flowed after him, full of expression but incomprehensible. People looked.

Brainbox had evolved a number of little games of his own. Ways of killing time, since he couldn't bear to waste it. Right now he was pursuing his self-appointed task of translating tannoy announcements, all the flight numbers and destinations, into what Amanda rather thought was ancient Greek. That would probably be for the benefit of his imaginary companion, Philip of Macedonia. Occasionally Philip's son Alexander joined them. Not often, though, for Nicholas thought he lacked the statesmanlike qualities, the sheer gravitas, of his less famous dad. Sometimes Nicholas could be heard chortling to himself as he polished a rather risqué bon mot in Latin for the benefit of one of the bawdier and more murderous Roman emperors. That suited Nicholas to a T, to embellish a dead language for some imaginary dead old man. Not just any old man, mind, only despots and prime villains were worthy of the effort. Brainbox never cared what other people thought even if he noticed them, which, being him, he didn't. He didn't look to see if wife was following. He knew she was.

Amanda was trailing slightly behind as she turned the corner and wondering if she could let wife lose her balance altogether, just by removing the hand which was stopping the skis from rolling. Tempting though this was, she decided against it. Wife was so vulnerable and she did not want Amanda's exaltation to be spoilt by wife's tears. One of the strange things that still happened was the kindness of Brainbox, which could come quite unexpectedly just when his usual irritation was expected. His gentleness, so characteristic of the old, unformed Nicholas she had married, just broke her down. Wife had wept in many public places recently, too many. Fortunately, Nicholas had decided not to notice or, if he did, not to care. He could be in the same room and could even sit beside his wife on the sofa while tears flowed unstoppably down her cheeks and carry on reading the paper. Perhaps he had loved her once, but he had not kept faith. Instead, he had encouraged her to play the wifely part without ever defining terms and conditions. To behave as though everything was in order when, being so intelligent, he surely knew better, this was a grave fault.

Something caught her eye. Just ahead of her walked a big, shaggy looking man, walking arm in arm with a woman. He looked very familiar. Her heart gave one huge thump, then carried on at double speed while her brain relayed the rational message that of course it couldn't be him. But her internal organs set up a bowel-twisting little dance. The man who couldn't be Charles glanced sideways at the newspaper stand, then veered over to it. Her stomach churned. It was him. She stopped dead.

On went Nicholas in full polyglottal flow, expecting wife to be present and willing as she always was. Amanda was immobilised, watching Charles Beauregard. Twenty years since she saw him last. There was a huge lump in her chest of misery and longing. Breathe, go on. She forced out an exhalation. Better. A sharp pang of need and desire sprang into the air, it crackled live and electric across the space.

He stopped dead, as if stung. Dear God, he knew. He turned to look, saw her, said something to the woman and came towards her. He shimmered across the waxen floor, a glorious mirage. As he took her hand, he examined her face very carefully. In those few seconds before anything was said, she received a simple but important message. Whatever she felt, he felt too.

The woman's high heels tapped over to where Amanda and Charles stood quite still, staring at each other.

'Amanda, how wonderful this is. May I present you Louise,' said Charles. 'My wife.'

His accent was just as strong as ever. He remained holding her hand and she had to retrieve it to shake hands with the elegant woman he had married. This person said 'Enchantée' and Amanda replied 'Bonjour, Madame' and could not help noticing how exceptionally well turned out and attractive his wife was. She was conscious of being observed in return. Jourbon Damma. The backwards language flowed.

Inside her shoes, Amanda's toes curled with the urgent need to exchange essential information. Yes, she had married that man, the one from then, whose name was Nicholas, who was over there somewhere, ha ha. They had children, yes.

'Deux enfants,' she said. Hilary was seventeen and the little one, Edward, nine. Her French was dreadful, his English worse. Stubbornly each strove to speak the other's language. She wanted to explain that the poverty of these communications was to do with the fact that the woman he was seeing now was not the real her. Inside wife with her nervous smile was the real Amanda, who was repressing the urge to lie down with him there and then. Any surface would do, the airport floor would be fine, if necessary. Or, there again, why lie down? Incredible that for so many years she had forgotten how it felt, to feel desire for a man. Her heart pounded painfully.

'My Michel is nearly seventeen,' he said. 'They like each other, les jeunes.'

'Oh yes. Oui, I'm sure. Young people do,' she said inanely.

The elegant wife was plucking at his arm, their flight was being called and Amanda realised that something had to happen. She couldn't possibly stand never to see Charles again, no, she very possibly couldn't stand to watch him walk away without lifting up her head and howling her loss and regret like a wolf. She had a vision of herself lying rigid and resentful alongside the skis on the trolley, being pushed away by Nicholas.

'Look, Amanda, I tell you this,' Charles spoke with great meaning. 'You send your Hilary to visit us, then we come visit you,' he said. 'Young people, they do it. Always. They like each other. You like it? We do this definite, yes?'

'Yes?' she said, without quite grasping the sense. From the corner of one eye, Amanda saw the swivelling head of Nicholas. Now he was a minesweeper, his manner on ward rounds, his face intent. This was how he searched his roses for greenfly. This gave her a jolt and made the blood flow into her face and concentrated her mind.

'A foreign exchange,' she said, 'Yes, of course, I know just what you mean. How wonderful, we must do it.'

'This summer,' said Charles. 'We do it. Yes. I call you.' He took from his wallet some little cards and pressed them into her hand. 'Write please your number. Address too.'

'Yes,' said Amanda. 'Définitivement, oui. And you will come to England, what a good idea, how lovely, Nicholas will be thrilled. My husband, Nicholas. He is mon mari,' she said smiling at Charles's rather beautiful wife, as though the word husband somehow legitimised the outrageousness of the plan, as though there were any possibility of this woman accepting it. Very carefully, she wrote down her name and address in capital letters. She tucked his second card into her purse.

Charles's wife smiled and nodded back in a very polite way. It became clear that she didn't understand English. Amanda took her hand and shook it with enthusiasm, unable to banish her foolish smile.

Nicholas had seen them and was bobbing his head in recognition and as he got near he inverted the stretch of his mouth into a smile. He was bound to be annoyed. For Nicholas punctuality was, if not the chief of all virtues, certainly one of the braves.

Charles's wife was looking at her watch, tugging at her husband's arm, with all the universal let's-go signals.

'This is Charles Beauregard and his wife, um, Madame Beauregard,' said Amanda, speaking very rapidly. 'Hilary's going to stay with them this summer. It's all fixed up.'

'Why, hello there,' said Nicholas with false bonhomie. Written all over his face was distaste at being pushed into shaking hands with complete strangers. His eyebrows telegraphed astonishment.

'You remember Charles, darling?' Wife put on her brightest tone. 'Of course it's years and years. Before we got married. Charles did six months at Guy's. Mon mari est médécin,' she added for Madame's benefit. She began to feel wildly exhilarated.

'Ah,' said Nicholas. 'Enchanté.' It was by no means clear that he did remember, but Amanda saw that this explanation put a different complexion on things. So, more glossily, did Madame Beauregard. 'Madame, I'm sure I would have remembered you,' he said gallantly.

Madame nodded and smiled. The goodbye handshake went on for a bit longer and he continued to look and smile admiringly as the Frenchwoman led her husband away, just as Amanda watched and absorbed Charles. She committed him to memory. She could hang on, for the summer. Now there was something worth waiting for.

'What was that you said? Amanda. For heaven's sake.' Nicholas shuffled with irritation from one foot to the other.

With deliberate slowness, Amanda put what he always called her scarf thingie on, carefully wrapping the long trailing ends round her neck, securing the whole fragile enterprise with a small knot. Then a bow. She made it all right and tight. As secure as it could ever be. She found that she was still smiling.

'About Hilary? Amanda?'

She gave her full attention to pulling out the ends of the bow.

'What do you think you're doing?'

'Putting on my scarf.'

'Don't be obtuse. Those people, who are they?'

'Look,' she said with a faint edge, drawing from him that and-what-have-I-done-now irritated look. No, she thought. Why should I tell him anything? 'Come on, darling. You know how you hate to be late,' wife said, very nicely, and set off at a good old whack. He came rumbling along behind.

'It'll never work,' he said.

'What?'

'Hilary won't want to go and stay with complete strangers.'

Things tended to come out in a rush and a muddle when she got seriously annoyed. That was why she didn't argue with him any more, because she always managed to defeat herself before the battle started. Amanda drew a deep breath. She wasn't going to argue. She was just going to do what she wanted.

'Amazingly lucky for him,' she said, mildly.

'Amazing,' Nicholas said in his deeply ironic voice, 'is thinking that Hilary will agree.'

'It's arranged.'

'Without asking him?' Nicholas snorted derisively. 'You're very confident. He'll have made his own arrangements by now.'

'Oh no, I don't think so,' said the sweet voice. 'He'll just have to unarrange them. It means I'll be able to concentrate on Edward, before he goes to summer camp, while Hilary's in France. Ed needs attention, you know how wild he is. Oh, and I've invited the parents to stay, when they pick up their son. We'll do a weekend thing, I expect.'

For years she had been setting up such joyless arrangements and he had always accepted that that was what a wife did. It was curious to see how little meaning the words offered compared to her powerful inner sense of what was actually going to happen. She could deceive him because, for a complex man, he was so simple-minded.

Nicholas's brow furrowed in disbelief. They were nearly at the front of the queue. 'What did you want to do that for?' He loathed guests in the house.

'Tickets, darling.' She smiled as nicely as she could at the – what did they call them? – the ground hostess. Nicholas muttered on and she shut her ears to him. Amanda thought that if they had arrived at the airport two minutes sooner, or later, then she would not have seen Charles. The little hairs on the back of her neck felt strangely sensitised by this idea. That she could by such a narrow margin have missed him made her feel dazed with the luck of it, the incredible, extraordinary, wonderful bit of good fortune. She had already determined to change her life. Nothing was going to stop this from happening. She let her mind drift away back to Charles and how he looked and sounded. It was essential to preserve as much as possible for the coming months. Her heart continued to thump madly while she began to think about what it had felt like to be held in his arms, so long ago.

Summer

'We ran into your maman and papa at Zurich Airport,' said Louise. 'We nearly missed our plane.' She'd been impatient, hearing their name echo tinnily through the public address system. *Please proceed immediately to Gate 34. Monsieur and Madame Beauregard. Immediately, please. Your flight is about to depart.*

They'd been the last passengers for the flight, they'd done their usual gallop down the stairs and onto the bus which had ferried them in solitary glory onto the plane for Paris. Familiar though this was from twenty years of being married to the erratic doctor, whose time was not so much kept as heedlessly thrown away, his wife had yet to come to terms with it. Then, when Charles had made casual mention of the foreign exchange, Louise had moaned gently. He knew very well how she hated guests and how nervous they made her. How could he?

'We hardly know these people.'

It had spoilt weeks of the summer, knowing that this was coming up. Having been brought up in a modest household where callers were subjected to intensely formal meals, she always felt that she would have to be on her best behaviour and that her best could never be good enough.

'Oh, I know them very well. English people are not like us. They are very relaxed.'

Charles had said this, or something like it, several more times in the intervening months. 'Her, the wife I know very well. You know it will be pleasant to have another child in the house.' Or, 'It's a big house, they will do whatever they like and you'll see, you'll have less to do, not more.' He'd smile or pat her hand, sounding so considerate, getting his own way. He always did. He had a particular tone of voice which stopped her from arguing.

There was something in him, some force that could not be resisted. She leant forwards and kissed the top of his head, thinking that this was almost the prime characteristic which defined him and it was precisely the factor which made him so very attractive to so many people. The reason, she supposed, for his success.

So. He'd arrived safely. So. Back in England, Amanda sat looking at the phone in the bedroom and waited for her rage to abate. Why had she not strangled her idiot son at birth? Her hands were trembling with annoyance and frustration.

She was staring ahead vacantly. Eventually through the open bathroom door she caught Nicholas's eye; he was well advanced upon his tooth-brushing routine. He liked to gargle with various green liquids and did so pre- and post-brushing. This second gargle would culminate in his singing up and down a scale with the stuff in his mouth and then doing a mega spit, at the end of which he would carefully examine his output for streaks of blood. Recent root canal work had alerted him to the need to preserve that which he had, drilled and filled, but still his. The spit came. The examination was a pass and now he looked at her with a bit of a gleam in his eye, evidently mistaking her interest for, well, interest. Without meeting his eye, Amanda reached for the remote control and flicked on the telly. Motor racing.

'You don't want to watch that.'

'I don't mind, really. I know you enjoy it, darling.'

This expressed precisely how Amanda felt about sex with her husband. Except that she did mind. Actually, if precision were required, it would be more accurate to say that he generally seemed to enjoy it and she almost never did. Once things had been different, but now they weren't and she always had minded and always would.

'You are sweet.' Kiss, kiss. His breath smelt of spearmint. He lay beside her with the earphones on, in order not to miss a single roar or whine as the bloody cars throttled up or down or did whatever they did and Amanda pretended to read her book. She was working out when she could call France tomorrow and making a mental check list of the questions she needed to ask to establish precisely when Charles might be in the house alone. Just what she would say to him she didn't know. It would be sufficient to hear his voice. She would have been very happy to hear him recite the phone book, indeed just listening to him breathe would be a fine, sweet pleasure. To feel his breath against her face, now that would be the summit of desires. To feel his cheek against hers. To feel.

Her imagination leapt nimbly on to other desires. Desire didn't begin to cover it. This was lust and it was unmanageable. It was so powerful a force that it leapfrogged all the usual fidelity and loyalty stuff that got in the way of this sort of thing, it lightly jumped every hurdle to do with her own physical two-children's worth of sag, those inhibiting lumps and bumps. Achingly strong, her lust even flattened those reasonable, indeed essential worries about the consequences. She didn't care. Whatever happened, it was worth it. Amanda was not beautiful but knew that he would find her so, that she would be so. He was beautiful to her. Her hubris was such that she even knew that it was impossible that she could feel such desire and Charles feel nothing. He felt what she did; that much was certain.

She closed her eyes. She lay very quietly and thought about Charles. There was so much to consider that she would ration him, she'd start with neutral territory. There was the unusually elegant way his ears slid onto his altogether delightful head with two tiny, lovable creases. Then there was the strip of velvet skin which ran behind those ears. She dwelt in some detail on Charles's honey-coloured skin and tried very hard to remember how it tasted and how it might be both sweet and slightly salty. That was the place to start tasting him, the tender flesh just near the nape of the neck. She thought about the particular timbre of his voice, so gentle and so sexy with resonances which shook her from head to toe. His mouth, the humorous curve to it.

With eyes shut tight, she began to imagine his body. This game involved a careful invocation of memory and imagination, thinking carefully about what she knew and remembered and then about how it would feel to stroke him and where, exactly, she might choose to start. So many places to start, only one to finish. She would not yet permit herself to think so far ahead, she would not touch him until near the end. Amanda sighed.

No, to begin with, she would lie next to him, very very quietly, and for a long time they would kiss, they would deliberately prolong the sweet agony of waiting, though the imagined taste of him pulsed through her entire body. Resisting the urge to touch herself, Amanda found that the now imagined touch of his bare flesh was enough, more than enough to make her quite giddy. Now came the speculation as to which particular set of reciprocal nerve endings he might choose to start with.

The game was arousing and dangerous and completely addictive. Amanda breathed in and out, to still her pounding heart, which continued its painful thump. She felt a great throb of heat rolling off her body and realised with astonishment that just thinking about this man was nearly sufficient to bring her to the point of orgasm. Not now – not yet. She would resist, until she was alone.

Nicholas shifted. This ridiculous state of arousal was somehow affecting her husband. She took another deep breath and froze. His hand reached under the covers.

'Darling,' he said in a tone of pleasurable surprise. The lust she felt for the Frenchman was about to benefit an astonished Nicholas whose exploratory finger touching her thigh felt an exceptional pulse of heat and lifted in disbelief, only to return, to rise, one centimetre at a time, delicately to penetrate its rippling source. She heard herself let out the long-held breath. Her disloyal body could not prevent its response and so with eyes tight shut she succumbed and thought and felt only Charles.

Hilary and Michèle were sitting at the old wooden table in the orchard staring at the stars and the moon over the château and waiting for Charles to bring out the coffee. Hilary was intoxicated. There was the wine, of course, but over and above that the night and the place and the ravishing Michèle. She was giving him that thoughtful look again, the one that brought back to mind the idiocies he had uttered at the station. These were the kind of heat-seeking missiles which were bound to home back in on him sooner or later. Hers was also the sort of look which made any number of fresh idiocies inevitable if Charles didn't get a move on.

Michèle leant forward and put her hand on his arm and half whispered with her warm breath into his ear with an assurance that was far, far older than her sixteen years. The touch of her hand throbbed through his entire body.

'Hilary,' she said. 'Will you do something for me?'

'Yes, of course, anything.' He swallowed. Battalions of messengers were racing up and down his body letting all the other nerve endings know that something was going on in the arm region and that there was a warm mouth very very close to his ear and a whole warm, silky gorgeous girl attached to it.

'I want you to pretend something, that we are having a little romance. You know. Just for fun and to fool the parents?'

Hilary nodded while he sought words which would handle the situation and enable him to deal with this shameless and totally acceptable advance without issuing wild whoops or war cries. Call this a favour? Thank you, God. He was in heaven.

Bursts of Gilbert and Sullivan erupted at intervals from Nicholas's shower. He had left the bathroom door open. Amanda, passing grimly with a pile of towels, saw her husband throw back his head and let the water run down his face while he carefully soaped and re-soaped all orifices. Nothing like a clean man. Nothing like a happy chappie. Nothing quite like an accredited red hot lover on a glorious summer Saturday morning, who would soon come trilling downstairs and give wife a special resounding and above all self-congratulatory kiss over the muesli. Would he wink? Yes, she rather thought he would.

Amanda had that night experienced something closer to real passion than she had felt in years. She felt very dark, both replete and sexually unsatisfied. She lusted, oh unreasonably, for Charles. Desire had woken her early that morning as it did every morning, beaming in with the dawn. Not fair, not right, when it also kept her awake at night. She was dreadfully tired, yet this combination of sensations was interestingly strange. I think I hate him, Amanda thought, and I'm alive. I've not been alive for years. She leant against the door of the airing cupboard and Nicholas, descending in his bathrobe, saw her standing there and winked.

'Love you,' he said and wife, quite unable to frame any kind of reply, smiled.

Down the path they wandered in the direction of the village, hand in hand, Hilary and this girl, who fitted him so well. Their arms swung to the same rhythm, she was the perfect height, as she was the perfect every-glory-be-everything. As soon as they were out of sight of the house, Hilary would make a move. The big tree, that was the place.

'Mm, Michèle, wait,' he muttered. Baise-moi, he had discovered, meant fuck me. Not that that idea was intrinsically bad, but it lacked subtlety. A person could by stages work up to that same excellent idea. But as soon as he got within striking distance of that delicious, that adorable, that incredible mouth she sprang away like a terrified gazelle. For Christ's sake. He wasn't going to rape her. One kiss. Goddamit. Romance included kisses, right? She had kissed him two days ago with thoroughness, with every appearance of pleasure.

Breathing heavily, Hilary tried to work out what it was he was doing that was so terribly wrong. People kissed in France, it wasn't contrary to the Napoleonic Code. The village was full of rustic snoggers, they were at it, open-mouthed, slobbering each other like expiring carp in the aptly named Café Necker in the village square. While he, the chosen one, didn't even get to give her the sort of kiss she got from Mummy.

'Tu viens?' she said, skipping merrily ahead. It made no sense. If he was so repellant, why did she grab his hand at every opportunity? This, it had to be remembered, was a girl given to removing her bra in order to sunbathe in full view of total strangers with a devastating effect upon his anatomy. He wasn't going to be able to spend the rest of his time here lying on his front which was already noticeably paler than his back. He was permanently aroused and ludicrously frustrated, oh, but totally bewitched.

She took his hand again. The back of his hand grazed her jean-clad thigh. OK. No need to think, after all. He concentrated on making this happen again. His knuckle, sensitised, was a new erotic zone.

A toot, at the bottom of the drive, signalled Charles in the old jalopy, off on his rounds. Were they coming with? Hilary looked at Michèle. He didn't have a brain or anything like that. Whatever she wanted, they did. She nodded at her father so they both got in and then at the last minute Michèle leapt out. Ah, she had forgotten – shopping for Mummy. You go, Hilary. She blew him a kiss and his head turned, a sunflower revolving on its stalk, seeking its sun. He watched her in the rearview window for as long as he could.

As Charles roared about the countryside, he sang old Prévert and Brassens ballads extremely loudly. Hilary was picking up the odd phrase and now and then joined in. They both enjoyed this. Occasionally Charles would put his arms round Hilary and hug him and this, to Hilary's amazement, was something he didn't mind. He'd never been hugged or touched by a man before. Charles smelt wonderful, of strong tobacco and a faint hint of aftershave and clean skin with a kind of after-hint of Louise and the teeniest trace of Michèle and it was perfectly obvious that he wasn't feeling him up. He didn't have designs on Hilary, unlike the multitude which Hilary had on his daughter. Would Michèle let him just hug her like that, lean up against a tree perhaps and just lightly feel the delicious length of her – hmm, if he didn't try to kiss, but just felt? Hilary, closing his eyes to think a bit more about this one, was startled by a roar in his ear. Charles was singing again.

This man, so utterly at ease in his own skin, had a mission to frighten passengers out of theirs. Hilary gripped the dashboard as the doctor once more overtook on a bend and at reckless speed, sustaining one high, cracked note for the duration of the adventure. Charles seemed to be addicted to danger or, rather, to running risks in everything that he did. These relaxed him to about the same degree that they tensed Hilary up.

They now turned at fairly unreasonable speed and with some protest from the tyres into a long unmade road which led up a thickly wooded hill to the modern house of the elderly Demoiselles Dupont. They had a farm but the house, a modest two-storey building sitting on a little hillock with a garage beside it, was pretending to be a suburban house. Fancy wrought-iron railings separated the garden from the animals and hens and stuff beyond, which were all housed in the kind of romantic barns and outhouses that any Brit would have chosen to make into the house.

Charles was there to cut their corns for the two elderly ladies. The elder of the two, the one with the quivering neck, came on tippy-toes to open the front door, walking along a long snake of towel which led from the front door into the salon. There,

Hilary was introduced to the second one, who was dressed just the same and was distinguishable from the first only in being less wobbly and in smiling more. He had come to like the way you were properly introduced and shook hands with people in France and they said something polite to you (often about the English weather and how you weren't missing it, ha, ha) unlike the British system of generally not bothering and pretending the other person didn't exist or, if you ignored them, would go away.

The ladies sat down on their green brocade sofa waiting and waggling their four parchment-coloured feet. The towel they had laid out beforehand was exactly the same colour as their flesh. Charles Beauregard was ransacking the battered old case for the tools of his craft, failing to find a suitable implement in its capacious depths. They knew their man. Number one sister smiled flirtatiously and whipped back a green cloth and there, laid out ready, was a whole battery of clippers and parers. Now, as one, they lifted their four feet onto a special bolster.

Hilary, once he had got the idea of what this little operation involved, let his attention stray and stood at the window watching through the railings a cockerel floating about the yard in the back and generally hassling the hens which were scratching away in their run. He was thinking about life and the universe, which mostly meant thinking about Michèle. The cockerel chased a nice fat hen up the run into the hen house. Good luck, mate, thought Hilary. You and me both. But the bird was too stupid to enter the hen house though Hilary at the window mentally egged it on. If the bird made it, so would he. The dumb cockerel just stood there.

Charles sat on a little footstool in front of the first mademoiselle and massaged her foot while she whispered into his ear and the second mademoiselle said four or five times that the chiropodist did not have his gentle touch. Then the doctor accompanied the two mesdemoiselles into their bedroom for an examination of whatever else might need looking at. Though he was never summoned for anything other than feet, Charles had implied that there was often some other, more delicate service to be rendered which, unlike corns, could not be mentioned over the phone.

Since he never produced a bill, for these services Charles was rewarded with a fine old bottle of Armagnac from les caves of Papa Dupont. He seemed loath to take it, but they went on insisting. Another rummage in the bag produced his packet of fags and his matches and he lit up and they all had a little drink which was generally the lethally strong fortified wine everybody offered as standard issue to round off the doctor's visit. If you were still alive and could drink this, then you'd make it. The demoiselles beamed and everybody clinked glasses and said 'Cheeyars' as a little compliment to Hilary and he said 'Salut' and 'A la vôtre'.

'My old friend Professor Vigne-Laval taught me to drink. Surgical spirit – bouf! Strong. Some doctors drink before the patient comes, some afterwards; he said you're a good doctor when you can drink with them,' and Charles winked broadly in Hilary's direction and the ladies giggled. This professor was the genius and mentor who had also taught Charles how to drive and drink and how to bed women, possibly all three pleasures simultaneously, and he'd supplied a bon mot for every one.

'OK,' he said, back in the car as they rolled up the windows to keep the dust out. 'Now we will have a little swim on the way back. Hilary,' always pronounced Eelaree, 'when I look at you, I think you could have been my son.'

This was the most intimate thing Charles had yet said and so close to what Hilary was thinking that it was eerie. He didn't know how to reply. It was a perfect day and the river, with its series of deep places and little beachy spots, deliciously cold. They parked the car on the road and walked to a place where Charles said nobody came and there lay in the shallows and talked. It was a fisherman's paradise. Hilary watched a shoal of small brown fish dart around inches from where he lay. Charles interlaced his fingers and caught one for an instant before letting it dart off to join its fellows. For such a massive man, with a substantial belly and a great bull's neck attaching the big head to the torso, he was very gentle, exact in all his movements. He knew when to be silent and when to sing. Everything was simple for him.

'I don't always like my father,' Hilary found himself saying. 'I mean I respect him and all that and I suppose I love him but he never lets you forget who's the boss. He has to win, that's his problem.'

'C'est toujours comme ça – all men have to win,' said Charles, for that was how they were made. His father was a good man, Amanda had told him so.

After that they swam in deeper places. Hilary was a natural athlete and Charles hopelessly unfit but gifted with brute strength. Resting naked on the bank beside that great mass of flesh, Hilary felt very young. Charles smoked, naturally, and wore his most serious face.

'Ta maman chose him as a father for you, this fine doctor, Hilary. She could have had any man. She wouldn't look at me, no, I begged her, but she would not let me give her a baby.'

Hilary tried to speak, producing a squawk which came out as a gurgling 'Hurhahmmmaaaaagh?'

'How do you think a woman like that gets to know a man like me? Just drinking coffee in the coffee bar?'

'But you're not like that – she's not like you – you're completely different. Mum's not that sort of woman.' He started again. 'Look, I hear what you're saying but believe me you're completely wrong. My mother is – is – très comme il faut.'

'Amanda?' Now Charles simply roared with laughter, so much so that his cigarette butt shot out of his mouth and buried itself in the undergrowth, a fire hazard which then had to be recovered. While he found it, he afforded Hilary a disconcertingly frank view of his hairy buttocks and balls hanging down – the same view, perhaps, that his mother had enjoyed? No, Hilary couldn't believe it. For Christ's sake.

In England, the conventional mother crept furtively towards the telephone.

The Lennox's house in Sussex was agreed to be absolutely charming, a perfect little Queen Anne house surrounded by lovely gardens. The manicured lawns were the pride of Nicholas Lennox, who at this moment was singing a Gilbert and Sullivan aria extremely loudly as he drove the motor mower back and forth. Every now and then he glanced over his shoulder to admire the newly minted velvet stripe. Amanda could see him through the narrow window in the hallway as she lifted the telephone.

A couple of feet away and very well hidden from both his parents crouched nine-year-old Edward Lennox, cradling a large water gun. Amanda, as she dialled, smoothed her hair. There was a series of clicks and stutters and then a considerable pause before she heard the ringing tone. She cleared her throat several times.

In the house on the hill, a woman picked up the phone.

'Oui, bonjour?' This was Madame Moulins the cleaning lady.

'Bonjour, hello, ici Madame Lennox. Bonjour, Madame Beauregard.' There was a pause, then the woman at the other end said something quite rapidly which seemed to imply that she was not Madame Beauregard, but that she would fetch her. Or so Amanda assumed.

'Ne quittez pas' meant don't hang up. These were the only words she could be quite sure of understanding. So she stood there, staring out of the window, saying 'Shit, shit, shit' to herself, over and over again. Why was it so hard to get through to him? All day she had thought about the timing of the call and planned in her head what she could say. So many useless days when she had not heard his voice.

At this moment, young Ed leapt out of the viburnum hedge in his Ninja turtle fighting stance and blasted his father in the face with a powerful jet. The machine swerved sharply, destroying the beautiful symmetry of the lawn.

Amanda, hearing Nicholas shouting but missing the cause of such fury, was shocked by the sudden gargoyle looming of her husband's wet and hysterical face which came from nowhere to rage and gibber at the window. At this nightmarish vision of uxorial revenge, she leapt up and in her guilt dropped the receiver which swung and banged backwards and forwards against the hall table.

Pointing and frothing, Nicholas rushed by. Amanda ran to the front door where the cause of the commotion and the full extent of the carnage upon the lawn became all too clear. Nicholas continued to chase after – and fail to catch – his jubilant, dancing demon son. As he went, Eddie was laughing fit to bust, flailing one hand over his head and shrieking 'Ex-ter-min-ate' over and over again. This was his favourite way of mocking his father's authority. Amanda found herself pacing forwards and backwards at the front door in impotent rage. It took a while before she – or they – quite realised that she was screaming 'You're destroying me' over and over again. Amanda knew it only when Nicholas came up to her and took hold of her shoulders.

In France, Marie Moulins shuffled back to the phone, picked it up, shook it, then shouted at it. 'Oui, oui, Madame?' she bellowed a number of times. She continued to repeat this louder and louder before finally putting down the phone with a shake of her head.

On the river bank, Charles shook his head at Hilary.

'C'est ça,' he said, laughing. 'So you think a woman like your mother doesn't fuck?'

2 ∫

Louise carried in the usual plate of eggs with swimmy yolks alongside thick slices of bacon and as Hilary thanked her he wondered if she'd still smile at him so nicely if she knew Charles had slept with his mother. Look at these prisoners of the kitchen. That these women had been young once and had experienced the passions he did was both obvious and grotesque when the object of those passions sat in front of you, dipping a vast tartine into a big bowl of coffee and shoving the sodden brown mass into his gob. And was his mother intending to relive the experience? If she'd had it? He swallowed, hard. Please. He was overreacting. He peppered the first egg.

'Chérie,' Louise said to her daughter, 'don't go out just yet, the Dutroncs are calling.'

'He's so boring. Oh, all right,' and sulkily Michèle snatched another roll, buttered it on the wing. Out she marched, bowl of coffee in one hand, bread in the other, opening the door, oh yes, with her hips, the most delicious roll of all.

'You know, for a woman her age, my mother is very shy.' They hung around the orchard. 'Is your mother shy?'

'Yes. No.' When he was twelve she'd beaten off a big black dog that had bitten him by hitting the snarling beast with her hands. Then she'd gone into the road and stopped a passing car for help, insisting that the driver take them to a hospital. He couldn't even begin to explain her.

Two heads came a bob-bob-bobbing past the apple trees. Michèle's warm breath on his cheek, whispering that Monsieur Dutronc was the mayor. 'He is the owner of the ironmonger's down the hill and very old. You watch, how he holds the hand of his wife all the time. You see, she is his new wife. Come on, then,' and she pulled him gently by the hand.

In the salon, Hilary shook hands with two small gnarled folk with almost identical pointy ears and smiling brown faces. They could have been twins. He settled down for the statutory hour of sweet nothings and the old chap's visit to London in 1934 or was it 1949 and/or his membership of the Résistance. Most of France had belonged, well, many in the neighbourhood – well, certainly in this village. Bravely Dutronc upheld the honour of his people vis-à-vis the English. Of course one could not speak with certainty of the newcomers and the mayor shook his head sadly. Michèle winked at Hilary.

'Monsieur Albert?' she said and Louise tutted and Dutronc spread his hands as if to say, who knows? He had a way of pausing before he spoke as though he was thinking very hard about the reply and as though it would be worth waiting for.

'Who knows?' he said at last, with the air of a sage. 'About Monsieur Albert – who knows?' So who was Monsieur Albert?

Madame Dutronc, whose manner reminded him of those nodding dogs with rigid bodies you got in cars, gazed with brimming eyes of love at her husband while keeping stumm herself. Louise disappeared to the kitchen, abandoning them. There was a very long silence. Hilary cleared his throat.

'Vous avez beaucoup souffert,' he said, 'dans la guerre.' Madame nodded and smiled. Behind her back, Michèle cast her eyes to the heavens and suppressed her laughter.

'Ah,' said Dutronc. 'Ah . . .' There was a long silence. 'Non. Non . . . J'étais jeune,' and he squeezed his wife's hand. Young people did not, could not suffer. That was for the old. She brimmed and nodded. Hilary had noticed this sort of thing before. That was how they thought, in vague generalisations. The language lent itself to a sort of charming blither. La vie est pour vivre, they would say – la jeunesse, ah, long pause, c'est pour les jeunes.

The little something came back and proved to be a fortified wine and coffee, black and very strong with lots of sugar lumps. Routine dictated that Louise would offer round prettified plates of petits fours which were to be admired rather than eaten. These, duly admired and politely refused, circled while they went on to discuss the weather in England (very bad) and people's babies (so ugly nowadays) and what French republicans thought of the Queen (remarkably little) – subjects on which Hilary was evenly ill-informed. Monsieur Dutronc paused and laboured through his hour, determined to show them all what a man of the world he was.

After they'd all embraced the air four times and the old couple had trotted off, Hilary discovered that this was the cut and thrust of politics, petits fours style. The elections for mayor were imminent and Dutronc was counting on the Beauregards. This visit affirmed as much. Dutronc represented the old guard, the villagers of yore, among whom the doctor and his family held an honorary position. Representing those unreliable and by implication collaborationist newcomers was the pharmacist and opposition candidate, the selfsame Monsieur Albert.

Only half an hour later the petits fours recirculated. The opposition candidate so far forgot himself and the etiquette of canvassing as to snaffle up the entire plateful of goodies as though he were starving. Monsieur Albert was a pharmacist but his father had been a communist and worked on the railways all his life and had always worn a jumper and scarf hand-knitted by his wife. Jean-Jacques was passionate about the terrible mistake his father had made. In old age he had had to survive on almost no pension while his sharper workmates all got promotion and were better off and index-linked, though less clever than he. He had recanted, but too late. To live nearly your whole life according to a false belief was bad enough, but to realise it was tragic. Hilary, agreeing, preferred this man of passion to the old bloke with the hippy-happy smile and the charisma bypass, even if he did have three first names and an absurdly fluffy wife with the yet more ridiculous name of Héloïse.

'I'd go for him,' he said when he'd got Michèle on her own. 'He's got some oomph in him.'

Michèle knew better. 'He's nouveau riche and Papa says he has ambitions because he has no children,' she said dismissively. 'Everyone knows it's Héloïse who makes the money. People who like my father won't want to vote for him.' This was illogical, quite barmy.

'You mean people prefer the old one with a new wife?'

'Of course. And the remarriage business, you know, it helps.'
'What happened to Dutronc's first wife?'

'Madame Dutronc picked and fried a basket of poisonous mushrooms and ate them – with butter and herbs. Very fat and greedy she was, she ate them all on her own. Nobody liked la prétensieuse. Elle se donnait des airs. Dead in twelve minutes. Six weeks later he married the other one. They love each other like crazy.'

And people want to vote for him after that?'

'Why not? You don't get it. Dutronc is what he is. But Jean-Jacques creeps around being nice to everyone. But really we all know he just likes money. It is a big business, you see, the sale of drugs. That's why he comes courting Papa, because he doesn't prescribe drugs so often. So really, Jean-Jacques can't stand him.'

And the mayor doesn't like money, then?'

'Bouf,' he loved that sound, the expelled hot air. 'Of course he does. But he isn't a hypocrite about it. Come on. Let's go to the village.'

Again, Michèle took his hand. Hilary had plans. These centred on a particular segment of the drive which just took them out of view of the house. Every inch of gravel was as familiar to him as his own house, if not more so. Here any number of rich emotions had been expended, here more had happened in four days than in a lifetime in Sussex. So at the big tree, on cue, he took Michèle in his arms and sort of leant with her against it for a glorious, giddy instant, delicately, resisting the urge to lean too hard and definitely he should not grind his pelvis into hers.

For four seconds this warm, lovely creature allowed him to hold her in his arms and he felt the whole length of her lightly touching him. Then Michèle chuckled and did her usual trick of shoving him off. She hopped off ahead, laughing and skipping. As though she hadn't a care in the world. If lust could be said to grind a person down, then he was just a small heap of pulverised ash at her feet, a molehill attached to a giant, painfully throbbing and permanently erect member. Sighing, the legs attached to the organ walked it down the hill. He could watch her for ever, from any angle, even the way the little bit of ankle he could see between the jeans and the shoe was made. The extraordinary elegance of those bones deserved study.

Louise watched her daughter and Hilary drift past the window and then set off down the drive hand in hand and, without thinking, remarked to Madame Moulins how charming the young couple was. Marie, who was on her hands and knees scrubbing the flagstones, now rose panting and groaning to her haunches, where she remained, breathing heavily, for ten or twenty seconds. From this position she rose slowly, levering herself up with both hands against the kitchen dresser.

Louise, who knew what was coming, wished she had bitten her tongue. Marie would hang her head as if in contemplation of those big raw fingers, slack with exhaustion, for a further ten or fifteen seconds. Then, wiping her hands on the towel that she wore permanently slung round her right shoulder, she would lumber to the window. By the time she got there, the young couple would be long gone. So she would give her employer one of her special seemingly blank but actually faintly accusatory looks and, instead of returning to her former and entirely self-imposed labour of cleaning the floor by hand (any number of long-handled implements had been provided for this purpose), would need to have a glass of water and a bit of a sit-down and a moan about her legs. This, generally, was accompanied by such suggestions as sit down, Madame, you have a rest, don't you worry, I'll just catch my breath. Why am I so stupid, thought Louise. Why don't I know when to be quiet?

As Marie slowly sipped the water, Louise would offer her coffee or a tisane. Marie would refuse with loathing. She was there to work, that was the implication. Yet she would always sit down and have lunch with the family, managing to put away each course, not refusing second helpings and even – for it would never do to leave that little bit – greedily polishing off all the leftovers as she did the dishes afterwards. The plates were scoured before they got near the water. This disgusted the more abstemious Louise.

And then it occasionally happened that later in the afternoon Marie would have one of her funny turns and need to sit down and naturally Louise would offer to make tea or a tisane and somehow over the years it had become a matter of course that Madame would offer Marie a little something. Marie always demurred at length but sometimes after a lot of persuasion might eat a little piece of tarte aux pommes, say. She ate very slowly, needing like a child to be urged for each mouthful. In this martyred manner she always managed to finish every last morsel offered, infuriating Louise who had insisted that she take it. She was as greedy as Louise was inconsistent.

All afternoon Louise danced around her, torn between the desire to get rid of her and the feeling that she ought to get better value for money. Sometimes, in her haste to see the back of Marie, Louise would find herself running her down to the village in her little car. Every time, she could not help noticing the old plastic carrier bag that had been coming up the hill empty and going down full for years. She'd never looked in it; she had her pride, after all. And it was no good, no good at all Charles saying that she should simply not give her lunch or, more contentiously, sack Marie. Charles didn't understand that, tedious and indeed horrible though she was, Marie was utterly reliable and always came and needed the work. How could Louise, with all her blessings, sack a horrible fat old woman who was poor, whom she disliked and whom nobody else would employ?

Slowly Marie sat down, breathing heavily, looking down at her fat fingers. The whole thing now followed its allotted course. Today, however, Marie was in a particularly vituperative mood. It couldn't be the legs, though they were bad enough. Whenever she felt more than usually put upon, Louise thought about how dreadful it would be to have been born with such shapeless tree-trunk legs and to have to clean as Marie did. Sometimes her own slim, long legs could reconcile her to the tyrant of her kitchen when nothing else could. Louise sighed. Ten long years since she'd first looked at Marie's legs and for their sake excused the inexcusable.

Over the sip of water, Marie was making a snuffling noise. That was her way of expressing derision. 'Why do you permit it, Madame? An English boy. Everybody knows about the English.'

Louise said nothing. It was so stupid, to try to reply to something as pathetic as this. It wasn't as if she cared what this stupid woman thought. Only a complete idiot would listen.

'Ah, poor Madame, you smile but of course things are far from easy for you,' said Marie, smiling herself with false sympathy, 'How does even the most careful maman protect a young girl like Michèle, one with her, you know, her . . . well, and then to have a young man like that right here in the house.' She shook her head knowledgeably and clucked and sighed and Louise drew a long breath at the cunning of this double, no, triple insult.

'Oh no, Marie, you're joking. I mean to say, really, you can't say these things.' Louise turned on her heel and went out of the room. Seconds later (she could be nimble when she scented blood) Marie heaved into the hallway ready for battle and snuffling louder than ever, her hands crossed on her substantial chest in a praying position.

'If only you knew all that I know, Madame,' she said rapidly. 'But the good Lord has spared you much, indeed he has.' Her bosom heaved, she made a sign of the cross. Louise paused, turned, looked at her.

'All that you know? What exactly do you mean?' she said sharply. Mention of the divinity made her nervous. 'What do you know?'

'I – I?' said Marie, whom injured innocence ill fitted, starting to wheeze as prelude no doubt to one of her little attacks. 'I? What should I mean?'

Louise ground her teeth. At moments like these she understood how easily a person could chop up another person with an axe. A good sharp butcher's knife would do it, though it might be more enjoyable to run that person over with one's little car, back and forth on the gravel, reversing over the silly old fat head until it popped.

Hilary understood nothing. Not even at the hour of the apéritif when much Frenchness explained itself, in vino veritas. Half an hour before dinner, when for two hours, nothing had been consumed, Charles would emerge and do his stuff with a bottle of cassis or fraises des bois and some white wine or champagne, depending on the general mood. He drank a lot without ever getting drunk. Two or three glasses before dinner, and plenty more with it and brandy or whisky afterwards, a little digestif to settle the stomach. Coffee came with plenty of sugar cubes and perhaps one might have a little je-ne-sais-quoi in the marron glacé line. Hilary, nothing loath, stuffed his face from dawn to dusk.

Why weren't they porkers? Michèle tucked in as did Louise and they both had more curves than the Grand Corniche and not an inch of excess. That old saw about living to eat held full sway in this household. I eat, therefore I am. Full intellectual vigour was applied to the discussion of what to have and where to buy it, hours went on cooking and serving it, clearing up and starting again and the whole point was that it all had to be fresh every day, or else honour wasn't satisfied.

When, thinking to emulate Charles, Hilary expressed some interest in what they were having for dinner, Louise took him into the kitchen. There for ten minutes she explained precisely how to bone and stuff a duck with full mime effects, gesturing around and skewering an imaginary quacker.

The thing about Louise was that she just didn't have that mechanism which told you when people were making a polite inquiry and when they were really seriously needing to know the precise number of pine kernels you crushed in a basin with how many leaves of tarragon. She also unnerved Hilary by looking directly into his eyes in a very serious way, as though she genuinely cared what he said or thought and was very possibly committing his words to memory. These in his experience were the well-known signs of off-your-trolleydom, particularly the female sort and particularly unnerving when the face staring at yours was as lovely as hers still was.

Yes, Louise was very, very watchable, particularly in the kitchen and he much preferred her in her big butcher's pinny tied up round the waist nice and tight with a little bow in front to the way she was when got up in one of the immaculate silk numbers. There was something quite interestingly erotic about Louise palpating a chicken breast or coming across the kitchen towards you with a handful of liver dripping through her fingers. It was a treat to see her faintly flushed and daubed with flour with a little wisp of hair escaping at the nape of her neck, Louise nicely mussed with her hands deep in a bowl doing a bit of pastry-crumbling or whatever. Cooking was a sensual art, no doubt about it. In her case there was just a shorter than usual hop from kitchen to boudoir, from stew pot to sex pot. Lucky old Charles, eh?

Mentally, though, he couldn't quite get her straight. In other respects she wasn't afflicted. Unlike his parents' pals, she never volunteered views on how much bigger he would or wouldn't be or on what it felt like to be young/old/growing up/past it, with it/having it/not having it. Nor did she find herself hilariously entertaining, hee-hawing at her own jokes. She didn't do anything really in the joke line. Charles was the fun and games merchant. Louise was pretty quiet, not speaking except when spoken to. She didn't lecture him either, except when he made the mistake of asking about something – and then, unlike his mother who could boomerang from dirty smalls and A level revision round AIDS and back to car borrowing and room tidying in one swoop, she stuck to the subject.

Louise was refreshingly indifferent to whether or not he washed or had washing or needed anything, nor did she ever expect him to nip down to the village for a pint of milk or a newspaper. She seemed to expect nothing at all from him and to be absolutely thrilled whenever she got a bit of praise. When you thought about it, she was remarkable. Just like her daughter.

'One day you will be old, Hilary. Même toi. You see these old fools, they disapprove of everything, but it's just that they have forgotten. Many of them never had any fun anyway, poor salauds. They haven't lived at all and now they're dead above the neck and below the waist. What's life without passion? Always play for high stakes. Live on the edge. Your mother, now, she completely understood that,' and he shook his head remembering and looking with pity at the old guys who hung about the place. What did he remember, exactly?

Charles had taken Hilary off for the afternoon to play boules. They stood in a shady bit of dust, throwing their balls around. Charles never stopped going on about his feelings. What a combination that'd make: the body of Michèle and the emotions of Charles. Hilary told himself that he couldn't seriously be thinking what he was. No. Well, he could, but not at those moments when Charles would keep going on about Amanda.

Hilary was concentrating on trying to discover exactly what

it was she and Charles had got up to all those years ago. The finer part of him didn't want to know, but there was a pushier, lower part which was very nosy. That part had decided that their goings-on – if they had gone on – presaged him and Michèle having some. Of course his mother had slept with men. Twice. She had two sons, didn't she? Obviously, there had been some sort of friendship with Charles. Some sort of something. There was no hard evidence. Let's just rephrase that, yes? No proof that it had included sexual intercourse. Sexual intercourse was high on his personal agenda. Why should his mother have been any different? Because most girls, nice girls, pretended that they were?

'Charles,' he said, 'where exactly was it that you met Mum?'

'In hospital, of course. Didn't she tell you?'

'Sure, sure, of course she did. It's just that some of the details have slipped my mind.'

Charles ambled up to the end of the boules ground, examined Hilary's ball, paced back slowly. His mother had told him nothing.

'She was so sexy, it was unbelievable, it took your breath away. Tu comprends?' He fumbled for a cigarette, lit it, exhaled slowly. Hilary smiled and nodded. He could not imagine it.

'Oui,' he said.

'I wonder if you really know what I mean. Women, you see, in some ways are profoundly unknowable. So much is intuitive. Women experience real pain, mental and physical in childbirth, for example, more than a man has in a lifetime and they can be so strong. I've seen them do incredible things. But in other ways they are hard to understand. When I touch a person, with my hands, like this,' and he laid both hands on Hilary's shoulders and pressed down on them, firm and hard, so that it almost but didn't quite hurt, 'I know whether they are lying or not. I can tell you from touching a person if they are really sick or not, if it is serious. The soul and body are linked, you see. Things like cancer, you can feel the heat through the flesh, man or woman. But mentally – ah, it is very different. When I look into a man's eyes, I generally know what he thinks, and he with me – but a woman?' He stared into Hilary's eyes and Hilary, dazed, stared back.

● ● ●

Caution had long since given way to a reckless abandonment of care. Amanda, ruled by needs she had neither the desire nor the ability to control, scarcely waited for Nicholas to go upstairs before she lifted the telephone to call France. Let him listen, she thought. Let him think whatever he thinks. Just leave me alone. Nothing Nicholas might say or do could matter.

Engaged. She put it down. Try again in a minute. Nicholas came down, went into the garden and sank into a deckchair. He waved to her to come out. She waved back and made some gesture, designed to imply that she had something to do. He lay back and closed his eyes. Something stirred. She looked at his upturned face, drinking in the sunlight with a strong sense of déjà vu. There had been a day like this. She closed her eyes to think – and then she had it. Fifteen years ago a patient had died on the operating table and Nicholas had come home for the bank holiday weekend and lain in the sun like this.

She had treated him as a convalescent, brought out cups of tea, had remained in the dark of the kitchen with Hilary teething and fretful, shushing him so his father could rest in the brightness outside, from which they were excluded. Nicholas was in pain and she thumped pieces of Play-Doh and boiled kettles and stole out to hang nappies on the line and stood, just as she was doing now, to watch the man outside. There was one helpless little creature pulling at her. Here's the train with the eggie on it, down the little red tunnel we go. For Nicholas wanted to give up. He wanted to jack in the career, the house, go away, be something different. She had said all the obvious things. She told him that he saved lives, that his training would be wasted, that he was needed and so on. Silently she was screaming: what about me? One of them had to be a surgeon, or everything she had chosen was a waste of time. Yet this never occurred to him. So, in her bitterness, she said nothing. Not then, not later when he went back to work quite normally without any further discussion, for she was frightened to give him the slightest opening. Silently, the train continued down the track and there was no knowing what other direction it would have taken or where else it might have ended up.

Amanda moved through the days in a kind of dream state,

conscious of how strange it was that to the outside she appeared
to be the same. Nicholas had noticed nothing different about her,
nor would he while dinners appeared as usual. If anything, she
was more attentive than usual, inquiring about his work and
showing an unprecedented interest in his tedious college of
physicians politickings. She wanted him to talk so she could
let her mind drift to Charles. Time alone, that was the precious
thing she yearned for, time to sit and think. Perhaps she was a
better wife to him now than before. Perhaps being disconnected
was the secret of happiness in marriage and everybody knew it
but her. Every day a new secret seemed to reveal itself in her
private consciousness. She noticed the looks people gave each
other, felt the meanings behind words.

It was Ed, whom she had put down as intrinsically incapable
of noticing anything outside his own, highly selfish, personal
boyworld, who gave her pause. 'There's something different
about you, Mum,' he'd said in a thoughtful manner. 'I know.
You're not telling me off so much.'

Amanda saw that this was true. She was so filled with her
inner, secret life that she didn't have the time to feel as annoyed
as she had before, things had a new perspective. So that was
how spies managed. It was perfectly possible to lead a double life,
providing you kept it all in your head and told nobody anything.
Silly little wife with her dull moments and her chores was good
at protecting Amanda that way.

The phone rang only twice before a female voice answered.
Amanda asked to speak to Charles. 'C'est Madame Lennox,'
she said.

'Oh, what a pity,' the voice said brightly. It was Michèle. Her
father and Hilary, she said, were out playing boules. Amanda
sighed heavily, said goodbye, put the phone down and turned
with leaden tread back to the kitchen where there was, as ever,
dinner to cook, and where she snapped a tea towel at a fly and
got it, for a change.

'Boules-shit,' she said.

Louise was in a temper, she paced up and down in front of her
dressing table. As she took off her clothes and creamed her face,
she was replaying the scene for Charles's benefit.

'Your problem is that you have no problems,' said Charles in his weary voice. This infuriated Louise.

'Of course,' she said snappily. 'I of course have no problems, know nothing and am nobody. Why should anybody care? Why should the daughter of a hairdresser from Rennes even aspire to know anything? Evidently even a stupid country woman knows more than me about everything, including my house and my daughter and has better manners. And is perfect in every way.' She started to brush her hair with violent strokes. Charles groaned. She rounded on him.

'Life is very easy for you. You have a position in society. You don't have to get excited about stupid women, you can keep your famous calm. You and your beloved Professor Vigne–Laval have all the best lines. But even an ignorant country woman is permitted to tell your wife what's what.'

'What did the old bag say that was so terrible?'

'Oh, she is always cunning, I told you, it was all spite and innuendo. Nothing. But it was what she implied. As though the whole village knew that Michèle was some kind of tart.'

'Sack her,' said Charles.

'I hate it when you speak like that.'

'What do you want me to say? Why do you listen to her? Is this all you have to complain about?'

And so on and so forth. If there was one thing Louise couldn't abide, it was being told how perfect things were and how wonderful. He never listened to what she said.

'Speak up for yourself. Answer her back,' he growled.

'That's what I am doing,' she said, 'and you DON'T LIS-TEN!'

'Dear God, what do you think I am doing? What more do you WANT?'

'I want to be taken seriously. Not treated as a nobody. A nothing.'

'You aren't a nobody,' roared Charles. There. This was how it always ended up, with him shouting at her. She went on trying to explain that he didn't realise, that he didn't really care. He just thought he did. Charles rapidly became quite demented.

'SHUT UP,' he said, 'JUST SHUT UP AND DO AS I SAY.'

He continued to shout on and rave that she WAS a SOME-BODY and must assert herself and so on until she was bludgeoned into silence. They stared at each other, each breathing deeply. Louise was flushed, hectic, trembling. Charles pushed her down on the bed, crushing her with his substantial weight, none too gently. He smoothed back her hair, kissed her when she protested. He was as aroused as she was, as she always was, by their arguments. Whatever the subject, they always had the same outcome.

A startled Hilary, woken by the din, was sitting bolt upright in bed. His room was directly above the parents' one and he could hear them screaming at each other, at it hammer and tongs, with emphasis on the hammer.

The shouting stopped. He could hear the springs of the bed going dzigga-doo, dzigga-doo. Quite slowly at first but yes, inevitably, speeding up. In the sudden silence the noise of the springs was very loud. Dzigga-dzigga-doo, doo. And, getting louder and louder, came an accompanying noise. It was a gasping, throating sort of moan. This might well indicate the utmost throes of pleasure. Or not. Dzigga-dzigga – aahh, dzigga-aahh, dzigga-aahh. Aahh . . . He lay down on his side. Firmly, he pressed the pillow over his free ear.

The next day, when Michèle and he rambled off on their usual walk, she took him down to Café La Fourchette and didn't come in. 'A tout à l'heure.' A little wave and a smile and off she went swinging her shoulder bag and did not invite him to accompany her.

Hilary, drinking the usual Coke at the usual table, waited and when she did not return he grew impatient. Twenty minutes passed, thirty, forty and he refamiliarised himself with the mental gymnastics that went with this sort of clock-watching. Ten minutes at the cleaner's, maximum, twenty to buy fruit for Louise, five minutes to press the flesh here and there, another fifteen minutes to remember to go back and pick up the daily baguette and so on. Then it was an hour. He stared into the windows of the Boulangerie Lardon opposite, watched the continuous flow of baguette-buyers with no Michèle among them. Then it was an hour and ten minutes.

Not the most generous of calculations could account for the hour and forty minutes she kept him there, returning empty-handed and smiling. He felt stupid about it, he felt that the time had been stolen from him somehow. He'd been conned.

'You were gone a long time.'

'Was I?' They walked up to the house. The bag went on swinging and swinging.

Dinner was a quiet affair, served by a pensive Louise who funnily enough seemed to have exactly the same problem on her mind.

'Hilary? On s'est amusé comment? This afternoon? You know, you forgot the bread.' Louise dragged deep on her inter-course cigarette. Hilary glanced at Michèle, who continued to rip apart her piece of bread, giving him a bright and slightly inquisitive look, as though she didn't know herself.

'Nothing much, the usual,' he said.

'For instance?'

'The café, a walk. You know.' He shrugged his shoulders.

'Did you meet anyone?'

'No.'

'Not anyone? Are you sure? None of your acquaintances in the village?'

Hilary shook his head. He looked at Michèle, who smiled boldly back at him. Oh, her mouth.

'Nobody at all,' he said. The phone shrilled out and Charles leapt up, while Louise ground out the stub with her usual extra thoroughness, frowning as she always did, each phone call the harbinger of annoyance. Charles returned a moment or so later and clapped Hilary on the shoulder.

'Vite, vite, come with me. Call out. Maybe you can help.'

Did they want coffee? Louise was on her feet, brandishing the pot as Charles left the room.

No, he called and they were off, Charles snatching up the old bag near the front door, loping across the gravel. Hilary hurried behind. Bang, they were away, the wheels skidding slightly on the gravel. Through the bright window, he saw the two lovely women moving about the table picking up plates. In the large, elegant room, they were like figures on a stage set. Did they speak to each other when he wasn't there? Did they exist at all? Perhaps they would disappear into a void. Perhaps it was the same one that had swallowed Michèle this afternoon.

They were through the village and out, picking up speed. The headlights flickered along thick white bands painted on grey bark all the way along the avenue of lime trees. The night lay waiting, caged beyond the bars.

'Thanks for taking me,' said Hilary. Charles smiled and lit up and the car filled with the acrid, comforting smell of his Gitane. If he weren't Michèle's father, Hilary would have asked him for advice. He thought about asking for it anyway. They were going to see a pregant woman, Charles said. Slight problems, nothing serious but the husband was worried. It was not far away, but difficult to get to.

The long tree-lined avenues rose and fell, hill after hill, through early-to-bed villages with their shutters drawn tight and then they turned off onto smaller roads. At last they came out on a road so rough it was scarcely more than a track. They were crossing a plain with only a few lights in the far distance. The Peugeot bumped along more and more slowly. Charles cut the lights and engine.

'Now we walk,' he said. 'Look'. He was pointing to the stars, brilliant in the inky dark. The night was quiet and warm and there was no sound but their own footsteps and an occasional rumble of a motor in the distance, where the road snaked by. Charles had a torch but they didn't need it for the moon lit up the track. On they went, silently. Hilary felt how small he was in the world. He listened to his boots crunching and felt the pressure of the slight unevennesses under his feet, the wind in his hair. These were delicious sour-sweet minglings, like sugar dissolving to relieve the acidity of lemon juice, new sensations transmuting the old bad ones.

Up ahead they saw a light swaying from side to side. The man holding it was keeping a lookout for them and he hallooed as he heard their footsteps. Charles hailed him cheerfully. The farmer spoke rapidly in a local dialect Hilary couldn't fathom, pulling at Charles's arm. He was nervous and jittering. Charles laid his arm over the man's back, half escorting him into the house that lay ahead. Hilary understood him repeating the word 'douleurs', pains, which the man pronounced as though in Latin. 'Dolors,' he said. 'She has bad pains, very bad,' and he shook his head from side to side. In the light, they shook hands and Hilary saw that he was in his early thirties, bony and sallow with a long face with flared nostrils. Hilary sat downstairs and kicked his heels and looked at things while the man led Charles up the stairs. The room was all brown: a brown piece of carpet on brown tiles, eight chairs round a table, a huge television set, a dresser. Hilary looked at the wedding photograph, which showed the man with his wife who was pretty and small and young and dolled up in a big frothy white dress. He towered above her, unsmiling, the long upper lip drawn down.

In a matter of just a few moments Charles was down again, looking for the phone, dialling, rapidly speaking. He was saying it was an emergency, an ambulance was required. He began to explain how to get there, interrupted by the farmer, adding and changing instructions. Patiently, Charles made sense of these, incorporated them. 'Get here as fast as you can,' he said. 'She hasn't long to go.' The man began anxiously to pluck at Charles's arm as he put the phone down, saying no, doctor, surely not, she's not even seven months gone, and it was startling to see his nervous smile reveal his huge yellow teeth, real horse's teeth with big gaps between them. He was terribly ugly when he smiled.

'You know, Monsieur,' Charles said, very calm, very polite, 'sometimes babies cannot wait. Sometimes it happens like that.'

The two men went back up the stairs and as they did so a whimpering cry floated down. For an instant Hilary thought it was the baby, but of course that was ridiculous, it was her, the woman upstairs.

A few minutes later Charles was back, phoning the hospital again. Emergency, he'd said, and couldn't they hurry – just get a move on? The farmer came clunking down the stairs.

'They'll be as quick as they can,' Charles said. The man stood very close to him, staring at him with huge scared eyes. He swayed slightly and looked as if he might faint. Charles looked at his watch, threw Hilary a glance.

'What will happen, what is going to happen?'

'Do not concern yourself, it will be fine. I think the baby will come soon, will come early, but probably not before the ambulance comes. They have been warned, they have all the equipment. You know, my friend, trust in your wife. Nature has designed woman well, inside and out. My old professor, Vigne-Laval, used to say that nature was the artist, and man merely the paintbrush – women are designed to make babies.'

'Tell me, what will happen?' the fellow repeated, pawing at Charles's arm. He was not capable of taking anything in.

'First we will get everything ready. Come with me.'

Back upstairs they went and now Charles set the man to work, calling for fresh linen. The big wrought-iron chandelier shook as Charles's heavy tread passed back and forth overhead. Five minutes later, he came down again and opened his bag, stared thoughtfully into it. The farmer tumbled down the stairs after him and stood too close, looking from Charles to the bag. His hands were shaking.

Charles rummaged at length, thoughtfully. He pulled out a packet of cigarettes, offered them, was refused, went outside for a smoke. Silently, Hilary and the father stood and watched his broad back through the window, until another cry from up above drew the worried man back upstairs. Hilary went out.

'Will they come in time?' He was whispering, though there was no way she could hear, upstairs.

'I doubt it. Come on, you can help. She's nine months gone, but he doesn't know that. I won't tell him either. The waters broke this morning, she didn't dare tell him. Lying in a wet bed for twelve hours . . . She's half dilated now, it won't be long. She's very narrow, too, and I have so few instruments . . .' He sighed heavily and shook his head and blew an elegant smoke ring to the heavens. 'Poor little thing. Let's go. You find me towels, lots of them, and boil up some water. Put it in anything you find, jugs will do or bowls. Ça va? You're not going to faint, are you?'

Hilary smiled and nodded and turned to go back into the farmhouse. He caught the merest glimpse of Charles's bowed head and the flash of a hand as it formed the sign of the cross. A shudder passed from the crown of his head right down his spine, the touch of an angel's wing.

It got worse. He'd seen hospitals before, plenty of them, had hung around waiting rooms and chatted up nurses, but he'd never been close to anything like this. The bedroom was gloomy, filled with dark furniture which seemed to come from another time. The young woman lay on the bed propped up on pillows and moaning. She wore a silly nightgown, a pink thing with ribbons, above which her white face and terrified big eyes seemed all the younger. As each pain came, she gripped her husband's hand and screamed and her whole body tensed and arched upwards. At the end of the contraction, she lolled back and the whites of her eyes rolled up. She seemed to be exhausted already and she kept asking for something, but her accent was so thick he couldn't understand. Yet she spoke with such urgency. Hilary strained to make it out while her husband sat silent and grim, staring at her face.

Hilary came in and out with jugs. He found ice. He ransacked the big old-fashioned wardrobe in the room for towels. That was the only time she appeared to notice him. A contraction ended and she struggled up to a sitting position and stared at him.

Then she fell back onto the pillows, letting out another of those terrible cries, which sounded as if she was being pulled apart. Her calf muscles knotted up with cramp each time. Bunched, like athlete's legs, they looked to be in agony. When that happened, Charles at once began to massage her feet and legs. How huge her belly seemed, unnaturally distended. Hilary looked away. Tears were running down her face.

At the next opportunity, Charles gave the instruments he had to Hilary to boil. When he got back with a steaming bowl full, Charles was sitting beside her. He was like a cat, the way he got himself so precisely into a small space. He was talking soothingly and Hilary saw that he was trying to stop the father from panicking and frightening the mother yet more. The three of them took a deep breath. Charles exhaled slowly and counted with a raised finger, meanwhile resting his big hand on her head. Hilary found himself copying him, counting in his head. She took a breath. She was trying, she was, but every time she turned away to her husband and saw his scared face, his terrible yellow rictus of a smile, she began to whimper again. The pains were now very bad.

'Excellent, very good,' said Charles cheerfully, beckoning Hilary to come out with him. Outside the door of the bedroom, he whispered to him to go down and put the lantern out, next to the car, for the ambulance men, then to find the very sharpest kitchen knife. He was to sharpen it as well as he could and as quietly as possible and then boil it and bring it upstairs. Hilary's heart was knocking painfully against his ribs, he was in a sweat of fear. He had to swallow before he could speak.

'What are you going to do?'

Charles touched his face tenderly, as a groom touches his bride, as a lover touches his beloved. Poor frightened, small Hilary let his face rest in that warm hand for a moment. 'Probably nothing. I might have to cut her a little, to let the baby out. The ambulance will never come in time. I have an old scalpel, but no new blade.' He smiled ruefully. 'Be quick with the knife, but don't let our friend see. He's in a bad state.'

Hilary hurtled downstairs. He ran, his breath panting loudly in his ears to the car and back. He clattered through the kitchen, pulling out all the shelves until he found it, a wooden-handled knife with the slimmest and meanest of blades. He put a pan of water on the stove to boil and searched on. An old-fashioned grindstone. He turned the wheel, it groaned. Another terrible scream rang out from upstairs. He nearly sliced off his finger, but just stopped in time. With one trembling hand, he stilled the other. He held the blade in the boiling water for a couple of minutes and then like a murderer stole upstairs with it behind his back.

The girl lay on her back and round her open knees stood a circle of old-fashioned smoky storm lanterns. Heat and light shimmered off them in the big, dark space. Beyond the lights, like sentinels, stood two huge jugs of water, steaming, beside the piles of towels which Hilary had banked up. The farmer sat rigid on a chair beside the bed, staring in horror at his wife's contorted face, while she gripped his hand so hard that the knuckles were white round squeezed red sausage fingers. He kept saying how sorry he was, how sorry.

The room was filled with her, with the hoarse sound of her moans which stiffened into screams each time the pains came. She was still asking for something. As he slipped the wicked blade into the disinfectant, Hilary understood. She was begging her husband to kill her for she could no longer endure the terrible pains. He kept shaking his head and saying forgive me, forgive me.

Hilary began to pray, continually, in his head, along the lines of please God, make it be all right, please God, please.

As he moved across, he saw the incredible sight of the baby's head, or rather part of a head of dark hair appearing between her legs, an impossible bulging curve of head that couldn't possibly get through there, couldn't.

Charles seemed to be pushing down on her stomach with one hand, his ear pressed to one side of her belly, listening to the heartbeat of the foetus. It looked as if he was trying to push the baby out. Jesus. It must have hurt like hell. Hilary watched, with clenched fists. He was sweating himself, like a pig.

The noise was now terrible, screams punctuated by moaning gasps as she drew breath, only to scream again. She was drenched with sweat, her hair plastered to her head, she writhed and twisted. That a woman could endure it – it was unendurable. That a man could do this to a woman – that was also unendurable.

Charles reached out for the knife. 'Be quick,' he said. 'Quick.'

Carefully, Hilary fished out the knife and put it into Charles's hand. Please God, please.

The father saw the knife. He stood up and moved forward a few paces and then fainted dead away, crashed onto the chair he'd been sitting on and smashed onto the floor. Hilary tugged at his boots, shifting the dead weight a couple of inches along the floor to lay him out straight. He was so heavy, a dead lumpy weight he could barely move. Was he dead or concussed? Neither of the other two seemed to have noticed. Hilary knelt beside him, saw that he was breathing and stood up again.

Charles was cutting her, and again, blood spurted out everywhere in a crimson gush, terrifyingly, and then savagely he reached right inside her body and still he was cutting at her and Hilary stood there, frozen with fright. The butchery was appalling. He felt sick and giddy. All at once, the baby slid out of her body and the mother stopped screaming instantly. She knew.

Something was terribly wrong. The baby was a boy, a tiny skinny thing covered in greasy wax stuff but his skin was a horrific bright purple. It was a colour so unnatural that Hilary had never imagined skin could be like it. He saw the severed cord and then the marks where it had been wrapped round the baby's neck and pulled tight. Now he understood.

With incredible speed and gentleness, Charles took the little thing and laid it down on the towels and bent over it.

'Take the cord,' he said to Hilary. 'Gently, don't pull, just hold it, the afterbirth must come now. It is a boy, Madame, a lovely boy, the image of your husband, a wonderful boy. Just one moment, Madame, I will give him to you.'

There was complete silence. The young woman just lay there, waxy-faced, strangely still. Yet a moment before she had been so loud, so violently in motion. Her eyes were fixed on Charles's broad back. She stared at Hilary and her face was so white and stricken, her look so appallingly full of pain, that he could not bear it and knelt down, out of her sight, still holding the cord. The bed was a mass of blood, otherwise he would have rested his head against it. He was so very tired.

He was very careful to make no noise but could not prevent tears running down his face, which they did, on and on, unstoppably. She was silent. He kept his head well down, so she would not see. There was another huge contraction, he could feel it through her whole body, but still she made no sound. It was the afterbirth coming out, a great white spongy mass at the other end of the cord which like some hugely sophisticated electrical cable was a complex spiral cord with red and blue in it. He curved it all round carefully into one of the bowls.

The only sound in the room was Charles pummelling and stroking the baby. In the new quiet, the slapping noise was very loud. He was cruel, Hilary thought. Why hurt the little thing, even though it could feel nothing? Hilary wanted to say stop, it's dead, we all know it's dead, let it be. He was crying too hard to say anything.

Charles began to hum. It was a strange noise, a kind of sing-song incantation. Then he was talking, quietly under his breath, and then louder. 'Come, little one, that's right, that's good, that's better, oh, that's very good, that's the way, come, little one.'

On he went and on. Through the bones of his head, through his flesh, Hilary heard the voice and concentrated on it, so gentle and so kind. There came the sound of a little cry, which turned into a wail. Hilary drew a great sobbing breath, gulped, smeared the fresh tears which would not stop falling with the back of his bloody hand. He began to sob out loud, uncontrollably. The baby cried again. He found himself saying thank you, thank you. Thank you, God.

The little mouth opened, drew another breath and began to wail even more loudly. The eyes were squeezed tight shut in the little purple monkey face and, carefully, Charles wrapped him in a fresh towel and presented him to the mother. She took the baby in her arms and stared at him. Incredibly, the little thing stopped crying for an instant and opened up its little eyes, which were a watery blue, and stared at her. As though it knew who she was. And the way she looked and looked back at the baby boy made Hilary want to laugh and cry all at once.

They heard it, distantly, then ever nearer, the siren wailing in the distance. They had forgotten the father. Charles now picked up one of the jugs of water and poured some of it on a cloth and dabbed at his face. As he came to, Charles helped him to his feet, wiping him down. Surreptitiously, Hilary washed his own face.

'You fainted, Monsieur, very understandable. Look, you have a little boy. Premature, but nice and big for his age so he will be fine. We must get him to hospital though, and your wife also needs some attention. She has been so very courageous. Come along, mon brave, you help Monsieur.' He winked at Hilary.

Hilary supported the farmer down the stairs. He was groggy, but all right. The ambulance men were at the door and organising matters. Within minutes they had taken the little family away.

Hilary and Charles stood at the farmhouse door and watched the tail lights bumping slowly down the track. Charles yawned and stretched and went back inside and helped himself to a glass of brandy. Hilary had one too, which made him shudder and then warmed him. The terror was subsiding.

They drove slowly through the lovely pre-dawn. Clouds of mist swirled and eddied across the fields. Over the horizon a faint streak of light heralded the day. They turned onto the tarmac road.

'It was a miracle,' Hilary said. 'You made that baby live.' Charles shrugged his shoulders. 'Did you know it would be all right?'

'I hoped.' He smiled. He had prayed, too. Hilary felt like embracing Charles.

'So did I.' God, yes, and how. Especially over the knife.

The day grew and grew and Hilary found that he was no longer tired, but exhilarated. His hand hurt. That, too, was good. He sang 'Jerusalem', belting it out, all the way through, at the top of his voice. Charles put his hand on his arm, delicately.

'J'étais bien content que tu étais là.' He sighed. 'That poor man. Somehow, I can't see it being his baby. Who knows. A man, you see, never quite knows. That is the prerogative of the woman.' He fumbled for a cigarette. Hilary struck a match, held it for him.

'I loved your mother very much, it was a most passionate affair. I could never forget her. I never have forgotten her.' He cast a sideways glance at Hilary. 'I feel how much you are like her. Perhaps that's why I feel as I do. Cela te gêne?'

'No. Go on, I want to know. Really, please. I don't even know how you met.'

'Look, I tell you, for maybe six months, I was a student in London. It was for fun, it was the place to be. All young, all medical students all together. Your mother was beautiful, clever, everybody was in love with her. She chose me, it was incredible, wonderful. Then, I asked her to come to France and stay with me, I had two years to go in medical school. She said no, she had to be free.' Charles was driving slower and slower.

'You see, she understood me very well. I wanted her, but the fact was, I also wanted to be free. Later she wrote and said she had met your father, she was going to marry him. Well, I didn't like that at all so I went to England and saw her. I met Nicholas. I don't think I liked him very much, nor him me. But I saw that he was clever. Brilliant, some said. I could see that he, who was going to become a great doctor, was an eligible parti. Whereas I, you see, was erratic, a bad student. I wasn't even faithful to her. Of course I didn't tell her that, but she knew. I loved her, but I was not the better man. So I said that to Amanda that she was right. Partly it was true, partly I wanted to hurt her. I knew, you see, that she still loved me.'

He sighed heavily, lit a new cigarette from the stub of the old one. The car stopped at the roadside. Hilary stared out at the sunflowers, all on automatic compass and swivelled the other way.

'If I had not been a naughty boy, you might have been my son. She was clever, your mother. It was her choice – not me. She made the right choice. She chose your father.'

Charles started up the car again and they moved slowly off. Hilary looked at the sun shafting across the early morning mist and the promise of a brilliant day. He thought about his mother, who had never finished medical school, who had married the wrong man and had his babies, screaming in pain like that woman. She had had choices, more than most people did, because she had brains and looks. With all that, she had got it wrong.

He couldn't see that clever, beautiful, free-spirited student at all. He didn't believe in her. His mother was a nice conventional woman who dressed badly and was a good mother and who spent her days doing things for other people. And on and off so unhappy that she cried in the middle of the day for sheer misery. She had been destroyed. The world was a tragic place. There was the smallest gap imaginable between getting things right and getting them hopelessly wrong. It all made him feel old and incredibly sad.

'I'm not so sure,' he said. 'That she was right, I mean.' His voice came out very small. 'I'm not sure if she is happy,' and he said this quietly, because it was clearly very wrong to tell this man that. Charles, accelerating as he cheered up, laughed and it seemed that he hadn't heard that bit. Hilary felt a pang at his own disloyalty.

'Oh, I didn't do so badly,' Charles said. 'I had a lot of fun instead and later on I met my lovely Louise. Besides, at the time it seemed to give me an excuse not to go on. I knew, you see, that any healing powers I had lay in these hands. They couldn't teach that in a lecture room.'

'So why did you go on?'

'I didn't.' He shook his head. 'I never qualified. It was easier for me to find a way to have the papers forged,' he said calmly. 'That was how I got registered. After all, it was necessary for me to have the papers somehow. To have a dossier, a certificate number.' He shrugged his shoulders in a very matter-of-fact way. 'You need that to practise as a doctor.'

'It's usual, then, in France?' Hilary swallowed. He didn't know what he was supposed to say. Was this some joke? Charles then explained that of course it was not usual. Nobody knew, not Louise, not Michèle, nobody. Only him, Hilary.

'Je comprends,' said Hilary. His throat hurt.

'I knew that I was meant to be a doctor, you see. That was obvious.' Smilingly Charles reached over and gripped his shoulder for an instant in a playful, friendly way. Hilary covered his eyes as, turning the next corner, the sun hammered through the windscreen with painful brilliance.

3

Hilary caught glimpses of the old lady's frail body stretched out on the shiny stuffed counterpane, saw Charles bending over her, his hands soothing and stroking flesh that was dead white, only the forearms brown, like long gloves. The door had been left ajar. He paced about the tiny room, unable to stop himself from watching through those couple of inches. She had groaned to begin with, had let out a little cry, collapsing stiffly forward onto the bed. Now she was very quiet. When they arrived she'd kissed the doctor's hand before he could stop her.

Madame Ourlandes was eighty-nine and lived alone, having buried her contemporaries, her husband and all three of her children. Her house was tiny and wooden, with a verandah and a sprawling garden grown wild. There was a small area in front which was immaculately tended and she was generally there, weeding or planting, when they arrived. It pained Hilary to see her nearly bent in two as she carried the heavy watering can along the path. How shrunken her world was, how vast the wilderness she kept at bay. The house was very isolated, but Madame was not troubled. She had been born in this, her grandparents' house. She intended to die in it.

She let out little sighs of pain all the way up the stairs which she ascended with terrible slowness. You could see how she suffered. It was in every inch of her, in the deliberate positioning of feet and hands. Years of experience had taught her the least painful ways of doing things. Madame Ourlandes had acute arthritis and it had knotted her up, had taken further inches off her height, turned her hands and feet into big knobby branch stumps which looked as if they were made of wood. Her eyes, though, were alive and bright, her mind acute despite constant pain. She spoke in a very small voice, high and sweet like a child's. She had a way of giving you her utmost attention, of looking at you with wise eyes.

Three times a week Charles Beauregard came to the little house and soothed her with massage. She was his last call. Madame blessed him for it, kissed his healing hands. Gently, she took Hilary's hand between her tortured palms and whispered to him that God must bless the doctor and keep him safe. His calls soothed her to sleep and real rest which was precious for coming without pills. Charles always left her fast asleep. Like the old countrywoman that she was, she rose at first light, put herself to bed when it faded. She had no electricity and did not miss it. Quietly Charles and Hilary crept away from her house. Like thieves in the night they would tiptoe down the little staircase and gently close the front door.

Charles knew to park a little distance away down the quiet lane, for fear that the noise of the engine starting up would wake her. Her hearing was acute. 'When God calls me, I shall hear him,' she said to Hilary. He particularly wanted to see her face at repose, smiling, and wondered if she looked like that when asleep. He hadn't dared to ask if he could go in and look at her, but the idea grew in his head.

'She always asks me the same question. Why does God keep her alive, an old woman, no good to anyone, when he took her children?' Charles lit a cigarette, eased the car onto the road.

'What do you say?'

'It's hard. I don't know. She is a pure spirit, you know. She is nothing really but pain, inside and out. It has refined her down to the essence. Perhaps we need that – we others who are coarse and rough.'

'Is that what you say?'

'Ah, no. Never. I would not presume. No, no, I tell her I do not know her purpose but surely she has one. For we all have one.'

'But if we don't know what it is?'

'Ah, that is precisely the human condition. Not knowing. If we knew those things that God knows, we would not be human at all, but angels. Perhaps the precious thing about Madame

Ourlandes is just that at her great age, with all her wisdom, she still asks such questions. My old professor used to say that there were three things you should know about a person. What they know, what they don't know, and then what they don't know that they don't know.'

They were quiet then, the warm air blowing in as dusk fell, the same mild air filling the room where the old woman slept at peace. It would be invaded by the real dark of the woods and countryside by the time they were home.

They had finished dinner when the phone rang and Louise's habitual shrillness softened at once into warmth.

'Bonjour, Madame, oui, oui, I can guess who you want to talk to – vite, Hilary, ta mère!'

Hilary, who felt both a compelling need to talk to his mother and dread of any more frankness from anyone, rose slowly.

'Mum,' he said.

'Hello, Hilary.' She sounded a bit flat. 'How are you, darling?'

'Fine, terrific. Couldn't be better.' He felt a bit flat himself. 'Something I wanted to ask.'

'Yes?'

Not easy, this. He turned over various ways of phrasing the next bit. Did you sleep with Charles, Mum? By the way? Or, mind if I ask a rather personal question?

'I was a bit curious, I just wondered how well you really know Charles? I mean – how, well, ah, well?' He let out as false a laugh as any he'd ever heard.

'Quite well, Hilary, or else you wouldn't be there, would you?' She laughed lightly.

Hilary asked himself how exactly he proposed to check out Charles's account of their relationship. *'You see, Mum, I'd like to know whether he tells the truth or not. Can we start with something non-controversial. Sex. You and him. Are we talking numero cinq? Numero seven? Hecky thump. So you did it all. I see. Thank you. Really glad I asked. Next question. Would you describe your old "friend" Charles as a liar? I mean, do you think of him as being a cheat? A fraud, a pathological criminal?'*

'Darling? Are you still there?'

'Sure, sorry, just a second, hang on.' His hand, holding the phone, was sweaty. Hilary knew that he, no chip off that old block, was incapable of Charles's appalling frankness. Through the glass door, he stared at Michèle, sitting at the dining table, as she leant forward and picked up a glass. The curve of her throat, swallowing, could move him almost unbearably.

'Hilary, are you there?'

'Course I am, Mum. Where did you meet Charles?'

'At Zurich Airport, darling, I told you,' she said wilfully. Another long silence. 'Aren't you happy, Hilary? You did say it was wonderful, before.'

'Fine, sure, yes.'

Once he told anyone Charles's secret, it would be in the air and somehow people would find out. And if Charles was betrayed, he, Hilary, would be responsible. He alone. Visions of an arrest, of Charles being taken away, danced through his head, the family ruined, tears on Michèle's face, hand-wringing, bailiffs at the door, silk dresses being carried away in bundles, Louise in rags and a shawl. Dickensian squalor and distress. And if he kept quiet, didn't that make him an accessory to the crime? Why had Charles told him?

'Hilary, what is going on, darling, this is long distance,' said his mother sharply.

'How is Dad? And Ed?'

'Ed's asleep. Well. I must be going. Goodnight, Hilary.'

''Night, Mum.'

Both receivers were plonked down simultaneously. What now?

'Pear tart with just a little Calvados? Or apple?'

In the kitchen, Hilary dithered about while Louise went into the pantry and selected from its cornucopia of good things. She slipped the tart onto a plate while he chose words and discarded them and then, because in a minute they'd be back in the other room, he blurted something out.

'Charles is an extraordinary man—'

'I think Michèle—' she started and stopped.

Think, Hilary told himself. 'Go on. Please.'

She turned the tart on the plate and turned it again until the position was right, for a thing had to be perfect or it wasn't worth doing. 'I think – mm, well. Michèle really likes you,' she said. 'I know a mother mustn't say those things. Never interfere, you know. But we are pleased you came. Good. What were you saying?' She picked up the plate with a kind of apologetic little swoop and dip and waited.

'Ce n'était rien,' he said. Of course he wasn't going to tell her anything.

Amanda looked at Ed. Head down, her boy went on forking stuff into his mouth blindly while attempting to extract a piece of paper which had unaccountably become stuck down the rim of his bird-watching binoculars. His extraordinary patience and concentration were only ever applied to his own very small and personal interests. Not unlike his father. Who, again, would not be home to dinner and had only just rung to tell her so. Another man might have been having an affair. Nicholas? She thought about it. On the stove, the pans were bubbling away. One by one, she turned them off. Not Nicholas. Incapable of it. He didn't have the juices necessary for passion.

Too low a flame. How could a man as clever as her husband choose such stupidity as a modus vivendi? She turned to look through to the dining table laid for dinner. She went up to it and gave it a malicious little shove. Silver-plated and spotless, knives and forks and serving spoons winked and trembled.

In the kitchen, Ed focused the binoculars on the wall telephone. They were too heavy for him and his hands trembled. Slowly and triumphantly, Columbus sighting land at last, he read off the number he knew by heart.

When the oven pinged, Amanda removed the fluffy, golden mass. Nicholas's favourite pudding.

'Soufflé, Ed?'

'Ech, echaah, ecch, aagh. Ugh, ugh ugh.'

The vomit noises went on for some time and were then transmuted into Apache war cries by her discovery of one remaining tub of vanilla-chocolate-fudge ice cream. She spooned it out, without bothering to rebuke him. Ed shut up after a bit and looked at her. She sat dreamily on the edge of the table and stared at nothing. He let the ice cream melt into a pool and then with loud gasps and slurps drank most of it. Inserting a straw into each nostril, he blew as hard as he could into the beige puddle. A sort of tune bubbled through. He looked at his mother. Still she did nothing. He did it again, much louder.

Nothing Ed could do really bothered her any more. He did the theme of Thunderbirds twice and then managed to draw the remaining liquid up into his nose. He held his head back to keep it in. He now waved at her, permitting it to drip out again, gesticulating meanwhile for tissues.

'Gotta bad gold.' Silently, Amanda observed the twin flow of matter. Without comment, she passed the box of Kleenex. She started to clear the dishes away.

'Bathtime,' she said mildly. 'Upstairs. Off you go,' She found no need to urge and coax as she used to, just as he found no reason to argue and refuse.

Amanda waited for Ed to get out of the bath, a process complicated by his recent discovery of modesty. The water seemed to run interminably. She had swum naked with Nicholas on their honeymoon, centuries ago. Clamped together, kissing, letting the bubbles rise as they did. Closing her eyes, she thought about how it would be to swim like that with Charles.

Inside the bathroom, Ed knelt damply upon the bathmat and gazed at the soapy meniscus which was on the verge of flowing over the rim of the bath. He had blocked the overflow with soap. He controlled the bath by judicious manoeuvrings of a trickling tap and the plug, which was held in the plastic beak of a long-handled parrot's head. This was supposedly designed to open and close when the grip was squeezed. Often, though, because it was a very cheap toy, it failed. This potential failure was what gave excitement to the project. The trick was to lift the plug at the precise second of the bath overflowing. He started the countdown in his head. If his grip slipped that was it.

'Come on, darling.' It was quiet in there. Amanda tapped on the door. For a long time there was silence. At last, she heard the sound of water gurgling down the pipes. A pink shrimp completely wrapped in a sheikh's robe towel, Ed sidled into his bedroom, closing and locking the door to keep her out.

Leaning against it, Amanda remembered the long gone era when she and Nicholas used to pay attention to what the other one said. She'd loved him then, or at least she'd thought she did. To be precise, she'd not had to think about whether she did or not.

'Ed, you ready?' She tapped on his door.

She had been amused by him, that had been the essence of Nicholas. Fun allied to sharp, dazzling intellect. Sexiness which was linked to words, the mind rather than the body. The pleasures of intelligence. Whereas Charles just emanated that extraordinary physical allure. Whereas Charles just . . . *was*. She closed her eyes, to aid concentration.

'Mum?' The shrimp unlocked the door and appeared, hair combed, pyjamas on, smiling. He jumped into bed. She tucked him in. With the astonishing display of passion which arose magically each night from the deep sea of his self-centredness, he hugged her tight and kissed her and told her how very much he loved her. She loved him, too.

'Mum? Why've you gone quiet? Are you happy now?'

'I'm always happy. Don't be silly. Time to go to sleep, darling,' but he propped himself up on one elbow and gave her his deep, disconcerting stare.

'You won't do anything dramatic, will you, Mum?'

'Why on earth should I?'

'You promised me you'd tell me when you were ready,' and he at once turned over and closed his eyes. Within a minute, he would sleep.

Back in the kitchen, Amanda thought about the immense tenderness she felt for her children, never more strongly than when sleep or absence freed her from them. Whatever it was that linked them to her, it was stronger than everything else. It was as powerful as life itself.

There on the table stood the concave collapse of what had once been a perfect dome. And what was to become of it now? She lifted up her fist and smashed into the middle of it. Bang, to the bottom, ouch, a frill of substance jumped into the air and she felt the stored heat from inside burn her hand. A satisfaction, of sorts. She let cold water run over her hand, watching each frothy splodge of soufflé fall from her skin, swirl round the sink and then carry on its journey, down the plughole and ever on, down to the sea.

Amanda ran a bath. She contemplated her legs which rose

pinkly from the foam, long, yes, if a touch Rubenesque. She wasn't twenty any more, but things were generally speaking in the right place. Or not too far from it. Her hand, which had to be kept out of the warm water, which hurt it, splayed on the rim. She breathed in, watched the waist reappear and a rib or two and the breasts jut forward. Men liked bottoms and curves anyway. Men had always liked her. Funny. She'd forgotten that. There were many things, even very important ones, she had forgotten and which it was crucial to remember, if only she could remember how.

Over at the dressing table, she stared for a long time at her face, too pale with such light coloured hair. Such terrible hair. The bright blonde stuff was ridiculous and she would tell Georgie to tone it down. She pulled it back, frowned. She smoothed back her forehead with her hands to make the little frown lines and crow's feet disappear. She brushed her hair forward, back, then forward again. Carefully, absurdly, she applied make-up.

Not that terrible old nightie. Slowly, she extracted garments one by one from her cupboard, trying on this and that. She sprayed on scent. Still humming, she floated around the bedroom, finally arranging herself voluptuously on the big double bed. A woman ready for adultery. There was no place where she and Charles had not made love. Her parents' house, their faintly Spartan queen-sized bed, her skimpy single bed, the drawing room floor, the bath – closing her eyes Amanda tried to recapture the details of that memorable weekend of her parents' twenty-fifth wedding anniversary. While they made love with closed eyes in a darkened room (if they did it at all) in the Grand Hotel, Brighton, their wild child did better. Their good girl Amanda, left to guard the house. You won't be lonely, darling, will you? No, Mummy, I won't. You have a lovely time. Don't worry about me! I'll be glad of the quiet to work, Daddy. Sex was something that to this day they had never mentioned.

So long ago. Over twenty years. Amanda had been a good student, hard-working, always in the front row to be sure of not missing a word of the lecture. She had made careful notes with different coloured biros to underline major and minor headings and this, in medicine, was crucial, for nobody sought originality or inspiration. They wanted facts, dry and well-ordered.

That summer morning as she sat down, she had become aware that she was being stared at and had to turn round and there was Charles, two rows behind. He had smiled at her in so suggestive a way that she had blushed. And for the remainder of the lecture she had been unable to concentrate for his eyes on her back. She knew that he would ask her out and that she would go – that he wanted to make love to her and that she felt the same. All in one glance. Incredible.

Opening her eyes, Amanda was saddened to see her 45-year-old body reflected in the mirror where she half expected the long hair and the absurdly young face and Mummy's pearls. The little blemishes and marks of life, everything losing its lustre, even the gums beginning to retreat. She had been pretty, very – she knew it now, even if she hadn't then. Charles had made sure that she knew that she was beautiful; he had made sure that she felt all the important things. And the upshot had been that she had cut all her lectures, had six glorious weeks of passion and the following year had chosen to marry Nicholas. Charles had made her need a man. Why had she not chosen him? She frowned, thinking hard. She had known one day that she shouldn't marry him. On such a meagre basis, lives were decided. It had all started and ended on intuition. But why? How? When? Why couldn't she remember?

Pudding plates clattered (soufflé, his favourite, not a patch on Amanda's) and Nicholas saw that they would be out of the restaurant with nothing ventured or gained if he didn't get on with it. With something not unlike a prayer he leant forward. He looked intently at his dining companion. Fearful of being overheard, he lowered his voice.

'After all these years. First time I've done anything like this. You see, Amanda,' he paused, feeling uncomfortable and disloyal. He looked imploringly at the face opposite. 'It's hard to put it into words.' There was another long pause. Get on with it. 'There's something wrong with her,' he said.

'Physically wrong?'

'I don't know.'

'Has she seen her doctor?'

'No, no, that wouldn't be – you don't understand. She doesn't say a word to me. Not even hello. I was hoping you'd have some idea. Of what it's about,' and Nicholas waved his hands about, helplessly.

Professor Jameson lit his cigar and rolled it in his square-ridged scholar's fingers and then sucked at it, luxuriantly. He smiled in a kindly manner. Nicholas wondered if his wife was mad. It seemed a long time before his companion spoke.

'She doesn't speak to you? I see. Why do you think that is?'

A bluish aromatic cloud lay over the table where they sat. In frustration and annoyance, Nicholas spread his hands to signal that he didn't know and looked at them, his long, strong fingers, helpless on the tablecloth.

The pharmacist spotted them through his big plate-glass window, came running out of the pharmacy and right up to them, face wreathed in smiles.

'Wonderful news, Mademoiselle! My first little nephew.' He shook hands with Michèle, offered his faintly damp hand to Hilary. 'And you were there, young man. You see, I have heard the whole story. Fernand is my cousin, you know. You didn't know? Ah. On my mother's side. Second cousin really, almost a nephew. Well, he's a fine healthy boy, thank the good Lord. Mademoiselle, your father's a genius. Ça alors! What can't the man do? First of many, I hope. Young blood, that's what our family needs. And without the doctor, who knows what might have happened? Nearly a tragedy. What a man, no?' Drawing out a handkerchief, he blew his nose.

'Why are you so surprised about the baby?' Michèle's tone was tart. She got out a Marlboro and inched it between her lips. What was it with her and the smoking? 'My father's been doing his job for twenty years. He should know what he's doing.'

'No, no, no, Mademoiselle,' Jean-Jacques wagged a playful finger. 'That is so often not the case. You'd be surprised. Doctors get prescriptions wrong. They make mistakes, oh, all the time. Not your papa. You know, he doesn't prescribe a lot of medicine, not him, I should complain for that's my business but no, I respect him. Twenty years, you say? Twenty years. It's true, yes. Why, I have been here twelve years. I can tell you, Mademoiselle, I have not in that time made a fortune from your papa, but still I consider him the best doctor I know. The very finest. And you – you helped him, young man. I thank you.' He grabbed his hand again. Hilary shuffled bashful feet. The pharmacist's penetrating eyes, which occupied the exact midpoint between the shiny dome up top and the compensatingly hairy luxuriance of the moustache below, swam with unshed tears.

'Oh, it was nothing. Really.'

Bored, Michèle puffed restlessly on her fag. Hilary thought about the cord round the baby's neck, its purple skin. What if it had died? How would he be feeling now? Could a proper doctor have prevented the whole crisis happening in the first place? A real, qualified one?

'So, there was a real emergency, I hear. Well?'

Hilary began in his stumbling French to tell him the gruesome details, half waiting for him to say, ah, but that was the wrong thing to do, surely, normally a doctor does this and that. He might betray Charles inadvertently. Oh God. But Jean-Jacques went on listening attentively while Hilary gave him a blow by – no, a cut by cut account, while incurious, rude Michèle backed slowly away. When he got to the gory business, the pharmacist shuddered.

'Ah, poor Fernand could never stand the sight of blood and nor could I. Excuse me, please – twenty years, eh, that is something.' He backed smilingly off and, in increasingly morose mood, Hilary ambled on.

The problem was the daughter, not the father. Hilary had thought it couldn't be possible for him to exist in this state of permanent dizziness while she remained unmoved. Well, he'd been wrong. She could be indifferent to him and continue to play strange and cruel games. He had a permanent lump of misery in his chest, a hopeless feeling that he couldn't do anything at all, that he was doomed to follow her about and slaver at her heels like a dumb dog. And this incredible combination of raging, unsatisfied lust and total lack of knowledge of the other person added up to being in love. Love was the reverse of knowledge. What he knew about her, he didn't necessarily like. How could that make sense?

And yet it did if he thought about girls he liked but could not desire, as opposed to those whom he had made love to who were often not likable at all. Julia. She had allowed him to do some quite astonishingly bold things to her on her mother's kitchen table, a place that was deeply uncomfortable yet inarguably less cold and hard than the alternative, the quarry-tiled floor. Julia, who was athletic and bright and quite pretty, yes, and whose parents were in the house. He didn't like her particularly. Nevertheless, at Julia's instigation they had gone into the kitchen and boiled the kettle and steamed up the windows and put the radio on. Every now and then he had laughed loudly. For the benefit of the parents upstairs, who could never have allowed mirth to coexist in their minds with the kind of animal behaviour it was accompanying. Girls were in conspiracy with his prick, which chose instant gratification, however sordid, every time. The world divided into girls who never would and girls who definitely did, and while the latter existed on the planet, his hormones wouldn't let him waste time getting to know the other sort. Then there was the incomprehensible Michèle who managed to be everything at once and whom he could both love and hate with the same terrible intensity. Why was she so cruel?

Héloïse sat with her legs crossed in front of her gilt and curlicue dressing table laden with lotions and unguents. One fluffy mule was swinging, she hummed nasally to herself. Slowly, she rubbed cream into her forehead, then streaked it lightly down her nose. Dipping into the pot for another smear, she dotted it about her cheeks and on her neck. She threw her head right back and stared down her nose at her reflection. Then she patted her cheeks with both palms, fingers curling back. Jean-Jacques, approaching slowly, bending to kiss her neck, encountered a dollop of substance. It was always the most expensive of substances, too, always the tiny jar at 150 francs. The little minx. Not that he begrudged her a thing, she should have the very best, the finest. He bent forward again.

'Mon ange, be patient. Don't you want me to be beautiful for you?'

He did, of course he did. But beauty took so long and so many greasy creams and then he was frightened to approach her and often, too often, after another exhausting day, he fell asleep before the creams had been absorbed. Not tonight, though. The news of the new little baby cousin had put ideas into his head. These ideas were old friends. He twinkled at her in the mirror. She smiled back.

'Not long, my darling, my chéri.'

Waiting, he began to pace about the flat, thinking for perhaps the thousandth time that if there were a child, as there would be, of course, eventually, since there was nothing wrong with either of them, then they would move. It was very convenient to be right above work, but a child needed space and light and a garden. Life would change, for the better.

'Chérie,' he said, 'when I am the mayor of this town, I shall reorganise everything, every last bit of it. This place needs action. New blood. Old Papa Dutronc is past it, he's had his day. We need to put the place on the map. Make things happen. You would like that, wouldn't you, my darling?'

No reply came from the bedroom. She was concentrating of course. Trying out new products was part of the job. A woman had to look after herself, especially one as good-looking as his wife. Beauty was her profession, she made a nice little living from the parfumerie and the beauty treatments. Looking good was part of her professional armoury. Though the money never quite came out at what he thought it should be, considering the clientele and the prices she charged. It was just enough to give her a nice little allowance, nice clothes and her little fripperies. Not enough for the basics. Still, that was fine by him. It was a husband's job to provide for his wife. When they had children, when she had to give up her work, she would find him just as generous.

She would not lack for a thing. No silly, pretty thing she fancied should ever be denied his Héloïse. To this end, the pharmacist worked as hard as he could, always looking for new business opportunities, doing many menial jobs himself, always up early and to bed late.

'How to make one's mark, eh, that's the question, isn't it, my love? How to make people think. They just do the usual thing. Good old Dutronc, they say, fine old fellow and they vote for the nice old man. Without thinking, you see, what could be. Without progress. They don't realise what I am capable of. How to be known as a go-getter. Ah, that's the thing.'

Still muttering to himself, by now he was in the kitchen, opening the fridge door. There were face creams in here, too. A fridge should have some food. He gazed mournfully at the ampoules of collagens, the gels and vitamin supplements, the extracts of lamb's foetuses. Never any protein or vitamins in their more usual form. He fumbled through a couple of pieces of paper. A slice or two of ham, a little sweaty. A few green beans in a bowl. An old orange. His wife could not be accused of extravagance in this department. Jean-Jacques sighed. He was often hungry. Héloïse said that he needed to lose weight. He hardly had any belly at all. He sucked in his stomach, inflated a manly chest. What was that in the back, in that little Tupperware box?

As he carefully felt with outstretched fingers past the beauty treatments to the very back of the shelf, he thought about the new little cousin and the great good luck of Fernand. What a hard time that poor Marianne had had. But a boy, a dear little boy. His Héloïse would be in the most modern clinic, yes, and early too. With the finest doctors in the land. What had Mademoiselle Beauregard said? Her father should know his job after twenty years. She was right. A good man, the doctor, though Jean-Jacques regretted his tendency to under-prescribe. But he had achieved a miracle. With a little shiver, the soft-hearted pharmacist thought about what the English boy had told him, about the purple baby and the cord and the nearness of disaster. Without the doctor, what would have happened to the baby? Dead no doubt, the little thing. Twenty years' experience. Healing hands. Truly, he was a good man. In a sudden access of generosity, the pharmacist decided that Dr Beauregard might be the man to deliver his and Héloïse's future son. A man to be trusted despite his great fault.

It was a sauce, a tomatoey kind of sauce. Jean-Jacques opened the lid and dipped a finger in. Not bad at all. It needed just a touch of pepper. He found a piece of bread left uneaten from supper and dribbled drops of sauce onto the bread. He was stuffing this rapidly into his mouth when inspiration struck. He called out to his wife.

'Listen, chérie, a magnificent idea. What if I organised an

event to honour the doctor? Twenty years in the village.' He
swallowed. 'You know, it's a pretty important anniversary – he
must be the most popular man in the place. I think I am the first
to think of it.' He got a spoon out, returned to the sauce. A little
salt helped, too. 'What do you think, my angel? An inspiration,
isn't it? What do you say to a dinner, a banquet?' She probably
couldn't hear him. He raised his voice.

'For the doctor. A banquet. Ten courses. What could be
more appropriate than for the pharmacist to organise such a
thing? People will remember. They'll see it's something between
professionals, those of us in the medical profession. Something
that would hardly do for an ironmonger. Ha.' He was feeling
more and more pleased with himself.

'Did you hear, chérie? I said they'll see, then, a pharmacist is
in that club too. A professional. Naturally it must be beautifully
done. Only the best of everything. Nothing but the finest.
Foie gras. Homard. Champagne!' His mouth was watering.
Jean-Jacques tore off a large piece of bread, dipped it into the
tomato sauce. He chewed and swallowed it rapidly.

'The cream of the place will come, not just from here, either.
This will be a tiptop medical occasion. You know, I could talk to
the big hospitals, get a list together. Surgeons, doctors, a professor
perhaps. For you – a lovely new dress.' Pacing backwards
and forwards in excitement, Jean-Jacques now dribbled the
remaining drops of the sauce onto the last piece of bread. He
could scarcely believe his good fortune. There was a kind of
muffled bleating noise from Héloïse in the bedroom.

'You know what? I'll find out where our good doctor qualified
and invite his contemporaries, to honour him. His professor, his
best friend, all his colleagues.' He stuffed the last piece of bread
into his mouth and with élan skimmed the empty Tupperware
box onto the draining board.

'Did you hear, Héloïse? Dutronc will think himself lucky to be
in such company. As for that sweaty pig of a baker, Lardon, he
needn't aspire to it. They'll all see who counts and who doesn't.
Me, I shan't be too proud to shake hands with old Limousin the
farmer, no. People will see. What do you think, my angel?'

Lardon with his shiny big red face, his hairy back, his string
vest, his overgrown loutish son, would not be invited. Young

Lardon was a randy goat and notorious in the village for his womanising. He made eyes at every woman. Once, approaching the parfumerie, he'd caught the young man with his too-tight jeans and gaudy shirt staring in through the window at Héloïse and licking his lips. The thought made Jean-Jacques shudder. Disgusting though he was, the young baker knew his place. His father, who never met the pharmacist without embracing him as a confrère, was a very different proposition. Lardon with his coarse red face and his rank armpits needed to be shown who the real professionals were—

There was another bleating noise, this time much nearer. Rapidly, Jean-Jacques turned round, calling out, 'Did you hear, my darling?' He found himself just centimetres away from a green-faced ghoul with huge white eyes staring at him.

'Chérie?' He blinked. How silly he was. It was just the darkness of the kitchen, the thin unearthly light from the fridge, the greenness of the mask. His wife was pointing at the sink.

'You idiot,' she said. As she spoke cracks began to appear in her face. Fine green powder showered down her front. 'You fool, what have you done? My special mask. Human foetal tissue, very pure, and white of eggs and vegetable extracts. And you just throw it away, as though it cost nothing.'

Jean-Jacques' face quite suddenly took on a greenish hue all on its own, quite without any artificial aid. He staggered to the sink and bent over.

'Baargh,' he said. A long spasm shook his entire body. 'Burghth.' Then, with a great heave of his shoulders, to his wife's horror and disgust, his mouth opened and a stream of reddish liquid gushed out.

Descending as usual in the direction of the village, Hilary and Michèle passed the pharmacist toiling up the drive in a smartly pressed grey suit. He shook hands, explaining that he was coming to pay a call upon the doctor and Madame Beauregard. So he would find them at home, that was very good. He gave off an air of suppressed importance. As they reached the gates, Charles roared past. Toot toot, Mr Toad. He had the gleeful smile on his face of one who'd got away with something.

Thursday was market day, a little breeze fluttered the pennants on the stalls and the sun danced over the porcelain ornaments and glittered on a thousand butcher's knives. Hilary and Michèle wove their way along the high street. The place was stuffed with people as half the countryside took its basket for a saunter along the cobblestones and paused to say a newsy hello to its neighbours. The delicious aroma of chickens roasting on slow-turning electric spits made his mouth water.

A jostling bunch of grannies were queuing up to select their cheese and eggs at a vast caravan. You could scarcely see the assistants behind the pyramids of cheeses. Hilary couldn't resist a nutty Pyrénées cheese, grey-brown rind and inside pale yellow, delicious with the dark gold crust of his bread. A goat's cheese rolled in herbs followed. A woman selling foie gras gave him a taste of the aromatic pinky beige mass. Pure goose. Look, Monsieur, here is one with truffles. It was smooth and rich and irresistibly good even at six quid a tin and he bought a couple for Mum. Then he needed a bag and saw a granny's green string one which meant he could manage a couple of slices of smoked ham for the pleasure of the dexterity with which it was cut and then, because they were so pretty, a huge bunch of red and white striped radishes with feathery grass-green fronds. Louise would find uses for this stuff.

He'd lost Michèle. No, there she was over in the little square where the T-shirts and tops and swimsuits swayed brightly against each other. All the mademoiselles of the village seemed to be there pouting at the boys while they flicked their way through rows of sexy little tops. Yes, teeny knickers were big. You paid more for less, 'FF255 le set' it said against the row of evidently crowd-pleasing matching bras and pants in astonishing designs, all satin and lace in lurid colours.

Michèle smiled at his shopping bag. Like him, the shops were getting into the spirit of the thing. They had set up their own stalls in front of their windows, blocking the pavement and spilling people onto the street which offered the additional excitement of making cars swerve all over the place. This gave Hilary an excuse to take Michèle's arm and she, all smiling compliance, held on to him, so close that the wind flicked her hair in his face.

How perfectly the brilliant day combined its glories and then added one more, a warbling bird. A nightingale? He looked. No birds, no cages, but a crowd clustered round an agile-looking wizened old darling selling bird whistles in clay. He wore a wizard's hat. The whistles were shaped like birds and some of them were fired and glazed in brilliant colours. Their maker had laid them out prettily on shelves covered in velvet and he snatched up first one then another, putting two of them to his mouth at the same time and making one bird call to the other. He watched the crowd carefully and smiled at Hilary and beckoned him closer. The melodic warblings sounded genuine. Hilary bought one, it was just the thing for Ed. He blew on it. Tu-whit, to-whoo, it warbled. Owl-shaped as well, nicely made. Another item for the string bag.

Café La Fourchette was nearly full. Over coffee, he tried to explain to Michèle what Ed was like, with his bird-watching mania, his mad interest in all feathered things so oddly allied to total disrespect for anything else in nature. His totally destructive genius for practical jokes, his Superglue and tripwire antics. All the time he was waiting for the right moment. He'd know it when it came. Then he'd tell her about her dad. If he was to confide in anyone, it had to be her. She stared out of the window with those extraordinary eyes of hers, her air of having everything sorted out.

Would he, ever? Hilary worried, sometimes, that there wasn't much to him beyond a certain facility with book-learning, a good memory. He had thousands of opinions, ever shifting sands there, but what were his real passions, where were his commitments? He changed his mind about things all the time. Like, from minute to minute. And was it proof of his shallowness that whatever he started thinking of, he tended to end back with himself? He had half an eye on the greaser over the way who seemed to be attempting to stick his long yellow tongue down his girlfriend's throat while lighting a cigarette.

'Tu restes?'

His attention was recalled. 'Where are you going?'

She gave him her most dazzling smile as she stood up. 'Just a couple of minutes – I forgot to get something. Wait for me?'

Hilary nodded. Lightly, she touched his shoulder and then went out of the café and down the street, swinging her shoulder bag with her usual cheerfulness. He turned his attention back to el Fumato, who was now sharing his fag with his girl. Lovingly they blew smoke into each other's faces. Hilary now realised that what he'd taken to be a strawberry birth mark on the hussy's neck was the largest love bite he'd ever seen. A real whopper, a rosy red swelling three inches round. Old Nicotino was having a proud prod at it, presumably the most recent token of his esteem. She was slapping playfully at his hand, on which two guitarist's nails stuck out like horns, cracked, yellow and hard.

Amazing, really, all that Michèle knew about these people. Georgie, his mum's hairdresser, looked gay but wasn't. There was a girl in the shoe shop with huge tits. That was his local knowledge. Very subtle. But Michèle was pretty sharp in her observations and then all of a sudden he realised she wouldn't come back.

Hilary got up and went out into the main street, looked up and down it. What a fool he was. She wasn't in the Boulangerie Lardon opposite, nor in the mini supermarket. He looked up and down, but all the market stalls were in the way. He went up the street back towards the house without seeing her until he reached the turning in the road from which he was bound to see her if she was going up the hill to home. No Michèle.

He retraced his steps, passed the café going the other way. She wouldn't get away with it, not this time. Why did she have to spoil everything? Why couldn't he trust her?

Hilary speeded up until he was somewhere between a saunter and a jog. The village came to an end fifty yards on at the T junction. Beyond was an old stone wall which carried on for another hundred yards and beyond that lay the forest. Way up ahead, he saw a little figure in the distance which could only be her. Slender, jeans, the hair, moving quite fast. Panting a little, getting into a good rhythm, Hilary accelerated further until he was running. Another few minutes and he'd catch up. She was walking quite fast, the shoulder bag bouncing against her hip. He thought about whether he'd grab her, playfully of course, give her a fright. Though any second now she'd hear his footsteps and turn.

Another figure appeared out of nowhere, or rather out of the woods, and boldly walked side by side with her. Blue jeans, bright shirt, a man, tall and broad, dark hair though Hilary couldn't see any detail, it was too far for him to see the face. They were talking. Michèle was gesticulating. Some jerk. She was giving him the brush-off.

Straining a little, Hilary increased his pace. The man suddenly reached out and simply pulled Michèle off the road and into the thick woods. Yanked her, by the arm. One minute there were two people in the road and the next second they were gone. Shocking.

Hilary shouted her name while he ran as fast as he could. He kept his eye on the place. It could have been no more than a minute before he was at the spot. He shouted again. Nothing to be seen. Panting, he sat on his haunches for a few seconds to recover and stared into the trees. Nobody. His heart was pounding. He felt completely panicked. A catastrophe was happening, she was being attacked, he was just sitting there in anguish. Rape, murder. Dear God Almighty. He felt his heart skip painfully with fear. Standing up, he took a deep breath, then another, to calm himself. Be sensible. Get your breath. She can't be far. She'll hear you.

'Michèle!' Not loud enough. He called again as he walked forward into the wood. No sign of anybody. And was this the place where they disappeared? He looked at the carpet of bracken and twigs. No signs of a disturbance. Had the man dragged her through here? No, he must be in the wrong place. He went on, then on some more.

Hilary plunged deeper and deeper into the woods as fast as he could. Running, though, was nightmarish on the uneven ground, with stumps of trees to trip you and hollows and dips. He went crashing through the forest, bursting through brambles and bushes which whipped at his face and body. It took all his concentration to avoid falling, jumping over logs, swerving through the trees and all the time bellowing her name like a wild man. No sound came back, nothing but the thump of his heart, the crisp noise of twigs breaking, a couple of startled pheasants, whirring aloft. His legs were hurting, his heart and throat sore, he was full of terror. So easy to get it wrong, the narrowest of margins between everything being all right and catastrophe.

There was what looked like a riding up ahead, its smooth expanse of green pulled at him and he turned, sure that that was the way to go. It would be easier to run on. Jumping and swerving over a deep ditch full of bracken, he failed to spot a log. It tripped him. He lost his balance and cannoned into a tree, falling forwards, head first. The thick bark simply jumped out of nowhere and hit him, hard. Thump. He fell heavily and then lay like an idiot, amazed to discover that he didn't seem to be able to stand up.

Jean-Jacques had felt a little twinge of disappointment when the doctor drove past, when he waved but did not stop. No doubt he was on his way to see a patient. An emergency perhaps. For a little moment, he stood and mused. Should he turn back? And then it occurred to him that it might be no bad thing to have a private little word with Madame. Perhaps she had already arranged a party for the twentieth anniversary? And it certainly would be convenient to know the correct date without asking the doctor himself. Actually, he had no particular desire to meet the doctor who, good though he undoubtedly was, never quite hit it off with him. How could he, when the man so thoroughly rejected his métier? Not that he bore a grudge, for that was not his way. Why, he hardly ever said a word about it, not even to Héloïse. Doctors were his business after all, it was his job to support them.

Perhaps, and he rubbed his hands together at the thought, it could be a surprise? There was something glorious about the idea that Jean-Jacques Albert might enter into a secret correspondence with professors and specialists. He began to visualise the winks and nods, the special greetings. He imagined the old ironmonger shuffling up to him, when he knew. There was a man incapable of penning a good professional letter. He'd be well and truly out of his depth.

'Monsieur Albert,' he'd say, 'I'm getting on a bit. Out of touch. I wonder – look, I know it's presumptuous to ask, but have you ever thought of doing my job?'

At the front door, Jean-Jacques spent a little moment combing through his hair, neatly removing the stray hairs and dropping them onto the gravel. He wiped his hands on his trousers and checked his face in the little mirror he always carried for shiny spots. Héloïse always fussed. His bald head shone, but there was nothing he could do about that. He picked a number of imaginary pieces of lint off his jacket and straightened up, putting onto his face what he hoped was a respectful but friendly smile. Madame was always immaculately turned out. And she was a healthy woman. Headaches, yes, aspirin was sometimes required. Sticking plasters, the usual female stuff. She was an infrequent visitor to the pharmacy. She had never yet brought in a prescription.

Finally, he knocked on the door of the doctor's house, coughing quietly to himself once or twice and resisting the urge to smoothe his fringe of hair When nothing happened, he rang the bell.

'Madame! Ça sonne!' Nervously, he frowned and then again prepared his smile. He waited, swallowed. In another little moment, he heard the rapid tippety-tap of high heels hurrying towards the door.

'It is you, Monsieur. Come in, please.'

Madame Beauregard was wearing an apron, clearly she was busy in the kitchen. Jean-Jacques was ushered into the salon and there he paced from the doors to the far end of the room, continually threatening to knock into something and thus making himself nervous and alarming his hostess.

'Thank you, thank you, Madame.' He paused. Breathily, he sought the best way of explaining his plan. He noticed, as no man could help but notice, the delightful curves of Madame's figure as outlined by her robust but to him alluring garment, its strings pulled tight. It was a very long time since he had seen his Héloïse in one of those. 'I am thinking – I am thinking of organising a little event to honour your good spouse, Madame—'

'Ah Monsieur, excuse me, my stew will burn . . .'

Alone, Jean-Jacques did a number of turns upon the carpet. The most wonderful smells were floating through the open door, smells to make a man's stomach rumble and his mouth water. Back she came.

'You must tell me more, Monsieur,' she said. 'Please sit down,' and, reluctantly, he did. Jean-Jacques explained about the twenty years – his good fortune in finding that out. 'You see, Madame, one must never be too busy for the good things in life,' he said softly and it was true, very true, he felt himself how often he had made that mistake. So many good things that he had missed . . . he leant forward and softly began to speak his heart. 'Permit me to tell you of my dream.' His mind began to buzz. His plans began to seem a little understated. He would elaborate upon them. His head began to race ahead. 'Something exceptional, something the village has never seen. I am talking about a banquet – a magnificent occasion,' and Jean-Jacques sprang to his feet.

'A dinner fit for a prince – a king, Madame. An occasion to do honour to the doctor and to the esteem in which we hold him – the guests all very important personages . . .' Was she laughing at him? 'Of course,' he added rather stiffly, 'I am not in a position to choose who shall and shall not come. Your husband has so many medical colleagues, all his contemporaries. I have thought that perhaps, to save you the trouble, I should be the humble organiser. A mere functionary, Madame—'

'I would be so pleased if you would organise it. You know why I am smiling, Monsieur? It's because I am truly delighted with your idea.'

Pacing back towards the fireplace, Jean-Jacques spotted a silver cup upon the mantelpiece. He went nearer and looked. Turned, looked at Madame. She nodded her permission. It was a trophy for lifesaving, awarded to the young swimmer Charles Beauregard.

'I don't believe it,' he beamed, shaking his head. He read and re-read the inscription, simply charmed by it. He couldn't put the thing down. If he had needed to be convinced of the rightness of the cause, this trophy would have done the trick. 'Ah! There must be a presentation, naturally – if only I could think what to give! And I need the date, of course. Something fine, something which can be inscribed upon, something – just like this.' He nearly laughed with pleasure. The more he looked at Madame Beauregard, the more he felt in his bones the rightness of the whole wonderful venture. 'What a man – ah, what a man he is!'

Madame Beauregard broke into a most dazzling smile. 'I've just had a wonderful idea. Professor Vigne-Laval must be your guest of honour. Charles has mentioned him, oh, a thousand times.'

'That's a name I recognise,' he smiled and rubbed his hands together. 'I have an idea. Let us make a surprise for your husband. We should try to keep the whole thing a secret for as long as possible.' For the glory and the honour was to be his, all his. He didn't want anybody else taking over his party.

'Now, you want me to look up the date, I suppose, you need the one on his diploma. I will come and bring it to you tomorrow, with all the names and addresses I have found.'

'Tomorrow.' He nodded. He lowered his voice conspiratorially. 'Perhaps you could come just when the pharmacy is closing, Madame, then we will have a moment to talk.' There was a very loud knocking on the door, which made them both jump.

The bleak eye of the femme de ménage fell upon them.

'Bonjour, Madame Moulins,' he said. He knew her well. Bunions, elastic stockings, ointment and plenty of it. Piles and plenty of them.

'M'sieur,' she said coldly. 'I thought you might like to know it is lunchtime and no sign of the young people.'

At once Madame Beauregard jumped up. 'Thank you, Marie. Please come with me,' she said, beckoning to Jean-Jacques. 'I really must insist on helping as far as culinary matters are concerned – the kitchen, cher Monsieur, is the province of a wife. You'll see what supplies I already have.'

He followed as she led the way past Madame Moulins who glowered on in the hallway. With modest pride, she led him into the larder. Jean-Jacques, a man starved of sensual pleasure, was fairly intoxicated by what he saw and smelt. Shelf after shelf of good things rose into the air. The ham, the cheeses, the pickles! Jar after jar of homemade condiments, of preserves and jellies. They rose up in all their shining, dark beauty. And there, with cheeks flushed a lovely rosy pink, was Madame Beauregard. She closed the door of the larder behind them.

'You see? Inhale, Monsieur,' she said in a low voice. He obeyed, staring at her. Alone in this tiny room, alone with Louise – he knew her name, of course – he sniffed the heady mixture of perfume and pâté and truffle, of ham and cloves, ginger and cardamon. She stood so close and looked at him so intently. He felt himself rock forwards and backwards, gently, on his heels. He felt slightly dizzy. Very, very gently, he rocked forwards.

'Monsieur, at last I have found something which perfectly combines my tastes and my inclinations. Perfectly.'

He gazed at her full lips, oh, full of hope. He rocked back one half a centimetre.

'Something to astonish my husband,' she went on.

Dumbly, swallowing, Jean-Jacques nodded.

'He always gets what he wants. But now it is my turn.'

There came the sound as of a sack being dragged along the floor. Madame Beauregard sighed loudly and pushed open the larder door, ushering the bewitched pharmacist out into the fresh light of day. He nearly fell over Madame Moulins who was on her knees doing something to the kitchen floor. As she moved forward with a great, shuffling, heavy groan, dragging her feet behind her as though they were a dead weight that happened to be attached to the ends of her legs, he understood the source of the noise.

'We must discuss everything, please stay for lunch,' Madame Beauregard said firmly. Dumbly, he followed her back into the dining room. 'Look, there is a place already laid. Four of us and you.'

He looked. Yes, the table was laid with five place settings.

'They are late today – we must begin without them. Sit, Monsieur,' and she was gone, returning a moment later with a steaming pot. She lifted the lid, releasing the most tantalising aroma. 'A simple potage, just some asparagus, that's all. Rabbit stew with a few herbs. Some noodles with it, very simple, just tossed in butter. A little salad, then perhaps a sliver of cheese? A morsel of tarte tatin, perhaps. Please, sit down, Monsieur.'

He spread his hands to say no – no, he couldn't. His stomach was rumbling loudly. Not a word came out. The femme de ménage was still standing glowering in the doorway. She coughed, twice. Madame Beauregard half turned and bestowed upon her domestic a most glittering smile.

'Thank you, Marie, that is enough for today. Perhaps you would like to go early?'

How dazzling, how wonderful the smile of Madame Beauregard was. The soup was yet more wonderful. The asparagus was heaven. Soon she returned. She ladled out a generous helping of the stew. Her hips moved provocatively as she tossed the salad, they rolled as the noodles received their buttery coating.

'So much, Madame, too much,' he said weakly. But the juices in his mouth were swimming in anticipation. Behind Madame's back, he saw Madame Moulins crossing the hallway clutching a large carrier bag to her ample bosoms. As he took his first mouthful, half-closing ecstatic eyes, there was an incredibly loud report, like a shotgun going off. He looked up, alarmed. Slowly, a beatific smile spread across the face of the lovely Louise.

'Don't worry. It's only Marie, Madame Moulins going home,' she said. 'She shut the door, that is all. I expect she is hurrying to catch her bus,' and she laughed. It was such a lovely, joyful sound that he had to laugh too. 'Please, Monsieur Jean-Jacques, you need a napkin,' and he felt her hand graze his knees as she laid a snowy white cloth across them.

Charles Beauregard came roaring through the woods and, just as he flipped the indicator for the left turn into the village, saw his daughter kneeling at the edge of the road and slammed on the brakes. She stood up. A green string shopping bag dangled from her hand. He reversed back to where she stood.

'Perhaps I've lost Hilary,' she said, spreading rueful hands.

'How very careless. What d'you mean, perhaps?'

'This is his, but I left him in the café,' she said in a noncommittal tone. He looked at her.

'And how long ago was that? Where did you find it?'

She shrugged. 'In the woods. Back there.'

Charles flung open the passenger seat door and without a word she got in, sitting silently while he drove to as near as he could get to La Fourchette, wove his way through the crowd, looked in the café, spoke to the waiter and, finally, telephoned Louise. With some difficulty, he negotiated a three-point turn, set off down the road again.

'Yes, he followed you. And what exactly were you doing in the woods?'

'Nothing.'

'Were you with that stupid Lardon boy? Tell me, now.'

'I gave you my word, didn't I?'

'Yes. You gave your word.' Charles stopped the car abruptly

and, reaching across her, he pushed open the passenger side door. 'Go home,' he said, with suppressed fury. 'I'll find him. Tell your mother we'll be late. I will talk to you later.'

Michèle stood in the road and watched the car disappear. When it was gone, she hoisted the bag onto her shoulder. She stood for some minutes before turning and walking very slowly back into the village. Very slowly, she plodded up the hill towards home. Halfway up, while still hidden from the house, she burst into tears which would not stop. Still sobbing, she sat down and then lay and looked up at the leaves and the sky. She touched her face, which was red and shiny. Michèle, who had no need to check her appearance, did not carry a mirror in her bag. She knew how she looked and was and she waited. She would wait. Soon everything would revert to how it had been before.

Deep in the forest, Charles transcribed a second circle. When he failed to find Hilary, he decided to cover the same area, but following a slightly larger circle this time. He called out Hilary's name as he went. Next, he expanded the search zone to include the broad riding which led straight to the heart of the forest. Some instinct drew him to walk a way up it first. Perhaps it was merely the fact that the going there was so much easier. Then he saw Hilary. He was lying behind a log, very still, very white in the face. When he saw Charles, he gave a lovely smile. It occurred to Charles that the boy looked a lot like his wife.

Charles knelt down and examined him. He checked bones, pulled him straight, tested reactions. An ugly bump on his forehead.

'I feel sick,' he said, 'I knew you'd come. Can't walk on my own.'

Charles slid his arms under him and braced himself to lift him into a sitting position against a tree. Another effort, and he was up.

It was tough going. As he half staggered and half walked with his burden, Charles took deep breaths to steady himself, to set up a rhythm. In, out, one, two, he counted out loud.

Hilary's head throbbed. Blood pounded through it to its own crazy rhythm. He was in motion, he felt sick. He was on an animal. Its warmth, the mane. He was on the sea, rocking, in the hold of a ship. He was sea sick, horribly so. No wonder, the swell of the sea, throwing him from side to side, the motion was terrible. He became more and more aware that his body was swaying and throbbing.

'Michèle. Something happened to her. A man grabbed her.' Urgently he clutched at Charles's arm.

'Something happened to you. Michèle's fine, I've seen her. You banged your head hard. A miracle you didn't pass out altogether.' Charles patted Hilary's arm, unclenched the fist that was balling together the fabric of his shirt sleeve and placed Hilary's arm around his shoulders. They set off once more. 'Steady now,' he said.

Very slowly, they moved through the wood. The shafts of sun beating down through the trees were so bright that Hilary had to shut his eyes. Even from behind his lids, the sun pierced him with its dazzling lances and made him wince. Bird song trilled its torture. The wizened man in the market was warbling behind the trees. He felt the patterns the sun-dappled leaves made on him, like lace. It was all so strange. He could smell fresh bracken. He was concentrating with his whole being on walking straight and not falling over. This made his head thump. Everything was overlaid by the presence of the big man, soothing, holding him together.

His head was full of strange, incoherent thoughts, pain and pleasure mixed, relief and surprise. It felt so good to be held by Charles, so safe. His mother. Michèle. The purple baby. All in his arms. Charles had saved them all. Without him, what?

'The thing is,' Hilary said. He struggled to make it all quite clear. What was the thing? He squinted at Charles's face, received a flash of woodland brightness which made him close his eyes again. 'There was a man,' he said.

'He hit you?'

'No, no, I went into something, a tree, I don't know. Why isn't she like you?' Charles had to realise that he had to say these things. Later might be too late. He might as well say everything. Nothing to lose, all lost, the world lost for love. The deep chest swelled and receded. Was Charles laughing? Hilary thought he might cry. He quite wanted to. He had never felt more serious in his whole life.

'Be quiet,' Charles said. Hilary wasn't going to cry, no, he was made of sterner stuff, so just in case he squeezed his eyes tight shut.

They were coming out onto the road and there was the car. Charles helped him in. They were at the house and he was being carried inside and up the stairs and put to bed with painkillers inside him and a cold compress on his head. All of this happened from very far away. Hilary heard himself sleepily agreeing that he would be fine in the morning. Then he drifted away on the faint whispers of Charles and Louise conferring.

In her room, Michèle lay awake and listened for the noises of the house. The owl's cry hooted out from the orchard. The wind was rustling up a summer storm. No sound from downstairs where, by candlelight, her parents held hands and whispered.

Hilary woke perhaps a dozen times and each time felt the tide drawing him out to sea again until at last he woke very hungry and knew that he was better. In the shower, he felt carefully at the lump on his head which was shiny and blue-green and dramatic. It hurt like hell. The towel on his head was interestingly acerbic. Putting on his shirt, he discovered how stiff his back was. His head set up a thudding counterpart to his feet, descending the stairs in gradual rallentando.

They'd had breakfast. A thermos of coffee and a basket of brioches were waiting for him. He consumed them ravenously, tearing them apart and loading the frail shells with butter and jam. Chewing hurt. Little pink rosebuds clustered winsomely in a vase on the table. For no good reason, the sight of them also hurt. Something to do with his mother, who also did arrangements like this. When he had eaten, he stayed for a long time staring at nothing. Eventually, Charles came yomping past and skidded momentarily to a halt when he spotted Hilary through the glass door.

'You all right?'

When Hilary nodded his head, a hammer inside it suddenly fell onto the front of his forehead, bouncing off to smash the cranium and then thud back again.

'Will you come out with me? Sure you can manage it?'

'Yes,' said Hilary very quietly and carefully. He didn't want to see Michèle. He followed him out. Was he so slow or was it that everything else was going so fast? Behind him, the door crashed cataclysmically. Instead of starting the car, Charles hammered the car horn impatiently. Hilary winced.

'Ah, here she is. Get a move on, can't you?' Charles bellowed out of the window at his daughter who came running up. She got in. Crash. The bang of the car door reverberated through Hilary's eggshell skull.

'Make up your mind. I have to stay in. I have to go out. In. Out,' said Michèle snappily, leaning forwards between the seats to kiss Hilary's cheek and say her 'Bonjour' to him. 'Hilary, how are you?' He didn't manage a reply. She was thrown back as the car roared away. The loud scrunch of the gravel shivered up through the framework of the Peugeot. Hilary sat in his personal hell and waited for the next thing to happen. The car stopped abruptly.

'Out, I think. You go and help your mother. Go on.' Charles sounded peremptory and there was no gainsaying that tone. The big arm reached over, banged the door shut and they were off, leaving Michèle standing there, slowly pushing her hair back off her forehead with that gesture he knew so well.

For of course Hilary turned to watch her. He had to look, despite the pain in his head, despite his certainty that she would not turn to look at him. Because knowledge of its hopelessness didn't cancel out passion. He was not going to let himself be involved, but this purely intellectual decision did not connect with his guts, which churned on regardless. And so he looked and looked, seeing, as Charles did not, that far from turning up the hill to help her mother, Michèle merely waited for them to be gone before continuing on her way.

Lunch was prepared so Louise hurried back to her work in the surgery. She knelt in front of the great box of papers, discarding some, sorting others into neat piles, slipping yet others into files, unable to prevent herself from sorting and clearing as she went. Behind the big desk and thus hidden from the patients, stood four large cardboard boxes full of unsorted papers. More paper spilled out of the files proper. At each new piece of evidence of incompetent clerking she tutted and sighed happily.

Charles followed a system of sorts. It consisted of jamming

everything current into the right-hand side of the desk until this was full. At that point, the older papers were transferred to the left side, where with luck they could remain, yellowing and crumpled, for years to come. In due course, however, one of two things would occur: either Charles would need to find a particular piece of paper or an over-full drawer would jam, perhaps the one which housed something important. His matches, say, or his Swiss Army penknife. Then would come a roaring and stamping, a drumming of feet and rattling of handles. A hand would descend to hammer and bang and rip out handfuls of paper from both sides of the desk. These discards were then shoved pellmell into boxes which mingled what was current and what was long forgotten into newer and greater obscurity. Charles always claimed that he could find anything he needed within five minutes.

Another X-ray. These really did belong in the patients' files. Smoothing out the crumpled report which came with it, Louise undid the dusty green-ribboned concertina. Patients' files were haphazard affairs, not always containing medical notes, but crammed with bills for things Charles had bought from people's shops or businesses. Thus old Limousin's file had nothing on his rheumatism but a whole sheaf of papers relating to his application to convert the old barn into holiday houses. His seizures being more and more severe, his medical notes were in the right-hand side of the desk.

Ah, there was the card of the neuro-surgeon at the teaching hospital – she slipped it on top of the pile on the desk. A glass paperweight compressed the booty. Three or four pieces of paper, the top one scrawled upon a leaf torn from an exercise book with Vigne-Laval's address written in Charles's hand. She'd done well to find that. There were a couple of letters from consultants and the list she'd written out of all the eminent doctors she knew or had heard of. How pleased Monsieur Jean-Jacques would be.

Looking at her watch, Louise hurried to the kitchen to turn the oven down and down the hill she went, swinging her basket with the precious papers in it. She felt important, imbued with a sense of purpose. Jean-Jacques was hovering at the plate-glass window and, seeing her, threw the sign to closed and, ushering her inside, closed the white vertical Venetian blinds.

'They will all think we are having an assignation, Monsieur,' said Louise, laughing, and he blushed furiously from the crown of his head right down to the V of his crisp white overalls. It took the entire time that they spent talking, ridiculously enough in whispers, agreeing a date several weeks hence, passing over the list and studying it, adding the names of people the pharmacist knew – all of twenty minutes for that blush to fade. Leaving the papers with him, Louise set off on her second errand, which was to pick up some bread. Passing the Boulangerie Lardon, she averted her gaze.

Jean-Jacques watched to see the lovely Louise pass once more. Sweetly she waved. With a sigh he went up the stairs to the flat. Nothing was cooking in his kitchen. That morning's dirty breakfast dishes still lay on the table. He opened the door to the fridge and, with a grimace, closed it again.

Louise checked her watch. Charles liked his fish golden brown and piping hot, just flaking inside, but completely plain with just a sprinkling of parsley and a dash of lemon. Very simple, but it had to be just so. Setting the fish on a very low flame, she decided she'd just take five minutes to look in the attic. Up the stairs she went, humming to herself. There was a box of old papers she'd seen a year or two back.

With a conspiratorial glance left and right up and down the corridor, Nicholas tapped on the door. A cry of some kind encouraged him to enter and, as he did so, Jim turned, his face streaming with tears. Nicholas made to go out again.

'Hayfever,' Jim wheezed. 'Forgot my spray. Bloody nuisance.' He waved to him to sit. Nicholas waited for the seizure to pass, which it did, slowly and messily. Boxes of tissues lay about the place.

'How are you today, Nicholas?'

'What? Oh, fine. Well. I don't know.'

Jameson finished the job of wiping himself down and most of the desk and then sat down and looked at him.

'Silly,' Nicholas said. 'I don't know why I've come.'

'Don't you?' Jim smiled. 'Old friends should help each other, right?' This emboldened Nicholas to start the speech he had prepared.

'I think,' he said slowly, 'I think what I'd really like from you is some kind of analysis of the kind of state my wife is in – well, a diagnosis I suppose of what those symptoms represent. That should be quite simple, shouldn't it?'

'Sorry. I can't do that.'

'Jesus. Then what kind of help can you offer? What am I supposed to do? Jesus.' His hands were trembling.

'Talk to me.'

'What about? My primitive sexual fantasies? Penis envy? That I want to get back into my mother's womb, having killed my father first?' He should never have asked a friend. No, better to go to a stranger.

'If you like,' said the old man, still smiling.

Louise was singing. It took a mere two minutes before she pulled out a file inside which was a letter with a university crest. Then another. And another. A moment later, a piercing scream rang around the rafters. Louise threw all the papers up into the air, then scrabbled around for them again. She snatched up the first piece of paper and read it out loud: 'Regret to inform you that in these circumstances it will not be possible for you to continue as a student here.' With appalled disbelief, she read and re-read this and a number of other pieces of paper with the same crest and the same message. 'Would not readmit you to this or any other faculty' – 'lowest ever marks in a public exam' – 'failure to attend even a single lecture during the course of two semesters' – 'unusual for a student to fail each exam so unequivocally' – 'lack of application, lack of all the qualities desirable for a medical career . . .' Expelled. They had expelled him.

Spreading out the contents of the file, she examined each piece of paper. Every one spoke, not just of failure, but of a dogged determination to fail on the part of one Charles Beauregard, a student who refused to study but would not give up his right to do so.

At the very bottom of the file, she found a letter addressed 'To whom it may concern'. This was an official document which gave the date and place of issue and number of the diploma which qualified Charles Beauregard as a doctor. It was precisely what she had wanted to find. Except the date was that of his failure, the place the university that had kicked him out.

She read it four or five times, frowning, then stared at it for ages without it making any sense. She looked at the piece of paper very carefully and then held it to the light. It looked genuine enough. She held all the rejections in one hand and the certificate in the other, as if she could make them balance out in some way. Then she saw it. The crest on the certificate, at first glance identical to that on the other papers, was not. There was a horse's head on it – and the horse was winking. A forgery, a stupid joke. No, it was too much. It was so typical of Charles. His unmistakable thumbprint stamped across it.

She threw the thing down. She felt like screaming. Her chest was pounding away. The shock of it had made the blood drain from her face, she knew she had turned pale and suddenly felt terribly cold. She took a deep breath, let it out, but still her heart knocked crazily against her chest. She felt sick.

Now came rage. How could he? How dared he? How could he deceive her like this? For all these years? Not to mention the patients. Thousands of them. The man in the white coat wasn't a doctor at all. How many thousands of incidents had happened, the near misses, the non cures, the – my God, how many deaths? The implications multiplied with horrible speed. She was finished, ruined. He was a murderer – a monster. Should she have known? Their life together, everything she owned, everything she did, everything they were – the meaning had drained out of it all.

Louise sat back upon her haunches and opened her mouth, throwing her head back, ready to scream again, but only a feeble squawk came out.

'Madame! The fish is burning!' A thin but piercing cry floated up as from another world.

'Madame!' It seemed to Louise that this cry had been coming up through the house for some time, had been in her head, without her quite taking it in.

'*Madame!*' Slowly, she went downstairs. The kitchen was full of smoke, the fish had long since burnt. She needed to think. Marie stood with her head on one side, staring at the fish pan as though it was some alien creature that had flown in through the window. She had at least had the sense to take it off. Her triumphant smile creased up her stupid fat face. Louise looked at her, looked at the charred fish, through the black veil. It was all of a piece.

'It doesn't matter,' she said. Nothing mattered, not even the stupid face of Marie. The whole world had suddenly turned black.

4

Madame Ourlandes waved at Hilary who smiled back.

'In old age, Alain Ronsard remained the idealist he had been all his life,' Charles was saying. There was a faint sigh of agreement. Some people were nodding. There was a big crowd in the non-denominational crematorium, a modern concrete building which had a sweeping tick of a roof and a reverential driveway, tricked up with the symbols of religion but lacking the content. This made people uneasy. Hilary watched them. As the room filled up, people made polite remarks about how efficient the whole business was or how much more pleasant it was than they had expected. Then as they sat and waited, there was nothing to look at but the coffin, placed just where you'd expect an altar to be. It rested on a solid metal trolley, an ugly monster designed to take great weights.

'For this we can envy our friend, he who had no envy in him. To live so long and still to love mankind, that is a kind of grace. May we all come to such a state of grace in the end.'

Spreading big, deprecatory hands, Charles stepped down from the little stand, which was hardly big enough to be a pulpit but had pretensions in that direction. Music swelled up, heads bowed, people were saying prayers and Hilary, who had none, stared at the coffin instead. The whole business was bizarre. That a doctor should usurp the job of a priest at the funeral of an atheist made some sort of sense, but they had been short-changed. The fake spouting idealism insulted the dead idealist who had had such belief in mankind. Or were words so pure that it didn't matter who spoke them? He saw that the thing about Charles was that he was so often right.

He went on staring at Charles, who beckoned to him to come forward. Hilary had never seen a dead body and didn't want to start now, but he went.

A uniformed attendant opened the double doors, another came forward to take the trolley and the music got louder to cover the noise. There was a shuffling, a repositioning, people stood. The trolley was taken to the back of the building and wheeled into position facing the furnace, tilted slightly to enable the coffin to slide off and take its position on a raised dais. They watched from behind the stable door which kept onlookers at a safe distance.

Now a heavy steel plunger leapt out like a metal tongue and thrust the coffin forwards and down the slight incline. Simultaneously, the metal doors slid open letting out the roar of the furnace and a bright flicker from below. Hellfire was glimpsed for seconds before the tongue snapped back and the doors banged shut. Gone, he was gone, irrecoverable.

The dead man's son held his hand over his eyes, then turned away. This was what lay at the end of the journey. It was perfectly mechanical, a shunt in a box, and the faces lit by that fire would be people in uniform, who hadn't known you, who couldn't have described your face. Hilary felt pity prickling round his eyes for the old man who had gone on this terrible journey alone, as all must go. He'd met Monsieur Ronsard once, in the village, and had already forgotten what he looked like.

He had forgotten the ashes. It took hours for the body to pass through the furnace and come out, sieve-sized.

Quite a few people waited for the work to be accomplished. When an attendant made a discreet sign, everyone got up. They all trooped outside into the sunshine and stood in a respectful circle on the concrete discs which, like thought bubbles, drifted together to make up an idea of a path. With a quick glance to see that they were ready, the attendant turned the base of the metal container. Calm and steady in his blue uniform, he paced and swung it to and fro with a practised hand. Like incense, the cloudy issue, finer than sand, rose into the air. It shimmered in the bright light, tiny flakes blew up and away to settle beyond on the roses and flowers. The earthly remains of a man who had lived all his life in this place as had his father and his father's father. Dust to dust indeed.

Hilary thought of the brilliance of their roses at home, which were not the equal of these. They bloomed iridescent orange and yellow, these daily recipients of human fertiliser. It was over in half a minute. Madame Ourlandes leant on her stick, apologising for the traffic jam she caused as the group of people walking to their cars down the narrow path bunched up behind her, not liking to overtake, not wanting to walk on the grass. Her hands were shaking. She crept along like a snail, her back so bent that from the rear her head almost disappeared

'I just want a minute,' she whispered, taking Hilary's hand in her bumpy claw. Every step was so precisely taken, her small weight shifted from foot to foot with infinite slowness and care. Her eyes were wise. 'I would have liked to fly like that up in the air. Do you know, my dear, that I have never flown?' She twisted her head up and laughed at him sideways and squeezed his hand. 'A country woman, all my life. I have never got away from the earth, me. Now I never shall. Please. Call him for me, Monsieur le docteur. I need him.'

People shook hands and said their farewells with that generalised sombreness of things ending. Charles spoke for a while to Madame Ourlandes then helped her into her neighbour's car.

As car doors banged, as the more timid smokers lit up and mourners called out see you there, or back at the house, he could see the upbeat reaction was starting. There was a kind of easing out, a shrugging off. On with the next thing.

Charles was gloomy, it was in the way he held his cigarette, the tilt of his head expressive of loss. 'You see? This man couldn't believe in God, but all his life he believed in human beings and what they could do. Incredible, his faith in humanity. In spite of the evidence. Me, I'm too cynical for that. And when you can't believe in God or humanity, what is left? I'll tell you. Nothing. Even Madame Ourlandes doesn't believe any more. Today I wrote a prescription that will kill her.'

Hilary looked at him. 'You can't do that.'

'She asked me – why should I not help her?'

'You can't.' Hilary clenched fists. He felt sick and angry and it flashed across his mind that Charles could not have taken the Hippocratic oath, would never have sworn to protect life. 'That's murder.'

'She suffers terribly, she wants to die.'

'She's a Catholic, she believes suicide will send her to hell—'

'So for something *you* think *she* believes in I should let her suffer? Poor Madame. Lucky for her that I am not such a hypocrite. It is for her to decide what happens to her, not for you and not for me either.'

'But what's to stop you from giving,' Hilary didn't know the phrase for what he wanted and so he invented one, les pillules de la mort – 'death pills to anyone, then?'

'Nothing.'

'But if anyone could get them from you, there's no morality in it. You have to protect human life, that's your job.'

'Please, let's not be too exalted. You have to do the best you can. Sometimes you ease pain and sometimes not. Sometimes people are in such pain that nothing helps it. And then it's not for me to judge if what they suffer is bearable or not. I am not God.'

'If you hand out death pills, you are.' He's the devil, thought Hilary.

Neither of them said much after that. Hilary went on feeling sick and anxious. In certain circumstances it might be not just conceivable but imperative to tell on Charles. The very thought of doing that made him feel like shitting in his pants.

Charles soon recovered his equanimity and by the time he dropped Hilary at the bottom of the driveway he was singing again, the hit of the season. Appropriately enough, it was a bit of advice from one man to another: 'Never-ever-ever-ever-ever tell her that you lur-urve her!'

'Sure you won't come on my rounds – see the baby you delivered?'

Mutely Hilary shook his head and stood for a long time where he had landed, staring at the gravel and at his own two feet.

Sunlight streamed into the ward, making the white coats glow with undeserved brilliance. The old man, propped up on pillows, half of him under a large cage, stared at the surgeon and held his breath. At last, Nicholas shook his head, alarming his patient who uttered a hoarse cry.

'No? Doc? Whaddayer mean, no?'

'I'm so sorry. Thinking about something else. Of course you're going home. I'll lay money on it. A fiver says you're out in, let's see, three weeks at the latest? Make that ten pounds. Nurse! You're my witness. Done.'

The old man cackled and did a jubilant high five and looked from side to side at the pleasant faces of the nurses and the junior doctors to say what a one he was, oh he was, he was. What ones they all were.

'Good, good,' said Nicholas.

Mr Coghill, pleased by so little, had had all the bones in his leg smashed by a lorry driver. This was an opportunistic moron who liked to thunder down the bus lane and whose small child had been allowed to stand, unrestrained, in the front of the cab and drink out of a can. When her dad did his bit of last-minute braking at the naturally wholly unexpected, indeed unreasonable, sight of a bus ahead of him, veering off sideways into Mr Coghill's mini, the little girl had gone spinning through the window and had bounced off two cars before picking herself up from the pavement, face shredded, arm broken but, miraculously, alive.

Not one scratch had harmed her dad, though some Coke had splashed onto him. He had experienced what he liked to term mental anguish, notably the inconvenience of his solid bulk being trapped in his cab for half an hour while rescuers tried to get out the old man. The little car had split apart like a burst paper bag. Nicholas had saved the old man's leg which had splintered through his flesh. He believed that he might walk again, eventually, on crutches. This was very unlikely, though Nicholas had no intention of telling him the truth. Medicine had made an inveterate liar of him. Besides, it was possible. Physio could do a lot but would not be able to stop the leg from hurting, always. Moron had made a cripple of him and Mr Coghill said he was lucky, Doc, wasn't he, that his dancing days were over.

The child, fortunate in being brought in very fast to one of the best plastic surgeons in Europe, might with luck eventually look something not so very far off normal, though several more operations would be required. Because of the way her nose had been flattened, she would always have breathing difficulties. The best hope was that she would merely look ugly.

And the father, unscathed and unrepentant, who had yet to visit his elder victim and was notorious in the children's wards for complaining and foul language, wept when he was told that he might lose his licence and with it his livelihood. That destroyed a man, he kept saying. He'd not failed his breath test, had he? It was the brakes what done it, not the man who never checked them. Not having a job destroyed a man. He was a victim of circumstances, that was what he was. He was immensely sorry for himself. He brought the family in to look at the kid and sympathise with him. Nicholas had had him removed from the ward when the moron had attempted to tell him these things. It was entirely possible, for the world was a cruel and remorseless place, that he might keep his job and driving habits intact. That being so, it would probably all happen again.

Smiling vaguely, finger tapping conspiratorially on nose, Nicholas strode off to the next patient followed by his customary phalanx. As usual, he paid his camp followers no attention whatsoever. He was thinking about Jim, who only that morning had asked him if he'd spoken to Amanda. After all, talking to Amanda was but the apex of the problem. Or, to be precise, her talking to him.

Jim's Cheshire cat grin stayed with Nicholas as he continued round the wards. These bedside visits involved no medical element whatsoever, for the actual business of treating these people was far too serious to be incorporated into his floor show. The point of the round was to reassure people that they were under the daily supervision of an expert and that that expert was cheerful about their prospects. Nicholas, smiling and nodding, saw that Jim's smile wasn't precisely supercilious or patronising. It held trace elements of the seen-it-all-before, though. Had he? That, of course, was also what attracted him. Increasingly he felt the urge to give in and tell Jim all his fears and hopes and dreams, yes, to cry on his shoulder like a little babby.

'Morning, my dear,' he said, looking at the old dear whose hip he'd done a week ago and using his universal appellation, for who could remember their names? It was their medical notes he needed to keep in his head. She smiled back at him and nodded. 'And how are you today?'

'Very well, Doctor, thank you.'

'Good, good, excellent. We'll have you doing a tango before the week's out. Nurse! Make a note of that, please. Put me down for the foxtrot.'

Today, the hips and knees were all friendly, all doing quite well. He tended not to listen to what the patients said unless they complained of something specific, which on the whole meant that their suffering was intense. His experience was that there were few hypochondriacs among these old folk given to British understatement. It was extraordinary, how brave people were. Naming of parts, that was what he did between wards.

Down the corridors he strode, with lyrics dancing through his head. Mrs Femur may I introduce Mrs Tibia and her charming relation Miss Patella? Miss Fibula, are you perchance connected to the little Tarsals? Everybody on their tippy-toes for the dance. Tunes bobbed up and down, acquiring words. The Scapula thinks it's humerus and the Tarsals merely numerous for we hardly dare articulate the hamate and the capitate. Yes, the drivers who are pissed, they never would be missed for I've got a little list – yes, he's got a little list.

Heading it was little Annie's dad, who should be gagged and made to spend his remaining years in some menial capacity on his knees, probably swabbing floors, in a position which would enable passing Coghills in wheelchairs to run over his hand; arse-in-air would also allow passing doctors to give his fat bum a kick and upend the big red head into a bucketful of grey suds. Perhaps that might give the blockhead a dim notion of cause and effect. Head down, elbow-greasing, bum up and frothing dirt, he might just get an angle on what he was worth.

Slowly Louise walked down the drive. She was ruined. They were finished. Charles would go to prison. For how long? A very long time, evidently. A lawyer would know. There would be lawyers, all right, judges, a court, the weight of justice would crash down upon their heads and crush them to dust. She sniffed the air and smelt their dusty robes, looked at the gravel and saw the flinty look in their accusing eyes, heard their archaic language.

A catastrophe. Yet the chasm had been there all along. She had stepped across it every day of her married life and not known that it was there. She could have carried on for another twenty years and not known. She could have died without ever discovering the truth. She could that very day have been organising his retirement party to mark the end of a long and successful career. Her hands were clenched tight and it took an effort to force herself to loosen them. There were red marks where her nails had scored deep into her palms.

She stopped and shook her head in sheer disbelief, then went on, dragging her feet. The whole of her body felt rusty and locked. The first thing to do was to see Monsieur Jean-Jacques and call this fiasco of a celebration off, this mockery which had exposed her husband to her and would announce to the whole neighbourhood that he was a fraud and a criminal. Though exposure must come eventually, she would not knowingly engineer it.

For, as she crept down the hill, Louise knew that deep in some part of her being she had always expected if not this, then something like it. She was the daughter of a hairdresser from Rennes. She always would be. That she should be the doctor's wife was not fitting. It never had been. She was a fraud, just as he was. No wonder they had found each other. The journey to the point of exposure had taken her whole life and yet the surprise was not that it should have come, but that it should have come today. And the thought of the shame and humiliation of that exposure made her shudder.

Louise leant against the low stone wall to think for a little moment what she was going to say. Certainly not the truth. That would not solve the problem. Although the logical part of her understood that it was Charles who had perpetrated the actual crime, she blamed Jean-Jacques for it. Because this fool had decided to organise a celebration for the man he disliked, her life was ruined.

She felt both angry and sick. How unnecessary it all was. To sit and think up lies, in the heat. One moment the world was clean and beautiful and the next, everything was black and burnt and complicated, under a haze of smoke. And there was no going back to the clean pure time, no chance of recovering the happy person of the morning. When she thought of the trivial concerns that had seemed important then, she felt like crying. For she had been very happy and, fool that she was, she had not known it.

What would she say to Charles? It was a bit like discovering that you were married to a lunatic or murderer. Just what sort of man was he? Perhaps he had murdered people, dozens of them. To live this sort of lie each day was conceivable if it was merely a question of adopting an identity, but his deception went so much further. It took cunning. It took courage. Just what kind of mind could permit a man to live a lie that required a daily subterfuge of these dimensions? How often had he stood knowingly on the brink of disaster? It was a gigantic joke perhaps on his part, a massive piece of legerdemain, but it was the lives of others he juggled with, not his own. The more she thought about it, the more frightening it became.

Louise felt that she was walking on a cracked sheet of ice, hopping from one block to the next. The whole sheet was crazed and the cracking noise loud. Another little piece slid away under her feet, another little portion of truth and she was on the edge, staring into the icy black waters below. She feared her husband, just as much as she loved him. She had always known this without ever consciously thinking it. Fear was the blunt instrument that whetted their love.

With a trembling hand, she rapped at the plate-glass window of the pharmacy.

Jean-Jacques was returning from his errands and just coming towards the door when Louise Beauregard appeared as magically as if his wishes had grown wings and flown her to him. Her cheeks were pink and her eyes bright as if they had candles in them. 'Bonjour, Monsieur Jean-Jacques, I must talk to you,' she said. 'At once.'

'Come with me, Madame Beauregard,' and he unlocked the door and beckoned her into his inner sanctum. The dispensary was his shining temple, its hundreds of little drawers and glass-fronted shelves carried a munificence of pills and ointments and lotions. Everything the frailty of man or woman could possibly require was there, exquisitely arranged by his priest's hand. Each drawer displayed his careful lettering separating goats from sheep, not in lifeless Dewey Decimalisms, but with lovely curlicues and flourishes, with major ailments separated from minor, with alphabetically ranged brand names. Trusses and bandages, stockings and foot pads were defined and named by digit or by limb. It was his very own system and he adored it. In his ordered universe, he was creator and worshipper alike.

'People don't usually see my little cubbyhole, you know, Madame,' he said with his modest smile. 'You see here my supplies, Madame – ah, not as interesting as yours, I think. Nor so delightfully – aromatic.' There was a very particular smell, though proximity had deadened Jean-Jacques' awareness of it. It was a clean smell, combining lint and cardboard with a whiff of formaldehyde. It was faintly medical, the smell of authority.

Slowly, she spread her hands, paused, considered, made to speak again. Breathed in deeply and then out.

Jean-Jacques had had plenty of experience of things going wrong. He knew about the frail and elderly, those who sneezed or coughed or fainted, the chronic malingerers and those who came in denying all but hopelessly ill. He looked at Louise and noted symptoms. There was a pulse beating in her temple. Her hand was upon her chest which swelled and fell with strong emotion – and that hand trembled a little.

'Chère Madame,' he said, with a little self-deprecatory cough. 'I have already taken the liberty of using my lunch hour to write a number of little informal notes, to tell people of the forthcoming celebration, of the anniversary—'

'Already?' she said. 'But this is the limit!' The sharpness of her tone took him aback. She took a deep breath, supporting herself against the dispensary table.

'Why, Madame,' He shuffled his feet, 'you gave me the addresses yourself. I posted them just five minutes ago.'

'But it must be cancelled. You must stop them.'

Jean-Jacques did a little turn about his table and the presence of so many familiar things restored his nerve. He touched the ledger, admired his old-fashioned pestle; he let his hand drift across his spotless white coat lying on the back of his special chair. It was starchy crisp. He put it on and did the buttons up, one by one. His armour was impenetrable.

'Dear Madame, your charming modesty really won't stop me.'

Jean-Jacques continued to smile nicely while he delivered his ultimatum. '*Nothing* will stop me. I am going to find a way to honour your husband. I assure you that the whole village insists upon it. This celebration will happen. *I* insist upon it. I won't hear another word on the subject. You see, this is not a private matter. It is in the public domain,' and even as he uttered these words he felt how well they suited his mouth. 'Now, dear Madame, you must tell me what is wrong with you. I am not a doctor, I would not dream of aspiring to it, but I know a thing or two about simple ailments and I can see you are not feeling well.'

Amanda was sitting with a book on her lap for the obligatory half-hour between clearing up dinner and the time when she could decently go to bed and she did not look up when Nicholas came, newspaper in hand, into the sitting room. He came and sat beside her, so wife shifted slightly to make room for him and reached for the TV remote control and put it beside him. There, he was settled. She found it quite convenient to sit and rest and seemingly read while actually she just thought her own thoughts and so it took a while for her to realise that Brainbox wasn't watching the news, indeed hadn't even turned the TV on. She closed her eyes, to avoid him. It was easy to block him out.

'Are you asleep, Mandy? You're smiling. Mandy? Mandy? Mandy? Mandy?'

This was irritating of him and so she pretended it wasn't happening and it wasn't until he took hold of her hand that she saw she'd have to reply. She opened her eyes to look at him. He was staring at her.

'I was nearly asleep,' she said, with wife's silly-me smile.

'Why don't you talk to me?' Stupid, you see? When any fool would know. But little dimwit wife always toed the line and so she smiled nicely and even laughed a little. 'Mandy?'

Her eyes looked at him calmly while in her head, with growing exultation, she skied down the black slope, not just well, but magnificently. At the mogul where she had fallen, she jumped. She soared into the air, she flew. Mandy, Mandy, Mandy.

'Talk to me for Christ's sake.'

'Language,' she said, just as she did to Ed and that was rather amusing and so she smiled and looked at him quite calmly. His mouth opened wide when he spoke, she could see all the black fillings. There was no need to shout and rant. She didn't see why even wife should have to put up with that and so, blocking out the noise as best she could, she sang to herself in her head. When she grew bored with having to look at him, Amanda took the remote and turned the TV on and began to watch an old film which she had seen before. Vivien Leigh in *A Streetcar Named Desire*. She watched the great star with fascination and awe, her skin as thin as the floaty chiffons she wore.

'We've seen it before,' she said. Amanda knew, of course, that Nicholas, sitting beside her with his head in his hands, was in some kind of state. There was no need for wife to do anything about that. This particular scene was, after all, very familiar. 'You see?' said Amanda. 'We've seen it all before.'

Louise was unwell and the whole house was topsy-turvy. Hilary stared at the stars and listened to the owl, which like him chose the orchard as the place to express its feelings. Tonight, it was in full cry. There was a storm coming; the air was still and humid and everything was oppressive. Through the big French window he could see Charles in the kitchen busy laying a tray with cups and making coffee. They would have coffee outside, where there might be more of a courant d'air.

Charles had made dinner for the three of them, insisting upon serving them and in the process using every dish and saucepan and plate in the place. These were all left for Madame Moulins. This, he said with a wink, meant that the morning would bring her an interesting surprise which would relieve the monotony of her life. Somewhere else in the vicinity Michèle was presumably relieving the monotony of hers. Not that he cared. It was no longer possible for him to talk to her, any more than he could talk to Charles and yet he so much wanted to – like a child he yearned to be reassured. Hilary ambled inside.

'Give me that,' he said. Gingerly, he took the pot, which was very heavy and brimming with scaldingly hot coffee.

'Don't worry, I'll bring it. Would you take Louise a tisane? For her headache? Good, good.' Charles had loaded a tray with little delicacies. He loved his wife, he was all concern. 'Tell her I'll be along in a minute.'

Hilary rapped gently on the door upstairs.

Louise lay in her bed with some kind of compress on her head. She looked pretty ropy. He put the tray down and quietly backed away.

'Don't go.'

'What can I get you?'

'Nothing. Sit here.' They were both whispering. Plaintively, Louise looked at him. When an enormous bang came, they both jumped.

Hilary hung out of the window as the storm broke and he heard the thunder rolling their way. Flashes of lightning lit the horizon. A real summer storm, you could see it rolling up and over the hill until suddenly it hit the house. The rain pattering loudly on the leaves in giant drops then thundering across the roof. Ripples of wind across the bone-dry cornfield. A roar from below as Charles gathered up his belongings and made a run for it, laughing like the devil. Hilary watched him run back out again, pick up the coffee pot, heard him curse as he burnt his fingers. In those few seconds, his shirt was completely soaked and stuck to his shoulders.

'Something terrible has happened,' said Louise.

'What?'

She shook her head and winced. 'I can't tell you. I can't tell anyone.'

'Charles?' he said. She turned her face to the wall. How literal life could get. He sat for a bit then when nothing more was said, he got up and tiptoed away. For a little moment, he hovered at the door. Her face was a white blur in the fading light.

'Will you help me, Hilary? Don't go. Are you on my side?'

'Of course I am.'

He came back and sat on the bed. She reached out and took his hand in her cold one. It was nearly dark but the room was lit by the occasional flash of lightning – which coming simultaneously with the bangs meant the storm was right above them. In these flashes they studied each other. In this light, her eyes were black. Her hand gripped his hard, tensing up with each bang. He could not read anything in her expression beyond simple fear.

It seemed to Hilary that the terrible thing that had happened to both of them was Charles – but he did not dare ask. Not by one hint dared he betray the doctor to his wife. They looked on and on at each other. This exchange of looks was so heavily freighted with meaning that he knew that she must know and yet nothing was said, nothing could be said. He waited. Then, at last, the persistent drumming on the roof began to abate and after the flash he counted to two, then five, then seven seconds before the thunder came. The air was suddenly cool and fresh and it smelt green, of crushed leaves.

'There's going to be a party,' Louise said. Her white teeth flashed in the dark at his little exclamation of surprise, for of all possible revelations, this was the most unexpected.

'Here?'

There was a long pause. Louise stared at the ceiling. 'Of course it will be here,' she said very slowly. 'Where else? It is a party to honour Charles, you see. From the village – but of course it must be my party. I must be in charge of this. My God,' she said, sitting up suddenly. 'There is everything to arrange.'

'I'll help you,' he said.

'Will you pass me that book, please?' As if the electricity had just scored a direct hit upon her, her whole tone and manner had changed. She wanted the notepad near the telephone. At once she started scribbling and intent upon her task seemed to forget that he was there. Hilary backed away, slowly. He closed the door as quietly as he could, looking at the dark head bent, busy. How strange everything was. Coming down the stairs he passed Charles who touched his arm in his usual, confiding way and laid a finger to his lips – a finger that could have meant anything, anything at all.

Now Hilary could not help himself. He looked everywhere for Michèle, into each darkening room of the house, even the linen store, even the garage. He needed to see her. He needed her. He stood outside and let his head fall back and the warm rain poured down, making him close his eyes. When he opened his mouth he could taste the storm at the back of his throat. But the owl had stopped hooting and Michèle was not to be found.

'She was watching this old movie.' Nicholas looked at his friend. Jim didn't meet his eye at all, he just went on leaning back in his chair and very gently swivelling from side to side, never more than an inch or two in either direction, a constant motion which should have irritated but instead soothed.

'Tennessee Williams. *Streetcar Named Desire*, you know. Marlon Brando in a vest. We were just sitting on the sofa,' he said. There was a long pause. This was not the where and when of it, or even the how. He had to begin at the beginning. 'We've seen it all before.' That was what Amanda had said. He looked at Jim, who continued to study the contents of his In tray as a pleasant variation upon the lesser but no less impressive contents of Out. The desk, a handsome wooden affair, was covered with receptacles. Three jars of pens, pencils and the like, nothing uncontained. Chaos was ordered, kept at bay, was named. In and Out, yes. Nicholas began to talk very rapidly.

'You have to understand how we were, Jim, how far it's gone. I've never in my life had a friend, anybody, to talk to like Amanda. D'you know what I mean?' He thought that it had started with sex, with a complete knowing and trusting of the other person, with total honesty. His wife had been the only person in his life to whom he could say anything, anything at all. The first and last. He shut up for a bit and thought about it. He was suddenly clear-headed. How very strange it was that they had accompanied each other on this journey of life for over twenty years only to find that they were unable to speak at all.

'Professional help,' said Jim. 'That's what you need. Tell you what, here are a few names. I'll just jot them down. You have to get her to go and see somebody who can help. I mean, as a friend, I can't do what they can – I'm not a professional, am I?' He sneezed, suddenly and violently.

'God,' said Nicholas, watching him begin the business of rubbing the spray from the desk.

'You didn't really think I could do anything, did you?'

'No, of course not.'

Abandoned, Nicholas sat listening to the gentle exhalation of his own breath and the tiny scrape of Jim's pen on the paper while his solitude became a real fact in his head. He felt so sad. To be so terribly alone was sad even in his cruel world where little children could be tossed about like rag dolls, could crack their heads open and break their bones and not always be mendable.

Hilary had no time at all. He hurried and scurried and did a thousand errands for the mistress of the house. All week he scarcely caught a glimpse of Michèle. Louise had assessed what abilities her household contained. Thus Hilary became the messenger who fetched and the mule who carried, Michèle was the silver polisher, Madame Marie chief scourer and moaner, Louise the cook. The beneficiary of all this industry smiled and said a party was a wonderful idea and calculated on his fingers how long it was since they'd had one.

Charles, meanwhile, went his own sweet way. The tooting of his car setting off each day to visit patients was the signal for the delivery vans to start arriving, grinding in low gear up the hill and scattering the gravel yet further from its allotted resting place. There were deep ruts in the drive and still the vans kept coming. For there was no time to waste. The party was that very Saturday and there was no time, no time. Louise did not stop running and doing and cooking for one single instant.

This was serious food, this was the French showing off at what they did best. Her pride as a woman was at stake. And, when she wasn't preoccupied with the precise quality of sole or foie gras or the cheeses, when she wasn't off to choose between the Bordeaux or the Burgundy, they exchanged information in a cryptic manner. Hilary understood that her hand had been forced and how; he saw exactly why it was that the little pharmacist was going to get his way. What did Charles think of all this?

When the troops gathered, it was in the kitchen, the motor of the war machine. These days they also ate there, for the dining room paraded an ever-growing array of china. Whole cupboards of fine porcelain, carefully washed by Madame Moulins, drew up their ranks upon the table.

Louise would still dish up a three-course lunch. This was too important for a Frenchwoman to neglect, even in these hasty days.

'Charles – seems – so pleased with it all,' Hilary would say carefully.

'Of course. Did you think he wouldn't be?' she might reply. Hilary smiled at her. Then he dared to ask more.

'It's going to be a great celebration of him, then, with speeches and so on?'

'He's quite vain enough to enjoy that, you know.' Louise gave him a speaking look over the salad bowl – a shrug. She didn't look pale or wan any more. As the week wore on, as the supplies were delivered, not to mention the tables that would hold the groaning plenty and the chairs le tout countryside would lounge upon, Louise became more and more energetic. Each day she grew more purposeful and it seemed to Hilary that that febrile energy of hers had always needed something to feed upon and had at last found it.

Daily the pharmacist toiled up the hill with his growing guest list to discuss and his hunger alike to taste and be part of it all. He stood and sniffed at the larder door and his eyes were bright as he mentally counted and planned. He tried a little morsel of this and sneaked a fingerful of that. He went to the garage and stared at the crates of wine and, in the cellar, he inspected the tubs which were to hold the ice for the champagne. All the time his lips moved, as though he were praying.

Jean-Jacques was the bane of Madame Moulins' life. All week she complained that 'that man' was in the way, that he brought his dusty feet onto her clean floor, that he irritated her. She would follow him up the hallway, moaning on her knees, swabbing just behind him, practically falling over him in her eagerness to remove these imaginary traces of his passage. Hilary became her new favourite and when not fetching and carrying he was treated to long accounts of her various ailments, none of which the pharmacist had managed to cure with his costly ointments and creams. Yet when Monsieur le docteur came in, dislodging small stones and ridges of earth from the giant crenellations along his boots or trailing a dripping bag of fish from the surgery to the kitchen, why then Madame Marie said not one word. She had too much respect.

At night, Hilary had time to think. He lay in the brass bed and studied the rolling line of unnaturally blue flowers across the wall and up onto the ceiling. He had it by heart, each curl of a petal grown familiar. Mostly he thought about Michèle – nothing precise, more a glancing through of memories of the day, a recording of the glimpses he had had of her. They said their good mornings and goodbyes but otherwise hardly spoke. Hilary, grown expert in the analysis of the expressions of that lovely face, believed that she was troubled by something. Perhaps it was his hope that she, like him, should not be happy. Not that he cared, oh no. Increasingly, as the week wore on, he would wonder about Charles and his extraordinary sang-froid. How it was that he could face such an event so calmly.

Hilary came to believe that something must occur to unmask him, though he was not clear whether this was something he desired or feared. He had the strongest possible sensation of something coming towards them unstoppably. He could almost see the storm coming, the wind furrowing up the corn. In the quiet dark of the night, he felt that such an outcome was right; by day, in the presence of mother and daughter, he knew this would be a catastrophe they had not deserved.

'You're a good boy,' Louise said on the Thursday night and, 'This is supposed to be a holiday, you know,' and she ruffled his hair, just as his mother did.

So Friday became the day off, the day of the fishing trip. By seven o'clock in the morning they were on the road with a basket of food and rods in the back and Charles lighting up the first fag, singing the first song. Hilary, who had hardly spent any time with him of late, felt as nervous as a lover who, fearing rejection, both longed to touch and dared not attempt it.

Before they even got near the water there was the issue of what to put on the line. Charles had a whole box of flies, which all had special names. There was le jeune Clemenceau and, more whiskery, le vieux. There was la petite pute, a voluptuous little pink dolly, and her big sister, la grande. Did Charles invent these names? Delicately, as though he was indeed touching a woman, Charles attached the flies.

The idea was to flick the rod backwards so the line snaked up behind your head and then with another deft flick it came forwards, so the fly fell lightly on the water. Or hit you on the side of the head. It looked simple and was hard, the line looked light but was heavy and it was all too easy for the novice to wallop himself on the ear. To begin with, they lay on the river bank lazily casting flies. Every now and then, in an access of energy, the naked Charles would tug on his waders and stand in the middle of the river casting his rod over the lovely clear waters, an odd enough sight without the ever-present danger – to Hilary's mind at least – of him hooking his private parts by mistake.

When he got too hot, Hilary joined him. They stood side by side in the river while he tried to master the art. The cool water was delightful against the heat of the sun on his back.

When he'd given himself a thick ear for the umpteenth time, Hilary went back to lying on the river bank and contemplating the mysteries of the universe, watching Charles as with the utmost delicacy he dropped the fly just where he wanted it. Exquisite, the brilliant little clump of feathers bobbing on the bright water, the big man so still that there was scarcely a ripple, every stone on the river bed magnified and the flash of a bird overhead a startling gash in the blue. Hilary stretched out languorously, feeling sexy in the heat, the dry warm earth alive with tiny noises and rustlings. A parade of ants carrying a single glossy leaf grouped around his giant hand, which had descended so unexpectedly, to examine the intruder and plan their next manoeuvre.

He'd fallen asleep and was startled awake by a shriek, the sun high and hot, a bug up his arse practically, Charles in the shade of the big tree that overhung the river, laughing and pulling at the line.

'The net! Quick, bring the net!'

Thrashing and crashing, Hilary snatched at the net, got into the water, stepped on something slimy, stubbed his toe and fell on his face, dropping the net altogether while Charles suddenly yelped in a different tone and caught hold of the line and Hilary simultaneously saw that he'd somehow got the line tangled round his cock and that the cause of this excitement was a huge brown fish which was getting away – it was going – gone – and then it darted away at right angles and straight into the net which Hilary had dropped. With an exultant cry he caught it up. A beauty!

He scrambled back onto the river bank and waved it about. Charles saved himself from premature emasculation and then came after him and, dropping all, embraced him. Laughing and shouting they danced about like two demented savages. It was a brown trout. A brown trout, not the usual rainbow kind; a real catch and hardly ever seen in these waters.

Were they going to take it back, show it to people?

'Never! We'll eat it, here and now,' Charles said. 'Food you have caught yourself is the most delicious in the world. I keep an old pan in the car and we have butter, and there are herbs, in the salad. You'll see. Fit for a king.' He went up to the car, carrying the fish. 'Look for some nice twigs and little branches, there you go. What's the matter?'

'Nothing.' He couldn't look while the fish was being killed.

Charles scooped up an armful of kindling from underneath the old tree. Neatly and carefully, he built a circle of flat stones and laid a fire within it. Then he laid more stones on each other until he had built a little structure to hold the pan above the flames. A bucket of water was placed in readiness. With precision he gutted the trout, turned its innards out, filled it with basil and tarragon. Rubbed a little butter onto it. Carefully he lit the little pile of wood.

'OK. Never leave a fire, not even for a second. Always have some water ready.'

'You're not worried, Charles, that people will find out about you?' Killjoy couldn't leave it, Killjoy had to know.

'Why?'

'Isn't the party a risk for you?'

'You English. The conscience of Europe. I tell you, Hilary, I can't live my life worrying about what people know and think. Je m'en fous.'

'And what if Louise knew?'

'Eh alors?'

'But if people knew – you must worry, surely, because you'd lose your house and your family and your job . . . it's against the law . . .' His voice trailed away as Charles came closer and closer until he could smell his warm smoky breath. He laid his sinewy arm round Hilary's shoulders and held him tightly against him, shoulder to shoulder.

'Do you worry that I could come up to you like this, then I might wind this line round your neck,' and he looped it round his neck and Hilary felt it resting on his flesh and then pulling slightly and he stood as still as he could and stared at the large-pored nose inches from his. Charles's voice was very, very quiet.

'Do you worry that in the next ten seconds I might strangle you and hide your body over there, in the river bank – you see the place? Nobody would ever find you. How easy it would be.' He gave the tiniest tug on the line.

Hilary nearly gagged. He stared into the eyes which stared back. He could smell the summery hot smell of sweat on Charles's skin. He stood perfectly still. Charles's arm round his shoulders did not move, the line was taut. Charles's large naked body touching his. An uncontrollable tremor ran through him, a cold blade of fear shot from his head to his feet. He could not help it; his legs trembled a little. Satisfied, the big man let go and spread his arms in an expansive gesture.

'You see? It didn't happen.'

Hilary crouched down until the trembling had ceased and then he sat there for a long moment and watched Charles go about his cooking as if nothing had happened. The fish, its skin blackened, fell off the bone, the flesh was moist and aromatic. The scent of the herbs, cooking, filled the air.

'Come, taste.' Hot fish, cold tangy salad, the crust of the bread, the faint smell of sweat, the wine, cooling in the river. All quite unreal.

'This is possibly the very best moment in the best place in the universe,' said Charles. Like a spectre at the feast, Hilary sat on the river bank. His same too-thin body, reprieved and still sitting in the sunshine as it had before, felt strange and precious. As if he had been murdered but didn't know it, he found himself turning and looking at the river bank, to see if the mound of freshly turned earth was there. His skin was simultaneously hot and icy cold. He felt the sun on it, saw the goose pimples.

Charles uncorked and poured the wine, he rolled it round his mouth and swallowed in one huge gulp and poured again. A belch of satisfaction. Hilary had a slug. Cold and dry and delicious. They drank deeply. With the wine, some of the strange feeling began to evaporate. Something was left, some aftertaste. An invisible line had been crossed.

'Your mother was like you,' Charles said after a while. 'Is this right, is this wrong? You know what matters? Nothing,' and he waved a lazy hand. He was a little drunk. 'Today I am a magician and with these hands I can make anything happen. I can catch any fish. But tomorrow I may be dead. So every day I take what I want.'

Charles curled up like a dog on the car blanket and fell asleep. Soon he snored. Watching the big fleshy face quivering, looking at those over-sized limbs, Hilary wanted to hurt him. Yet when he woke, Charles smiled at him sweetly. There was something so pleasant and amusing in the way he lay, naked and vulnerable, singing to himself, that Hilary no longer knew where attraction ended and repulsion began, spiced as both were with a thread of fear.

They overheated, they swam, they idled out the day and let it shimmer into dusk. Not until the midges began their dance over the water did they think about returning to the house. It was dark, Hilary half asleep as the car crunched up the long drive. He woke up to see Charles go from the car into the house. Through the open windows of the dining room he watched Charles pick up his wife and then put her down and kiss her, a job done thoroughly and with real ardour. She kissed him back. Hilary couldn't stop staring. I want real passion when I'm that old, he thought. Oh God, I want it now. Why couldn't he take what he wanted?

Saturday dawned as perfect as its predecessor, the faintest of mists over the orchard heralding the heat to come. Woken by the noise of an engine, Hilary looked out to see a man riding a motor mower through the orchard, scything down the long grass, and he was out there in a flash to cut shiny green swathes and pick up an apple on each turn.

By the afternoon, the long tables outside had been laid with gleaming white cloths by Hilary and Madame Moulins who, working as a team, developed a certain synchronous ability. He lifted and flicked, she caught and tucked. Along that expanse a field artillery of cutlery was arrayed and an army of plates and she, demonstrating exactly what went where, would return more than once to find that Hilary had left out something. Who could eat that much? Ah, he would see.

Then he was the plate navvy, carrying the heavy load, for apart from the mere three plates that would adorn each place setting, a new plate would be required for each course and these had to be to hand. And then there were the glasses. White wine and red wine and water and let us not forget the carafes for the water, let us not omit the crab claw crackers and the langoustine forks. When he had done the right number of places – it was sixty-two exactly – Hilary went to tell Louise that she had over-ordered. Ah, non, she said. There would be more people. There would always be some local folk who would consider it an oversight that they had not been invited and who would turn up regardless. She had catered for them. Louise stopped, looked at him, fingered her chin. It would not do to seat them quite as well as the others. She would set up another table some distance away.

'Tu verras, les gens ne se gênent pas,' she said.

So, with this in mind, Hilary laid a table for a further fourteen of the free and unembarrassed. Louise was still as fresh as anything and Hilary sweating by the time they came to the doo-dahs and decorations. Fresh flower displays had been ordered and these he now lugged on vast platters from the cool interior of the wine cellar to the garage, marginally warmer, but more accessible for the evening. The butter dishes and items to be kept cool needed, now, to be prepared and taken downstairs. Singing, she departed to do this. Beyond, in the pantry, layer upon layer of loaded platter lay. Great tubs stood at the corners of the kitchen, stacked with champagne and ice.

From the open kitchen window, her voice soared forth. Hilary couldn't think of anything nicer than that sound of a happy woman. He lay for a moment in the long grass beyond the orchard and thought about his mother and how she had sung about God not making little green apples when she was busy in the kitchen and, years ago when he was a very small boy, about inch worms measuring the marigolds. She'd shown him a little worm, humping its back and flopping, arching its small length across a leaf. Now, with his hands clasped behind his head, one foot lazily swinging, healthily tired and the whole strange but glorious evening ahead – now, he watched a small, many-footed bug scamper past and saw the macrocosm in the microcosm.

Louise had thought of everything. The grass of the orchard had been mown and raked away and re-raked. Little sparkly lights had been hung through the trees. Two hours had been allowed for everyone to retire and sleep, if they could. Laid out in a generous U shape, the subsidiary table that crucial, socially dictated distance from the others – friendly, but not too convivial – the banqueting table looked like a huge face with a slightly lopsided smile.

Later, with the blue deepening day arching down behind, with the freshly sprinkled flowers so bright and dainty, with the tablecloths caught up in elegant swags and the silver sparkling, he set out candles. Beneath the twinkling apple trees the tables were festooned with an abundance of elegant white twists fixed into those special candlesticks which Charles's grandmother had kept carefully wrapped in newspaper for decades and which Louise had discovered in the attic. Michèle had spent the whole of the previous day polishing them. When they came in from fishing she was sitting in the kitchen, scrubbing away, her hands so ingrained with the blackness of the old silver that it had seemed impossible that they would ever come clean, her smudged face concentrated into a frown.

The evening came. Hilary stood in the orchard by the tables thinking that he'd never seen anything quite as pretty as that place set up for a party with the grand silver moon brightening. Deliciously at the upstairs windows flashed come-hither glimpses, nothing in the world more enticing than lovely women, dressing. Faintly her voice asked for the green shoes. 'In your cupboard, look, my love.' The fall of upended bright hair that hung down brushing the carpet to be brushed itself suddenly swept up to fly past the window, a bird seeking to escape, naked shoulders. How his heart pounded. For fear of being noticed, staring up so, Hilary turned away.

The trumpet of Chet Baker breathed its magic out through the windows of the salon and there came Charles absurd yet elegant in a dinner jacket that was slightly too tight, carrying a bottle of champagne and two glasses. From the kitchen came the faint clatter as a dozen young men prepared to serve. Charles was scowling.

'Stupid clothes. Tonight I'm going to get drunk,' he said, filling two glasses and passing one to Hilary who, behind his back, superstitiously crossed fingers.

● ● ●

Jean-Jacques was hunched in the kitchen, polishing his shoes which were a little tight but so very elegant that the pain was worth it. When he could see his smile in them, he slipped them on and walked rather carefully back to the bedroom. The bow tie, a struggle, right over left. A new tie, silk, a real beauty. There. Only the jacket remained. He patted the pocket, which crackled. His speech, practised in his head each day, rewritten every night that week until it and he were both word-perfect. People would revise their opinions of him. He could almost hear the applause. Now, to fill the remaining minutes, he polished his gold dress watch. This, his finest possession, which had not worked for fifteen years, certainly looked very beautiful.

Sitting on the bed, breathing gently on the gleaming surface, his eye was drawn to his wife as she outlined her little mouth with lipstick. It occurred to Jean-Jacques that the two shining surfaces, which opened and snapped shut, had something further in common. He wondered if he would say it. Why not? People changed, things moved on, they had to. It was ever the law of the tribe that new leaders arose and came forth to supplant the old. And leaders were firm and their wives knew it.

'Héloïse?'

'Mmnh?' She was using a little brush to draw the finest of lines along the outside of her lips. Then she would brush in the colour which made them look so full and luscious. He would say it.

'You are just like my watch,' and she looked up at him. 'Beautiful to look at, but you don't work. It is exactly the same. Your insides don't work properly, but on the outside you look so perfect.'

Héloïse stared at him in the mirror. She looked startled.

'Chéri,' she said, 'What is it? Mon amour, you know I long for nothing more than a little baby. But what can I do?'

'"What can I do?"' he said in mimickry.

She didn't know what to do. So. Carefully, contemplatively even, he started to unzip the dress she had just wriggled into, first placing his watch on the dressing table for safekeeping. He exposed the strap of the brassiere, the little panties. With his eyes still on her, he bent down, untied his shoelaces, kicked off the shoes. Just as carefully, not losing the crease, he stepped out of his trousers and hung them over the occasional chair. He undid the shirt button by button. Off it came.

'Come here, chérie.'

She giggled and didn't move and so he said it again, so she would see that he meant it. He draped the shirt carefully on the coathanger, over the jacket, and removed his underpants, playfully kicking them up into the air. He extended a hand to her and she came towards him, the dress dropping to the floor. He picked it up. It was new, after all, and had cost a pretty penny. How lovely she was.

'One instant.' While he rummaged for a hanger in her cupboard, she was gone, into the bathroom, but Jean-Jacques wasn't having any of that and he darted after her and heard the door of the bathroom cabinet bang, saw her eyes wide and startled. 'Come here,' he said again and, when she didn't right away, he picked her up and, staggering a little, for tiny as she was he wasn't quite accustomed to that sort of thing, he carried her over to the bed. He put her down and kissed her, as he hadn't in years, slowly and very thoroughly. He was going to take his time about this. He was going to enjoy it, and so was she. Her face flushed. She lay quite still.

'We'll be late.'

'Yes.'

'Kiss me again, like that.'

She hummed, afterwards in the bathroom, showering at length. Jean-Jacques lay on the bed, profoundly satisfied, and watched the door open and grumbled and fussed, just the right amount. Hurry up! Time to get ready! Then, letting his shower run, he locked the door and searched her bathroom cabinet which was stuffed full of toiletries and female stuff. This was a tricky operation, for things kept falling out and had to be replaced, precisely as before. With delicate fingers he picked through it all.

It didn't take him so long to find a little case at the back of the cabinet, with the diaphragm in it which she had not had time to insert. Hidden in a big pack of cotton wool balls. Wrapped in cotton wool. He got the cap out and looked at it and plucked its rubbery texture. He showered. Then, as he towelled himself, he looked until he had found a safety pin which he used to prick a dozen tiny holes in the cap. That should do it. Carefully, he put it back so everything was precisely as he had found it. His darling, whom he would wrap in cotton wool.

'I'm sorry I said what I did. About your insides. They are beautiful.'

'I know you didn't mean it, mon amour.'

'One day we will have a baby, when the good Lord wills it.'

'It is my dearest wish,' she said.

'Good, very good, my darling,' and as they turned into the gate and up the hill and their heels crunched on the gravel, Jean-Jacques thought that it was not so very difficult to obtain his heart's desires. The trick was to go about things the right way, with lightness of touch, with elegance. He transferred the large and elaborately wrapped parcel he was carrying from his left to his right arm so he could take her hand. Little hand, so small, like a child's soft hand. He began to hum to himself.

The guests were all there. There had been one particular easy chair empty and Hilary felt sick whenever he looked at it, for it was the place reserved for Madame Ourlandes. But, at last, she had come, leaning on a neighbour's arm and apologising for her slow ascent of the gravel. She was resplendent in stiff blue silk that crackled when she sat. Hilary ran to get a cushion to ease her bones and as she sat he whispered in her ear that she looked beautiful. He wanted to say more, to beg her not to take the death pills, but as he hovered, trying to find the words, Louise called him away. Tonight he was the 'son of the house' and his privilege was to serve.

The phone rang on and on as Hilary passed, carrying away the empty bottles, returning with full ones. Eventually, growing sick of the noise, he picked it up.

'Oui, bonsoir?' The hubbub from the kitchen where a dozen waiters were falling over each other and shouting was now so loud that he could scarcely hear a thing. 'Pardonnez-moi? Anglais. English. Je suis anglais. Voulez-vous répéter?' At the fourth repetition he more or less got the name and, assuring the disembodied shouter that somebody would come along and collect him, went to find Louise.

The guests had all drunk a fair bit of champagne. There were a dozen or so of the uninviteds, just as Louise had predicted, who were now milling around the far table squabbling about where they were to sit. In this they were being assisted, with exaggerated care, by Charles, who was already quite drunk but didn't show it.

Moving slowly along the big table where places were marked by names, Michèle lit candles. Her simple little frock was so ravishing that you wanted to weep or sing. Slowly Hilary went along the opposite side keeping pace, just looking as, one after another, the candles glowed into life as if their sole function was to caress her intent face. It was a perfect night, warm with the slightest of breezes. Beyond the orchard the old historic monument was about as lit up as he was. He waited as, bowing low, Monsieur Dutronc kissed his wife's hand and assisted her to her seat. Jean-Jacques in ebullient form was bouncing in and out of his chair, waving to people. Finally Hilary reached Louise.

'Some guest wants to be picked up from the station. Viande? Vivale something? Viande Lavende? He's waiting, at Tours.'

'Vigne-Laval. Oh my God,' she said.

'What? What? What is it?'

'The professor, the one Charles always talks about. I didn't think he'd come, he never replied. My God.'

'Oh, shit.' He stared at her helplessly. 'The one who taught him all he knows?'

She took hold of his two hands and looked at him pleadingly.

'I'll do something,' he said. 'Don't worry, I'll get rid of him,' and he extracted one hand and laid it on her arm and knew how the knight in shining armour felt when he got on his horse and said his piece. Louise put her two hands up and pulled his face down and kissed him on both cheeks and for an instant continued to hold his face with those cool hands and look at him with such gratitude and sympathy, such a heap of emotions, knowing that he knew that she knew and so on and etcetera. She smelt pretty damn wonderful.

'Give me the car keys.'

'Are you sure you can drive there? Have you ever driven on the right?'

'Absolument.' He felt powerful. He could do anything. Gaily, he clanged down his visor to go dragon hunting. Carefully he negotiated the drive, revving up a little, fiddling with the gears. Luckily Charles had moved the car, put it down by the gates. Right. Odd. He hadn't driven the Peugeot before, nor ever driven on the right. It was OK, it was cool. There was a fine demarcation between terror and elation and he was the dragon-slayer, on the right side of it. Learn from Charles. Why not murder the man?

Brake, indicate, find the gear lever, crunch, shit, turn left through the gates. Careful, he'd looked the wrong way. Go slowly, this was fine. The white-banded avenue of lime trees unrolled their careful stripes and then he was at the left turn leading to the crossroads, crunch, ouch, gears down, indicate, yes, this was the road.

He was climbing again, up in the cornfields, the moon brilliant and huge, the road undulating ahead so the headlamps of an occasional car, coming the other way, fired up the line of the horizon with flashes of light. He'd had one glass of champagne, enough for Dutch courage. The night smelt warm and dry. He was getting the hang of the gears. Hilary began to sing. No reason not to put his foot down a bit. He felt terrific. He was past the moated house and there were the old walled farms over there, he saw a tiny yellow dot, a light in the old wall, the blackness around it darker than that of the fields. A small animal, a rabbit or whatever stood in the road, picked out in his headlights. He slowed down. It didn't move, it stood and stared at him. He slowed, then stopped the car. It was a hare. It hunkered down again and took its time and at last hippy-hopped away into the ditch. He thought about his baby being born and life was good.

He came off the autoroute. Tours. City centre. Signs. He was going along the river, nope, that couldn't be right and so he turned off and went straight up the big shopping road, the Rue Nationale to the end where he recognised the pretty flower-power roundabout. OK, right here, and on he drove. No sign of the station. Hell, wrong again, so he did a U and came back on his tracks and crawled slowly along the Boulevard Heurteloup, looking for signs for the station. The post office. The town hall. Women looking at him. A hotel, the Printemps department store, gardens and there was the jutting hulk of the new Palais des Congrès which, more InterCity train than anything else, thrust its nosy snout into the square opposite the station. Indicate, right, there you are et Bob est ton oncle. He'd done it. He felt truly fantastic. He felt high as a kite.

Carefully, he eased the car into a parking space outside a little boulangerie. He got out of the car and stopped to have a look at the station and who was waiting there. A woman, middle-aged, only one man, an old guy with a beard and stick. Had to be him. Hilary looked around carefully, both sides of the street. Various young lovers. The old bloke had a briefcase, dark jacket, unmistakably conventional and top-drawer. Not a million miles from his dad. Prof written all over him.

There was a crowd in the square and crossing it he saw that the yoof splashing about on the beached whale of the under-lit water feature and those specimens lurching in and out of the careful grid of new, young trees were compatriots. Had to be. Best of British. It was a bunch of lager louts, half-dressed, bottoms sidling forth from little more than a pair of Union Jack shorts. They were heaving about the place, having a few drinks, nothing too terrible by the usual football standards, but rowdies all the same. They would be intimidating for a provincial who would prefer to look away and pass on the other side.

Hilary stopped near them and studied Vigne-Laval's goatee beard and the peremptory way he had of jerking his head from right to left to right. A man of opinions. Someone who didn't like to be kept waiting and who looked with particular distaste at the writhing slobbering British manhood before him.

'Hello, matie,' said one of the louts. This bloke, quite young, sported a heavy designer stubble that seemingly extended down from his skull in a dark corridor past neck and ears to broaden out into luxurious curly black hairs which covered his puny frame where it was not hidden by his Guns'n'Roses T-shirt. He looked wetly at Hilary, then put his arm round him. Fairly stunned by his badger's breath, Hilary did not resist. No sirree, he offered his friendship.

'Hello,' he said back.

'I hate France.'

'Yeah.' Badger-breath was pretty drunk and had a tattoo of daggers and hearts on his arm, very black against his pallor. The crease of his other arm had swallowed some Gothic script. There was a further tattoo on his wrist: RUDE! it said. Hilary did a few approving nods. Bloke leant blokishly forward, sharing the emanations of many previous pints. He made a stabbing gesture at his arm.

'I wuz having rouse. R-A-U-S. German. But the bloke wot done it couldn't spell, stupid fartarse. R-U-A he done before I noticed. You see where he gone over it?'

Hilary shook his head. 'Nar. Looks very good to me,' he said. The avenue of possibilities this opened up. Visit the dyslexic tattooist for Mam and Dud. Op the gonners. I love yuo.

'I hate foreigners.'

'Yeah.' An idea could not be suppressed, it rose up until it frothed irresistibly over. 'Do you want to earn a few bob?'

'Year. Yer wor?'

'D'you see that bloke over there?' Hilary said, pointing.

'Year.'

'He's a foreigner. Look at that beard. How can anyone walk the streets looking like that?' And, warming to his theme, Hilary began to whisper into a yellow, waxy ear. 'Not and expect to get away with it. What a poofter. You see the stick? Terrible.'

'Yer wor?'

'I know him. He's a real arsehole. Do you want to earn a few bob?'

'Yer wor?'

He began to lay out his plan. Laid it out again. As, slowly, understanding dawned in badger's teeny brainette, the prof took to pacing up and down and did some more looking at his watch. Loitering at the high-technology bus shelter, Hilary waited to see how the Kommandant would marshal his troops. With charming simplicity, Badger-breath rallied his fellows with a shriek. He pointed.

'See 'im? Lez gerrim. Kumon,' he yelled.

Vigne-Laval couldn't believe it. They came lurching across the road in a bobbing bundle and in one swoop they picked him up. He was borne away, protesting, over the heads of the mob, which gave him the bum's rush into the station and surged onto the platform, passing him bodily into the train that stood there. Hilary, coming up behind, watched the prof's stunned disbelief turning to helpless rage as they hustled him onto the train.

He protested, the goatee rose and fell. He had no idea of why and what.

One of the lads picked up his little case and, wiping it on his bum, flicked it in. One of them began to wave. They all began to wave, twinkly sea anenome fingered. 'Byebyee, don't cryee! Byeee!'

Oh, happy synchronicity, the TGV was off. The prof snatched up his bag. Hilary watched the doors of the train close with the mob protecting it by leaning against it and pulling faces. Vigne-Laval now started thumping against the door with his entire strength and making no impression. All the passengers were staring from him to the mob. The prof ran frantically along the train to the next door, as the train slowly pulled out of the station. His baffled little face peeping out. No hope of him escaping. Hilary watched him peering out, still scarcely able to credit the idea that this bizarre thing really had happened to him, until it disappeared. The TGV didn't stop until Orléans. There was nothing more to fear.

Hilary gave them every penny he had. They were worth it.

'Yer wor, matie,' said mein Kommandant and the whole lot of them suddenly began to squabble over exactly which particular brand of liquid refreshment they'd spend it on and they were off, out of the station and across the road and streaming unstoppably into the Atac supermarket to seize more of the right stuff quickly, before it closed.

Behind him, leaning against the orange pillar where travellers validated their tickets, stood an old bloke with long strands of grey-white hair falling over his collar, wearing a Nehru jacket. With a faintly knowing look, he turned his head to watch Hilary pass. Crossing the station concourse, Hilary was aware of the man following. Outside, as he waited to cross the road, a hand touched his sleeve.

'You are English – we spoke on the telephone. So you have come for me, very nice. My name is Vigne-Laval, but you must call me Gaston,' and he held out his hand and Hilary, gobsmacked, gripped big swollen knuckles, yellow-stained.

'And your name, my friend?'

'Yes,' said Hilary, swallowing. 'Hilary, my name is.'

Gaston walked with a slight limp but was nimble and quick.

He could have been anything from late fifties on. He had a sallow face that was gaunt and covered in wrinkles and creases and laughter lines, a face as lived-in as a tramp's sleeping bag. Close up, his neat-looking jacket was stained and threadbare at the collar and Hilary could smell the fags and beer on his breath. Gaston said *tu* to him, straightaway, very pally. He was disgusting.

They crossed the now empty square and got into the car. Shit, shit, shit. What was he going to do now, crash the car? Spend the evening driving the man around the countryside or what? Hilary couldn't think. Panic rose up and had to be suppressed.

'The young men at the station, friends of yours?' Hilary found no adequate reply. Gaston here didn't need much prompting, he leant over and pinched his arm, lightly. 'Ah, youth can be severe. So, my English friend, you are staying with my old pal Charles?'

'Yes,' he said. He was filled with rage. The unfairness of all this was powerful, stronger than any guilt he might have been expected to feel at propelling that other old innocent on his way to Orléans. He thought about all the appalling consequences of turning up with this bloke at the party. The motorway lay up ahead. They turned up the ramp.

'Professor, he calls me. Well, I will tell you. A long time ago, Charles and I were medical orderlies together. I, being so much older than him, taught him a great deal, I can tell you. He was so young, he didn't even have a beard. Like a girl, he was. He didn't even know how to fuck a woman properly. Sixteen he was when I met him.' Not getting a reply didn't put him off, he carried on regardless.

'But already he had a mind of his own. Now. I will tell you a story about those days that will pin back your ears, my friend. I will make you jealous of me. Me, him and four girls. One was English, long hair she had. Gee-lian. Never I forget her. What, don't you believe me? You wait.' Hilary saw the sign for Orléans, then for Paris. What if he drove him to Paris? His mind was racing, his heart beating fast. Not that he had the money for the journey. There wasn't enough petrol in the car. Think, for Christ's sake, he told himself. Think. Meanwhile, with the lunatic, this sex maniac sitting right beside him and now – please not – with putting his hand right down his trousers – Jesus, was he going to pull his plonker out? Eyes on the road, he drove on.

Nicholas reclined on the deckchair in the middle of the lawn. It was getting late. He had always loved these midsummer evenings when like an old friend the light lingered in the sky for just a little longer than you might have hoped.

From where he sat, he could see the light in Ed's room. Amanda was up there saying goodnight. Ed never wanted to sleep in the holidays, never wanted to do anything sensible. Nicholas had done bathroom duty and said goodnight to him earlier and he had called out for his mother. Like a little boy, like a baby. For some reason this had given him a pang. She had come up, of course, as she always did, was even now kissing and tucking him up, as a good mother did. She was a very good mother to her boys. Nicholas felt any number of uneasy sensations gripping and turning at his heart, squeezing his stomach somehow, not pain but a kind of foreknowledge of pain. The body could feel limbs that had been amputated. Scratching the place where it itched was helpful, even if it was a void, so strong was the brain's ability to create an image, an aura of what had been. Pain went on for ever, even when its cause was long forgotten. Perhaps when something strong or strange was going to happen, a person might experience some kind of precursor of it. He hoped not. He sat and looked at the light until it was quite, quite dark and waited for the feeling to go away.

Inside the house, Amanda looked at Ed.

'You're bonkers, Mum,' her son said, turning over sleepily.

'What?'

'I don't mind. Dad does, though.'

'Don't be silly, Ed,' she said, smoothing down the duvet, but he merely sighed and stretched and recomposed his sleeping position.

Soon he was asleep. Amanda stood at the window of Ed's room and listened to his regular breathing and stared out at the motionless figure of Nicholas, stretched out in his deckchair in the garden. She thought with a sudden rush of anger that while she didn't particularly care what he thought or did, this buddha in a deckchair lark was something she did resent. So in due course, she went through the quiet house in a malicious frame of mind. Alongside those tasks left for her to do, she would see whether anything of his had been left unprotected.

'. . . Nurses, especially in their uniform, all nicely starched up and nothing underneath. We were a fine couple, share and share alike, say I. I was a good-looking fellow in my young days. Well, Charles was always an ugly mug, but women loved him. To see him in his married state, that will amuse me. Well, he was always a lot cleverer than me. It's no fun being on your own. Nobody to warm your back. Not that I sleep on my own so often. Now where was I? After I taught him the card tricks, one time he got me into trouble, plenty that cost me, plenty, not just money.'

Chuckling to himself, the man got a little flask out of his jacket pocket and had a slug. He'd been on the booze ever since they'd got in the car. It was the bottle he was fumbling for down there. Dirty pig.

'Yes. Look, Charles has a daughter. He lives a responsible good citizen's life.' Get the message over quick, while he was drinking, the only time he shut up. Hilary put his foot down. He'd speed past the motorway exit.

'I know it. The daughter, the wife, they are too good for me. Hey. What's this?' Gaston was dangling Hilary's watch in front of him. How had he done that? He got it back and with difficulty he put it back on, one hand steadying the wheel. The old rogue laughed and wheezed at his great joke, very amusing.

Hilary had another thought. 'D'you have any money on you?'

'Sorry, no cash.' He leant back, made a big show of turning out his pockets which were full of crap. A rusted up Swiss Army penknife – how had he achieved that? – a bottle opener, various pencils and bits of paper.

'Nothing?' And now the silly sod was holding up Hilary's wallet, he was rifling through it, chuckling away to himself. 'How did you do that? Give it back,' and with difficulty Hilary wiggled it back into the back pocket of his trousers, where he trusted it had to be safe.

'Leave the motorway here. Charles is my oldest friend. Did I tell you that? Why don't you call me tu? I say tu to you. Here! Turn here!' He snatched at the wheel, they came dangerously close to the next car – Jesus, they were going to hit it – a blare of horns. Hilary elbowed him out of the way and grabbed back the wheel and the idiot jerked at it again. They fought for control – Gaston was strong – and with a jerk and lurch, they turned off. Hilary's heart was pounding like mad. As soon as they were off the slip road, he pulled up. He felt sick.

'Never do that again. Do you hear me? You could have killed us.' His hands, on the wheel, were trembling.

The maniac fumbled in his pocket, lit two fags, passing one to Hilary which he took and threw angrily out of the window.

'Don't get so excited. You would have missed the turning. Look,' and he pointed to the road sign. 'I know, I come here before.'

'What?'

'Oh, but Madame doesn't know,' and he tapped his nose with one long yellow-stained finger. 'Madame goes away and I come, two times. But this life is not for me. Really, Charles and me, we are bachelors together. Real men. Let me see, this girl, was it nineteen seventy? Seventy-two?'

Hilary drove on. What was he supposed to do? Kill him? Yes. How? Far too rapidly, they were approaching the lime tree avenue. He braked. His passenger had wound the window on his side down and had stuck his head out of it. How about ramming it against one of the trees?

'There, you see the turning. Slow down there, take the next right. I do not think, my friend, that there is a future for you in navigation, no. Why aren't you stopping? You stop! You turn! That's it.' He reached for the wheel, Hilary elbowed him back. Again, the lunatic took the wheel, swung it round.

'I said not to do that,' Hilary roared.

They had turned into the lime tree avenue.

'What was I saying? This girl was called Madeleine and she had an incredible body and an incredible flat. Tits like melons. We are talking in the centre of Paris, mon pote, in those days a place like that cost, ouf, let me see . . .'

The problem was this guy's unerring sense of direction, which worked in inverse ratio to his conversational sense. Oh shit,

Hilary thought. Gaston again stuck his big stupid head out of the window.

'Look, my friend, I am trying to help you. Yes! I know this one. Nearly there.'

Bloody wonderful, this was.

'Here, OK? You turn, just there. RIGHT, take a RIGHT.' He hung onto Hilary's arm like a weasel, all sinew and tug, shouting, 'Turn! Turn! Turn!'

'All right, lay off, leave me alone.' Hilary tried to shake him off. He was like a rat. Grimly, Hilary clung to the wheel and drove past the house. At the crossroads, where he had to stop, Gaston opened the door, hopped out and loped off back the way they'd come. At this Hilary lost his cool. He roared after him.

'You're not a doctor! What are you? What is this?'

'Me? Don't be so stupid,' he shouted back at Hilary. 'What d'you think I am, you little shit?'

Hilary let his head rest upon the wheel. He thought, that's it, I'm finished. In the rearview mirror, he saw the mad old fart moving rapidly along the dark hedgerows, his jacket a paler blur. Hilary reversed at speed, hoping nobody was coming the other way. The bugger was even quicker. Leaving the car at the foot of the hill, for the whole driveway was blocked with cars, moaning to himself, Hilary ran after him. Gaston had a surprising turn of speed.

They came up past the house with Gaston clucking and panting. He stopped to get his breath and Hilary grabbed him. Last-ditch stuff, this. They wrestled for a moment in what Gasbag clearly took to be a playful manner and then he broke loose and loped round the trees and into the orchard shouting, 'Charles, j'arrive!'

Now things were beyond any control. Up stood Charles and he opened his arms and let out a great gurgling cry. They embraced. They swayed and turned together. They kissed, four cheeks, they slapped each other on the back, the works. Charles was drunk.

Louise rose and Gaston took her hand and kissed it. Then he and Charles went arm in arm round the table. Tenderly, Charles held onto him.

Hilary and Louise stood there, banjaxed. 'I'm so very sorry. I couldn't – didn't – he wouldn't – he's un maniaque.' Laughing, re-arranging chairs, Charles busily fixed things so his old pal could sit opposite him. Gaston crossed arms, stuck out a paw to each of his neighbours and fell upon the food and drink. Charles leant forward over the table and filled up his glass; the man emptied it in one vast gulp, tilting his head back like a hound and letting the wine run down his throat. Charles laughed and filled it again.

'Jesus,' said Hilary. He watched with horrible fascination. In his dad's hospital, he had seen old tramps eat like that, with a mouth full and a forkful ready and one hand busy on the bread and the other curled protectively round the glass, because somebody might snatch the food away. Gaston's gob was kept full as he chewed busily and rapidly but also kept a bulging eye on the main chance which, in this instance, was his neighbour, Héloïse's swelling décolletée.

All around there was a general easing of waistbands and wiping of mouths, a laying down of napkins and raising up of glasses, a fumbling for cigarettes. A mountain range rose next to the kitchen door, as plates were cleared from the table to join their fellows in the pre-ordained spot, each peak rising as happy testimony to the powers of knife and fork. Hilary carried another pile of plates over and set it down.

Gaston had now hoovered up so much and so fast that it seemed incredible that he hadn't yet thrown up. The more he filled his belly, the more confiding and pally he became. Behind his chair, Hilary hovered and looked at the white hand of Héloïse who was fingering her blonde curls.

'What tricks I taught him. He has good hands, you see, big but very, very careful – skilled. Now you, you I think, let me see – ah, you could be taught, oh, many things,' and his hand slid up her arm and towards her bosom and she, giggling, pulled it away though not, by Hilary's reckoning, quite as quickly as she could have done. He caught a glimpse of the pharmacist turning in time to clock this. His face turned a deep red colour.

'I love you, mon vieux,' yelled Gaston to Charles.

'Moi aussi, je t'aime.' Tears welled up in Gaston's eyes. They clasped hands across the table. Charles again filled their glasses. By Hilary's reckoning, Charles should by now be extremely drunk, but you wouldn't know it, the hand was steady, he looked normal. Another bellow came from the riff-raff. Hilary moved reluctantly towards them.

'. . . try this. You'll see. Not as fine as the langoustine we had for Martine's birthday but not bad either . . .' At the uncouth end the uninviteds were cleaning up various platters of odds and sods which had been left near them for precisely that purpose. They had finely honed culinary senses and were particular about their sauces and condiments. One big buck with a cheeky face had even had the gall to suggest to Hilary that next time Madame might like to get her baguettes somewhere different, laughing at his own wit. Boulangerie Lardon, that was the place. Hilary shouldered their cast-offs, as requested.

'. . . Never saw a nurse with a nicer arse and what fabulous tits . . .' The return journey past Gaston, audible at some distance. Hilary looked at Louise. She no longer seemed upset. She looked fine, sitting nearly opposite quite calmly and looking from face to face as if measuring them up for something. He went over to her. Waves of noise were coming off the table and rolling through the trees and the branches swayed with it, the silvery-green leaves twinkled and the little lights trembled.

Close up, he realised that she was after all in some sort of state; she was gritting her teeth so hard that the whole of her jaw was locked and a muscle in her cheek twitched. He poured her some water, put the glass in her hand. She gulped it down.

Gaston winked at Hilary and then, as if that wasn't enough, stagily raised a finger and laid it along one side of his nose. This, which should have been reassuring, had the opposite effect. He followed this with a slow, deliberate wink at Héloïse which did him no good whatsoever with her husband who looked as though for two pins he'd poke him in the eye. Charles, sitting opposite, winked back.

'Eh! Mon pote!' roared Gaston, 'Think of the ones we did for – in our day!' They both roared with laughter.

Jean-Jacques's emotions were in conflict. He felt as though he was the victim of something, a shipwreck perhaps, being tossed about from one side to another. But the dinner was a success, excellent. They were on the home stretch with two-thirds of this long and copious meal in his belly. He watched as the guest of honour, this vulgar, nasty man, this professor, again pawed his wife. This concentrated his mind upon his loathing – yes, it was that strong – of the medical profession.

He loathed the way the long greasy hair curled over the collar, the bleary eye, the mouth that never stopped, whether chewing or talking. Every pore of his body disliked this man, this insult to humanity. The wine rose to his head in an angry surge. Jean-Jacques looked again in the direction of Madame Beauregard who nodded at him and gestured that he should rise. Charles Beauregard was not a bad man, no. The other. *He* was a bad man. The pharmacist felt a new and pure sensation, a small tenderness towards his old enemy whom he was about to honour.

He stood, cleared his throat, swallowed. The lank and silvery head of this professor fellow swivelled to look at him. Again, he swallowed and cleared his throat. He opened his mouth. Then he closed it again.

For this was not what he really wanted to do. He wanted to make his mark more literally. What would satisfy him would be to take that fellow and hit him, not so hard that he was permanently damaged, but enough to mark him. The man was a shit. And Jean-Jacques Albert was no speechifyer.

Everybody was looking at him. This made him feel powerful which in turn made him feel more real than he usually did. His toes, in the too-tight shoes, tingled slightly. He would suffer for it tomorrow, but that day had not yet come. It was still today and his heart was beating rapidly, so much so that it seemed to have swelled beyond its normal size. Feeling in his pocket, he drew out his carefully prepared papers and waved them at the other guests, smiling. He felt a dropping away, the absence of a weight on his body. The speech fell onto the grass and the pharmacist spoke from his heart.

'What a party!' he heard himself say. 'Isn't this something, ladies and gentlemen? I'm not making a speech – you needn't worry. We're here to raise our glasses and celebrate twenty years of our good doctor here. Let us drink to twenty more – and to Madame his wife! A good doctor, a wonderful wife, and as you see a most wonderful cook! Ladies and gentlemen, to the doctor! And to Madame!'

As glasses and voices were raised, Jean-Jacques leant down and under cover of the general hubbub shot a remark over Héloïse.

'Touch her one more time and I'll plaster you across the table.'

Professor Vigne-Laval stared at his glass as if he hadn't understood what he'd been told and then, swivelling slowly, he returned his bloodshot gaze to Héloïse.

'Quel magnifique châssis,' he said breathily.

Yes, he would hit him. This knowledge sang louder and louder through Jean-Jacques. The tingling spread round his whole body, as though his flow of blood was invigorated by the very thought. His right hand began to bunch itself into a fist as though he had no control over it, to unbunch and bunch again. He saw the doctor looking at him, saw on Charles Beauregard's face a kind smile. Yes, he smiled at him in sympathy and in understanding, oh, the sweetness of it swept over Jean-Jacques. Let this oaf drink and wink and nod. The pharmacist, who could have been burdened through the years with an idiot like this one, realised that he was a lucky man. The doctor was laughing. With the utmost pleasure, Jean-Jacques laughed back at him.

Charles rose and held up one hand. At once the noise died down.

'Friends,' he said loudly, 'you're all friends tonight, every one of you. I'll drink to that,' and round the table the glasses were lifted and drained. Jean-Jacques stayed on his feet, his fist still in its state of expectancy. 'Twenty years we've been here and tonight I'll tell you the truth. I'm no doctor, I never was.' Charles Beauregard's voice boomed out and, getting the joke, Jean-Jacques laughed out loud, he even leant forwards and banged on the table though his Héloïse shot him a disapproving glance. There was a little ripple of laughter round the table.

'Listen, all of you,' the doctor said. 'I never qualified to treat you. All I've got is what you see here.' He held up two empty hands. 'That's all.'

'No! You've got more than that, my friend.' The idiot beside Jean-Jacques had the effrontery to get up on his hind legs and start braying like the donkey he was. Vigne-Laval was visibly swaying and, face on, Jean-Jacques was repelled by his pungent breath.

'Shut up! I know nothing, do you understand? *I know nothing at all.*' Loud as the doctor shouted, the other voice was yet more powerful.

'*He's a fucker, ladies and gentlemen,*' bellowed the professor. 'Let us not forget,' slurring his words and shrieking so loudly that nothing else could be heard, 'his wife! Never forget the love of a woman! I drink to woman, to wine, and to women everywhere!' He laughed coarsely and wiped away the flecks of spittle from his mouth with a sleeve. 'Women, unforgettable, beautiful, lovely, I love them all. They have been my university and I have a PhD in pussy.' At this point Héloïse started tugging at his jacket, hissing at him to sit down. And at this moment, with utter astonishment, Jean-Jacques saw that in his hand the professor held his own beautiful, precious gold pocket watch.

'Give that back,' he said, tugging at his sleeve. Vigne-Laval ignored him, leering across the table at Louise Beauregard. Jean-Jacques pulled back his arm and with a feeling of the most intense jubilation let him have it. With an upward jerk he slammed Vigne-Laval in the chin as hard as he possibly could. The professor, who was too drunk to see it coming, reeled back and fell heavily onto Héloïse.

For the second before his hand began to hurt like hell, before Héloïse screamed and the fool fell over and everything became messy – for that split second Jean-Jacques felt wonderful. Yes, he felt as good as he'd ever felt, about anything, ever. He felt pretty good afterwards, too, but that first connection, that crunch of bone against tissue, counted as one of the very best moments in his whole life.

Hilary, who had been holding his breath, let out a huge exhalation and dashed round the table, getting there just as Héloïse stood up and pushed away Gaston who now crumpled to the ground. He did this very neatly, knees buckling, head down between them as though he was practising for an airline disaster. Jean-Jacques was hopping about, nursing his hand. Gaston started muttering and thrashing with his feet in spasms. Hilary strained to get him up. He was much heavier than he had expected. Charles came up and between them they lifted him. From somewhere a shout rang out.

'Let the doctor deal with him! He can raise the dead, and the dead drunk!'

They staggered towards the house with Gaston mumbling and cursing and doing that classic drunk's thing of twisting his feet round and tripping himself up. The pharmacist came dancing along behind them. Charles was carrying most of the weight and with a good deal of fumbling they got Gaston into the study and onto the couch.

'I didn't think I hit him so hard,' said Jean-Jacques, exulting.

Outside, a wave of music burst forth. The dancing had begun. 'Good,' said the pharmacist, 'Good,' and with a swagger he turned and went to the door. He flexed his hand once or twice. 'So. For my part, I am going to dance,' and he went.

Gaston leant back on the couch and his mouth dropped open. Hilary looked at him. The man was white-faced, his skin looked slack and shone with a sheen of sweat. Charles, by contrast, seemed sober. His mood had suddenly suffered an abrupt change and he waved to Hilary to go.

'Go.'

Hilary backed away and waited just along the corridor, intensely curious to hear what might happen between these two.

'Toi,' he heard Charles say. 'Tu es une ordure.' He was angry and his voice was different, a calm, smooth voice which gave Hilary a ripple of goosepimples.

Charles closed the door with a quiet click. There came a noise, which might have been the sound of a clap or smack, it was hard to tell. Hilary waited nervously but now he could hear nothing, for the music outside was getting louder. He felt all at once how badly he needed to dance with Michèle, how overdue some pleasure was. The cooler air outside was refreshing and in search of Michèle Hilary went past the tables where coffee was being served, where people were getting stuck into liqueurs. No matter what had been before and no matter what came of it or didn't, he was owed this: to hold her in his arms once, to let his cheek rest against hers, to breath in the whole delicious smell of her. It wouldn't harm her, would it, to let him have this small pleasure, which meant so much? It wouldn't have harmed her to kiss him once properly, so he'd remember it. But he could not find her anywhere.

Hilary sat in a kind of stupor under the apple tree and watched the dancers, the drinkers, the surge and pattern of it all. Later, Charles emerged and Hilary saw him help Madame Ourlandes down the drive to the car – for she was the first to go. Hilary would have liked to say goodbye to her and now it was too late. Some force was pressing down upon him. Because of it, he stayed where he was under the apple tree and watched. He watched his host dance with his wife, he watched people applaud. Finally, with a disagreeable effort, he thought he had better see if Gaston was all right.

The couch in the study was empty; the man was gone. Hilary went from room to room and did not find him. He was not in any of the bedrooms or anywhere in the house. He looked in each bathroom, each cupboard and store, looked in the garage where there was noise and found a gang of waiters smoking and drinking, playing cards. As one, they turned their faces to him and just stared, so there was nothing to do but turn and go away. Not there, not anywhere.

Now Hilary went up and down the driveway looking in all the cars and, finally, walked along the perimeter of the garden. Then he traversed it up and down and did this twice. He did not find him. It was impossible that that man could have walked from there unaided, in his condition. Impossible. And only one car had departed with Madame Ourlandes in it driven by her neighbour. So he had not left. Hilary would have seen him. Again he walked around and now he looked for a mound of new earth but this, too, was not to be found, though the finding of it would not have been a surprise. Yet as he thought of how it would be to stumble upon turned earth, even to smell the tangy odour of it, he felt sick and his heart pounded with a horrible anticipation. The cars were beginning to leave and he stood, pale apparition, between the trees and counted them out.

At four in the morning there were still two couples dancing under the trees and a last half-dozen hardy souls sitting and quaffing Armagnac at the table. A halo of aromatic cigar smoke hung in the trees and the dawn was just signalling its intention of appearing soon.

Jean-Jacques had been sitting for hours supporting Héloïse, who slept with her head in his lap. He was nearly asleep himself. Now, he jerked upright.

'Time to go, my darling,' he said. With a little difficulty, he leant forward and his foot touched something. He hooked it out from under the table, a big box wrapped up in shiny paper. He edged it towards Charles with his foot. 'To think I nearly forgot. This is for you.'

Charles opened it and drew forth a shiny, new, big black doctor's bag. There was a collective sigh of recognition. Inside, it was full to the brim with packets of cigarettes. The mayor, who sat beside them, began to cackle. With slow pleasure, Charles drew off the cellophane, lit up.

'I like it,' Dutronc said. 'I like it. Eh, Monsieur? Not bad, eh? There's a sense of humour, eh? There's a bit of fun.' His wife nodded her assent as Jean-Jacques beckoned to Charles.

'My friend,' and now he began to whisper. 'You have your special gift – you know. Will you pass your hands across my wife? Down below – you know?'

Charles looked at him.

With another furtive glance at his sleeping wife, the pharmacist gestured from his chest downwards across his abdomen in a sweeping gesture. 'Please. There are things no medicine can do,' and he made a cradling gesture with his arms and rocked his imaginary baby to and fro.

Very carefully Charles pressed his hands against Héloïse, smoothing her down from just below the waist to the knees, passing his hands across her belly in curving movements. She smiled and muttered something in her sleep and turned a little. Charles did it again. Jean-Jacques watched intently. Dutronc, a little embarrassed, looked the other way. With one hand smoothing his wife's cheek, Jean-Jacques put the other in his pocket and felt for his watch. Carefully, he drew it out, held it to his ear and listened to its ticking. A smile spread across his face.

Everybody stood and now it really was over, the last people straggling down the hill.

'Remember,' Charles said, spreading out his arms to embrace Dutronc and then Jean-Jacques. 'Remember what I've told you, that I know nothing at all.' Nodding and smiling, they agreed. Whatever you say, Monsieur le docteur. Hilary remained outside as Charles went into the house and he watched for the bathroom light and the bedroom one to come on and go off again. Now he was alone but for the last two lads taking down the trestle tables.

He sat on under the trees. His heart was beating in a dull thudding motion which told him how tired he must be. He had long abandoned all hope of Michèle, who must have gone to bed hours ago. The magic was going out of the place. A grey-blue shimmer over the horizon showed where another hot day was coming. Somebody turned off the lights in the trees. There were shouts of goodbye from the last two young men, the crunch of their feet on the gravel, leaving. The sound of the owl hooting on the far side of the orchard. The last night. He began to think of things ending and his going and now he began to feel stranger than ever. The new day had come. He would be leaving for home in a matter of hours.

He wandered slowly through the orchard to the far side. A final tour of the place. Michèle's window dark.

He was walking backwards and looking upwards at her window when something tripped him and he fell over. It took a second to understand it was something warm and soft. A body – oh God. He had found the body of Gaston Vigne–Laval. Oh Jesus. A leg. He touched it and it was still warm. A moaning sound. He sprang away. A face half hidden in the bushes. He went closer, closer – with a shock of recognition, he saw that he was staring into Michèle's face. A horrible moment when he thought she was dead and his heart lurched and he felt sick, for her eyes were open. He went closer – too close.

Michèle was spread-eagled on her back half naked, her dress pulled up to her waist. A dark-haired man was fucking her, groaning, so intent he didn't even realise Hilary was there. Michèle, who did, continued to watch him, quite expressionless. White buttocks pumping up and down, up and down, the man had pulled his trousers down to his knees. He wore a white shirt and round his neck on a cord, slung over his back so it wouldn't get in the way, was a warbler from the market, just like the one that Hilary had bought for Ed.

Hilary leant forward, took hold of it and tugged and felt the sudden pull of the cord at the man's neck. He tugged again. The man might die, he might kill him, for he was starting to make a terrible strangled noise. He was struggling to get off her, up, away. Hilary pulled once more. It was right, what he was doing felt right. He pulled the cord tighter still. He pulled with all his strength so the man would die. So this was what he had learnt here. But they had to know why.

'Pute,' Hilary said and then he repeated it, louder. The word for prostitute. With his head thrumming with a terrific agony of excitement, he pulled at the warbler in sharp tugs, again, again, and the pumping intensified, and then the warbler came loose and he had it in his hand. Freed, the man collapsed sideways, panting and groaning and gurgling for breath. Perhaps it was merely that he had climaxed. When Hilary saw his face, he knew him. The big guy at the uninviteds' table, the son of the boulanger – the man of the woods.

Hilary turned and walked away and as he did so he found that he was blowing on the warbler. The cry of an owl came out. Dear God Almighty. He blew again and again. He was the owl in the orchard. He was the owl. He was the owl.

Tears began quite unexpectedly to stream down his face. He took the thing out of his mouth and threw it away and then he was running, faster and faster. He felt like screaming though he was also so stunned by the surprise, so shocked, that when he opened his mouth nothing at all came out, though some little insects came in and he stopped, spat them out and then he retched.

Hilary had the aisle seat. As the TGV pulled out of Saint-Pierre-des-Corps he leant back to have an hour's sleep before Paris. Couldn't, though he tried. There was the same pixie face in the mirror, the same bit of luggage shoved under the seat, the same leather jacket. Things bore the same appearance as before. Blood beat round his head in slow waves.

Madame Ourlandes had been found dead in her bed. Poor soul, Louise had said, poor old soul. It was a release from suffering. She had been gentle with him, had driven him to the station and seen him off quietly.

Secrets were strange things, they both filled you up and left you empty. They hooked and held you, like a fish on a line. You couldn't get away, you might have to live with the barb through your cheek for the rest of your life.

Hilary stared out of the window at the smooth green indifference of the fields. It was possible to live with intense desire that could never be satisfied. He knew these cravings were illogical. Sense and reason would soon intervene. He looked out of the window and waited for them to do their stuff. Michèle was a tart, forget her. But what he felt wasn't so much to do with her but himself, a kind of shock of recognition that he was just going to have to carry on with all these acute sensations surging around. Knowing Gaston was an old lag didn't stop the anxiety. Knowing Michèle was a tart did nothing to assuage his pain. He could remember the crisp sound that Madame Ourlandes' blue silk had made when she sat. The night had been so very beautiful, hadn't it? Meanwhile, other people couldn't be expected to know what bothered him or even that anything did, nor could they be told. It was shocking, that this could all be so personal. And now he saw that the only victim he could be perfectly sure of was himself.

This was a shock. How long would it take for this to fade? The shock would become something calmer as it turned to memory. Wouldn't it? His heart thumped away. How long would it take? Because he could still see how she had looked, lying there, the picture was exact. How long? Think about something else. After all, there was a moral issue, wasn't there? An angle. Watching the lush landscape zoom past, the little copses and mini woods, the gentle roll of the slopes up and down, he tried to find it. He could examine a number of issues. Firstly, there was the question of whether the conflict or difference wasn't as much to do with nationality as anything else. For he saw some kind of moral conflict, didn't he, he didn't just feel gutted on a personal level, there was a whole other business there to do with how a sixteen-year-old girl was expected to behave. He thought, too, about Charles, who had not said goodbye to him. Was that the right way to behave? Was that correct? But whatever else he had done, Charles had always told the truth. A strange thing to say of the fraud who so liberally handed out the death pills. Then he thought about Gaston. Always, though, it came back to the same thing, the cord round the neck, always that, back to it again and again, the back and the buttocks up and down and the cord and her face and the body and the cord and her face. He would never forget it, never, never.

Michèle. Oh, Michèle, how could she? She had broken his heart. His whole chest hurt as if he'd been kicked. He folded his hands across it to keep everything more or less in place and stared out at his reflection and felt the deep ache of it, felt a searing pain which burnt everything, even the insides of his eyes which wanted to cry but of course didn't. He would never cry again.

5

Michèle Beauregard was sunbathing. She could not remain still for more than a few moments at a time and now, sitting up, she loosened her hair, permitted it to flow down over her shoulders charmingly, and with a series of little shakes of the head and stretching movements eased herself over until she was supine. A moment later, she removed the skimpy little bikini top and lay down again. The earth, which had held its breath for excitement at this manoeuvre, once more let it out. The air was thick with the exhalation of atoms colliding as they, too, jostled for position.

Nicholas, twitching at his curtain, absorbed that her breasts were, excitingly, degrees paler than the rest of her. On the lush green of his well-watered grass, in the bright sun, her flesh was altogether paler than indoors. The glint of a thin gold chain on her ankle. Rosebuds, tips, delicate things, silken. He was too far away to see if there might be the faint mottling of the towel or the crease of a blade of grass imprinted on her leg. From his dry throat came an involuntary groan.

From the landing, he passed with stealth into Ed's room and there he rummaged. Months since he'd been in here. There, perhaps in his son's collection of weapons or maybe on his bookshelf. Drawer after drawer displayed his son's lack of taste, his consistency in that alone. Hilary had come home from France and mooched about for the last fortnight and in all that time had said nothing about Michèle. Incredible. Was the boy blind? Were both his sons daft?

Nicholas had bought the binoculars for his son's ninth birthday. A tight red rage was building at the remembered cost. Look at this rubbish he's accumulated, ridiculous waste of money, a boy his age, plastic trash and look at the state of this room, they must be here – look at this *mess*. While each drawer was rammed back with anger, the deep inner part of him was reverberating with its own ragings. Bonkers, it screamed, off yer bleedin' rocker, leave it out, mate – a coarser version of the same faux demotic he used on his rounds. Alien forces had moved in three days ago, the day of her arrival. They had found Nicholas and taken him over and they gave him no rest, they ran him up and down the stairs and in and out and all the time said hurry, hurry, hurry. Gerra move on, you bloody nitwit. Carpe diem, quam minimum credula postero. Michèle teased him with brevity in all forms. Michèle was staying with them for a mere two weeks.

Nicholas was sick. The sickness lay in his garden, the worm in the bud. Oh rose, thou art. Layer after layer of it, unreasoning, mad, impossible desire. Beyond each furl and curl another one, tight, below, fresh-minted.

He pulled at the last drawer, much too hard, and it jammed then jerked out and littered its cargo of rubbish, its old Beano annuals and plastic bits and half-done kits, all over his shoes. The trash stash. A little tin of paint in gun-metal grey rolled quietly away. He kicked it, hard. A thin grey smear laid itself out across the carpet and mocked him. A tiny oil slick dripped from the lid.

High on the roof of the handsome Queen Anne house there was a flash and a glint of binoculars in the hands of Edward, Ed the daring, Ed the bold – though he was wobbling a trifle insecurely on his dizzy perch. To get up there involved climbing out through the attic window, then over an overhanging bit, then edging up the roof tiles. He'd taken off his sandals and socks, so with bare feet he had a better grip. Sweaty, the soles, just a bit. He wasn't scared any more. The binoculars were a middling pair, not brilliant, but the lenses were OK. Carefully, breathing rather heavily through his mouth, Ed adjusted the focus and blinked as Michèle leapt out at him. He contemplated the faint golden down that lay along her arms and then followed the arm up and down and examined her armpits for a good long bit. He wasn't fussy, he wanted to see everything and he didn't know when he'd get such a good chance again.

Ed was experiencing a golden age. He was on holiday. A beautiful French girl who liked taking her clothes off was staying in the house. She did not seem to mind him staring at her. She never wore a bra. She had allowed him several puffs of a cigarette. She winked at him now and then. Neither of his parents was paying him the slightest bit of attention. His mother was always busy cooking and stuff, and apart from the odd session shelling peas, she left him alone. He was going away to camp, but that wasn't for a bit yet. His unfettered leisure stretched out deliciously.

The only black spot was the presence of his brother. Eight years separated them and had ever done so with great effectiveness. Hilary belonged to the country of the grown-ups, with the added bonus of indifference, exclusion from the wonderland of his room being an acceptable price to pay. But since he'd got back from France, and particularly since Michèle had arrived, Hilary was very funny peculiar. He'd never paid any attention to his brother in the past, beyond a certain amount of cuffing and cursing. Of late, more than once, Hilary had tried to talk to Ed when it wasn't at all necessary. Asking him how he felt, strange things like that. Ed could see him now as he sauntered up the lane. He looked at the hangdog way Hilary was coming along and hastily withdrew a little, ducking his head down as far as he could.

Ambling along, Hilary caught the glint of the binoculars and turned to look over the hedge. What a demon Ed was.

'Edd-wardd! You'll kill yourself, you dork. Come on down! Hey! Ed!' The boy on the roof retreated and put his head down further as though, ostrich fashion, that made him invisible. What a bloody fool Ed was. Pathetic little pre-pubescent.

There she lay, a slumbering beauty. No. She saw him too, for one eye, nearly closed, opened wider. She turned on her side, tossed her hair. Hilary stared down at his tennis shoes. Carefully, he continued his self-appointed task of walking between the tracks. The sun beat lazily on his head. The road which in winter could turn into a mudslip was now ridged with parallel prominences separated by the width of a caterpillar tyre. He walked between them, feeling the hard earth through his soles, fingering the cow parsley. He reached out and tugged at the odd greenish blackberry. He didn't go in through the gate. No, he would go round to the back.

So he kept his head down and did not see a blurred white oval of a face rise behind opal glass at the house. Nicholas Lennox had found the means to his end. The eminent surgeon had achieved his desired sight line by means of the wicker laundry basket, the cork-topped bathroom stool being too low, the crouch turning into a kneeling position. Down the knees went onto the wickerwork. Swinging open the window, he achieved the dream of an unimpeded view. Being on this glorious hot Sunday dressed for tennis, his knees were bare. He should have put a towel on the basket. Never mind. No time to lose. When in due course he went down for lunch, Amanda would notice the latticework pattern imprinted on his knees and would think in a distant way that perhaps he had hurt himself. Which was quite true.

'Mum?'

'Just give me a hand with the basket, will you. Thank you, darling, lovely day for it.' Amanda wiped her hand on her pinnie and took a breather, staring out through the open kitchen window at that one particular spot, peculiarly prominent, on which Michèle had chosen to recline and where, sitting up, she was lighting yet another cigarette. This nymph made the veins on the backs of Amanda's hands stand out. She exacerbated both the sagging skin around her throat and a certain ache inside it. Amanda wondered, vaguely, if she should take up smoking herself. She looked at her hands which seemed such a strange colour against the wedding ring. A dark reddish colour on the knuckles, almost as if they'd been injured. Perhaps if she took it off. She tugged and, when it wouldn't, started to massage hand cream into the red knuckles.

'Mum? Cup of tea?'

'What a star you are. Madame B's brought out your feminine side. Ummh?' Amanda sat at the table and looked at her son, whose beauty was intensified by his shorts, his semi-nakedness, his tan. She had always admired his looks, so very different from hers in every respect, most crucially in the way they went on improving with age. Even as a baby he had been elegant.

'Did you talk to her a lot, honey? She didn't look terribly chatty . . . Not like your Mum, I suppose, terribly elegant, that's what I thought. I mean. Not that I got a glimpse. You tell me.' There she was, looking at him again, waiting for his reply.

'Earl Grey?' said Hilary. 'Louise is, um, well she's not what I'd call chatty, not in the normal way.'

His mother listened to what he said about France with a stillness and attention that was, frankly, scary. Not terrifying as her silence had been – no, this was quite different. She no longer cried in silence, tears dripping from her cheeks unheeded making little damp channels down her dress. He said to himself that that stage was over. She was on to the next bit and now everything was concealed. Not from him of course, just from the others. But this business of him knowing made it impossible to tell her anything, had any telling been possible in the first place. Which it wasn't. Yet she would keep on asking. Ironic, really, when he so badly wanted to tell her everything and ask her advice.

So Hilary smiled vaguely and poured water on a tea bag and thought that it was wonderful, how she could stand in her kitchen, a rock, frumpily dressed in the summer uniform of her class – a print frock which revealed freckly arms and sagged rather but was a favourite. Then there were the ancient sandals, the hair pulled back in a pony tail because the heat wave went on and on – and none of it mattered to her. She didn't give a stuff about her appearance. All around were baskets overflowing with her produce, with sprigs of mint and strawberries and peas from the garden. Endearing, that was what it all was. Good for her.

'Give me the peas,' said Hilary, splitting them and running his nail down and eating half as he went. 'Food's her thing. The only time I saw Louise really passionate was to do with the size of the oysters and how they weren't fine claires number whatsits, you know. So you could never know what she might've been like when she was young.'

'She was beautiful. Like Michèle. You can see it.'

Hilary watched his mother as she stared into some alien landscape in her mind while gulping down the tea. She was always busy cooking, peeling, doing. She slaved over the hot

Aga, day in, day out. Today there would be the classic English roast lamb, pink inside, new and roast potatoes, gravy, two veg and salad, homemade apple pie, cream. With a bottle or two of claret. The best food in the world, really. Try doing that for a hundred odd people. Hilary uncorked the claret and put the bottles to stand. Tea break was sacred.

There were long silences. He was aware of a certain amount of marital stress here, quite apart from the Charles business. It was as if there was some primeval slime or bubbling stew in her which went on and on all the time, a kind of biological life force that just was. Creative and all that, but not so as you'd see. But every now and then the slime surged and threw up an idea, like a bubble rising slowly through mud. Then it would pop and there would be nothing to show you that anything had happened, but the idea would be there, in the air.

'Charles hasn't changed. I did think that – not that you'd know. Well. I mean, how could you, darling. But you can see – some people have a kind of strength that's just in them.'

'Strength, weakness – they're like two halves of the same coin,' he said. Dimbat.

'Tell me more about France. You've hardly said.'

'Oh, France. Well, you're right about Louise being elegant. A real stunner, she is. Amazing cook. She makes this great apple tart. Almost as good as you, Mum. But she's not half as pretty as you, Mum, not a quarter. You know, it's all, like, make-up and labels. And food is everything, it's their religion.'

She nodded. 'It's impossible for a woman to spend time on herself, when there's so much to do in the house and garden, Hilary,' and she looked as though she was going to cry. 'Hands like these – well, you can't stop it. It's just part of the aging process.' She blinked quite rapidly.

That was the thing which drove him bonkers. Hilary watched her with amazed affection. Did every remark have to relate to her? Wasn't it possible for a woman to take a compliment to another not as an insult to herself? Gender differences came down to this. Women never let themselves out of the beam of the critical spotlight, whereas men never took anything to apply to them. She sipped her tea and went on looking wobbly. No sense. Here was a woman who, told by the weathermen that there was a fifty per cent chance of rain on Friday and a fifty per cent chance on Saturday, would cancel her picnic because there was a total certainty of rain. He felt suddenly terribly fond of her for caring, just as fond as he'd been two secs ago for not, and went up and kissed her on the cheek.

'Mum. Please. You look gorgeous,' he said. The hand was really awfully red, around the knuckle especially. Perhaps she'd burnt it on something.

Amanda dished up lunch. They all ate plenty, Ed nose down in the trough and shovelling it in in concentrated feeding mode, then coming up for air.

'But it all gets mixed up in your tummy, doesn't it? So what's the big deal?' Ed was just trying to understand, you could see that. His eyes like saucers with mock amazement, his face all screwed up with the effort of it.

'No, no we serve separate the légumes. Not with meat. Separate the salad. Then some cheeses. Traditional, you know. Everyone in France do this.' She shrugged polished, bare shoulders.

'So you can never have gravy on your earth apples. Get it? Earth apples. Mum, pommes de terre, get it? Mum? Michèle's taught me lots of French. Dad? Do you know what gravy is in French? Le gravy?'

'Hilary's the expert,' said Nicholas, who'd got up to carve more meat and was offering the plate round, oozing charm. She looked at it. A thin pink fluid, in runnels, beyond the valley of the spikes.

'Mum?'

Would he have been like this, if he'd been Charles's son? Odd, to imagine a non-English Ed, a solemn little boy who would never mash up his roast potatoes and make a well in the centre for gravy. Which he always ate from the outside in.

'Mum?'

'No, Edward, she doesn't know the word. They don't have gravy in France like we do,' said Hilary.

'No gravy? Pas de gravy, Michèle? C'est impossible. Pas de gravy, quel disaster. I'm not going to France then. Pas de mint sauce, Michèle?'

Michèle smiled and shook her head. 'What is the sauce à

la menthe?' Her eyebrows flew up, for she was amazed by everything – the failure to peel all the potatoes, the way all the vegetables went on one plate with the meat, a highly uncouth practice to French eyes, the way that Nicholas dissected his meat, finding Latin names for sinews and knobbly bits which he liked to hold up to public inspection in a way she clearly found hilarious. And he was funny, his rubbery face pulled into expressions of utmost astonishment. Expertly, he forked a piece of meat onto his own plate. Smilingly, he took a little blob of mint sauce, put it on the girl's plate. Ed roared with laughter at her face as she tried it. She made a little moue, dead charming, of course.

Nobody noticed Amanda's face when Nicholas did his Latin party piece for perhaps the thousandth time in her married life. Nobody took their eyes off Michèle for a second, while Amanda cleared, helped intermittently by Hilary, and washed up and made coffee which, regrettably, she allowed to boil and which, like everything she did, was not quite good enough for her husband. She put the stuff on a tray and took it outside and the others sauntered out through the French windows onto the terrace and there she served it, smiling pleasantly. Then she went back in.

They sat on outside and had coffee and the afternoon was glorious and Michèle hoiked up the floaty pretty dress she'd put on to have lunch in and let her gorgeous legs tan a little more. Such skin she had, like a child's, which she of course was, just. Though in her soul that girl was ancient as Amanda had never been and still wasn't. That girl had lived her previous lives to the full.

'Hil, honey, take out some chocolates. Sweetie day, after all,' She passed them through the window. Ed with pillage noises of a Viking nature fell upon the box.

The mistress of the house sat in the kitchen with the door open and put her feet up because they ached, easing them out of the sandals and onto a chair and looking at the knobbly bones and the little veins, from childbirth, which Louise probably didn't have. Little dark lines, wispy, ugly, there. Nor those yellowy ugly heels which she particularly hated herself.

Her three men clustered round Michèle. They sought words for hazelnut and for cream fondant, which was French, wasn't it, and Nicholas led the laughter and fun in a manner which made it clear that only a bad sport would take his remarks seriously. Ho ho. And now and then a shout would come – buck up, Amanda! Come and enjoy the day, darling! Only a spoilsport would stay indoors and do cooking and clearing up on such a glorious day. Wife wasn't interested in the day, though, was she? The glories were hers anyway, wherever she was.

Wife got on with it. She made beds, loaded and unloaded the washing machine, went shopping with the ubiquitous basket in the charming local town. Wife got on with it. She organised more food, more meals, everything with a smile, always slightly harried, driving young Edward off to summer camp, back down the motorway. Get a nice bunch of flowers, cut the stems, dissolve the white stuff you got these days in warm water, arrange the flowers, fold the washing, see the place behind the machine where the powder fell, clean it, Betty bloody Boardman too old now, too stiff, and couldn't reach. Swab with the cloth, wipe down the cord, rewind the twisted bit of the kettle. Never had been any good, cleaning ladies difficult, this one very much so. Thanks, Mrs B, see you on Monday!

Saturday afternoon and wife sank with a sigh into the hands of the hairdresser, Georgie of the little-boy name and slightly wizened looks, who while an expert on appearances considered himself beyond all criticism. Wanted to say, just once, look, dear, we all know it's a fake tan and the trousers are so tacky. No, you couldn't, grateful that he came to the house. Look, Georgie, whatever made you think that anyone cared whose hair you'd done? On a Saturday, special customer, grumbled a bit, big tip required she knew, how kind of him to come. Amanda's eyes closed, she was far, far away.

Nicholas was playing tennis with something more than his usual competitiveness. He threw the ball a little to one side, caught it and started again. The serve thwacked away well, skimmed just over the net, Hilary scooped it up but returned it weakly, allowing his father to smash it back this time unreturnably. They were very alike in build and height but Nicholas felt bulky and old when he looked at his son. Hair, thinning on top, this year he had sunburn on the top of his head which had painfully brought home the truth of the matter. The business with the angling mirrors in the bathroom, compulsive, to look and then feel – what? Rage, at himself? Michèle ambled by and sat on a low wall.

'Come and play, Michèle, take this boy to the cleaners.' She shook her head. Nicholas was sweating. 'Ball girl then?'

Out of his mouth came casual nonsense which did not alleviate a painful series of double faults. Without ever looking in her direction and without even trying, Hilary now began to wipe him out. Hit inadvertently on one sensitised knee by one of his son's slam-banging ace serves, he leapt into the air and jumped about the court like a wounded frog. How high the boy threw the ball, how high. He squinted at it.

'Forty love.' Hilary served and hit a fourth ace. 'Five–one, same end.'

Nicholas was sweating profusely, he swigged at the bottle of water and choked a bit on it. He felt the heat of the sun on his bald patch, felt in his breathy gasp for air as his boy gave him the runaround that he was old and dead and buried and his brain was gone. Why else would the husk run around so, sweating and hustling and trying so hard? Why? She sat there and she knew bloody why.

Georgie expertly parted her hair with the comb and examined the roots as nobody since Miss Leeming had done, for nits, years back. Satisfied, he nodded, combed it through so the foul-smelling paste penetrated a squidge further towards the tips.

'Colour's taken really nicely,' he said. 'Lovely. Five more minutes.' He always congratulated himself fulsomely on whatever he did.

She gave no sign of life as the time passed, nor when he rinsed her hair twice and smoothed in the conditioner. It dripped a little on her neck. She pretended that his hands, which were adept but impersonal and which quite often hurt when he massaged her scalp, really belonged to Charles. Curious, then, that when he pulled her hair it was she who said ouch – sorry. He never apologised. Never said a thing even if the hairdo was grim. Lovely, he said. Suits you. Her fault, for putting up with it. Charles would never hurt a fly. She thought what it might be like, to be in his hands in this bathroom. She took a long time about that one.

'Sit up, Mrs L,' said Georgie.

'I've not had a proper orgasm in fifteen years,' Amanda replied. Her eyes were fixed on the white tiles with the rich blue pattern which she had chosen herself and, come to think of it, never liked. It was a speciality of hers, then. Georgie lifted his head and stared where she looked, at the pattern, whence no elucidation came. The hair, bunched up, had taken on the colour and sheen of an alien metal.

'I'd leave him tomorrow if I thought that Charles wanted me. Today. Charles has more sex in his little finger than Nicholas has in his whole body.' Her unseeing eyes closed again. The hairdresser, lost for words, stared at the little lines around the eyes and rinsed that final time and adjusted the temperature.

'Water's a shade too hot, Mrs Lennox?' Georgie said in tones more than usually deferential.

'It's not just sex,' she said. 'You have to understand I'm talking about simple humanity.'

There was a rough rubbing, a towel drying, then Georgie smoothed new towels – hers, naturally, to spoil and launder – round her, the whole with great care and she smiled at him, for he wasn't normally so gentle. The purse of his lips told that he would have said something, if only he had had some faint idea of what might be appropriate. Amanda's smile grew broader in the mirror.

'Well done, Georgie,' she said. It was the first time, even for a second, that she had felt that she had the upper hand.

As it dried, the alien colour changed into something which, without ever being natural or even pleasant, did approximate to the sort of thing some humans might have chosen to have on their head. Georgie pulled and smoothed and eased the dryer up and down and was careful, very. Amanda wondered why it was that these hairdressers, who spoke so much of condition and texture, who swore by this spray and that cream, who sold you things right left and centre, always chose to have their dark poodle hair streaked with yellow straw?

That was it, then, and the purse clicked and she gave him a

fiver which was far too much but he expected it and was satisfied, she saw it in his face. Mean little eyes he had, like a poodle's.

Wife sallied forth on Monday, hair newly minted, to chair the meeting of the Ladies' Committee of the Cricket Club. She hated Georgie for doing this to her and yet accepted that this was how things were and that he would do the same again, a matter of weeks hence. She would smile and thank him, just as at the club she smiled and nodded and did her impersonation of a woman with an agenda which could be written down.

'Are you sure, dear Amanda, that you can do all those lovely puddings as well as the flowers?'

'Of course, really, I mean I'd mind a lot if you asked any-one else.'

Ho, a little polite laugh and wife smiled particularly brightly at that. It was pleasing to her that she could make them think that this was what she cared about. Puddings and pie and make them all cry. At home, she would pick redcurrants and blackcurrants, basket after basket, until her hands were stained red. The violent red mulch which she would sweeten and serve up to them until they were sick on it.

Wife was the chairperson of the Ladies' Committee of the Cricket Club and it fell to her to organise the annual dinner dance, which the entire village believed to be the social event of the year. It had taken years for her turn to come, years in which – and it was astonishing to think of this – she had continued in the face of all the evidence to believe that such institutions had some importance. Wife spoke at length about prices she had paid for things and smiled in that particular way which caused those present to congratulate her, whether they understood the cost of things or not. She could make things up and they would not notice or, if they did, care. Charles Beauregard would be arriving with his wife in a week's time and, as she did not hesitate to inform Mrs Dobbs, the treasurer's wife, he would be coming to, if not at, this event. Following which she laughed quite a long time. Mrs Dobbs laughed with her and then fell silent. Later, Mrs Dobbs told her husband.

'I'd call it a really filthy laugh if I didn't know that Mrs Lennox is so obviously a lady. Such lovely puddings she makes too,'

Mrs Dobbs sighed, meaning in a vague way what she truly felt, which was that it was all a real shame.

'That French girl staying,' Mr Dobbs said. 'I've seen her. In the village. Wearing very short shorts and backless T-shirts. You know. I wouldn't like to even think of our daughter seen going around like that.'

His wife smiled and said, 'Quite right and it's just that sort of thing I'm thinking of, if you know what I mean. Poor Mrs Lennox.' They always agreed with each other and there was no need for anyone to remind anyone that poor Janice with her thunder thighs could never have got away with a mini skirt, let alone a pair of shorts.

Unconscious of such pity, Amanda sat behind into the sweet afternoon and, humming to herself, piled up the chairs and locked the committee room and was satisfied. It was wonderful to walk down the lane and feel the slight wind ruffle up the helmet she wore and take the lacquer out of it and the day was hers, for there was no Ed now for two weeks, and Hilary and Michèle had gone up to town with Nicholas to watch an operation. Dimly, fingering blades of grass and feeling the ruts of the track through the soles of her feet, she remembered that long ago she too had wanted to go and watch and that the moment had never come. There had always been some more pressing thing to do. Now, when she was completely free, there was nothing that interested her less. Why, she thought, she had forgotten so many things and how good that was, for her brain was still far too full and she wanted to strip the trivia out of it as, now, she stripped seeds from the husks of wild corn that grew in the hedgerows.

Hilary and Michèle looked down at Nicholas, who could not help knowing that he was the very archetype of an Englishman. He wore his green overalls and boots with aplomb, with a smile and a twinkle. In everything he did he breathed good humour. He blindly chose instruments with a patiently outstretched hand, dropped them if the nurse offered something that was not right and touched nothing if not with the utmost delicacy and concentration. Thus, he parted flesh, an act that could never be anything other than indelicate, with a gesture that was almost surreally light of touch and jocular. The irony of knowing and yet doing informed every breath he took. In Mr Lennox's operations, the atmosphere was ever light-hearted, even entertaining, for the surgeon was a well-known wag. The surgeon never let anyone down and especially not himself.

When he came into the operating theatre there was a wonderfully expectant pause. Eyes met in anticipation. There was no point being a character if you didn't enter into the whole thing wholeheartedly and give the performance every time. So he stood there in parody of himself and waited. Then, over the loudpeakers came a roar of Gilbert and Sullivan comic operetta and he joined in the choruses in a loud, nasal hum, let the odd refrain burst forth, gave the whole operation the tempo of the song. He knew all the words. He was counted on for that.

It was a new operation and there was a long waiting list for it and later Michèle would shake hands with an old woman who would hold her little hand tight and explain that it was a claw before, that she'd not been able to do that for years and the surgeon was a miracle worker, oh he was. Michèle smiled and looked away and didn't necessarily understand a word. From the other side of the ward, Nicholas felt that touch of her soft palm.

'You're a pretty little thing,' the old lady said. She stared at Nicholas adoringly. She held up her hand again and waved it about, seeking the great man's attention and admiration. Because of Michèle, he pretended not to notice.

Nicholas moved on to continue his performance elsewhere. It was a performance which brooked no added element, the whole was set and rigid, there was no interpretation in it. He excelled in the mechanical repetition of what seemed to have worked before. The operation and its aftermath, both sterile and both perfectly successful. Concave and convex, the perfect fit of two hollow vessels.

All morning Hilary had not been able to stop himself from feeling a grudging admiration of his old man alongside a full range of irritations and even rage at his grotesque mannerisms. The way his father talked to his admiring circle of students about the technology of the operation, which was what mattered, hardly glancing at the old woman's face, just giving her his standard cheery how-are-you-my-dear-fine-very-good line. The old fart, the old faker, the silly sod. The very stance of him, the very stripe of the grey suit, the very polish of a brogue sawed and grated at Hilary. The old dear wanted to talk to him and what did he care? All that and then there was the plus factor which tipped the scales, there was what he actually said. Crap from beginning to end. He was a bloody faker, he was unreal.

'Your father – he talks to his patients,' he said. Michèle looked at him, said nothing. So Hilary went back to the old dear and he hovered at her bedside and expressed his sympathy and regret and tried to say something personal.

'Do you need anything? I mean, can I get you anything?'

'You a student, dear?' she said. 'Just a mo, shush a minute, I'm trying to hear Mr Lennox,' and she flapped at him, meanwhile craning over his shoulder to see the great man doing his rounds, to hear the unintelligible banter.

'No, I'm his son,' he said, annoyed, whereupon she looked at him and saw his face and the resemblance, presumably, and seized his hand and shouted, not once, but several times.

'Oh look at this here! Lovely boy! Lovely! Lovely boy, Mr Lennox, lucky he took after his mum!' and by this means obtained her desire, which was that the surgeon should look at her and smile.

This day was different. It was screwed to a high pitch, tight and tense with expectation though Nicholas was not sure why until they were on the train and on the way home. Then, in front of everyone and while the train rocked and hummed and showed him all the usual places, Michèle leant over and put her elegant little hand on his knee with utter casualness.

'I love the English country, the looking,' she said. The corners of her mouth turned up in a wicked little smile. 'You like too, yes?'

Hilary read his book.

Nicholas felt his very bones dissolve with an acute mingling of pain and lust. 'Very nice.'

The hand remained on his knee. Sweat prickled everywhere. The warmth penetrated up and down, deep into his soul. She was just a little girl, she couldn't know what she was doing, she could not mean it. The hand burned through the thin fabric of his trousers, burned its imprint onto his flesh.

'So you think in France we don't have, no? Not so nice? You have to try, I think. Then maybe you like.'

'Yes. Indeed. Love to,' he said and swallowed. Oh Jesus. Wouldn't he like.

She looked straight at him with those clever eyes of hers and smiled out of her velvet face at him. Unmistakable the message of the hand, which now squeezed gently – yet she couldn't, could she? How and *when*? And his mind leapt ahead to think about that one and then came back again. She took back her hand. He composed a liturgy in his head of the little bones that made up her hand – bone by elegant bone he analysed and sang through her whole body, Gilbert and Sullivan or rather Lord High Executioner style, in his head, to the rhythm of the wheels. All the time she leant forward in the seat and looked at his face and he tried to stop his eyes from staring down the cleft between the lovely breasts, from sliding over the nipples which seemed, oh yes, to smile at him.

And Hilary finished his chapter and closed the book and put it down on the seat beside him and they all looked out of the window, for they were there. Polite as ever, Nicholas opened the door, held it, closed it afterwards with that sepulchral bang which went right through his head. That was it, but it wasn't.

Walking up the lane afterwards, she lagged behind.

'Nicholas? You know, I like the English gentleman, oh, very much,' in her lilting voice. She took his hand and held it to her breast. He stopped dead, for one long instant, held his breath. Looked at the way his son walked on ahead. Closed his eyes for an instant, just was, just was. Felt the air warm in his mouth.

'Don't you like me?' she said. 'I like you. Don't you want me?' This, in deep, warm tones. He nodded, dumb, dizzy, desiring.

Hilary ambled on kicking at the long grasses and the evening smelt dizzyingly sweet. Nicholas could not say a word. His hand, on her breast. Smiling, she took it away. This moment of anticipation made Nicholas breathless and, to be sure, the presence of his son was an added savour to it – the fact that his wife was a few yards away and could indeed have seen him from the bathroom window, had she been there, had she chosen to look. Nothing in the world could stop this moment, nor its inevitable corollary. His hand, which had touched her breast, which lay down his side and retained the shape in its palm.

Nicholas knew what was coming. He had nothing to say. It was in the head of that beautiful girl, what would happen, if she so chose, for he was whatever she might make of him. Her plaything, or so he hoped. Anything, just to touch. Just to be able to look at her, naked, that would be a great deal. To touch – oh please, to touch.

Nicholas had a wife. Sometimes people asked about her, patients for example. He had a stock response. He would say that he was a lucky fellow. He had a pretty, kind, lovely wife whom he adored, who was a wonderful mother and, last but not least, a great cook. He had said as much that very morning out of the blue to his barber, who smiled and wondered what he was up to. It was very strange and told Nicholas just how new he was to this game, that it should have taken him the whole day to realise that for himself. As if he hadn't known it, from the way he was hiding from Jim. How's the wife? Fine – better! Fine! He had already dismissed her and now he knew why. All this passed through his head in the short walk between one life ending, with that touch, and the beginnings of the next life.

It was a waiting game. He sat on alone in the kitchen, with his bundle of *Times* crossword puzzles which he solved in tens – for when a person was quite good at doing them, that person needed to save them up, just as he did with chess puzzles which he liked to lay out on the kitchen table a dozen at a time and get through in twenty minutes with closed eyes. His eyes were closed just as if he was busy in his head, but the moves could not be planned with quite such ease. It was a question of when, not if, and the tension of it was exquisite, oh, the finest, purest drawn thread of lovely anguished pain. He could still feel her hand on his knee. His hand on her breast.

So she reeled him in.

On Wednesday he mowed the lawn and tugged at her with each stripe, backwards and forwards willing her until, at last, she walked out from the kitchen in the lovely early evening with her long bare legs and a glass of lemonade. She sat on the old grey bench and watched him finish the job and then all casual ease she walked back to the shed with him and he emptied out the cuttings and put the machine away and wiped its oily surfaces. Look, she said. Grass stains on her bare feet. There, beside the weathered wall between the compost heap and the shed she leant forward and ran her hands down his back and up under his shirt and pushed herself up against him and guided his hand under her skirt and one finger touched the elastic of her panties. One finger. He thought he would explode. Before he could kiss her she skipped away.

The fine afternoon came when Hilary went out with his mother to the club and without even a smile, indeed with a very grave look, Michèle came over to Nicholas. She reached out and took him by the hand.

'Come. Now. You come please.'

She smiled as he stood and took off her shirt and showed him what he knew, which was that she wore nothing underneath. And as they went up the stairs, she disrobed and so in the doorway of his bedroom – for she led him to no other place – she was already naked and he was rewarded with an erection so large that it took a little moment to undo the zip, that task made yet more delightfully difficult by her insistence upon freeing him herself. His head was completely empty of anything else. That was the thing that was most amazing, the silence of his head which was never like this but which now held only the moment, the now and the urgency of need. He said not a word, nothing, there was nothing to say.

So it came about that that fine afternoon Hilary and his mother walked slowly back together from the cricket club up the lane, swishing at the cow parsley, silently but not because of any particular anticipation or unrest, each thinking their own thoughts. They were home earlier than planned and Amanda, thinking just quickly to brush her hair – for she took each opportunity to inspect herself, ever in hope, thinking to detect some improvement in some sphere – went to her room. She opened the bedroom door. She was touching her hair, shaking her head, she did not at first look at the bed, prominent though it was, because it had not occurred to her that there could be anything to see.

Hilary who had noticed Michèle's shirt upon the floor of the sitting room came swiftly up the stairs and round the landing to see what his mother saw and they stood and the pair of them watched Nicholas's back, dark with hair and with brown marks on the shoulders, Nicholas's white buttocks pumping between the brown legs agape and raised up of the girl, her hair tumbling loose and her face raised up, contorted with an expression which could not be read, her eyes open and staring over the man's shoulder. What a noise he made, he grunted and groaned and panted – and something must have alerted him to a presence, some change in the composition of the light, some current of air, for all at once the noise took on a different quality. The sound of an animal – Hilary thought of the owl and the whistle and his father was no different from the son of the boulanger.

Hilary shut the door. 'Right. Let's make a cup of tea, Mum,' he said with huge, with astonishing savoir-faire, putting his arms round her – for he'd seen it all before, hadn't he? He'd seen it all before. Just this view, dear God, he'd seen, just this, and Amanda paused a second – waited, and Hilary looked at her face. Flesh of my flesh, he thought, and she was no different to him in waiting, as he had waited, for the end of it. Yes, he had seen it all before. Waiting for it to be done. And when it was over, he went downstairs and put a tea bag in a mug and made tea, just as she liked it.

Unstoppably, unforgivably, above all noisily with groans that mingled the extremes of pleasure with existential angst, behind the door, Nicholas climaxed. He lay for a long moment face down on the girl, listening to the thudding of his heart and its counterpart, the footsteps not hurried, not hard, just soberly going down the stairs – and still he could not quite believe it. This had happened to him. Surely this had not happened to them. To him, to him? Had this really happened to him, to him?

'It was them?' he said to Michèle who, as soon as he was done, was busily wriggling her way out from underneath him. She walked away into the bathroom and began running a bath and started swabbing between her legs with toilet paper and called out to him – and this act, of all the least erotic he had ever seen, had a kind of deft purposefulness that was truly ugly.

'It was them,' she said, calmly and without any particular reaction or even any interest. She did not even look in his direction. It was them – it had happened to him. Any idea he had had of tenderness, of love even, any idea of anything died. She had not kissed him, not once. He hadn't noticed, before.

For Nicholas, who was so very far from being versed in affairs of the heart or of any other organ, had not imagined this. That they would lie together, yes, that the excitement would be unbearably drawn out, yes, that there would be words spoken – something – but not this. So matter-of-fact. 'Yes, it was them.' How banal, how sad it all was, that such intensity gave rise to this, to nothing, to something less than nothing.

He lay on the bed and watched through the open bathroom door as Michèle bathed, washing herself with thoroughness, not in haste but not slowly either, giving the act its due as he had received his due. He was too tired to move, certainly too tired to go anywhere. He thought that he might sleep for a thousand years.

She came out and picked up her clothes and he looked at her, naked, and then dressing without any self-consciousness. He felt no desire. He had so much wanted to just look at her and admire and now he had his moment and could look as much as he chose and that was it. There was no explaining. Unthinkable, the transition, from major to minor. She went away without saying another word and closed the door, firmly but quietly behind her. A deep lassitude fell over him, like a blanket of darkness.

He turned over onto his back and let his heavy body press with its full weight against the uxorial counterpane. He heard Michèle's faint footsteps go down the stairs and, incredibly, into the kitchen – on and through. No voices. Normally, with the windows open, he would hear something. He levered his head from the pillow and looked. It was a mighty effort, for gravity doubled and redoubled itself every second.

Michèle Beauregard lay in the garden, sunbathing topless; she lay in her usual place and stretched herself out as she had so often before. She could not remain still for more than a few moments at a time and so an instant after lying down she sat up and went through the series of little shakes of the head and stretching movements, and eased herself over until she was supine. The sun glinted on her hair as she spread it out.

Nicholas could not bear to watch. His head was so very heavy.

He fell back onto the bed and lay inert for a long, long time. He drifted into sleep and out again and let the thing pass over him and woke, then, in the dusky late evening and with a shamed, sudden eagerness showered for a long time and tried to make himself clean. He found no thoughts in his head at all, nothing but the same listlessness and heaviness and waiting.

Afterwards, not being able to gauge which offence was worse, he still lay on the bed, for surely to appear downstairs was unthinkable and, for the others, would be unbearable. In due course, there were footsteps. Amanda came upstairs and into the bedroom and in her usual manner undressed and brushed her hair and then went into the bathroom. There was the usual assembly of noises. The bathroom cupboard opened and closed and opened again. If he had lifted his head, which was no longer possible, he might have been able to see her go through her face-cleaning routine, which involved a white cream, then a pink lotion, then another white cream. She always stared at herself with intensity while applying a further, more yellowy cream to the tender area underneath her eyes. Last of all she would do her teeth. He listened to the familiar noise and finally the spit and rinse and she came and got into bed, all as usual.

'Goodnight,' she said. She turned over, plumped her pillow, let her head drop onto it – everything so normal, so deeply familiar that suddenly tears stood in his eyes.

'Oh, Amanda, Mandy, darling oh please,' he said, with a quiver in his voice.

There was a long silence.

'I have to sleep. Goodnight.' She turned over. Her tone was completely neutral.

The long weekend passed, the heatwave continued, everything continued as if it was just the same and Amanda said nothing to him. Hilary said nothing. Nicholas, wandering mournfully around his beautiful house and gardens and looking at his son and his wife, wondering if he had lost everything through his insane stupidity, was held in a torture of suspense by their silence. He could not stand to look at Michèle who was demurely picking currants for summer pudding. It was wrong to blame her for what had occurred when it was surely all his fault. However, he did attribute some measure of wilfulness to her. It was impossible to understand what had impelled this girl to do what she had done. Finally, because there had to be a reason and he could not flatter himself that it was desire, it crossed his mind Michèle had done this because of his son. Or – and this was a further turn of the screw – perhaps she had also fucked Hilary on this one-off, get it over with basis. Why had he never asked? He couldn't ask now.

In the garden, avoiding the spot where she lay, he marched up and down the stripes of the lawn. The grass grew lush and longer and so it would go on. He did not get the motor mower out. That side of things was done. It was all over. Let the forces of disorder prevail. He wanted it to run wild, he wanted it to be unchecked. Fiercely he imagined himself wading through knee-high bracken.

Saturday night came and after dinner the house was very quiet. Nicholas telephoned various friends and even, for the first time in years, met one of them in a pub for a Sunday lunchtime drink, finding out to his surprise that he could not confide in a bloke. It was early, the big mahogany bar of the Dog was nearly empty and it smelt of stale beer and polish and he supped his pint and spoke of the weather and wondered, as old Brian must have wondered too, just what they were doing there.

Sunday came and went and the long empty day held its usual pattern and food was eaten and drink drunk and the long shadows came across the garden and had no meaning. Monday came and he went to work and the day was as other days and there was no sense in it.

That night, Nicholas went home as ever, stretching out his legs in the first-class compartment, staring out at the yellow fields and the lovely summer's evening with a face of despair. He was terrified, but ready to listen – ready to hear. He was ready.

Amanda said nothing. Now, this was not the same silence as before. The wall was there, it had been there for some time, but it was of a different composition. Nicholas understood perfectly well that there were different shades and textures of white and black. His wife had acquired a different texture. She did not speak to him, not because she particularly meant to punish him but rather with the air of a busy woman who had many things on her mind and could not speak for good reasons. They sat together in silence. So it was all decided, all decided, all done and finished. That was what he thought.

Hilary avoided his father in a far more knowing manner and his eyes slipped past when they met. Hilary evidently hated him.

Nicholas saw that his life was unbearable and that it was without meaning. Then with a terrible jolt which took his breath away and made him feel for an instant that he had been seared inside, came the second recognition. Of course. This was precisely how his wife had felt. The silence and the tears. So something had happened to change matters for her. The only thing the poor, vain fool could think of was that it must be due to him. Now that it was too late he remembered that she had always been the only person he had ever really talked to in his whole life. The only one he'd always trusted and depended upon. The ironies of his position unfolded like Chinese boxes, each one containing a new and yet more intricately patterned one inside. Nicholas too cried, not like Amanda, but noisily, gulping and sobbing and wiping his nose on the back of his hand, snot runnelled, like a child.

It was the day when the Beauregards were due and wife had entered into a state of almost pure abstraction, in which everything was done which had to be. She swam through the air with slow movements of her arms and legs. Wife knew that responses were expected of her which she could not supply. Nicholas, for instance, with his hangdog miserable air was waiting for something. The French girl, for instance, should have received some sort of reprimand and she would keep looking at her hostess as if she expected her to say something. Really, it was absurd. Wife saw it all, but there was nothing at all which she could think to say to either of them.

Charles was on his way. It became a matter of hours, then of minutes. Amanda in this final, crystal moment of clarity could see that there was something different in the way that Michèle looked at Hilary and that this new thing was hurtful to him. The girl had taken to making little remarks which seemed to ask for a response. Someone who did not know her might have taken these for a sign of friendliness. Amanda, knowing better, felt deeply for her son. Shock was written all over him, in the coldness of that studied neutrality, the way in which he got through the day speaking all the necessary words, never once referring to what had occurred. Of course there would be some reaction and she would not rule out a potentially violent response of her own, but not just yet when there were forty, thirty, only twenty minutes to go. Couldn't he just realise that this was how things had to be? She could not be a mother now. It was cruel and harsh of Michèle to behave like this, and Amanda felt her newly active presence going through the house. This went on with intensity while wife performed the ritual dance of dinner and then with careful mannered ease sat to polish her silver candlesticks and waited and counted the minutes.

An hour and twenty minutes beyond the latest possible time, the car turned up the drive. There were voluble exclamations to do with timekeeping and ferries missed and caught and husbands and driving on the wrong side. Noisily, the Beauregards spilled out onto the gravel. Michèle came to be kissed and admired.

Charles lightly kissed Amanda on both cheeks and grasped her hands in his large, warm ones. He carried a big suitcase into the house. They walked together. Nicholas took the other one and politely listened to the voluble Louise who had much to say about the sandwiches on sale on the ferry and her husband's timekeeping and whose complaints and observations made her seem alive in a rather simple way that was now very remote from him.

Amanda with a pounding heart led Charles into the kitchen. This was where she lived. He closed the door behind them and looked at her. So many things she had forgotten, to do with texture and shape and the multi-coloured strands of his hair which were the colour of thick honey and the way the hollows of his neck moved when he spoke. The stubble on his cheeks, which she wanted to touch.

When Charles looked at Amanda, it was as though black and white was turning into Technicolour. He kissed her with thoroughness, heedless of anyone else, for they could hear that in the hallway Michèle was chattering on to her mother while Louise for her part tried to talk to Hilary and Nicholas kept saying something. Lapped by all of these sounds Amanda tasted the incredible sweetness of the man. She lay against his chest and his warm breath fell upon her hair and she felt the sensation of being alive course up and down her, simultaneously making her knees turn soft and her face burn, as though it would burst from so much sensation. They came together with such extreme naturalness. The extraordinary taste of him, which she could not get enough of, was causing some sort of chemical reaction inside her mouth. As wine should, excellent wine, the taste of the kiss grew and became rich and deep.

The evening would grow and bloom and Amanda blossomed, a slow-motion film speeded up until she hardly recognised herself. She was changing with startling speed. She understood that she was becoming much more vivacious, a kind of approximation of the woman he remembered, or rather her remembered approximation of the same. The taste of him was in her mouth. That and the unhurried grace with which he moved and spoke and the overpowering knowledge of all that was to come filled her up with intensity. This, then, was joy. So simple, so very strong.

While Amanda lived, so vividly, with Charles, wife became more opaque, dense or rather condensed into an abstraction of herself. This had to be. The wifeness was now so thick and heavy that, like heavy water, it could never be got rid of. The very molecules of which wife was composed might implode upon themselves at any moment. Meltdown would come, it was unavoidable. Amanda saw it all with dispassionate interest. Wife could barely speak, she went through the usual motions and people smiled and nodded and ate and said things through the thick green glass.

Every year the cricket club dinner was preceded by a one-day match between the Lennox's club and the neighbouring village's team, always the cause of much passion locally. The Lennox's side, ever hopeful, had never yet beaten the opposition village, which had the great luck of being home to a good county cricketer, Sandy Wicks. This match was seen as the climax of the season, despite all the cricket that would be played after it, for the grand dinner at which the home team entertained the visiting team was seen as a matter of great local pride and the only event in the year at which all local people sat and ate and drank together.

Nicholas was talking to Charles. He was trying to explain the composition of the team which included him and his son and which was once again doomed to failure. Charles did not understand why their team did not hire a better captain.

'The honour of the village,' Nicholas said, and, 'It's an amateur game.'

'You want to win, you get the best player, no? The other people have a good one. For you it is important to win, yes? So? You take the good player.'

Nicholas wanted very much to convince him and altogether felt that he wanted him on his side. He had only the faintest, dimmest memory of the French doctor from all those years ago. He had been much slimmer, younger, naturally. It seemed to him incredible that his wife had ever recognised him at the airport. Mind, the whole foreign exchange business was incredible, not least his own part in it.

Hilary's dreams at this time were exceptionally vivid. Not dreams exactly but something nearer to nightmares, for he woke sweating and with deep creases on his face where he had burrowed into the pillow and it had fought back. It was a shock to find himself in his own bed and not back in France and before he opened his eyes he expected each time to see the flowery tendrils of the wallpaper which he had so often followed along the ceiling and across the wall to the place of deliverance at the window.

He dreamt that he was delivering the baby. Charles was not there and he was the master of proceedings. He was in the kitchen, searching for the knife and failing to find it. Drawer after drawer was opened and he knew that someone had hidden the thin knife, the one he needed, hidden it where no stranger would ever find it. At last, he sharpened a wholly unsuitable knife, a serrated bread knife, on the old grindstone. When he turned the wheel, it groaned, as his father had groaned. The knife became blunt, not sharp. The teeth of the knife were moving along the blade, back and forth. They jittered and spun round. The young wife was screaming upstairs.

There was always a giddy moment, in the dream, when he thought he had looked away for an instant too long and in that terrible second the blade had done its work, had cut off all the fingers of one hand. It was a kind of delirium within the dream and he would have to remind himself that it was not possible and yet he would always look at his hand and then at the floor, one quick glance, to be quite sure that no fingers lay there. Then he held the knife with both hands like a dagger, pointing away from him. The teeth of the blade sang their own strange song.

Up the stairs he stole, to the room with the smoky light and the terrified woman in the bed and the yellow smile of the farmer. But there was no Charles there. He was alone, he would have to deliver the baby, and as the woman screamed once more he looked at the knife and knew that with this knife he would surely kill her. Then, lifting his head to say something and calm her, because he needed badly to calm himself, he realised that the woman on the bed was not the farmer's wife at all. It was Madame Ourlandes. She looked at him. Her stomach was swollen, pregnant, but her eyes were very old. The mouth, open to scream, closed. She fell silent. She knew that she would die. They both knew that he was going to kill her. Always, now, he refused the dream with violence and made himself wake.

Each time he found his teeth were chattering with dread and he had to calm himself by saying his mantra. It's all all right, it's fine, don't be silly. It's all right, it's over, it's only a dream. Over and over, except that it wasn't . Often, unable to sleep afterwards, he would replay the birth in his head to make it be all right, but always it came back to Michèle's open legs. Always, his discovery of her being fucked in the orchard, then back to the scene of her being fucked by his father. He did not just let himself see it all, he made it all happen, replaying, rewinding. He thought that this stratagem would eventually make it all bearable, oh, but it took so long.

On one of these nights, Hilary awoke with an idea in his head which would not go away. In the dream, he had the nylon fishing line round the head of the man fucking Michèle in the orchard but as he pulled it tighter and tighter, he heard the hooting of the owl right behind him and realised that it was his father he was strangling. This woke him abruptly. Perhaps he did want to kill him.

He turned on the little lamp, stared about the room grimly.

It was three in the morning. He still had an exact picture of Michèle looking at him over the head of the man from the boulangerie and then, with the same look, over his father's bent, desperate back. The two were connected in more than the obvious respect. She looked at him and there was a message in her eyes. Hilary sat up in bed. She looked at him and saw him. She had planned it. She had come to England and had chosen to seduce his father as revenge upon him. It was strange and horrible. But she continued to look at him with triumph.

The day of the match dawned as hot as its predecessors. Father and son dressed in their white gear in their respective bedrooms, alone in the house. The French couple strolled along the lanes and up to the club, with Michèle mooching along behind. Amanda was already in the club house, organising tea and cucumber sandwiches and slicing up seed cake. This day of endless activity had started for her at five in the morning and would go on till the small hours, yet she was calm and even happy.

In silence, Hilary and Nicholas walked to the match. At the last corner of the lane, his father held out his hand to shake.

'Good luck, then,' he said.

Hilary nodded but would not accept his father's hand.

'Come off it. Don't be so fucking sanctimonious,' said Nicholas.

'I've not said a *fucking* word.' Hilary pushed him in the chest quite hard. A moment later, Nicholas pushed back. Hilary jabbed at his face and missed, just. Nicholas jeered at him.

'You bastard.'

'Go on, go on, give it a try, you little shit.'

Nicholas, who would have been pleased to relieve tension in any way possible and would happily have been hit by his son if that made anything better for him, or for that matter for anyone, noticed that up ahead Michèle had stopped and was waiting. Did she want them to come to blows? His boy looked at her, desisting from the fight, which he was clearly spoiling for, with a curious, clouded face. Grief blurred his features. Rapidly, he went on past her. Nicholas now saw the odd, the expectant way the girl looked at Hilary who would not look at her, staring instead at his feet.

'Oh fucking fuckhead,' said Nicholas. He stood there in the

lane, clenching and unclenching his fists. He saw it now. Quite separately from what he'd done to his wife, he'd fucked the girl his son was in love with. He felt like crying, terrible self-pity prickled behind his eyelids. He didn't of course, no, he did his crying in private. Oh hell. With face half turned away, Michèle stood there. Tears brimmed up and began to fall silently down her cheeks. This was completely unexpected. He stared at her. That she had emotions was not something he'd exactly realised before.

Mr Dobbs passed with a cheery wave. 'What a day for it! Hot enough for you?'

'Yes,' said Nicholas.

There was a big crowd, for practically every inhabitant of both villages had turned out. They always did. Amanda in a sleeveless linen dress was slaving over tea urns in the big marquee erected next to the club house, where the evening's dance would also take place. Over the course of the past few hours, every dip and fall under her feet had become familiar. The urns hummed and buzzed with their own particular excitement.

At the open flap of the tent stood Charles who was not looking at the cricket. He was watching her admiringly. Before she turned and saw him there, she could feel it, felt all along one side of her body a kind of tingling awareness of his presence.

Over on the cricket field, Michèle was lying down on her towel quite far away and to one side of the pitch. She wriggled out of her skirt and T-shirt to reveal the skimpy bikini on her faultless body.

Before too long a couple of the local yokels were gawping at the French beauty from a couple of dozen yards away. Hilary, at outfield, felt suddenly acutely conscious of her and of their admiration of her. But then, everything was making him nervous today.

Teatime was nearly upon them. Amanda, who had gone to sit behind the marquee to have a rest in the shade, saw Charles appear, once more demonstrating his unerring instinct when it came to finding her.

'Hello.'

'Hello, you.'

He smiled and sat down on the grass beside her. It was very

peaceful here, between the guy ropes. He was there, it was enough. She didn't need to say anything. Because of other people, she used every bit of energy in her body to stop her hand from reaching out to touch him. She very badly wanted to touch him, but not now. It would wait, the touching would be all the sweeter for it.

'You are so beautiful,' he said, quietly. 'Always the same. Today I am so happy.'

'And me'. She closed her eyes and could have cried with it.

He was looking at her, she felt his look warm on her face.

'I never forget you, never.'

'No,' she said.

Amanda could hear the rhythmic regular thwack of the ball, together with the faint buzzing of applause and soothing comment. The sun was quite exceptionally hot, the smell of grass delicious, the whites in the distance dazzling. A huge fat bumble bee paused in its progress to look at them and then carried on. And, curiously, this was all quite astonishingly real, in a way all recent events had not been, in a way that nothing had been real for years now. She felt each breath of her body, each pore, each beat of her heart telling her that she was alive and that life was good and sweet.

Out on the pitch, the visiting team was making short work of the defenders. The score was up on the board. Somebody from the village called out something to her in passing and with a little effort she stood to see. It was the last of fifty overs. She rocked a little on the dry grass, feeling under her elbow the place where Charles's warm hand had rested as he helped her up. He stood next to her and the sleeve of his shirt just touched her arm. She was intensely happy.

Sandy Wicks was now batting. There was a mighty crack of leather on willow which made Amanda look up. He hit a ball which caught Nicholas neatly on the kneecap and he doubled up. She saw him rolling over and over in the distance some way beyond Hilary. The sun glinted on the batsman's spectacles, he waved victory.

The score was 230 in fifty overs for six wickets. The Lennox's side were never going to match that and the buzz in the tea tent was already faintly disappointed, apologetic.

Inside the tent it was hot, though all the flaps had been pinned back. Pitchers of lemonade stood ready, homemade, and the supply of cups of tea went on and on. There was no end to the thirst, she poured and poured.

A plume of smoke curled up from Charles's cigarette as he sat and watched Amanda. He was looking at her arm. She looked down and saw the way the shaft of sun coming in made the tiny hairs on her arm glint gold. In the distance, Louise was lying out on the pitch next to Michèle, the pair of them making a ravishing distraction for the yokels, who had doubled in number. Looking back, seeing the way Charles still looked at her arm, Amanda felt herself blushing deeply. It was the sexiest thing in the world. There she stood, next to the tea urns, in all the heat.

'What a scorcher, Mrs Lennox!' Wife smiled vaguely at whoever had said that. Dobbs. She stood on, for she could not have moved for anyone, for anything. Very slowly, Charles reached out his hand and began, very gently, to stroke Amanda's arm. Paralysed with pleasure, she stood there. Nobody noticed. Just the soft part of the upper arm, where the flesh was most tender.

'I am sorry,' said Charles, meaning something else entirely.

'Of course.' She closed her eyes and smiled back at him, closed her eyes in bliss, because she could not help it. 'The sun is very hot.' she said.

All the helpers were busy, there were hundreds of people in the tent, cups of tea to be done, and nobody noticed Mrs Lennox standing between the urns with the absurd smile on her face.

Over on the pitch, the local lad who was sitting closest to Michèle was talking intently. All the time his eyes flicked up and down her, for sheer animal amazement. He had told her that his name was John four times. Still she called him 'you'.

'So now they make the runs, they win perhaps?'

'No, no, you see they can't possibly win now. You'd need a miracle to win.'

'But they have the same time as the other people?'

He shook his head, patiently, started again to explain it.

'Why should they not win? You don't explain right, you.'

'Well, for a start, they never do.'

'Never? Look. I say this time they win.'

Louise stood up and wandered towards the tent. She soon came across Nicholas sitting on his own behind the tea tent with his head in his hands, not looking at anyone. He had rolled up one trouser leg and with a little moan was inspecting the wounded knee. He was a strange person but she thought him kind. His eyes smiled.

The second innings began. Hilary was in to bat and almost at once the other batsman was caught out. A desultory clapping greeted him as he walked back to the pavilion. The village had lost heart. Wicks, bowling, was cheerfully dismissing one batsman after the next as, very slowly, the local side built up its score. Hilary batted on.

Soon enough they had reached the last over, with Hilary still batting and Sandy Wicks still bowling. He raised his floppy sunhat, wiped his forehead with a rolled up end of a sleeve. The spectacles needed to be wiped. All this was done with the deliberation and that very English self-deprecation which was his hallmark. In a little moment now they would win. It wasn't county cricket but Wicks was a crowd-pleaser. Foregone conclusion, this was. There was enough of a showman in him to want to eke it out a little.

'Nearly had it,' said John, the young man sitting beside Michèle. 'See? He's a gonner.'

'No,' she said fiercely, looking at Hilary, who stood in the ready position, holding the bat. 'You know nothing, you.'

'Don't be silly, I was nearly on the team, wasn't I,' but she wasn't listening.

Michèle rose to her feet. With the first ball, the bowler got the last but one batsman out and now it was the turn of the last man. Nicholas strode onto the pitch with only the faintest hint of a limp. Behind him, looking anxious, was Louise. Slowly, she walked over to the main part of the crowd which had laid itself out on rugs and deckchairs all along the edge.

In the tea tent at this particular moment, Amanda was slowly stacking saucers on a tray. Charles came up behind her, reached round her for the heavy tray, just for one second cradled her back in his arms. Amanda's eyes closed as she sank into him, fitting together like spoons just for one instant. Nobody noticed a thing.

Out on the field, Nicholas made one run. Now Hilary was in to bat, the score four behind at 225. Wicks bowled a beauty and there was no score on the third ball. Getting ready to make his run for the fourth ball, Wicks fleetingly lost his concentration, becoming aware of a distractingly gorgeous girl – naked? No, in a bikini – crossing his field of vision and it was a little while before he recovered his concentration. He bowled hard and cleanly and it was all Hilary could do just to give it a touch with the bat. He was sweating like a pig.

No score.

It was the fifth ball of the last over and Hilary was steadying his bat. Michèle walked behind the sight screens. Just as she disappeared behind them, she removed the top half of her bikini and let it swing from one naughty finger. From her bikini bottoms, she drew a little tube.

Sandy Wicks prepared to bowl. There, straight in front of him, stood Michèle, looking at him, wearing only the skimpy bottom half of her bikini. In this position, only the bowler could see her. Slowly as he walked back, then faster, as he made his run, with immaculate timing and with undoubted erotic intent she began with both hands to rub cream into her wonderful bosoms, paying particular attention to the nipples.

The ball left Wicks's nerveless hands and, as it did so, it curved as though drawn to Hilary's bat. As he swung to hit it, Michèle slowly and suggestively rotated her pelvis and threw her head back. She did it faster, faster, one hand moved down towards the bikini bottom and then slipped inside it.

Hilary hit the ball as hard as he possibly could. Wicks was transfixed. He remained where he was, standing stock still and precisely in the path of the ball as, with unerring accuracy and huge velocity, it hit him between the eyes, neatly shearing his spectacles in two. He and they dropped, a roar went up from the crowd.

Spectators now started running over to help Wicks up. He was groping in the grass for his glasses as Michèle hooked up her bikini top. He managed to mend them, just, using a wodge of sticking plaster which one of the fielders had in his pocket. He put the glasses on. He was seeing double. He shook his head and blinked.

Over near the marquee, hope ran through the crowd and people began to sit up in their deckchairs. Some were even standing up to watch the match. Wicks steadied himself, for he was reeling slightly, and prepared to bowl the last ball of the match. He wasn't feeling quite right.

Hilary hit the ball with a mighty crack and started to run. Nicholas, also running, watched the ball wobble and bounce and jump its way right to the very edge of the field, and the young outfielder was running and he threw the ball back and Wicks, running backwards with his hand outstretched, saw one ball, then two and then three. A multiplicity of balls came at him and he tried to get hold of one of them and missed the catch. The ball bounced on towards the other side of the field and our men were still running. It was a five. Incredibly, they had won.

Around the pitch there was a hubbub. People were cheering and rushing up and down and there was a ripple of applause starting up. Young John Hardeman looked at Michèle who, ignoring him, now stood to put her T-shirt back on. For a moment, the head was gone. The blonde hair was pulled through the neck of the T-shirt and shaken out, smoothed. The head was back and it smiled broadly, the mouth curved up and when she smiled, she was staggering. The thing was, she wasn't smiling at him. He turned his head and followed her line of vision. She seemed to be smiling at the Lennox lad, but he wasn't looking at anyone. Unreal. Life was so bloody unfair. He thought of his girl friend, Angela, who was very nice and that, but not like this. Not like this.

Hilary saw but did not look at Michèle and instead he ducked his head, modestly. He walked slowly back towards the pavilion. Disbelief and pleasure and sun all joined up. The sight of people clapping, the smells and sounds of the day. A little avenue parted, of people clapping up ahead.

Nicholas made his way across the pitch behind his son and as he did so something inside him gathered momentum. He started to run and to shout. Whooping loudly, he threw his cap in the air, caught it, threw it up again, rushed up and in a totally unEnglish way caught up with and embraced his son.

'You're bloody marvellous,' he said.

Hilary smiled back. He didn't want to, but there was no

negotiating a position with his traitorous face. What was he going to do, pretend he wasn't pleased? He hit Nicholas in a sort of playful way on one arm. It was a blow, but without heat. His dad smiled in a curious way. He got it. Hilary hit him again, a little harder, but smiling, still. Father and son walked back together. Something was eased through this, somehow, or was beginning to ease.

'Enough?' said his father, raising mock coward's arms.

'Yeah.' Hilary felt all right. Actually, he felt as good as he had for ages.

In the tent, Amanda busied herself and rapidly prepared an ice pack which Sandy Wicks gingerly placed on his bruised head. Then she went back over to the tea urns.

Lying flat on his back with eyes half closed, feeling like hell, Wicks could not help watching with great interest the way that Mrs Lennox stood completely still, staring deep into the eyes of a big shambling bear of a man who stood beside her and very slowly and hypnotically went on stroking her arm. His head pounded. Perhaps it was a mirage, as the girl had been, or then again not. The girl had been so beautiful. She was worth it, sort of. Almost. If he'd had the strength, he'd have gone looking for her. Meanwhile he looked at what was there. Knew the husband. Funny, this business with the wife. Pretty woman, she was. Funny, that she didn't seem to care who looked.

Mrs Lennox and the man split into two and then four then six and it was a long moment before they reassembled into the right number of arms and legs.

6

The day cooled as the sun dipped behind the huge oak tree and threw its shade over the pitch where the score would stand triumphant over lesser matches for respectful weeks to come. The field was empty, as was the pitch. Only Amanda was there, absent-mindedly jingling the keys to the club house and staring aimlessly at a courting couple lost in an embrace. The crowd was down at the White Hart. The pub spilled them out of every window and door and still they came. Total strangers, thrusting through, caught some of the glory of it and were buoyant by the time they got to the bar. Winners and losers sank their pints and toasted each other. It was a fine sight, the men in their white flannels and the long day still smiling at them, the shadows lengthening against the mellow stone.

On the green the local lads and lasses sipped at their halves and eyed each other. Half a dozen tough leather lads on motorbikes rode slowly through the village, much admired in secret but sneered at in public. It was a famous night. The whole countryside was wound up and ready. Tonight, a hundred sets of parents would go out, releasing their houses and gardens for youth to spring upon its moment. All tumbledown merry, a dozen romances would start and two finish. Three virginities would be lost, two babies conceived, one marriage broken and another saved.

From house to house, warm Sussex water which had once bubbled through chalk now gurgled perfumed anti-clockwise down pipes. The ladies bathed. Louise rose from her bath and Michèle slipped into hers. Milly Dobbs puffed powder on her nose and cleavage and Betty Boardman tripped on a pebble as she hurried up the lane, ten minutes late. The sandals were to blame. These were the height of glamour, gold and high-heeled with Roman thongs which clung to her ankles and dug into her round countrywoman's calves. She had known that they were stupid. If you did them up loosely, they fell down. Betty equally cursed the chafing tightness of her girdle which left red weals round her waist and thighs. It was the new one, fancy, lacy and a little too tight. What night, if not this one, to christen what was new and special? In the name of beauty for miles around innumerable curlers unsprang in victory rolls. Betty's feet were in torment and by the end of the evening her toes would be red raw, ten uncooked sausages squeezing through a net. Yet, if she had to choose between comfort and beauty, Betty still took beauty every time.

In the pub, Old Spice clinked against Coty. They hurrayed Hilary. Strangers shook his hand and lined up more pints than any hero could manage. Nicholas bought a round and was bought several by people he barely knew. He gave a pint to Charles, who picked up Hilary and hugged him in the public bar, kissing him on both cheeks. The village roared and thundered its childlike joy.

In the rose garden behind the White Hart, a local lad and former reserve on the team, John Hardeman, gave the heave-ho to his childhood sweetheart, who loved him as nobody ever would again, for the sake of Michèle who had already forgotten that he existed. He said that he needed to be free. This betrayal was so urgent and necessary that it caused him not one pang. The French girl had smiled at him and all else was eclipsed. Upon the bowling green, Charles challenged Mr Dobbs to a game of boules and Dobbs, who was on his fourth short, kissed Charles on both cheeks. At his bathroom mirror, Sandy Wicks inspected his shiner through part-closed eyes and then shut his eyes, all the better to think about the mirage girl. The glory hour was on them.

In the marquee, where the heat of the day still hung, Amanda smoothed the little wrinkles in tablecloths and arranged pink bud roses on each table. By the time they sat down to eat, the buds would have opened. Her roses, gathered in the last hour, brought in at the last minute. A number of silver-plated rose bowls had been borrowed for the evening and she wished now that she had polished them.

Betty Boardman, so butter-fingered, had broken two glasses – tripping, jolting a table, down they fell. Those heels of hers, absurd. Could be worse, could be worse. Amanda felt happy. The band on their narrow dais were making a mess, with their electric leads winding off all over the place, but they were nice young men. Morris dancing they said they did, at a pinch, smiling at her disbelieving face. Oh yes, they did, nothing was too foolish. Whatever people wanted. It was a living. The bread rolls were either too soft and doughy white or poppy-seed-sprinkled and too hard. Never mind. One on each plate. Betty, she said, you do it. Thinking, of course, that they at least could not be broken. Betty set about doling them out using tongs, dropped one and with a sideways glance and a grunt, bent to recover it and quickly blew off the dust, popping it back with her fingers. By the third table it was fingers only.

The room looked very pretty. Hitherto undreamt of heights of sophistication had been reached. The village had never had a do like this, nor so much to celebrate. Her luck, the evening turning out so well, such weather and a famous victory. Her luck was that she would dance with Charles. He would hold her in his arms. She stood still for a moment and let her arms hang at her side and her skin remembered how he had touched her, in this place.

'Stress incontinence, that's what she said. That new doctor. She give me the name for it.' Betty Boardman started down her last row. 'Never heard of it meself, before Dr Cross said. Lovely dress, Mrs Ell. Belle of the ball, you'll be.'

'You could have rubber pants,' said nasty Amanda, thinking yes, she could, but it was very sharp of her and it was as well that just then the throbbing of the acoustic guitar drowned her words.

'What was that? Sorry, Mrs Ell? Butter pats?' Remorseless, Betty was, and for that alone, plus the remainder of her sins, wife appreciated and Amanda disliked her. Not that Betty ever seemed to realise.

Amanda worked her way along the long VIP table which was six eight-person ones pushed together in a giant U shape, folding the napkins. The team plus their wives, the president who sat next to the treasurer and their ladies. Ladies, it always said on the invitation, and the stupid word summed up how they thought of themselves and what she thought of them. The central places for the captains of both teams, naturally. For them the special centrepiece, with sprays of flowers projecting from her own silver bowl. It looked very pretty. The VIPs had the good damask napkins. Why not? Her finest, starched, ironed by Betty. Creases in the corners. Should have done it herself. Sod the napkins. Still, as she folded, she sang.

'Most women get it, after babies. Stands to reason. You know,' and Betty lowered her voice, though there was nobody else there to hear, 'sometimes, when you sneeze. Or laugh. Suddenly, you know.' Betty and her bitter butter, remorseless, had caught up. Amanda's old affection for her had been worn so thin by it. She needed oiling, smoothing out. Perhaps she needed a man. Curious thought. Betty had a lascivious cleft between her front teeth between which two miniature gummy dewlaps hung. Betty had a man, not that he did her much good. Boardman lived down to his name, thick as two short planks. Never did a decent day's work in his life. That was what he was famous for.

'Primrose oil,' Amanda said. It was a cure-all. Why, since all Betty's complaints were unmentionable, had that never stopped her from speaking about them? Why were unmentionables so patently the reverse? She was old, past pensionable age. Naturally, Amanda had never suggested such a thing. The only possible outcome would have been that Betty would have received a pension from her while ceasing to do any work at all.

'The thing is, Betty, you don't need a pension. What you need is a man,' Amanda said, wandering on and out of the tent to look for the lark. She was sure she had heard a lark. The sky called her, it was the richest, deepest blue streaked with gold.

Betty stared after Mrs Ell. She had probably misheard. Wax in her ears, needed syringing again. Dr Cross would do it. Tartar on her teeth, built up fast. A little bump on her foot one day, a bloody great corn the next. Nails which grew like wildfire. A blooming human dynamo, she was. Betty loved Mrs Ell, kindness itself and unfailingly good to her, as her own son George was not. Her husband Alf was an old husk of a man, useless at everything, always had been. You could say he was consistent, mind. Blue dress she wore, new, electric blue they called it. Bright against the tent. Betty decided that probably it was the Change. That explained primrose oil, didn't it? Needing a man, well, who didn't? Vitamin E Mrs Ell took, on her bedside cabinet it stood, new make-up and undies, she'd noticed, couldn't help it. From that lovely shop in Brighton, such a price in there, gorgeous things they had. Poor Mrs Ell. The Change on its own was enough to make you wish you'd never been born.

But Amanda, outside, heard a lark, saw the shimmering day fall through the trees, felt the warm earth through thin-soled shoes. The earth rotated through the black universe so that night should come for her alone. The very stars were up there, waiting behind the thin blue air, preparing to come forth for her personal delight.

She looked back through the tent flaps and saw that it was good. The tables were all done and the plates out, everything ready to serve. Chilled soup first, then the salmon. All ready in the club house by the time the men left the pub and walked back to the house through the lanes. The dog roses were in flower. Brambles and hedgerows had been newly cut and the green smell was heady and strong.

Nicholas did his rubber face as he tied his bow tie in the childrens' bathroom. Big grimace of a smile. He was whistling in a thoughtful sort of a way. His jacket hung on a hook on the door. He felt cramped in here. But his bedroom was full of dresses. Some kind of female explosion had taken place in it, a scattering of underwear and stockings, frills which he hadn't known his wife possessed. The things all looked new. Was that possible? Keep out, the room said. Keep away. Which was more than she had said to him of late. She said it with her face, with her rapid steps hurrying about, with her back. Busy. Amanda was very busy, with guests and the dinner and so on, and he remembered about the speech. It was traditional that the chairwoman of the Ladies' Committee who organised the dinner spoke a few words and then there was a toast to her.

He stopped tying the bow and thought about it. How the hell was Mandy going to make a speech?

Banished from his usual domain, Hilary had ended up dressing in Ed's room. The Eric Cantona posters on the wall laughed at him. Tied the bow tie a second and a third time and still didn't get it quite right. Needed one on an elastic, like Ed's. For tuppence he'd have worn that and his Spiderman outfit. What was it like, then, to be nine? Deeply self-centred as he was, Ed was nevertheless a prey to all kinds of strange ideas and fears. Couldn't stand to be seen naked, terrified of a woman seeing him without his clothes on. Wouldn't play football, claiming it hurt your brain, but loved rugger. Said he was afraid of the sound of the flute but mad about birds. Wouldn't sleep in a room in which the waste paper basket had anything in it. Neurotic, that was what he was, which was to do with the boy and not his age. As a baby Ed had been what he already was, an eccentric of the first order.

Hilary looked at himself in the mirror. He felt a bloody fool and, hey presto, now he looked like one. He opened the door, paused in the corridor. Somebody humming. Louise,was it? Funny thing, he thought. Something else. He used to think about sex. All the time, really. Not that that had gone, no, he was as interested in leg-over as the next man, but over the summer his horizons had expanded. Goal posts had shifted. Sex and neurosis. Love and death. He intoned the words in a deep, husky voice. Winning was good for you, it made you feel better. His heart was broken, but that didn't mean that all life ceased. Just that it had no meaning.

It was Michèle singing. A small, sweet voice. Cheerful, then, was she? Ha. He had never heard her sing or even hum before. He leant against the wall and listened with closed eyes and felt that this was as intimate with her as he had ever been. As he might ever get. He let the sound trickle through his head and sweep over his sore, sad heart.

There in the garden was a plume of smoke. Hilary went out. Charles was wearing the same too-tight evening clothes he remembered from before. It gave him a curious little moment when he saw him like this, with his cigarette and his glass, all as it had been but in the wrong place. This version of Charles went with the orchard and that huge moon. The big man put his arm round him and hugged him. Hilary felt the old warmth, felt the old familiar tug, the dance. Magnetic whatsit. Charles had got a bottle of wine from somewhere.

'Your maman gave it to me. What a woman, eh? Drink?'

'Sure. Doesn't it remind you of your party?'

'Maybe. No. It smells different here. England is full of flowers. English roses, like Amanda. Look at this,' and he waved a hand at a whole hedge of them. Yes, marvellous, wonderful, amazing. 'Your mother does the garden, no? Everywhere she makes beautiful.'

'About that night, about your party,' Hilary said, 'I never knew – I mean, you never said what happened to your friend. Vigne-Laval. You know, the professor.'

'Professor, yes. Ha. Like I am a doctor. Funny, huh, that he came?'

'Yes.'

'He came, he went. Such people, you know, come and go. Un clochard.'

'Vagabond?'

'Yes. Man of the streets, you mean? No real home, no place. You know what it is, Eelaree? I remember him better, so very different. When we was both so young. He was not like that. Sometimes it is better that way, when you remember. Better than seeing. You know, he is not a real person at all. Not having any value to anyone. That is his problem. But when I thought I knew, really he was always like that. Then I felt angry with him and with me for not seeing it before. But maybe mostly because we were young once and now not. You. You live it. You know?' The big man smiled and shrugged and sighed.

'Youth's not all it's cracked up to be,' said Hilary. 'What happened to him then?'

'I think maybe he just became more of himself. And now he is too strong. Too concentrated.'

'No, look. I mean, did you say anything to him?' He was bottling out here, and he knew it. It was hard to ask the question he really had in mind. Unsurprisingly.

'What do you mean?'

'He talked to me about girls, you know. In the car, when I

went to pick him up. How they were all mad about him and so on. This fuck and that fuck.'

'I can imagine.'

'Tits like melons,' said Hilary. He screwed up his forehead and remembered. The wiry forearm on the wheel, the infallible sense of direction.

'The professor of pussy.' Ironic, Charles's tone.

'Yes.' He swigged his glass down. Slowly, they walked back towards the house. That same smell Charles had, of Gitanes and warmth and him and some kind of lemony perfume.

'I know. Sure, he was a pig. Sixteen I was when we met. He was twenty. I loved him. He told me everything I wanted to know about everything. Treated me like a man. Introduced me to his friends, taught me how to drink, how to talk to women. How to screw them. I loved him for it. Everything that was worth knowing. So I always loved him but later I stopped liking him, because he was such a pig. Dirt, I don't see why a person has to live like an animal. His teeth, nails, everything, like an animal. Une ordure. Then I was angry, you know, to see him again in this state and remember what I rather would have forgotten. So. Now we go to see your maman?'

'She's up at the club. Wait, you didn't say . . .'

'What? Why are you looking so worried? Don't do your face like that.'

'Look, never mind. I mean, what happened? I didn't find out what happened. I mean, that's what I wanted to know. He'd gone, you know, after that bit of a punch-up.' Hilary jabbed the air with one fist, to show. Charles looked thoughtful. 'You know. We put him in the house – you remember, don't you?'

But Charles was shaking his head. 'I don't remember, exactly,' he said. 'He came. He went. Come. I am anxious to go and see your maman. What she has made for us for tonight. What a woman, you know? Exceptional. Look at this garden. Everything.'

'My father does the garden,' said Hilary, rather foolishly, screwing up his courage, saying now or never, now or never, over and over in his head. Charles scared him.

They looked at the garden. Hilary noticed that the grass was very long. His fanatical father, king of the pinstriped lawn, was letting it run, quite literally, to seed. He felt too much rage at his dad to wonder how he was thinking, but it did occur to him now, just briefly, that the old shit was suffering and was punishing himself. That he should express this in dandelions and meadowgrass was strange but not unsuitable.

'You know, it's idiotic and everything,' Hilary said, ten paces on and a bit breathlessly and quickly, 'but for a minute I thought you might've done him in. You know. Killed him.' He drew a line across his throat and smiled and moved a step away as Charles moved a step nearer and grabbed him with one arm.

'For being un clochard?' Charles held him clamped with one arm. Now he squeezed his shoulder, tight. Hilary breathed in and out rapidly, looking up and seeing, strangely, Michèle's face at his bedroom window. She was leaning out and watching them. This made him do something and he jerked away from her father.

'Yes.'

Charles inhaled, let out a warm rush of air, laughed. Gitanes smell and lemony warm, he wasn't going to kill him.

'Silly, huh?'

'No. You think like me. Good boy. That is what I think he deserves. Nothing. You see, people who give nothing deserve nothing. What is his pig-life worth? Un rien.'

Louise blotted her lipstick, twice, and was ready. Charles had zipped her into her beautiful white silk dress. She had done her face, put up her hair. Now, she went in to Michèle's room to see if her daughter needed help. She was conscious of the faint rustling sound. She wore thin silk stockings. She didn't like bare legs, even in the summer, for evening wear. Not elegant. Her shoes were an extravagance and very beautiful. She looked down at them admiringly.

The bed was full of dresses. Discards. Michèle was rather soberly dressed in a demure frock which set off her flaming beauty. She was leaning on the cill, looking out of the window. Down below, Hilary and Charles were walking in the garden. Louise went to look and followed the blue line of her husband's smoke through the topiary.

'You look beautiful.'

'Thank you. You too.'

'Nothing compared to my daughter.'

The two of them stood at the window and looked down. Louise felt the same old tug between love and fear. Charles so tall and big, the grumbling deep laugh, the charming boy beside him. Always something held in reserve, something not quite right. Apart from her husband, her daughter was the only other person who could inspire such ambiguous feelings. Yet she loved them both. She could not quite love them as she wanted to for those reasons, for knowing too much. Yet perhaps if they had been more straightforward, more ordinary, she who hated herself for that might never have loved them at all.

'Chérie? You are coming down?'

A shake of the head.

'Madame has gone on already. It is her special dinner. You know.'

'Maman?'

Louise looked at her daughter, whose beauty was so extraordinary. 'Mmh?'

'Did you ever do something stupid with Papa – you know, to mess it up with you and him? So he didn't like you any more?'

Louise paused. It was such a long time since she'd been honoured with her daughter's confidence. Not through the whole of the boulangerie boy affair. She wanted to say something that would please Michèle and bring her close. The silence was heavy between them and she tried to think how to fill it. But even in the brief pause before she replied, in one second of her not being quick enough, her daughter's mood turned.

'Don't tell me anything. Not you. Not you – I expect you always did everything exactly comme il faut.' She turned away. The bitter note in her voice prompted Louise's anger. How wilful she was.

'I think I did. Always. As you say, just what I thought was right. You like the other approach, don't you? You know, it didn't make any difference in the end. What do you want me to say? I'm not like you. You can't cut against the grain. Your papa – well, he is the other kind, the kind who does as he feels, right or wrong. Me, I always worry about being right. And in the end it makes no difference. To what happens. Believe me. The strong take what they want. They are the winners in the end. So don't complain. The weak, they can complain.'

In silence, they went down together.

So the little party walked up the lane to the club, Charles walking alongside Nicholas in front. Hilary thought that neither of them seemed to know what to say to each other. Both were slightly tipsy. So was he, for that matter. One glass and he was anyone's.

Behind them came the two women, Louise and Michèle, both so pretty, arm in arm, but they too were silent. Last of all Hilary who dreaded the whole business and had got out of accompanying the walk by going back to lock up. He loitered in the lane. Two elegant women, so like each other in figure and height, so different in every particular. The lane was quite full of people. Silk dresses, high heels, laughter.

The marquee flew its flags, the buzz of English polite conversation was punctuated with the sound of popping corks. How warm it was, they all said, thirstily drinking all they could. The village was dry-throated as much from its need to celebrate as from the much-discussed heat-retaining properties of canvas. Keeps the heat in, bit of a breeze, wait till later, yes, yes, yes. They bored him and perhaps even themselves.

Service came courtesy of Betty and Flora and Flora's three big sons. Every place had its bowl of chilled soup with a swirl of cream and mint, its bread roll. Wine was being poured, water jugs were full. Hilary lived it all through a dream-like state. It seemed to him that the evening was overlaid with the noises of France and himself carrying the plates backwards and forwards and it was curious that he wouldn't be doing it tonight, though he had volunteered. His mother had said she did not need him. He smiled at her, even waved, but she didn't seem to see him.

She sat at the main table and her eye floated from side to side and saw everything and nothing. Hilary could see that what she mostly looked at was Charles. Now the Frenchman, catching her eye, raised a glass to her and they toasted each other, silently, across three tables, and nobody seemed to see or care but him. His father did nothing. Not a bloody thing. Just sat there. Hilary gave him a hard look. Not a muscle moved.

Jack O'Brien, the president, rose to his feet and coughed and laughed and held up his glass until they had all hushed. They opened with a toast: 'The winners – and the losers!' he cried. They all held up the single glass of champagne, which was all the budget allowed.

Hilary swigged his down sharpish. 'The losers!' That was his party. Get drunk, that was the thing. Fizzy, a bit too warm. The blob next to him wandered away, so he sank his drink, quickly. He was two tables away from his parents who were at the main table, three from the Beauregards who were on the honorary table. Nicely placed to view them all. How delicately, when it came, Louise filleted her fish. Hilary drank what there was.

Compliments flew on the salmon and its mousse, on the new potatoes and on the mint peas, always so delicious, so English, and afterwards there were strawberries and cream and summer pudding which clever Amanda had made for everyone. Marvellous, your mother, they said, and 'Dee-licious!' Old Betty was bringing in trays of stuff, going out with pudding plates, coming in with decanters of port. A large Stilton cheese stood proudly to one side.

The dinner was said to be the best ever. Belts were undone. Speeches began. Hilary feeling only slightly drunk went outside. To have a slash.

Sandy Wicks looked slightly ill and felt more so.

Dobbs was conscious of his wife's cheeks aflame, as they always were when she was in public and excited. Apple round and red they were, not that she could help it, poor thing, though he always felt the same twinge, something between annoyance and embarrassment for her. She was a woman who could not stand to be wrong or at fault in any way. Funny, then, that her own body so often betrayed her.

O'Brien stood and waited for them to fall silent. When they didn't, he spoke up. 'Gentlemen, ladies, members, guests,' he said and smiled his rather foolish smile. 'It's been a wonderful match and a wonderful dinner and I'm not going to spoil it by going on now, but just to raise a glass to Mrs Lennox, the chairwoman of the Ladies' Committee, who's given us all such a fine spread. And not to mention her two men, two members of the victorious team and our winning batsman!' He looked around and beamed. 'Ladies and gentlemen, Mrs Lennox and young Hilary!'

Over in the corner, Betty Boardman put down her pile of pudding plates as Mrs Ell rose. She wouldn't have missed this for anything. People were clapping and pounding their feet. The new corset now hurt like crazy. She thought about the other, old, soft one. It had a tear in it, a kind rent, which made it very comfy. Still, fat stomach, not pretty, was it? Oh, so long since she'd had a figure. Bit of a stitch too. Still, she didn't like to sit down and stood throughout instead, staring fixedly at Mrs Ell and nodding and smiling in case she looked over, and meanwhile sipping at a little celebratory glass of port she'd kept ready, over to one side.

Amanda knew exactly what she was going to say. From her vantage point she saw it all. Among the faces turning to look at her was the guarded one of Michèle. Nicholas's betrayal had given Amanda her carte blanche. But she would never bring herself to tell Michèle that the person she had really hurt was herself. The daughter was wilful and stubborn, she was a creature of passions like her father. She would have to learn that when you lived that way a price had to be paid. People were clapping and she surveyed them. For her and Charles, there was no going back, no remaking of the past; for them there was the present moment and its glories. She caught his eye and smiled.

Nicholas was in agony as his wife rose. All through the eating he had felt acutely aware of the coming speech. He had been unable to stop staring at her, it was so long since he had studied her, but she did not once return his gaze. Part of his face was almost numb with not being looked at, cold and ignored. As he deserved, but still his heart raced with anxiety for her.

She stood and looked perfectly calm. Not a flutter. And now, with the aplomb of a seasoned speaker, Mandy waited for the noise to die down. She looked around, smilingly, held a glass up. For her, they fell silent. In that moment, Hilary came in.

'Ladies and gentlemen, members of the club and of course members of the teams, let us pause for a minute and raise our glasses to the unsung heroes and heroines of tonight.'

Mandy spoke fluently. She was bright as fire, radiant in

her dress of brilliant blue. Nicholas understood that she was transported out of herself by all that had occurred. She turned her head and for an instant stared at her husband, just as if she was indeed aware of the high degree of attention which he, unusually, was paying her. Attention unequalled in years. He looked at his wife and thought that she was like somebody else, somebody very familiar but whom he had forgotten. It was a funny feeling. As though she wasn't his wife at all. As though he was seeing her for the first time. And he remembered how beautiful she had been, her hair long and blonde, and how when he first saw the laughing girl among the crowd he had felt that strong taste he got sometimes, of the thing being perfect and wonderful and true to itself. Three or four times he'd felt that. His wife, really, and the children – the same when the children were born, each perfect, each so different. The strongest feeling in the world, he could almost taste it thickly in his mouth.

'Not the players, they get their applause. No, my toast is all the people backstage. Those who put up with so much – the wives who are forced to see and to hear such a lot about activities they may find, well, disgusting, those who stand and wait, those who serve their lordships, those whose job it is just to open doors,' and she turned and looked at him now and people laughed. Nicholas felt as though he was turned to stone. His tongue was suddenly fat and thick in his mouth, swollen up. As if he was having an allergic reaction. His blood pounded slowly and heavily round his head. His fingers had gone numb.

'My husband knows what I mean. Well, we the ladies of the team. Women, I'd rather call them. Oh, so many things we women put up with. I don't just mean the domestic service. My husband now, there's a man of action for you. Marvellous action as we've all seen today on the pitch. But he is one who does know about the very special view of things you can get from my angle. I mean the rear view – well, you know, don't you, Nicholas?'

He smiled and nodded and laughed, turned his head from side to side in order to meet the looks of idiotic people who looked at him and winked and smiled and raised glasses. In celebration of what? It was nightmarish, as though they knew what she meant inside those words she was saying about him, though of course they couldn't. Two tables away, Hilary sat with his head in his hands.

'Ladies and gentlemen, tonight is special for everyone and particularly for me. It's my chance to speak up, I suppose. My moment to say what I really think. And that is because of the actions of two people in particular who are here tonight. Two people who have done so much. They both know who they are. Stand up, please,' and heads swivelled across the room and Nicholas felt his heart pounding. 'My toast tonight, ladies and gentlemen – to Betty Boardman and Flora Jones!'

Betty, who listened hard and nodded a lot and yet did not expect this, sank abruptly onto a chair while Flora, more intelligent, quickly scuttled out of the tent without knowing what she was doing or where she was going. Thus outside, sprawled between two guy ropes, she heard the low murmur and the applause for her name. There was a good deal of it, dying down, then almost at once a burble of conversation which was almost as loud as people set to the port, the wine and cheese, the whole overlaid by the low rumblings of the guitars being plugged in. Then Flora knew that it was safe to go back in.

Nicholas was safe, too. He knew that he was alive, just. She was letting him off, sort of. He saw how, politely, the French couple applauded the applause. He saw his son raise his face and look at him with a curious expression. Nicholas saw the old Amanda, the woman he'd married, meet his eye, hers sparkling with wit and sharp intelligence and glee at having said what she had. He stood up and went towards her.

Amanda was already on her feet and walking away from him. Nicholas saw the intimate manner in which bloody Charles smiled at her and lifted his glass and toasted her. Then she said something to the Frenchman and he got up. They stood in the middle of the dance floor as the band twanged up, the first couple there. They began to dance.

Purposefully, Nicholas moved over three or four seats. He sat again. There was a bottle of brandy there, one he recognised for it had come from his house. It stood just beside the floral arrangement and right in front of Sandy Wicks. He took his glass with him.

'Sandy? Mind if I?'

'Not at all, help yourself. Wonderful woman, your wife.'
'Wonderful.'

'Still seeing funnily, you know. Two of her. You know, that ball I got. Two of her.' He chortled. 'One for you and one for me, eh?' Sandy laughed at his joke and blinked a lot. He had an enormous and perfectly circular bruise between his eyes which was a kind of greeny-purple colour. Lucky not to have broken his nose, from the look of it. His glasses accordingly were being worn somewhat lower down his nose than usual. Over the top of them he peered short-sightedly round the room.

'Looking for someone?' said Nicholas.

'Oh no. No, not at all,' said Sandy, continuing to look. Now he spotted the glorious girl, who was better than he remembered. He wondered if he'd get the courage up to do anything about her. A drink, for Dutch courage.

Nicholas poured a liberal helping for himself and his companion in suffering and let the liquid roll smoothly round his mouth. He would sit there and he would wait. Nothing else for him to do. Dance floor was filling up. Dobbs was there, dancing with his missus. Her face was a funny colour, bright purply red. Heart and lungs working too hard. All the people dancing were middle-aged. He watched his wife dance with the Frenchman and saw how he held her in a kind of embrace, wrapping his arms round her, and how she seemed to enjoy that. The brandy had a faintly anaesthetising effect, thank God.

Nothing to do but wait. Something in her face told him that everything had been decided, as far as she was concerned. She never looked once in his direction. Clear enough message there. He sipped at the brandy and waited for it to still the unhappy knockings of his heart.

Hilary watched Michèle. She too was very silent. He'd not said a word to anyone yet, nor did he feel the need. He was aware of his father, his mother, of her, her parents. When anyone from his lot moved, some sensor registered it. A whole set of vibes came from his mother dancing with Charles. They bounced off his father's face. He had no desire to look himself.

He was conscious that from time to time Michèle glanced at him, but he did not respond. He was aware of each glance brushing his face, like a flicker of flame running down it. Still he stayed where he was. Various local yokels came up to her and were given the brush-off. She stayed where she was and sat and watched Hilary. He thought that she looked very demure in her dress. He had not seen her like that before.

He kept an eye on John Hardeman, who'd have been reserve on the team if he'd not broken his leg earlier in the season. He'd been sitting next to the Beauregards all the way through the match. John had a very stupid look on him, he was staring at Michèle as though he'd like to eat her up. In due course – and the whole daft progress was wholly foreseeable, from his loiterings over near Betty, from his idle pausing and gazing at the band, to his sudden purposeful but seemingly unpremeditated start across the room – John went over to Michèle and asked for a dance. She shook her head. He looked at her for a moment in complete disbelief. Inside, Hilary smiled grimly. Silly sod. Could've told you.

Hilary looked around, no Angela. John was a fixture with Angela from the post office, had been for yonks. Hilary stared dispassionately over at the poor sap. He was pleading with her, practically on his knees. Pathetic. Poor Angela. Michèle lit a cigarette and, with those impatient gestures which were so familiar to him, blew out the smoke. Again, she turned to look at Hilary. Again, he failed to respond.

Now the acoustic guitar was thrumming and the four young men were right into the old favourites. These thrashes would always culminate in a number of them – 'Brown Sugar', 'Jumping Jack Flash', 'Knights in White Satin' – but there'd be other stuff in the meanwhile, the crowd-pleasers prior to the big numbers. His parents, who always claimed this era as though it were some kind of personal achievement of theirs, would be dead chuffed. Hilary ignored the music and sat on and with sardonic pleasure watched John Hardeman get his, lumps and all.

As Charles danced with Amanda, she felt a kind of shuddery feeling through her whole body which she could not resist. She felt herself blush from her toes to the crown of her bright blonde hair. She had forgotten what it felt like to be intimate with another human being. Long ago, they had held each other like this. All those years ago when she was young and free they had spoken to each other as lovers did, who cared about each thought and each emotion the other might feel.

'Mon amour,' said Charles and his breath was warm in her hair and this alone made her intensely happy. Over his shoulder, dreamily, she was aware of Nicholas sitting with his drink and his stupid expression, poleaxed, very satisfactorily so. It was curious, to think that both these men were truly there. She had thought so much of Charles that she was not sure that he was real, for all the warm breath and the weight of the arm which held her. Tonight Amanda had a second chance. She frowned a little. Still she could not think why it was that she had chosen Nicholas over this man. She remembered that Charles had given her an ultimatum.

Charles tutted at her. With one finger, he smoothed the wrinkle in her brow and smiled at her with such a delicious, naughty face that she could have laughed out loud for sheer delight. She felt consumed from the feet up by the most intense lust for him, the urgent need to touch and taste him immediately.

'Where can we go?' she said into his hair.

'Now?'

'Now.'

He looked around the room. Louise had gone up to the main table and was holding out one hand to Nicholas who, with the rictus she knew too well and the air of a condemned man, rose to his feet. Smiling, the elegant Frenchwoman pulled him onto the dance floor. He stumbled a little near the edge.

Charles looked back at her with a broad speculative smile.

'Here?'

He shrugged. She began to push at him, very gently but firmly, steering him to the far edge of the dance floor and away from his wife, her husband and the band. Once there she swivelled him round and looked over his shoulder. She felt weak with longing.

She surveyed the room. The noise was now intense. The band were doing their utmost, the strobe lights were on and at least three-quarters of those present were dancing. The remaining ones were getting stuck into the drink. General clamour and clatter and from one second to the next people disappeared in slow motion under the flashing lights.

'Here,' she said and nodded at the table. The cloth hung low. 'You go from there.' She pointed.

The lady president and chairwoman of the annual dance dropped to her knees at one end of the long U-shaped table. The Frenchman entered the space from the other. She did not know if anybody had seen them. It did not matter if they had. From their separate directions, they crawled under the tables towards each other, towards a meeting in the middle. The noise was intense. The strobe flashed. The long white tablecloth hung low. She felt the juddering of the feet, so near, pounding the ground and it jolted up her knees. As she went she pulled up her dress, so she could move more freely. She left her shoes somewhere near the entrance place.

The darkness beneath their white tent concealed them but was nevertheless bright enough for them to see each other. He did not smile. He looked at her with such intensity that she felt that she could have fainted. Carefully, they arranged themselves. It would be possible to lie, yes. Feet, those of Sandy Wicks, were safely a few feet away. Charles knelt before her, keeping his head low as he must and they kissed, the delicious taste of him flooding through her. She felt his hand reaching to unzip the dress and it was with joy that she felt it fall away from her. He smiled. Now, languorously, carefully, they lay side by side, he clothed, she naked, and looking intently at her he began to stroke her, beginning with her ear lobes and working with slow patience down.

Amanda felt all the delight and unreality of this, the coldness of the ground, the intense pleasure of her own nakedness allied to the incredible intelligence of his touch. Here were hands which seemed to have studied her pleasure. All this was so powerful that she could have fainted. Her imagination, so powerful a force, was doubly intensified by its collision with real pleasure. The strangeness of the time and place intensified it yet further, as did its illicit nature, as did the noise which allowed her to groan faintly, unstoppably as he pleasured her and yet not be heard. With slow, practised movements, he stroked and stroked. Her skin felt incandescent with pleasure. She was vibrating, like a spinning top, and she heard the humming sound he made, the sound of purring. The world could end, but not until this sweet pleasure had finished. She began to climax almost immediately, and as he felt this his mouth fastened upon hers and she was flooded with piercing sweetness. She was a comet in outer space, she was a streak of flame through blackness of overwhelming intensity. As the first shuddering subsided, as he continued to stroke her, she begged him to enter her but he shook his head.

'First I make you come again,' he whispered.

To feel all this, a woman had to be Amanda. No young person could have this experience. The whole quivering rawness of acute sensation which went with youth had been overlaid by layer upon layer of conscious memory. So everything that happened was informed by something else. His warm breath, his touch like this, the tablecloth and its pattern belonged to her, her reward for having lived her forty years, their patterns ironed into her and possessed by her and as inimitable as the whorls of his fingertips. The flickering ecstacy of his tongue, remembered and now. Her acute consciousness of everything, above and below, even to the shape of the field upon which the tent stood in which all this could happen, even to the shape of the moon in the night sky. The waiting and wanting which made today so intense. All this came as a blinding revelation of interconnectedness of which these sweet deep feelings sweeping through her from head to foot were only one part. She alone, here and now and with this man, could feel such sweet sure intensity of pleasure doubled and redoubled almost to pain. The whole giddy universe was created for her at this minute of that day and all the connections were hers alone.

She cried out, she could not stop it, her body shuddered violently with blissful sensation.

At this moment precisely things stopped being unreal. She was here, now, this was the reality of her life. Wife and Amanda abruptly fused. It was no game. What was happening was real and serious as much as it was physically extraordinary – and she knew it.

The table heaved and the centrepiece jumped. Sandy bent down, lifted the cloth. He looked through the legs of the rough trestle table. He blinked.

He saw the ecstatic face of Amanda Lennox, eyes tightly closed, blurring into double vision then back again. He blinked, pulled back. Then looked again. She lay naked and with her back arching, spread-eagled on the floor under the next table. Her large breasts were exposed, they seemed to be fighting their way up. Partly on top of her, with his face buried in her loins, was a bare-chested man who was not her husband. Her husband was there, glum-faced and no wonder, dancing over in the corner. Mrs Lennox's hands were clutched in this bloke's hair. It seemed to be his attempt to remove his trousers which had caused the commotion. Yes, there he went. He was about to manage it. She moaned and thrashed about. Fine. All clear then.

Sandy dropped the cloth once more and stared at the jug of water which, yes, was trembling. Though this could have been from the vibrations of the noise. Which was considerable. As he knew from his thundering head. The table jerked and then was still. Right, he thought. He didn't exactly want to look again.

Sandy stayed quite still, sitting in solitary splendour at the table where he had been indulging in a cigar and brandy. Practically everyone else in the room was dancing. He had been feeling sick for some time, too sick to go, or stay either. He felt queasy as hell. His smoke and drink were not a good cure though he had not been able to resist either. The sick feeling heaved up in a tidal wave and left a nasty taste in his mouth before subsiding. This caused him just for an instant to lay his head upon the table. For some reason, the thrumming noise, wherever it was coming from, entering his ear from this piece of wood, found some other resonance and only then did it occur to him how powerfully erotic that scene had been. But he felt so very sick.

With a trembling hand, he poured himself a glass of water and had a drink. He got out a handkerchief to wipe his glowing brow and winced. As he did so, his glasses, which were still held together with sticking plaster, fell neatly apart. He moaned to himself, mended them, just sticking the ends into the wodge, put the glasses on, carefully tweaked the sides of the frames, which were very wonky. At once, the glasses came apart again and fell off. He cursed some more. Put them in his pocket.

Sandy had had enough. The room split from double to quadruple vision. The tidal wave rose and fell again, a bit quicker this time. He began to think that he might be about to throw up. Years and years since he'd done that. He got up and, sighing deeply and shaking his head in disbelief, he slowly made his way out of the tent. Fresh air. That was what he needed. Mrs Lennox, eh. Well. His erotic fantasies would henceforth involve tablecloths, a degree of voyeurism and the lovely breasts of Mrs Lennox. Oh, but how his head hurt.

Coming out of the tent, Sandy saw his dream girl, the girl of the pitch. Pity. As he blinked she swam in and out of focus. He was probably concussed.

They lay for a long time quietly. With his healing hands, Charles was stroking her face and hair and throat. Her eyes never left his face, she had a beatific smile. Eventually, without urgency, they dressed, helping each other.

Amanda emerged quietly, discreetly, and as far as she knew unseen. In the cricket pavilion loo mirror she looked the same, but felt quite different. Charles's touch had done something to her. She felt it all over her, like a second skin.

Staring into the mirror, she thought about him. The smell of him on her. There had been a morning long ago when she had gone on duty, the white coat fresh but she herself rumpled from his bed. From his hands, as now. So this was it. She closed her eyes and leant against the door and waited for the picture to return.

Why had she married Nicholas? That night, she had still been on duty after a twelve-hour shift and Charles had come into casualty looking for her. White coat and stethoscope and she'd laughed. He didn't have the right, not that that ever stopped him. He took what he wanted. That piratical side was what made him so alluring.

She was a junior doctor on the ward. He was a visiting student, he should not have been there. He had his wilful ways, his arrogance, his spirit of devilry. But she had told him off for the imposture. She remembered that he had laughed and stuck his tongue out at her.

A tramp had just been brought in off the streets, a desperate creature with feet in an appalling state, dead drunk, a middle-aged man with lank dirty hair and a face covered in bruises where he'd fallen. Blood oozed from a nasty cut on his head.

Suspected fracture of the arm, she'd touched it and he'd winced. He didn't want to undress. Years, probably, since he'd taken his clothes off. Boots, half off, with a terrible stench coming from them. Ingrowing toenails, scurvy, filth, emaciated, liver disease for sure, with the meths bottles he had, one in each pocket. He'd fought the nurse to keep those, one in each hand. A lot of his body was covered with bruises. He'd fought to keep his clothes on, had scratched her face.

He'd stunk. She'd wrinkled up her nose, not meaning to, and he'd got huffy with her and then obscene. He'd used obscene gestures. Tried to put his hand up her skirt. She had been roughly pulled at by him, his breath was rank and unspeakably foetid and so she'd drawn the curtain, told him she'd fetch another doctor to help. Told the junior nurse outside with the basin to deal with somebody else. Leave him be, she'd said. Because he would maul her too. He was mad, drunk, you name it.

Charles had gone into the cubicle then. She'd seen it from the corner of one eye as she was leaving. He'd been angry. Hadn't liked the way the man spoke to her. Seeing that, she'd gone back. 'You shouldn't be here. Go and wait somewhere.'

Charles had sat down beside the neat little trolley on which the stinking human relict lay, glowering at him.

'You don't speak like that to a lady,' he had said.

She'd hovered in the curtains. He'd waved a hand to her to go away. 'I will stay with him,' he'd said.

'Fuck the lady,' said the tramp, laughing. He had terrible eyes, dark and bloodshot and was completely mad. He'd blown his nose with his fingers, onto the floor. Disgusting. He'd laughed at her face. 'Come here,' he said to her and, 'Nice bit of skirt.'

'Go. Go on.' Charles had flapped a hand at her. 'You need a consultant, yes? Go and get one and then you can get off.'

So she had gone. She'd wanted to get a senior doctor to look at the arm. Everything always took longer than you thought and it had taken time to find a doctor to come. There'd been more obviously urgent cases in casualty that night. There was a child, badly burnt, a nightie had gone up in flames.

When she got back with her clipboard, with her papers ready and with a senior doctor in tow and still busily apologising for troubling him, the tramp was dead. She knew something was wrong. From outside, even before she drew the curtains, she had smelt the acrid smell of his vomit. He'd lain there, so very still. Choked to death on his own vomit, the coroner had recorded. There he'd lain, on his own. All alone inside the cubicle.

Charles had told her that he'd got bored, he'd gone home to wait for her. But Amanda had known, had felt in her gut and belly, without ever being able to be sure of course, that Charles had struck him. One well-placed blow to the gut would do it and what was one more bruise among so many? She had felt with cold dread that it was on her behalf. That her French boy friend had killed the old man to avenge the insult.

She'd said nothing to anyone. What could she do? Accuse him? Tell people her boy friend had dressed up in a white coat and stethoscope to kill an old man? Unthinkable. But she knew, then, what to do. She had married good, decent, safe Nicholas and she had given up medicine since one of them had to look after the baby. She had let him deal with the dirty stuff. She had been too scared to deal with it herself. So. So that was why.

Slowly, she went back across the field. The noise was intense. The band was playing up a storm, people were going mad. The tent looked beautiful, all lit up in the darkness like a giant inflatable that had come to rest. She went in through the back, past the table full of her china, the place full of her and her house, her flowers and her tablecloths. She looked at it all. Then one by one across the faces until she found Charles. Cupped hands, lighting a cigarette. Such big strong hands, like the rest of him. So strange, that the healing, in his hands, was still so powerful a force. Good and bad alike were there, two sides of the same thing.

He didn't see her. He went outside through the main entrance for his smoke. Amanda began with increasing urgency to look for her husband.

Nicholas was sitting on the ground near the oak tree, not doing anything really, just waiting. As she rounded the edge of the tent she saw others about. Michèle was also nearby. Charles said something to her and behind them a couple kissed. The band finished. Silence fell and there was a whooping yelling storm of applause. Then the sound of voices. Somebody shouted ha ha twice, very loudly.

When she was nearly at the tree, the band struck up one of those ridiculous Roger de Coverly-style country dances which obliged the participants to meet and part and sweep around with a fol-de-rol and so on. Amanda stopped and bowed to her husband. He stood up. Very courtly. She looked at his face. Nicholas by moonlight was pale and his nose left a shadow like a crater, a hole in his face. They looked at each other.

'You're arrogant,' she said. 'Opinionated and often offensive. You don't take much notice of people at all, for all that caring profession stuff. I think the worst thing you do is to pretend you don't notice things. Sexually, you're selfish. Morally, well not quite bankrupt, that's what they say about politicians, but bloody low in the scale. In the red, that's for sure. You've lost the sense of right and wrong in some deep way. I mean, not because of that girl, but anyway. Perhaps it's middle age or the male menopause, people say that stuff, but I don't think so. I think it's self-indulgence. Cut off, cold, miserable.' She paused and looked at him. He nodded.

'You know better, that's the worst bit. If you were stupid or insensitive one would, well, understand. All that point-scoring. Like a child.'

'Yes,' he said. Nicholas studied his wife intensively. He felt like a child, just wanting to sit with her, feel her warmth, hold her hand maybe. He wondered if she'd let him hold her hand.

'Do you know that I've just fucked Charles? On the floor, just over there?'

'Oh,' said Nicholas. 'Is he the one you want?'

She cocked her head, looked at him, did not reply. 'No,' she said at last. 'I think it's you. You were the better man always. That's why I chose you.'

'Oh,' he said.

There was a very long pause. They both sat down and leant against the oak tree. 'Can I hold your hand?' he said, after a good long moment. In the distance, they could see Charles. They both followed the arc of his cigarette as he flicked it into the air.

In the marquee, Charles cut in on the fellow making up to his wife and took Louise in his arms. She was so lovely, his wife, she understood him so very well. She smiled at him so very sweetly.

'You've been so long. He was standing on my foot. A medical emergency, was it?'

'Perhaps.'

'You always rescue me.'

'No, you me.'

'Anyway. Together, that is all I care about,' and she thought it was true and how strange, that so many different things could be true all at once. They danced on wonderfully, perfectly synchronised. They had always had that ability, from the first moment. People looked and they would remember, afterwards, and remark upon them and say what a strong, indeed striking, couple they made.

Hilary pressed out the smouldering cigarette some dope had left just near the canvas. Yuk. Michèle was out here. There was a kind of trace of her in the air, the Gauloise, the perfume, whatever. Maybe he was just over-sensitised or something. Anyway. He looked around. There she stood, just round the corner, the flare of a match cupped in her hands, the light warming her face. For heaven's sake. He wandered round the tent in the opposite direction.

He kicked at the guy ropes, made the canvas shudder, thought that there were things he should be thinking about and wasn't. Like his parents. For the first time in his whole existence he felt sorry for Ed, so indulged, so weird, such a pain, but the one who was going to bear the brunt of their bust-up while he was safely away. From the back of the tent, where Betty laboured with coffee cups, he got a glimpse of the activities within. A lot of smooching was going on. He saw Charles and Louise in a slow embrace. Le slow, as we call it. No sign of his parents though. As if.

Coming round the other side, he heard the peevish tones of John Hardeman once again trying his luck. Michèle was bored with the lad. She dismissed him. 'Go home. Go away. Go on. I don't need you.'

The local boy, dumbfounded, tricked, astonished, grew angry at such venom. 'What did I do?'

'You're the wrong one,' she said.

'Don't you like me? You cow. You liked me this afternoon, didn't you?'

'No, I don't like you. Go away. I never like you.'

'You little slut.'

'Go away!' She was shouting.

Hilary's heart was beating fast. What did she think she was doing, standing there? It was her own lookout. Not his business. He was going to do what he did for himself alone. To please himself. Oh yes, very likely, and he jumped the guy rope and rounded the corner with fists up and ready, Mr Confrontation. Yo!

But John was walking away, hunched up, hands in pockets.

Michèle looked at him, blew out a smoke ring. Unsurprised, just as if she was waiting for him. Waiting, who knows, for what. They looked at each other. She pulled on the cigarette with a deliberate air.

'What took you so long?' she said rather pugnaciously.

Waiting for him. So. His heart began to beat a little faster.

Inside the tent, the hokey cokey started up with a roar and a bellow. But outside the long-awaited breeze blew. The night was fine and calm and everything was as it was before and nothing could ever be the same.

'I don't like smoke,' he said. 'I hate it.'

'I will give it up.'

'All right. Go on.'

Michèle threw the cigarette away onto the grass, its arc bright, and then bent forward as Hilary did and the two of them practically knocked their heads together, thinking to stub it out. The country girl. She was a country girl, after all. His heart was beating like an express. Incredible thumpings and poundings which went right up into his throat.

'Anything else you want?' she said.

'Yeah. Who's the right one?' he said. Mr Hard-to-get.

She wasn't having that. She tugged at him and pulled his arms round her waist. Fine. This far he would go. She pulled again, so they stood as close as possible. She laid her head against his shoulder with a sigh and closed her eyes. He looked at that curve of cheek, the way the mouth turned up. The blue vein of her eyelids which fluttered, slightly.

He closed his eyes too and without trying particularly hard, their mouths met. The strong taste of tobacco mingled with something incredibly sweet and powerful. Like honey. Like wine. Whatever. She hugged him so tight, he felt breathless. They stood there for about a thousand years and embraced, came up for air, did it again.

The air was sweet and slow. From within the tent, they heard the thudding, rumbling roar as the hokey cokey reached its ludicrous finale.

For the first time, he was holding her in his arms. Slowly they began to dance in the little space between the guy ropes. Well, move around. More of a lean than a dance. His prick, on full aching alert, let them both know just how interested he was. What was he to do? She pleased him, as she always had.

He kissed her again. She tasted incredible. Astonishing, really. She knew it, she opened her eyes and looked at him; he looked back. Hilary felt mesmerised. They stared at each other's faces, mouths, he watched as her eyes closed voluptuously, saw the way the long lashes lay above the delicate curve of her cheek. There had never been a girl like this. Never would be. He smiled.

'Funny, huh?' She'd opened one eye and squinted at him.

'Maybe.'

Gradually the faintest flicker of a smile grew on her face. Hilary laughed. They both started to laugh. A gurgly, real thing, this laugh, with the head thrown back to expose that kissable throat. A wonderful sound. Pure pleasure. But he wasn't going to say anything. Nope.

Over her shoulder he saw a strange sight. His parents, wandering away down the lane. Hand in hand. For Christ's sake. Hand in hand. He'd have said something to her, but she didn't care. She was giving him that look. She was wanting his full attention and, fair dos, this she could have. He took her face in both hands. Her eyes were closed, waiting for a kiss. She smelt incredible. Whatever it was in the perfume line, however much it cost, it was worth it.

'Please, do it again.' The eyes opened. 'What is it?'

'You have to say something to me,' he said. 'Or I won't kiss you.'

'I never say things. Please? You mean please?'

He shook his head and stood and waited until her eyes looked away and were abashed and then looked back again.

'You are – oh, I don't know,' she said, in a small squeaky voice. 'I can't say things.'

He waited.

'You are – impossible.'

'No.' He shook his head.

He was silent for a long, long time, just standing with her in his arms and waiting as the whole world did, for a word. In this moment there was no breeze, the hare on the hill sat with its paw up, alert, the stars paused in their orbits. His breath in and out the only movement in the universe.

'Bon. I see. *I* am impossible. Now you kiss me?'

The grass grew up through the soles of his shoes and the seasons changed and the tent could fold upon itself and all crumble away. But he was a rock, a fortress, a hard man.

'You want more?'

'Oh yes, much more.'

'Oh. Oh Hilary. I am so sorry, so very sorry, so sorry, very.' A warm tear, just one, trickled out of one eye and lay on her cheek. It was salty, delicious. It was surrender. Her breath was so warm, so sweet against the sour, he wanted to cling to the moment, but already the stars were in motion and the hare had thumped its alert and the world turned on its axis towards the new, the coming day.

The warm summer's night laid itself out over the hedgerows and fields. The sound of the music grew ever fainter and fainter as they walked away, hand in hand. The smell of the dog roses in the lane. Three babies made. A marriage broken and another saved. A love story beginning.

Halfway down the lane Nicholas stopped and made a ridiculous fumbling lunge at her, something which had not happened in twenty years, no more. Amanda started to laugh. Then he kissed her. Not bad.

She felt a kind of deep laughter inside, a rich full feeling, a laugh waiting too far down to rise up. It would come out later. The main thing was that it was there. It lay there like a deep grinding feeling within her. Giant tectonic plates being pushed. Continents which had been separated, meeting. Silly, she thought. But in her head, she was already singing the new tune.

£9.50

HARVESTING THE MOON

HARVESTING THE MOON

AND

OTHER

STORIES

URSULA PFLUG

2014

PS Publishing Ltd
Grosvenor House
1 New Road
Hornsea, HU18 1PG
England

e-mail: editor@pspublishing.co.uk • *Internet:* http://www.pspublishing.co.uk

CONTENTS

v

DIORAMAS AND MIRACLE FISH
An Introduction by Candas Jane Dorsey

WHEN I WAS A KID, WE HAD TWO CARS: A 1949 MORRIS Minor convertible, and a 1961 Panhard Dyna. In one or the other of them, my family used to go driving. Weekends, we'd go out of the city, but on weeknights, we sometimes drove around other people's neighbourhoods and looked into the lighted windows of cool houses we passed. Sometimes they were neighbourhoods like ours, and sometimes we went to rich areas, "seeing how the other half lives". This was in the late 1950s and early 1960s, when simple pleasures abounded, our city was small and trusting, and houses still had milk chutes. So it was still OK to crane our necks to see what art was on other people's walls, what colours they painted those walls, and people still left their curtains open after dark, so we could see them walking and talking, playing or working, sitting at dining room tables or welcoming visitors into the living room, kids doing homework while adults read the paper or watched their clunky console TVs.

When I went looking for an image to define how I felt as I re-read these stories of Ursula's, the image that came to me was of those drives, of passing fleetingly past the dioramas of other people's lives, seeing momentary glimpses but imagining the rest of the narrative.

Maybe I thought of this because there are so many familiar objects in Ursula's fiction. Maybe because my mother had one of those big old Singer electric sewing machines that the protagonists find in "Sewing Forgetfulness". Or because I had intense relationships with platform-soled and coloured-suede shoes ("Airport Shoes" and "Sewing Forget-fulness"). Or because I feel I have handled or watched with fascination those same robots, toys, fish, or walked the streets where those same young hippies, drug dealers, would-be revolutionaries and tired street-walkers formed my view of city life. But that's all too simple an answer really. What's familiar in Ursula's work is often the most profoundly strange to me too: the city through the dream, the spontaneous mysti-cism, the bravery in the face of revolution, the urge to childbirth.

Maybe the amount of my own fiction that began by bursting through from dreams with colours unseen in the waking world has opened my awareness to how much of her fiction comes through those same myste-rious doors. All of her work, whether realistic, futuristic or fantastical, has a tone of emerging from a dark mystery, as if it is reclaimed, sentence by magically-realist sentence, rescued, in fact, from a well of history.

If it is a well, an unfamiliar metaphor for me who was born and raised in a city, it is a deep, mysteriously-familiar well—but dark and dangerous too. It is the well where the giant cockroaches or the dying fish come from, the well in which, perhaps, one's childhood friend once drowned. Or let the metaphor be the land, a field, a woodland prairie. If so, it is a land at once bright with sun and dark with the knowledge of what is buried there. I'm always surprised again that in her hands, the darkness remains deep, but not despairing, helping me understand yet again that dark journeys are simply part of life.

The people and things and times we love die all the time. Being born is beyond our control, but the rest of it is, in one way, all about dying. Parents, children, lovers, sisters, brothers, rock stars, saints, heroines and heroes, cats and dogs, entire decades, entire countries, entire worlds—they all disappear into what Samuel Delany called "the great rock and the great roll". Our entire history is a vortex pulling everything down in a blur of memory.

Ursula Pflug knows a lot about that vortex. Her stories are full of sadness and loss, and yet, I feel as if they are returning to me so many things that life makes us lose. Reaching into the vortex of the past, Ursula comes up with an incredible salvage of heart, humanity, imagery and truth. The real stuff.

Sententiously I suppose I could just say, "That's how art works, when it's good—it's paradoxical." But really, that's too too boring to say, and too far from the full truth. Even more, it's a statement that's put out there to defend me from the reality, from telling you the main thing. I admit, I'd love not to reveal the treasure I bring in my hand out of Ursula's work. Sometimes I want to keep the core of my relationship with a writer a secret, you know? Maybe in case I break it, or maybe because I fear it will be stolen from me. But that's what I'm doing here, isn't it? Offering you the truth of my relationship with Ursula's brilliant work. So okay, I'll share.

Here's the main thing.

The main thing that has me looking through those windows again, very far away from the here and now, whenever I read Ursula's fiction, is some quirk of perspective that is special to Ursula, a tone, a sensibility that I perceive with some kind of literary synaesthesia as if it is a relationship to time itself. When I read a Pflug story or novel, even when (or perhaps especially when) it is about the future, I feel as if I never left the past, as if I were able to bring the past with me, to this moment and then to the future, not just as a memory or a dream, but as a way of life, a realisation of all hopes. The illusion that such possibilities exist is the great gift of Ursula's genius.

It sounds simple enough now that I've said it, but if you think it's simple, try and do it.

Ursula does it, and makes it look easy, but let's not, you and me, be fooled by our own pleasure, or nostalgia, or satisfaction as we finish reading each story. Nor should you, dear Reader, who perhaps do not, as I do, spend time building the same sort of edifices in fiction, be fooled by the quiet, deceptively additive small sentences that make up the multiplex entirety. This is hard-won, dangerous, beautiful, revolutionary, world-changing work, and Ursula does it.

Ursula is willing to take risky forays into dark neighbourhoods and strange worlds, in familiar yet exotic vehicles, but not only that, she will bring us along and direct our attention to what can be glimpsed through strangers' brilliantly-lighted windows. The process is even more entrancing to me than were those evening journeys when I was a kid in my parents' care, because now I know how transgressive it is to eavesdrop on the secret lives of others, no matter how important it is for our future to make those empathic journeys.

To borrow some of her own striking words: "'I brought a fish through the door, across the border,' and watched the indescribable looks on [their] faces as she removed it from her pocket and unfolded it on the table where it began to swim in slow lazy circles. She knew then that all her training and all her defilement were to this one end, to be a translator, to propagate miracle fish, fish smuggled across the border from another dimension, another world, in her own community."

How lucky that Ursula Pflug is willing to brave these frontiers and smuggle back what she finds, to share generously of her vision with us, so that we too may take home in our pockets these brightly-coloured miracle fish.

Candas Jane Dorsey

HARVESTING THE MOON

for Doug Back
through thick and thin and so many interesting portals

THE WATER MAN

THE WATER MAN CAME TODAY. I WAITED ALL MORNING, and then all afternoon, painting plastic soldiers to pass the time. The sky was painted red when he finally showed. I turned the outside lights on for him and held the door while he carried the big bottles in. He set them all in a row just inside the storm door; there wasn't any other place to put them. When he was done he stood catching his breath, stamping his big boots to warm his feet. Melting snow made little muddy lakes on the linoleum. I dug in my jeans for money to tip him with, knowing I wouldn't find any. Finally I just offered him water.

We drank together. It was cool and clean and good, running down our throats in the dimness of the store. It made me feel wide and quiet, and I watched his big eyes poke around Synapses, and while they did, mine snuck a peek at him. He was big and round, and all his layers of puffy clothes made him seem rounder still, like a black version of the Michelin man. He unzipped his parka and I could see "Gary" stitched in red over the pocket of his blue coverall. I still didn't have a light on; usually I work till dusk to save on the light bill for Deb. But I switched it on when he coughed and he smiled at that, like we'd shared a joke. He had a way of not looking right at you or saying much, but somehow you still knew what he was thinking. Like I knew that he liked secrets, and talking without making sounds. It was neat.

Seemed to me it was looking water—a weird thought out of nowhere—unless it came from him. He seemed to generate weird thoughts; like he could stand in the middle of a room and in everyone's minds, all around him, weird little thoughts would start cropping up— like that one. My tummy sloshing I looked too, and seemed to see through his eyes and not just mine.

Through his I wasn't sure how to take it: a big dim room haunted by dinosaurs. All the junk of this century comes to rest at Synapses; it gets piled to the ceilings and covered with dust. If they're lucky, they'll make a Head; weird Heads are going to be the thing for Carnival this year, just as they were last, and Debbie's are the best. Her finished products are grotesque, but if you like that sort of thing, they're beautiful. The one she just finished dangles phone cords like Medusa's hair, and gears like jangling medals.

Shelves of visors glint under the ceiling fixture; inlaid with chips and broken bits of circuitry that hum like artifacts from some Byzantium that isn't yet. There are two-faced Janus masks with their round doll eyes removed; you can wear them either way, male or female, to look in or out.

Gary was staring at them, a strange expression on his face. Like he wanted to throw up.

"Do you think they're good?" I asked to stop him looking like that.

"Good enough," he said, "if you like dinosaurs."

"I like them. They are strange and wonderful."

"But dinosaurs all the same," he said, his eyes glinting like the mosaic visors. I looked for the source of light on his face but couldn't find it. Maybe he was one of the crazy water men. You hear things; like that's the way they get sometimes; it comes from handling their merchandise too much. Fish heads, people call them. After the deep fish, the ones that generate their own light.

"Whose water you gettin' now?" he asked.

"I never called a water man before today," I said.

"What do you drink?" he asked.

"Town water. But I just couldn't do it anymore."

"Yeah." It was sad, the way he said it.

"Only cold. For hot we have pots on the stove."

"Uh-huh. Baths down the street at the pool, am I right?"

"Showers, mostly. They don't clean the tubs out too often."

"I guess not."

"I heard your water was the best," I said, threading through the junk to the desk where I keep my check book. I am a little proud of them, my checks. My buddy and I designed them and he printed them up for me. They're real pretty, with phoenixes and watermelons. I had to clean his kitchen for a week in trade, but it was worth it.

Gary looked interested, his pop-eyes studying the tracery.

"What do I owe you for this fabulous water, Gare?" I asked, punctuating my signature.

He moved his tongue around in his mouth so that his face bulged. A bulge here, a bulge there: his cheek a rolling ball.

"That is some way out bank you belong to, miss. What did you say it was called?"

"It doesn't have a name. It's my own personal bank. Very secure. These checks are not affected by the stock market."

"And a good thing, too," he nodded, agreeing with me. But he had his doubts. "I tell you what, miss. First delivery's usually free. You see how you like the water, you let me know. But the deposit on the bottles, I got to have that." He glared at me, wanting cash.

I hemmed and hawed, and took him on a tour of the premises. Thing was, we had no cash. Well, we had a little, but Deb took it this morning to get her hair done. Half a dozen places in town would rather do your hair on account, and Deb has to pick one that only takes jazz. She can be a prima donna that way. But then, she is the Artiste.

The store is a kind of a hodgepodge. I think she must have a call for the garbage, like a dog whistle; a supersonic whine that only it can hear. Because she cares about it. Garbage is her job. Deb rebirths obsolete appliances, toys, anything thrown away, and nonorganic. It's recycling, only more so; this way they get an extra life on their slow way back to Earth. She makes them into art: sculptures, costumes for Carnival; Heads, mostly. She takes hockey helmets, the domes from those old hair dryers, hats, and headbands. Anything to go around a head. Hot glue gun, soldering, she glues things to them: taken apart washing machines; orphan computers; microwave ovens. The grunts love it. Come February, they buzz in here like flies, picking up a couple of Heads apiece. Grunts have to wear something new every night of Carnival. A good thing, too: jazz.

When it first comes in, I just like to do nothing but hold the money all morning. It makes my skin happy. Deb doesn't like it; I don't do any work. She comes home, and I'm sitting on the floor, playing with the jazz. She yells, sends me out to the co-op for a year of rice and beans.

Gary and I pass a rack of toys; thirty years of Christmas, stacked up to the ceiling lights. Between the caved in Atari monitors and the bins full of busted GoBots, almost like an anachronism, was a shoe box of those little plastic domes where the snow is always falling. Gary stopped and picked one out, held it up to the light; a striped yellow fish danced among ferns. Once there had been a thread holding it suspended, but now it floated on its side: gills up, dead. He turned it over and over, like if he just waited long enough, and prayed hard enough, that fish would leap to life.

"It's nice," I said, my feet betraying me, shifting me from one to the other. "I don't think I ever noticed it before."

"Nice? It's amazing! You don't know how long I've been looking for something like this! Look, here's the slot for the battery. It's got a light bulb—this one lights up in the dark!"

"So it does." His enthusiasm made me edgy. I waved the check like a slow flag, hoping he'd change his mind about my watermelons.

But he didn't. "Look, miss. I'll take this fish for the deposit. But from now on it's got to be jazz. If you want to keep getting the water."

"Hmm. Maybe town water's not so bad."

He laughed. "It's your funeral."

"I'll give you a call, Gare."

"Sure. If you can find me."

I'd gotten off easy and he was mad. It was just his luck I'd had something he wanted. "Thank you for coming so soon after I called," I said, trying to placate him.

"It's very rare," he grumped. "Collector's material. I can sell it for a week of jazz uptown."

But you won't.

"No problem. I didn't even know we had it."

"No kidding." It was that look again, only in his voice; his hand wrapped around the toy like he was saving it from something. From me. What did I care? He was almost out the door and then he stopped, staring at the shelves of Heads again. "You make those?"

"I put them together. But my partner, she's the designer."

"She a healer, right?"

"Uh-huh."

"It shows." He nodded at the Heads, looked down at his opened hand, at the fish. He

chuckled. It made me look at him; his handsome face with a big grin cutting it in two. You wanted to like him when he grinned. And his hands knocked me out. The brown backs opening to velvet palms, soft and shocking baby pink. Yeesh. I wished I could have hands like that.

He did his other voice, cradling the fish like a baby. "I is going to fix this fish," he crooned. "This is a poor sick fish and needs mending."

The guy was not for real. But his water. "You a fish doctor too, Gare?" I asked, only half sarcastic. He turned on like a light bulb when I said that.

"That's very good, dear. Very, very good." He laughed, a happy laugh from deep down, and for once he didn't look like I made him sick. I was even afraid he wanted to give me a hug; his huge padded arms windmilling toward me like that. I backed away into the warmth; it was freezing standing there in the open door. "It's a kind of a sideline, my fish doctoring," he explained. "Like a fiddle. You know what a fiddle is?"

"Yeah, yeah," I said, "Economics 101." I slammed the door while I had a chance, and stepped back to the big window to watch him leave. He grinned, turning to cross the road; his feet leaving boat-sized holes in the slush. In the middle he stopped to turn and wave again. He was still chuckling when he gunned the van, his big head rolling like it was on bearings. "Pure spring," read the hand-drawn sign on the side. "A drink for sore throats." Weird. Like "a sight for sore eyes".

Three weeks to go.

Deb sleeps at the studio, brings me the new designs in the morning. Flavor of the week is headbands; I've been stringing plastic soldiers onto lengths of ribbon cable. You know the stuff: rows of tiny colored wires all stuck together, for connecting computers and all. When they're strung each soldier is painted to match a different strand of wire. "Rainbow Warrior," Deb calls 'em.

Two grunts came in this morning and bought Heads. Red Heads, blue Heads; color is big this year. One also bought a box of old electronic parts; said he wanted to make his own. An arty grunt, yet. He was pale and like his friend wore a grey, knee length wool coat. They both looked young. But lately it seems like all the grunts look young; young and spooked.

They make half scared google eyes, tell me it's their first time in a non-grunt place like Synapses. Say they work for banks. Tellers, they had to be; their coats too thin for managers. It almost doesn't rate as a grunt job, being a bank teller. Too servile. Seems like it takes less and less to be a grunt these days. How sad.

"You mean there still are banks?" I ask them while doodling on my creative check book. I know there are still banks; I just want to make them nervous. I'm bad when it comes to young grunts. But jobs. For money. Geez.

The secret life of grunts. I do wonder what they think about. They must be on town water. I can't imagine ordering it in and still being a grunt. I can't remember ever even wanting to be a grunt, but I guess grunts want to be grunts. They must. Or else why would they? It's not like you have to be a wage slave. There are other ways.

Another one came in this morning: a creepy, older one. He bought my window. It's something I do to relax, when I'm on break from Deb. I climb into the display window and arrange the junk into scenes, make a little chaos out of the order. Or is it the other way around? I forget which. Anyway, this time I'd found a plastic Doberman and hot-glued its mouth to a Barbie's crotch. I know there are worse things on this Earth than a little dog cunnilingus, but even Deb thought it was maybe a little much.

The grunt, however, loved it, asked me if I did gift wrap. I did by ripping a strip of red off the velvet curtains left over from Synapses' previous incarnation and tying it around the dog's neck. He loved it, he told me, in that creepy voice; he loved the store and he loved me. "Sure," I said, but I had to get a glass of water right after he left just to get over his face. Maybe that's how it happens to grunts; they get old when the inside faces out too long, when instead of being scared they're scary. And to think I cater to that market. Yeeagh.

I used to think all water was the same. It was what you drank for breakfast with a little coffee to stir in if you were lucky. It was a grunt drink. From Gary I learned otherwise. This morning I brought a quart up to the kitchen where I was working. I heated it up on the stove, and sort of meditated, tried to think how Gary would think. While I was waiting I amused myself pushing the eyes into a couple of old dolls. I sliced the faces off, attached them to one another with bands of elastic. One male doll, one female, the way you're supposed to do them. A type of Janus. It's not a big seller, but it's lasted; every year we do a few. When the water was warm I put the mask on and drank, using a straw. I'd pierced the lips for straw holes—grunts won't buy anything they can't drink in. The water went down, warm and wet, and I felt like there were revolving doors inside me, turning, and all of a sudden I could go out the other way. And then I could see the whole deal: how we lived; how we did up our place; what we wore and what we ate all because of drinking the town water. And this thing about getting your own water, it really worked. I could see how tacky it was: Synapses, Deb's and my life. A cheesy, no-class deal, except for some of the Heads. Like the Janus Head. It was clean, a nice idea made flesh. I kept it on, poking around the place, looking out the eyes of Gary's water. It was fun. I saw things I hadn't seen before, like which things fit together and how come. I poked around in shoe boxes all afternoon, looking at junk.

Every day they bring more in. I wonder where it all comes from. Junk out of plastic, junk out of metal. They don't make so much junk as they used to, but boy, when they did, was it ever a going concern. It must have employed thousands of people, the junk industry. I wonder where they got the raw materials from. I mean, what is that cheapo plastic made of, anyway? What natural substance has been humiliated in its service? I kind of got lost in the beauty of it, the beautiful ugliness of the cheap plastic objects I was handling. It occurred to me then they were beautiful precisely because they were ugly, and I even know a few people like that. And the more my thoughts headed off in that direction the gladder I became I work for Deb. Because, you know, I used to feel sorry for them. We'd be shopping for clothes at Thrift Villa or wherever, and there'd be shelves full of broken-down toasters and waffle irons, and I'd think how nobody cared about them, not even my Mom. Everyone always wanting the new one, the clean ones, without any scratches or deformities, in good working order and with high IQs. That is why I love Deb so much. She was the first person to see that all that old stuff wanted to still be used; it wanted so badly to have a purpose for us. So Deb thought and thought of how to use it, and finally she came up with the whole style of wearing garbage to Carnival, and now everyone does it, us and all the grunts.

Things have been different lately, I don't know why. Funny thoughts come to me while I work. That we are like fish in an aquarium, looking out at the world. I think it's since Gary came that it's been different. I never did any of that computing but my buddy Danny, the one who does the checks, he told me it is like that. Programming. It is like going into inner space. And I think maybe Gary's water is like that too, like going into inner space. To think I never knew. No wonder he was looking at me like that.

Two weeks. Carnival soon. I've started a new window. I work on it during breaks. TV sets done up like aquariums. Somehow they look the same: a clear glass box. I have a milk crate full of plastic fish; I string them from the inside of the TVs so they look like they're swimming. Take the picture tubes out, of course. And one real aquarium. A glass fish bowl I found upstairs that fits perfectly into one of the smaller TVs. I went down to the store and bought live fish for it. I paid for them with some of the grunt money. The dog grunt money, to be precise. I lied to Deb, told her Danny gave them to me when I washed his floors for him. She doesn't like me doing anything that costs money. Also she doesn't understand I have to make my own art sometimes. The windows. That's my art. That and the thoughts, the weird water ones.

Out of water. Once you get the new water, it's hard to go back to the old. I haven't thought so much in years. Even Deb likes me better, gives me time off in the afternoons to work on the window. It's very beautiful, now, almost finished. I wonder how I ever did dogs and dolls. I could never go back to that now. Phoned Gary but there was no answer. Shit. Town water sucks.

Don't forget to dream. To bring in the new world. Otherwise the old one just keeps rolling on. Death as predecessor to rebirth. The seed sleeping in the earth. The purpose of winter. Subtle changes taking place, deep in the darkness underground. Winter, Carnival, bringing back the sun. New windows. Fish televisions? But what is the death? The underworld. Being fish. What will we be, when we're not fish?

First day of Carnival. The grunts pour into the street, displaying their wares. Who will buy, and who will be bought? The one time of year they get to ease up. Bread and circus. For two weeks they live what is ours the whole year through. I felt so still, so empty inside. Deb was out, being photographed for something. I sat in the window, watching the grunts parading, wearing their garbage regalia. They were beautiful: moving in slow motion, with dreamy smiles on their faces. They looked happy. I recognized some of their Heads as ones we'd done. They smiled and waved at me, sitting among my fish TVs. Who is looking in and who is looking out? It is like the Janus mask. Tomorrow I will wear it.

I feel so still. In Carnival they act it out, the death and rebirth. But this year it's like it's real: Janus eyes in the back of my head. Gary came. He grinned and gesticulated, stamping his feet on the other side of the glass. He waved his hands. I wanted to see it, his beautiful skin, but he was wearing mitts. He brought the water. He carried it into the window where I was sitting, and we each had some. It was cool and clean and good, running down our throats in the cold morning. When we weren't thirsty anymore he made me come outside, showed me how Synapses' window was like a television too, or an aquarium, and I the fish in it. I knew where there was a big box of grease crayons in the back, and we drew it onto the glass: the outline of the screen and the control panel. I even found a fish costume in a drawer of stuff Deb did before the Heads.

He sat beside me for a long time, and we looked out the window, part of the display. A big, quiet black man and a thin white girl dressed up as a fish. The Carnival faces passed us, a white dressed throng, wearing Heads made of all their old stuff, and I was content as I've ever been. Finally understanding it, the meaning of Carnival. The old flesh dying to the new. They passed with the skeleton then, an effigy held high above their heads.

"Whose death is it this time, Gare?" I asked.

He put his big mitten out, covering my knee. "It is the death of Death."

"And the birth of Life?"

"Yes."

"That's what I thought. I'm glad I'm here to see this one."

"It is an interesting time."

He rose stiffly in his great padded knees, wearing a parka and thick quilted pants like always.

"I will be going then."

"I'm glad I know you, Gary."

"I, too. I will be coming by from time to time, to see how you are doing."

"Goodbye, Gary, goodbye."

Roses. It will be the next window. Flowers will bloom out of all the televisions there are. In the meantime it snows. Soft white snow falling like it does in a plastic bubble of fish, its string repaired. It sits on top of one of the televisions, where Gary left it for me to discover. Its light bulb glows softly in the darkening day.

VERSION CITY

I T'S BEEN SUCH A SLOW, SLOW PROCESS THAT UNTIL QUITE recently we hadn't noticed it at all. They kept telling us on the radio and in the occasional newspapers that it was turning to snow, but every morning when I woke up it was still raining. They told us the downtown sectors had been evacuated, but no one I know went anywhere except to Gus's bar.

There's a lot of people at the bar these days, and I know most of them from somewhere. I remember Lina from school days at McGill. She was studying economics then but now she's got a chicken connection and does her business at the bar. She has the best chickens available in our part of town, and like everyone else I'll pay her higher prices to avoid the Chinatown chicken hustlers and their rotten birds. It's been over a year since anyone's seen any beef other than the buffalo herds on Gus's back wall. He's been running scratchy, faded prints of old movies, and, except for the occasional sci-fi flick, all he can get are westerns.

I spent the morning sweeping dead bugs out from under the refrigerator. They've been growing in number since November and I don't know how long the cockroach powder I've been using will continue to work. It's a number seven red and should be good for another week, but the latest bugs are a size I'd hate to see anything but dead. They told us just last week on the radio that a special task force has been set up to deal with the bug problem. I've never seen a task force in my life. Maybe they don't come this far downtown.

When I got to the bar the film had already started. Gus was showing "The Swarm". I saw it years ago when I was going to school and it didn't seem so funny to me now, so I picked up the week's chicken from Lina and sat down at the bar next to Oswald, her bodyguard. Oswald's a big guy but friendly enough if you're a good customer. Other than Lina herself he's the only person I know who still wears new clothes.

"You here again?" he slurred at me through his scotch. They both like their whiskey, Lina and Oswald. She never used to drink so much in the McGill days. Neither did I; none of us did.

"Not much to do but drink and watch movies."

"No kidding, Jack. That and squish bugs."

"Yeah, I just finished loading up a garbage bag full of them. How're yours?"

"How are mine? Don't be funny, Jack. Mine are humongous, invincible, and fear nothing made by God or man. If we could develop immunity that fast we wouldn't have to worry about Harry Chung's dirty chickens."

"If we didn't have to worry about Harry Chung's dirty chickens you'd be out of a job, Oswald, so count yourself lucky."

"I count myself real lucky, kid, and just to prove to you how lucky I count myself I'm going to buy you a drink."

"Thanks, Oswald, I could use one."

"Don't thank me, Jack, thank Lina. She's the one with the chickens." Oswald was watching three young Chinese wannabe toughs who were standing around Lina's chicken booth, looking itchy. "Gotta go make myself useful, Jack. Talk to you later." Oswald got up and moved slowly across the room. The kids vaporized before he got there, but Oswald sat down with Lina anyway.

You can never be too sure that those types won't be back.

I let my eyes travel the room. Everyone was in back watching the film except for a newsgirl I spotted sitting alone at a table across the bar. I had the bartender send her one of whatever she was drinking and put it on my tab. He brought her a shot of tequila and I watched her heavy-lidded eyes scan the room until they met mine. She nodded. It was a shadow of a nod, but a nod just the same. I crossed the bar and slid in opposite her. She looked bad. Her small hands were fidgeting with a nervousness I didn't like, but I needed her information. I lit two cigarettes, one for her and one for myself.

"They're getting bigger," I said.

"Uh-huh." She woke up a little when I mentioned business. Tearing a piece of paper from her notepad she scribbled down an address and slid it under the table into my waiting hand. I peered at it in the dim light; it was a Chinatown address. I knew what that meant. The insecticide dealers aren't a bad bunch of kids but when they start dealing with the Chinese you know they're getting strung out. No one else will sell to a bug powder addict. They get into the business for the living it brings them. It's a good living except for the stories they keep hearing about the worlds locked inside the coloured powders they sell, worlds much prettier than this one. Sooner or later their curiosity drives them to it, even the best of them. This newsgirl looked like she used to be good, but in another month her little hands would be spinning like epileptic windmills, and from then on they're not much use to anybody except the Chinese. The Chinese don't pay them and they get cut off right around the time too much of the merchandise starts going up their noses. When they get cut off you find them down by the waterfront, climbing into bonfires and cutting themselves up with razor blades until they bleed to death.

I looked at the newsgirl. "You haven't got anything else?"

"It's all that's available this week. How's the other stuff holding out?" She had a ways to go, yet. That made it worse.

"Good enough, but I can't expect more than another week out of it."

"That should be about right. If you think you can wait until next week I might have something better for you by then. Nobody likes to deal with the Chinese but this stuff they have is serviceable. Ask for Lee, tell him you're a friend of Tanya's, and that you need a number three blue."

"He cuts you in?"

Tanya smiled. She knew what I was thinking. "We work it out."

I got up to leave. "They could offer you a bath once in a while."

Her eyes went vicious. "Chinese don't take baths, asshole."

I sent her another tequila from the bar.

Oswald was back at his stool, talking to Jayne, the poster girl. She had an old offset in her warehouse and printed up information sheets and posters for the parties.

"Hi, Jack. You running with the riffraff again, or what?"

"My bugs are getting to be the size of doorknobs, Jayne, and I'm afraid they're getting wise to my current supply. I've gotta do something."

"I'll bet you anything her connection is Chinese. I hope you feel good cutting that poor girl's arms and legs to ribbons."

"She's already gone, Jayne."

"Right on, Jack."

"You've never done it, have you, Jack?"

"Me? Are you kidding?"

"I did, once. It was when I was living with Gerry. He was a newsboy for six months. Before he got into it. We lived well for those six months, but I moved out right after that first time. I could see he wanted to go."

"What was it like?"

"What's it like?" She laughed. "It's not like anything at all." She stared hard at a spot just above my left shoulder, and then her eyes went cloudy. I knew that look.

"Jesus, Jayne." I shook her arm. "Snap out of it."

"I might go back, Jack. You never know. It's a hell of a life while it lasts."

"Don't scare me, kid."

"I scare myself, but forget it. You going to the dance tonight?"

"I hadn't thought of it."

"Then let's go together. The Insect Men are playing, I did the poster for them."

"Good enough."

They'd had the first dance one full moon night in August. The cockroaches had only started to become a problem back then, and the dance coincided with the appearance of the first of the new bug powders, a number seven orange. Half a dozen newskids showed up high. They danced like crazed woodpeckers and didn't bother anyone until they started to come down and sent a kid by the name of Sleeptalker out to score some more. He never came back. They found him strangled in a Chinatown alleyway late the next day, but that night at the dance a couple of kids slashed themselves to bits on the dance floor and another one tried to set fire to the stage. The others went home to sleep it off, telling us they'd never touch the stuff again. We didn't know at the time that there was no such animal, just as we hadn't known about the previous fires and the razor blades. The newskids don't get let in to the dances anymore unless they can prove they're clean. It's not hard. All you have to do is look at their eyes.

On our way to the dance hall Jayne told me that some joker had called the cops that night in August.

"So?"

"So they were told the police don't come into evacuated areas."

"Same as saying they stay out of Chinese territory."

"We're not in Chinese territory, Jack."

"We're close, kid, real close."

We arrived at the hall. The outside walls were plastered with Jayne's posters. They were beautiful. They were white and silver and you could get lost in them.

"Hot posters, Jayne," said the doorman, a fat guy called Brian.

"I tried to get it as close as possible."

Brian eyed me suspiciously. "You haven't hooked up with another newsboy, have you, Jayne?"

"Don't worry, Brian. This is Jack and he's as clean as you'd ever want to be."

"Keep it that way, kid." He waved us in.

We danced the Bug Shuffle. Our hands fluttered about our heads, miming feathery cockroach antennae; our legs found the rhythms of scurrying insect dancers. In becoming like them, we felt almost free of the changes they had made in our lives.

The band would counterpoint their songs with threatening percussive riffs, and we would all fall crashing to the floor, where we'd lie dying. When the music changed again we'd all get up and dance some more, till they came out with the newest powder.

At sunrise we were filthy and exhausted. Jayne wanted to walk, and led me toward the waterfront. We found a bench and sat down. The tail end of a fire was reducing the last buildings on the other side to ashes.

"What happened?"

Jayne laughed. "You don't know? Some newskids went over there a couple of days ago. They heard there was a whole warehouse full of number six green. They didn't find it so they burned the place down."

"Who started that rumor?"

"Probably the Chinese. It would seem like a handy way to take out a couple dozen of the greediest kids."

"Maybe they're happier there." The voice came from behind us. It was Tanya. She sidled around the bench and sat down beside me. "You got a smoke?" I lit her a cigarette. I couldn't trust her hands.

"Why don't you go over, then?" asked Jayne.

"I think I might, in a little while. You want to come with me?"

"Thanks, Tanya. Maybe some other time."

"They did find it, you know."

"I'm glad."

We walked home through the rain. Jayne's hand was damp in mine. Back at my place I went to the kitchen to put on some coffee. Something huge dove down the drain. They were alive again. I put some of Lina's chickens on to fry and brought Jayne her coffee in the bedroom, but she was already curled up under the covers, almost asleep. I took the chickens off and climbed in beside her.

"I gotta go to Chinatown this afternoon," she mumbled sleepily.

I brushed the hair out of her eyes. "Me too, honey, me too."

TELEPATHIC FISH

THE EYES OF HIS HEART, THE GRAVE OF HIS GAZE. MELANIE didn't know him from Adam, but it turned out he knew many of her friends. She didn't know yet that people like her knew each other, or would come to know each other in the years that followed; it was what took the place of destiny in those days.

His landing fluttered with mailbox overflow: discount pizza flyers were holding a séance. The spirits of departed anchovies whistled high and thin. Melanie stepped over a telephone bill; ripped open at the door and discarded. It rustled now with old leaves that dreamed, like everyone else in unswept winter corners of the tropics. In the dim light she made out the names of cities, each one farther than the next. She recognized them from her own phone bills, for hers too betrayed the secret loneliness. Her friends were strewn half across a world, and were, perhaps even now, thinking of her as she climbed these unfamiliar stairs in the dark wool night.

She could see her friends, lounging in bars in Montego Bay, in Belize—what was the name of that city?—it didn't matter. There they sat, pen in hand, lacking in ambition, completed letters, money; lacking everything except what they wanted: the death of time.

She'd seen rooms like his. They were serviceable rooms: all contained a bed, books, a few empty coat hangers. There were rooms like this all over the world, and all of them were easy to leave. Melanie had left rooms like these so many times she was now beyond counting. Years. What were the years made of?

They sat down on the edge of the bed, talking and drinking Jack Daniel's from the mickey he carried in his jacket pocket. On the ceiling above her head he'd pinned a map of the oceans of the world. Her gaze traveled the Earth's waterways, connected one to another, transmuting from sweet to saline. She thought of those anatomy drawings of the venous system, how blood was transformed by the human hand, for the sake of clarity, from red to blue. She told him.

It was Melanie's ability to think of these things, to be amused by them, that made her capable of going home with strange men. She liked the adventure of it. She only did it with the ones she liked, unlike her friend Jane, who'd go home with angry men Melanie didn't trust. She feared for her friend. In the mornings they sometimes compared notes on the telephone. They did this even when one of them was away. Their long distance bill was a taken for granted luxury—it was this young man's long distance bill that made Melanie recognize him as one of her own on the stairs, made her feel her choice was a good one. There is always that moment of truth on the stairs, at the door.

They talked about Mexico, where Melanie had never been, although she traveled to many of the world's out of the way places before they were built up. Danny (this was his name) stayed in Cabo San Lucas, at the southernmost tip of Baja, when it was just a fishing village. There are big hotels there now, he said. Perhaps the locals think this is good for the economy, perhaps they are pleased, but Melanie is sad she never saw it the way it was before.

"And anyway," she said, "who owns the hotels? All the money is probably siphoned out of the region, and the locals just work as maids and janitors, for peanuts."

"Maybe," he said. She felt familiar with him, trusting, as though she had known him for a long time. But she hadn't. She'd only known people like him, wanderers who'd learned to create intimacy in a short period of time, because they never stayed anywhere long enough to do it the slow way, the way that lasts.

Still, the short way felt intense and real, and when she'd chosen well, Melanie wasn't lonely in those moments. She lay down on his bed, looking up. Pretending to make herself very small she slipped into the map, following its currents from the Indian Ocean to the Penguin's Pole, as a sleepy-eyed turtle or a sturdy, migrating whale. Once she'd sailed for a few months in the Pacific Ocean, and schools of dolphins had played alongside the boat. Was it enough? Will it be enough, she wondered, when she no longer travels? Even then she already suspected such a time would come, and both feared and yearned for it.

Water is everywhere; all the water on earth is connected through the convection cycle. It seemed to her as though some secret of geographical telepathy was contained in water, for sometimes swimming in a northern lake, she felt the proximity of those Hawaiian channels she and her friends had sailed in so intensely. It was as though a few drops of water from there were just then wetting her fingers, having traveled along just those currents she was looking at now on Danny's ceiling.

"And wind, and rain," he said, when she told him her thought. She liked this about him, that he was interested in what she had to say. He shared her thoughts, unlike the men she chose some nights, lacking enough discernment, who wanted the act of sex only, and, if they talked, somewhat hopelessly wished she would be impressed with them.

She felt Danny knew they were the same, knew if he wanted her to return it would be done this way; by listening, by sharing, by kindness, by fun.

The currents poured from the borders of the map in waves of blue; oceanic light, washing over the bare bulb, the full trunk, the half-empty bookshelves (William Burroughs, Paul Bowles, Samuel Delany, Elizabeth Eberhardt, Virginia Woolf), the single blue armchair regurgitating its stuffing like a penitent glutton. More blue: his blue jacketed arm pouring her a drink, this time into glasses from the bookshelf. They were very beautiful glasses, a deep cerulean, and old.

They smoked hash.

Because she was feeling too lethargic to move, and was ensconced in her map-inspired reverie, he knelt at her feet and pulled off her boots.

They began to make love, unhurriedly, kindly, their bodies speaking to one another of the pact they had each made with solitude, with wandering, and how important these moments were; their solace, their communion.

"No ties, right?" he asked.

"Right," she said.

"Not many women feel that way," he said. "They always want to have relationships, to move in, start cooking me dinner and telling me what to wear."

"So I've heard," she said, "but actually I have the same problem. One motorcycle ride and they want you to meet their parents. It would be easier to get my own motorcycle, I think."

"It's because you're special," he said, but very carefully not putting too much import on it.

Don't scare her away.

She smiled, not taking it the wrong way. Melanie wondered how she was special, but did not ask that aloud. She'd heard it before. Special because she was cute and the guy wants to show her off to his friends, have her on his arm at the bar? Of course it went both ways; Danny would have been a prize at any party. He was handsome, he was literate, his history was packed full of romantic penniless world travels.

Many years later she and her friends are all, much to Melanie's surprise, still as wonderful as they were back then, now trying to buy houses, with or without success, having finally tired of paying other people's mortgages. That much later, Danny says to Jane, running into her on the street: "I really liked Melanie. She was one of the only ones who could drink as much scotch as me."

Even though Melanie lives in the country now, she stills knows them all; that is the magic of it. All those people she discovered one by one when she was young, as though they were magic, a puzzle to be done, an inspired riddle, have all grown up and all know each other. It takes one to know one, of course. And of course, there are the ones who died.

Special how?

Later on the phone (they still phone each other) Jane will say, "You were special for exactly that reason. You weren't looking to fall in love, to have a real relationship; it made them want you. You played hard to get."

"Oh, it wasn't that I didn't want all that," says Melanie, "I just wanted to do it all in three days. And then go home and do something creative, happily alone. And then go find another, but stay friends with the first one, because, you know, just 'cause the sex part didn't last, doesn't mean it wasn't love. The love lasted."

"You're weird," Jane says. "Always were."

"No," Mel says, "I was just a happy drunk."

It meant something then, to drink scotch until five in the morning, to go to strange and mysterious booze cans, made stranger still by the sensual derangement. Now she thinks it is silly, how she taught herself to drink people under the table. Silly, but worth it. Because of those moments created, of intimacy, and adventure.

Her father says, calling her long-distance on the phone, that hers is the generation that suffered from the war. "I lived through it," he says, "the war came, and it went. There were bombs, and you were afraid, and then they were gone, and you'd lived. But it's as though your generation took it on, the pain, the meaning of it. The world now is worse, more terrifying than that war that came and went."

Melanie is glad to hear him say this because she is tired of people talking about their parents' generation, saying "they lived through the war, what have we done compared to that?"

She has so often felt she lived in a war of the psyche, the spirit. She thinks of the people who have died. Friends cut down in their prime and all that.

A war about love, the meaning of it.

Possession or betrayal?

Why always only those two choices?

People die, trying to make a third choice.

There was a conversation going on in her head, as she looked at the map.

A conversation. Water. About evolution. Yet another telepathy the water carried: one going back through time. It was as though she could inhabit the evolutionary process, follow it backwards.

A conversation going through time.

She was a little drunk, and vastly entertained by this moment, this man she had found, that she liked enough to love for one whole night; he had an ocean map pinned to his ceiling, a paper ocean she could play in.

It was all happening while they made love. The movements of their bodies seemed to synchronize with the thoughts in her head, with voices, bringing them in and out, like the musical cues in a play. New characters came and went.

The first chorus member spoke, an elderly sea turtle Melanie knew was named Jack. In her mind's eye she offered him some of the Jack Daniel's, which she knew he enjoyed.

"Intelligent biped! Long buried evidence sleeps in your reptilian brain! It hoards the memories of things seen through the transparent eyes of fish creatures. Do you remember the choice you made—so close to the very beginning of this game—a choice that was to carry you over the whole long haul, and what a long haul it was, to this moment where you stand upright, inhabiting an intelligent, still-animal body, in the familiar, breathless company of a male of your kind?

"What made you choose limbs over water? Why did you trade the proven dependability of gills for hesitant, air breathing lungs? For how many lifetimes did you lurk, like a hopeful teenage pool-shark, in the crevices of rocky shorelines, considering? How many generations were spent prowling the wet side of beaches, contemplating the big step, a step you would have to grow legs to make?"

Then the fish spoke:

"Say, George, you think we should go for it?"

"I don't know, Fred, looks awful solid. I'd say we put in a little more time on the feet angle."

"Okay, pal, no sense in rushing things. We'll put it on hold till the next time around."

"It's a date."

Back to Jack: "Did you say goodbye to your brother, who, having made the step, chose to return, to grow himself a whale or dolphin body?"

"I guess he didn't like legs," said Melanie.

"Like legs!" exclaimed Danny.

Suddenly she realized she'd spoken aloud, or perhaps, she'd done it accidentally on purpose, hoping to arouse his curiosity. Hoping to share.

"D'you ever get this thing," she asked, "when you're doing it, where you get timescapes going on behind your eyes, or, sometimes, I travel to this town I've never been to in my life, that doesn't even exist, but I'll return to it again and again, when I'm making love, even with different people." She said this carefully, knowing everyone's sensitive about it—everyone knows they don't belong to anyone, but for the moment they're with someone, they pretend they do. Melanie sipped her Jack Daniel's. "I wander the town until I know every street corner."

"Cool," Danny said. "What's the food like?"

"That's just the thing. I can't eat; I can't open doors; I can't talk to anyone; it's as though there's a screen or a wall separating me from them."

"You're a spirit," he said.

"Well anyway," and she closed her eyes again, to hear the rest of the story.

"Did you make a date with him to meet," asked Jack, "millennia hence, in some moody waterfront bar, over a drink that tastes strangely of liquorice?"

That would be anise, said Melanie, in her head this time. Telling Danny about it as she went disrupted the flow.

———————

"And find yourself grateful for a mammal tongue to taste it with? 'Why did you leave us,' your brother asks you sadly. 'I missed you most in the Palaeozoic.'"

"It wasn't me who left, it was him who went back! Rodhocetus. Forty-six million years ago, remember?" Melanie said, again in her head. She was perfectly capable of doing this, having one conversation going on in her head, one in real life, watching an interior travelogue and having sex.

"You toast his eyes, blue as the sea," Jack continued, putting words in her mouth again. "Ah, how could I but not have gone? The things we've seen, the creatures we've been, I know you would have loved them as I did. I wished you were there with us on the African plain, when we fell from slippery trees to roll in damp grass, and found ourselves, some centuries later, surprised and delighted to be standing upright, in posses-sion of clever opposable thumbs we could now, treeless, employ for tool making and for love.

"But I never forgot you, and often wondered what you were seeing, what methods you had devised for breathing, for singing, for making love and more of yourself."

So he tells Melanie about the blue.

Now, many years later, Melanie is with Mark, and has two children. She calls him her husband because they live in the country, where common-law is something drunken hillbillies do, and partner is the person you have a business with, or your hunting companion, if you're a guy.

It is sometimes difficult for her to be partnered.

She longs for the winged, brief partnerships of her twenties; the same song sung from adjacent doorsteps, but never a house shared. It is the complete one inhabiting of the other, without respite, that she finds so stifling about marriage. Also, conversely, its comfort. While she is lonely sometimes, being married, as anyone is, it isn't the same gut wrenching loneliness she used to feel, forsaken on some North African beach, asking herself, "Where does it all end?"

Now she knows it will most likely end with her partner, if she's lucky and they continue to get along. And while open to wonderful, winged trysts in her youth, she was also, occasionally, open to the predatory. This fact of marriedness closes off other possibilities, the good and the bad.

She weighs and weighs.

"I'm supposed to be somewhere," Melanie said, having just remembered she'd forgotten a date with Jane to meet for last call.

"We all are, kiddo, we're all supposed to be somewhere."

"But where?" This time it was a larger question, containing, just for a moment, all of Time. He kissed her: a wet, blue Jack Daniel's kiss. She listened to the surf drumming on all the beaches of the world, caught and tamed for the length of an evening by the blue cage of his ocean map. She heard her heartbeat in the surf, and lay back on his bed, laughing.

"What are you laughing at?"

But it didn't matter; she knew she didn't have to answer. His tongue in her mouth seemed enormous to her, like the tongue of a whale. Like a whale it swam in her mouth, tasting of liquor.

His hands cupped her breasts and a wave spilled out from the paper ocean and into her body, traveling upwards. It crested, breaking across her hairline. Surf washed across her crown, and she could see the phosphorescence of sea spray illuminating the darkness.

"There's sparks in your hair."

"I know. Let's make some more."

Another wave crested, and blue light snapped from his fingers to hers.

"What kind of fish are we?"

Danny didn't say anything this time, but he didn't ask either. A hopeful sign, Melanie thought.

Sometimes she felt they didn't move for hours, two carp floating inches above a riverbed, watching the orange moon float dishevelled high above. Waves rippled through her body, making no sound. There was no sound except for the occasional snap of electrical currents.

Presently, he asked, "Can you feel the waves?"

It surprised her; she hadn't known he was seeing with her. They were listening to old Grateful Dead. Terrapin Station, some nostalgic desire having compelled them to fish it out of his tape box, perhaps memories of California. Of San Francisco, where they'd both been, but not together. And then he asked, "Have you lost your tail yet?" Her heart jumped.

With each wave came an image, a picture of her childhood.

"Can you see them, too?"

A laneway behind a church, shaded by old apple trees. Her sister, a game they had made, drawing designs in the gravelly sand with a stick.

"What were you making?" Danny asked, and she realized this was all she had ever wanted, was someone to see with.

To share with. It had never happened to her before.

The image faded. "I don't know. I haven't remembered that in years."

They were quiet but when they moved again the picture cleared, like a fish surfacing for air.

"Now I know. It was supposed to be a time machine."

"Did it work?"

"It's funny but when I was a kid I always thought they did. I argued with my sister about it all the way home. 'We are in the future of when we started the time machine,' I said. 'Of course,' she said, 'but we would be anyway; time went by when we were working on it.'"

Danny was laughing, enjoying her pleasure in telling her tale.

"So then,"—she reached across his chest for a sip of Jack Daniel's to lubricate her story—"I said 'Okay, so what if we went a few minutes into the future? How would we know the difference? To me it feels like we did.'

"All our walk home up the endless summer evening, the way they are only in childhoods filled with large leafy trees and solid brick houses and the sound of crickets—as so well documented by Ray Bradbury, somewhat creepily—what a resonant moment it must have been," Melanie rambled on, drunk and loquacious, "to have been so often documented, shared in unwitting collusion by so many writers, and more importantly, does anyone still have that childhood anymore, or are there needles and condoms in every sun-dappled alleyway of the world now, forever destroying the possibility of those moments?

"But it felt different to me, all the way home to supper, and of course, the prosaic qualities of a family dinner eventually destroyed it, but sometimes I think those moments were real, that I was right, that it was all practice for moments like these . . . "

Inexplicably, she did something else she had never done before. Saw his image, his childhood. He was swinging on a rope in a ravine, over a small creek. He was twelve, she thought. In his picture it was summer too, and Melanie could smell wet leaves and wild raspberries. His summer, too, had the same leafy, time-stilled feeling. A fallen tree lay in the creek bed, reaching upwards like a huge jagged hand. The tree was dying, but here and there on the end of a twig were leaves, small and brave and new.

"So then what happened?"

The image shuddered away, and Melanie had to ask to get the rest of the story.

Now, ten years later, Melanie has conversations with her children about people with tails. Her son would like to have a tail, he professes, and she admits she has always wanted a tail herself, and that her mother wanted one too.

But they lost their tails, and that's that.

But perhaps, just as some of them shed legs to plunge back into the oceans, some of them, people like herself and her mother and her son, could go back and get their tails.

It's happened before, why could it not happen again?

Besides, she thinks, we need tails.

Or else we wouldn't want them so badly.

She feels her behind hopefully, the base of her spine.
Nothing yet.

Danny was explaining his story. He was on top now; now he was
reaching for his blood red glass of exuberant and excessive liquor. They
had reached that point you only reach when you're in practice, when
you drink a great deal, when drunkenness passes and a kind of clarity, of
serenity and joy seeps in. Melanie is glad now, ten years later, that she
has found other ways to experience this feeling, especially with her children, because drinking just doesn't do it anymore.

"I fell off the rope that day. I broke my leg and a twig scratched my
eye. I was lucky, I guess."

"But it didn't hurt your vision any?"

"Seems not."

He smiled.

They grew up and lost his room, walking together up the ravine. She
stayed with him for three and a half years, from nineteen to twenty-
three, when one does, unwittingly, grow up. Then they separated,
perhaps inevitably, not knowing yet what it takes to make the long haul.
And Melanie found Mark, whom she "married" and had children with,
but of course, she wonders, the way you do.

Except that isn't true, but in her shared dream with Danny that night,
she felt what it would be like, to grow up with him, to have traded the
brief winged journey for the longer, more earthbound one. As though
there was a part of her that could scoot ahead on various timelines, check
them out, see which she liked best. That night she woke in his room,
briefly, her head nestled on his shoulder. "What a sweet touch," she
thought, "as though I was his girlfriend or something."

Meaning, how sweet to make her feel that way, so briefly, just this
once. Although there was another night, that summer or another
summer, when they again made love, this time without time traveling.
Instead they traded stories about their lives and their boyfriends and

girlfriends who were disrespectful or clinging, and looked at each other speculatively. But then, as always, one of them went away on a trip.

And would come back, and the other, crossing the space of the bar or the party, a look of pleasure and wistfulness on their face, would say, "I heard you were away?"

"Oh? From who?" Looking for the links, the connections. Lovers, friends, partners, whatever they were.

"Oh, you know. The way you hear things."

They all did hear things as though there was an invisible web connecting them all, as though on some level, they shared a group mind. Perhaps all generations are like this. But looking backwards, Melanie thinks how the threads between her particular group were different, that they were made of light. She wonders if they still are.

She and Jane call only once or twice a year anymore. "Sometimes," Melanie admits, "I wonder where they all went, those people you could say anything to."

And Jane says, "They're scattered all over the world or they're dead."

"Just what I've been thinking about," Melanie says.

Later she thinks, in those days they were just scattered across the world. There weren't any dead yet.

Why so much brightness, and so much pain?

But doesn't everybody believe that of their generation?

Maybe, Melanie thinks now, she and Danny didn't need to spend three and a half years together. They did it all then, the compressed version. Maybe that was enough. Maybe it would have been boring to repeat something she'd already done. Three years in one night of lovemaking. Ha. More like forty-six million into the past, three into the future.

On the narrow muddy street of a frontier town, they were still together, close to the sea. On either side were small wooden buildings, their doors hanging open. Most of them housed one-room restaurants, but they also passed a travel agency that repaired bicycles on the side. The restaurants were full of people, most of them young. Wooden planks creaked beneath their feet, protecting them from the mud that was everywhere.

"D'you think they rent them, too?" Melanie asked.

"Bicycles in the mud?" He smiled. Maybe.

A young woman in a red skirt smiled at them in passing.

"She looked so nice," Melanie said, "I wonder who she is? If we'd asked her about the bicycles we could've found out? Are you hungry?"

"There're lots of restaurants, aren't there?" Danny asked. "Maybe they don't have kitchens where people live. Hey, you haven't said anything about the important thing—that they can see you."

"It's because I'm here with you," she said. "You're not supposed to come here alone too long—I just figured that out. D'you feel as though you've been here before?"

"I don't know. Does it feel so much like home to you?" he asked.

"Like the journey's end? Yeah," she said. "But if we went to the bar we could find out where everything is. Bartenders always know those things."

"It's too early. They'd still be closed. The shipyard is near here. It's a shipbuilding town."

"We could go and watch them build ships till the bar opens."

"Would you like to do that?" he asked.

"I would."

They followed the track till it turned sharply downhill. They could hear the ring of hammers. At the edge of a wharf they sat down, trailing their bare feet in the murky water. All around them wooden boats were being built. No one seemed to mind that they were there.

"Look," he said, "the fish are very interested in you."

She looked down. Two fish were poking their noses out of the water, investigating her toes.

He smiled, reaching over to hug her. His face in sleep was very nice. She wondered if he was still there. She slipped out of bed, careful not to wake

him. In the blue armchair she poured herself a glass of the remaining
Jack Daniel's and looked at the sky out his window.

She wondered again about the town, its streets she knew so well, its
paths as familiar as the neural pathways of her own mind.

Where is it, she wondered, that I am called there again and again?
Does it even exist? And if it doesn't exist as a real place, then what is it?

What is the point of this shared dream, the next step?

Phil K. Dick would have had fun with this one, she thought.

"What a nice place," she said aloud, "I'm glad I finally went there with
someone else. It makes it seem even more real. And I know how to get
there, anytime I feel the need."

When she'd finished her cigarette the light above the rooftops, toward
the east, was beginning to pale. She pulled on her sweater and closed the
door softly behind her. She would find a restaurant and bring them back
some coffees. In the hall and on the stairs she thought she could hear
people sleeping.

Alone on the street, blue dawn light painting the rooftops, she knew
this place was unlike the other one in her heart. She felt breakable
here, as though her body was made of glass. She walked carefully,
but not enough, for when she brushed against the brick side of a building
her little finger snapped off and fell to the sidewalk, a blue cut glass
stone.

Melanie picked it up and put it in her pocket. Like the other things,
she would fix it later. (When she'd lived enough to know how. Followed
this path enough. Grown her tail.)

"It's warmer there," she said, "and the buildings are all made of wood."

Now, ten years later, she realizes it was not for her to fix. She must give
the blue crystal to her husband. She grew a new finger to replace it, like a
starfish, and kept the blue stone in a box all these years, a secret. But he
is the one who knows how. He fixes things, things like machines. He will
fix her blue cut-glass holo-projector, the one that projects realities, so
that she won't just be able to walk her town, with its sense of familiarity,
of adventure and security all at once, only in her lovemaking reveries,

(she goes there with him too, but never again as she did with Danny that day: namely, together. Something she only did the ever once) but in the real world as well.

That is what he is for, in her life. It tastes good.

BUGTOWN

THE BUGTOWN NEXUS IS A WAREHOUSE IN THE MIDDLE OF a six block radius of evacuated Chinatown territory, full of shoe-string insecticide operations and street vendors. Many of the Chinese left with the evacuation; Lee and some of his family and friends stayed. It is my friend Jayne who asked me to describe them this way, more truthfully.

"Why?" I say. "Everyone trashes the Chinese."

"I know. I do it too. It's the stress. But you know it isn't really true, and there are, in any case, very few Chinese left to trash."

"Trash-talking is just another way of dividing us."

"I know," Jayne said. "But I'm afraid, too."

"Afraid of what?" I asked.

"Of Lee."

"Me too," I said. "And afraid of Bugtown. But why are we more afraid of Lee than of Max?"

"*Je ne sais pas.* But if we go, maybe we'll find out."

A lot of the buildings aren't on city plumbing anymore and raw sewage runs down the streets; just a little worse than on our side of Spadina. Walking down those streets in the middle of the night you feel like you're in the Third World; no, on another planet altogether. Mostly I can't afford to be too thin-skinned, but Bugtown always makes my head spin. Why

39

do they call it that? Ask Max; he named it himself, the night his little shop in the shadow of the Toshiba light board under the Gardiner exploded, and his face turned purple. Yeah, same accident.

In school we used to call him Blue Max. Not anymore. The beginning and end of it all. Some people would have run when a thing like that happened, but not ol' Max. He could've gotten a job at the Proctor and Gamble labs, a new face, a house and a wife and a credit card, but he decided to stay down here with us as our only public servant.

The city sends us a big load of Roach Motels, Black Flag and boric acid, and maybe even female roach pheromones on a really lucky month, but their shit don't do shit on our bugs. Maybe they're hoping if they leave us alone down here with ineffectual powders we'll come up with something on our own. Something they can swipe for themselves, take the credit, natch. Like everything they take of ours. Our music, our art, our clothes. We're like a little experiment for them, I think on the mornings when conspiracy theory looms large as the new cockroaches. Why do they let us stay? An experiment in adaptation. Give people the most adverse living conditions possible, and see what they come up with.

Mostly we come up with a life. I'd take the conviviality of the monthly neighborhood dances, or the bike repair shop that doubles as a repertory cinema any day over being locked in a box up there, staring at Super-channel, or whatever shit they've got spewing out of the box these days.

Max, one of their best and brightest, decided to stay. With us. He said it was the explosion that made him see things differently. He said it turned his head around. I'm beginning to think he meant it literally. I'm beginning to wonder what that explosion of wine-colored powder made him see.

Like I said, Max is our public servant. He took it upon himself to help us remedy the bug situation, having been in chemistry with me at McGill. Max, unlike me, drank like a fish even back then.

I miss him sometimes. I don't go over there much, because of what you hear about the newskids—teenagers who sell powders, working under Lee, doing street sales in the bars and cafés. Sleeptalker, one of them, was a friend of mine. Found dead in an alleyway last month—murder or suicide; no one's talking, least not yet.

A good kid; we talked often and went drinking a few times together, uncovering one another's secrets early in the whisky mornings. He had a fireworks concession. Made his own, too; measuring out saltpeter and magnesium on his sales table right on Spadina. You'd think nobody'd have time for luxuries like fireworks down here on the fringes of China-town, but it's more like the opposite. We make lots of art. And we dance. You know what they said about Damocles.

I miss Max's blue eyes, talking about the future. He was the big idealist. What if he is, still?

Well, I've seen the future, Max, and it crawls. Like tropical breeds, bigger. Some talk of a new strain, from the radiation. You hear these things. Is it true or urban legend? Who knows; they'd be the last to tell us. Max is a chemist, not a biologist, but he does keep a lot of bugs over there, in little aquariums, feeds them different colored powders. They're beautiful, those powders, of every imaginable hue, and once every month or so a new one winds up on the street. The newskids who sell say it doubles as a drug, paint it on their skin, wait for it to come on, dance when it does. Never seen anything like those dances. People say, sometimes at the end, they start fires and climb into them. Sometimes at the end there are dead; not just the burnt corpses, so lacking in dignity, but worse, young people with arteries slashed open with razor blades. Young skin so desecrated; I only saw it once, now I don't look anymore, let others gather 'round staring when the ambulance circles.

What makes them do it? Or is it done to them? Not looking, I have no proof, no evidence, unlike the tiny greasy footprints on my kitchen counter, mornings I didn't scrub out the night's chicken pan.

Proctor and Gamble canceled Max's job offer when they found out the explosion made him crazy. It gave him visions of the chemical chains for better powders, he said. Powders that worked. These things happen, he said, citing the famous case of the benzene ring. Maybe his idealism just changed, like his face, into something unrecognizable. Blue Max, newly Max Maroon, set up his new shop in an abandoned building on Huron Street, started mixing up batches. People don't go around there much; they say the air is so full of dust when Max is in production you get wired just walking down the street.

It was Tuesday night, I was out of powder; the street showed no sign of any sellers and so I was on my way to Max's shop, Jayne in tow. She wouldn't go there alone, she'd said. Didn't know Max like I did.

Tanya the newsgirl was sitting on a bench outside Max's building. You could tell they were working on Blue again, because in the glow of the sodium lamps blue dust was swirling out of the open windows, covering everything. Tanya sat with her eyes closed, her lips parted, a fine blue coating covering her skin, her clothing, every inch of her. Max in full production. Why didn't he let her in, I wondered? Not that she needed to go in. She had all she wanted here. Crazy Max must be more strung out than anyone. Maybe he knew she was wired by now, and he wouldn't let her deal anymore, 'cause there wasn't any profit in it for him. It meant she might be about to explode.

Except that Max doesn't deal, Lee does. Public sentiment runs hot and cold against Lee: people blame him for the newskids' deaths but they continue to buy from him because Max's powders are the best, the only ones that really work. I don't like the racist comments I hear about Lee, even when I hear them coming out of my own mouth, but the truth is down here everybody gets called names: for their race, their gender, whatever they happen to be selling. It's like the school yard: if you come home with anything less than a bloody nose you figure you're still ahead of the game.

I ran a finger through the dust on Tanya's nose. She didn't even blink. "Is she alive?" Jayne asked, in that sardonic way she has. We rang the intercom and someone buzzed us in.

In the hall at the top of the stairs leading to Max's shop a Chinese woman had a little booth selling last week's Orange. Cut rate: it probably only had a few days left in it. Jayne paused, but I wanted the good stuff.

"Wait," Jayne said. "She's selling books, too."

"Books?"

Laid out on the table beside the little twist-tied baggies of Orange were poetry chapbooks, a Xeroxed copy of Kafka's "Metamorphosis," and several copies of a story collection, entitled "Cockroach Culture."

"Art out of life," Jayne said, picking one up. "It seems so real."

"Your posters are like that, too," I said, complimenting her on them again. I can never stop myself. Jayne designed and printed posters for community dances; she ran an old offset in her loft. She had an orphaned laser printer too that still ran but said she preferred the Gestetner; the print quality was warmer, like vinyl sound. She had an uncanny eye for color; I used to wonder where she got it, even worry because I knew she'd used more than once.

"Thanks," she said. "They're Cockroach Culture, too. Here's to it; I like it better than the old one. Maybe if I have any money left I'll get it on the way out. It's not too expensive."

"Printed on recycled stock."

"Home-made recycled stock at that; it's the only affordable paper still in existence. I know; it's my business."

"Speaking of business . . . "

We abandoned our browsing to visit Max. No one answered our knock and the shop door was locked.

On the way back down the hall Jayne said, "You want to hear my secret fantasy?"

"I don't know. Don't you think you want to keep it to yourself?"

"I'll tell you. I'd be Max's girlfriend, lover, whatever. I could be strung out forever. I'd never run out. I could stay here like a pig in shit. Max is the big time, isn't he?"

"Jayne, you scare me. If you got strung out you'd end up on the beach, cutting up your arms at some bonfire party."

"That's never been proven. Hey, looks like I get to buy my anthology after all."

We each bought a baggy of Orange from the vendor and Jayne bought the book, too. "You buzzed us in?" she asked.

The woman pointed at the buttons on the wall behind her. "I do door for Max."

"Oh, and he has an intercom in his room too and you tell him who it is?"

"Yes."

"He must trust you a real lot."

"I'm Lee's sister."

"That explains it then," Jayne said wryly. "By the way, you know there's a newsgirl sitting on the street bench? Only she isn't doing much selling."

The woman sighed and shook her head. "Tanya. I've been telling her for days to go home, get some sleep."

On the way down the stairs Jayne read to me:

"It is the disfigured face that heals us, the monster who kills our monsters for us, those we have created. Lee. I never told the truth about him, never told the truth about Chinatown. We look down on those who carry our pain for us, who wear the face we hide from the world. We have always done this."

"Strong stuff."

"It's true, isn't it?"

Too true, I thought. Like me when I don't think about the butcher at the abattoir, every time I take a bite of meat. Like we also don't think of razors and bonfires every time we buy powder that works. Max knows this too; it's why Lee sells for him, wholesaling to kids. To hide our own part in the newskids' pain we prefer to make racist remarks. But it's not because Lee is Chinese, but because of what he does, that we owe him. It is this debt which is too painful to acknowledge. Not acknowledging it, Jayne and I parted ways to our separate apartments to kill bugs, each of us quite alone.

Predictably, the Orange lasted all of two days. Once again, I walked those brown steps, his steps. Looking for Jayne who hasn't been answering her phone; not looking for Tanya, 'cause I know where she is. She's the known quantity, the one I can't retrieve. It's Jayne who stands on the border, has stepped across it once or twice, always come back. So far.

At the beginning I used to work with Max: factory help, powder production. And then I got tired. Tired of the sleepless nights, the beer, the coffee, the endless low-paid drudgery up and down those dusty stairs of my Chinatown youth. It was only two years ago but somehow it always feels I left my youth behind, there, with that job. When the kids started to get hurt I quit, figuring it was the least I could do.

But I still bought powders.

Max is crazy like they all say to let those kids slash themselves, or have it done, as some say, when they get too greedy, but nobody else is doing anything about the bugs. There is always a price for the salvation we will not attempt ourselves.

Carry a flashlight up the stairs, in case of one of the frequent power outages. Look for my face in Max's own. Dream a new game.

Green. Green of trees, not of powders. Sleeptalker, listener. I dreamed of him last night. He spoke to me, saying, "Don't kill them, let them live." When I woke I said, in answer, "It's easy to be a Buddhist when you're not talking about foot-longs, and I don't mean hot dogs."

Not foot-long yet. But who knows what tomorrow will bring?

In my dream he wore ratty jeans and long, thin brown hair, just like in real life, just like in old photographs of us when we were in high school. Nobody listened to us then when we said the apocalypse was near and it looks like we were right.

Who is it we in turn aren't listening to now? Not forty yet, I still have a chance to do something. Some small thing. Save one life.

Tanya. I can mark the time by her colors, the layers of powder nicked away on her cheek where a piece of plastic from a candy wrapper or a dry leaf has blown against her immobile face.

I looked at her for a moment and went on, to the twenty-four hour Mr. Submarine on Spadina. I bought a large assorted which I somehow knew, don't know how, was the kind she liked. And a large bottle of Evian, although I'm sure she would have preferred Pepsi. I tried to give it to her but her hands remained clasped in her lap and so I set it down on the bench beside her.

A shadow of a smile.

Rich blue and green layered in the folds of her clothing, iridescent peacock colors. Judging by the layers of color she hadn't been home for a bath recently.

The green was a pale green; a Day-Glow with white in it. I'm starting to sound like Jayne, like colors matter. Just as colors. I'd bought extra and stopped by her place on my way home, as I should have done days ago. She was printing; the new posters were blue and orange; colors lush and familiar.

"I hope you feel good cutting those poor kids' arms and legs to ribbons," I said. "So when's the dance?"

"Saturday. You have such a perspective, Jack. So hip, so new, so now. It hasn't been proven. Maybe doing that is just what they do; nothing to do with the powders. How come we aren't doing it, is what I want to know? Not many reasons not to. The way I figure it, the whole ship is gonna be sunk any time now. So we might as well have fun. Cockroach Culture: the last people's culture. It gives a whole new meaning to the words 'save the last dance for me.'"

"Are the colors what I think they are?"

"Yes, as you probably guessed I'm using bug powders. Can't get hide nor hair of printer's ink anymore, and I thought I'd give it a try. The last couple of days of a powder run are never any good anyway, so everyone's got these little twist-tie baggies of colors lying around; happy to unload 'em to me for a song. Cheaper than printer's ink, in fact." She pushed the hair out of her face.

"So that's where you've been the last couple of days; shopping for colors."

"Not that it's any of your business. Also I'm feeling very ecologically correct as they're water based. The colors might fade but who cares: this world will be gone by then."

"But at least you'll have left a slightly cleaner water table behind for survivors."

"Exclusively animal and vegetable."

"One would hope."

"No kidding, Jack."

Watching a really proficient woman work always gets my gonads going so after a while I asked her if she wanted to go out for a few beers when she was done.

"Sure," she said, "but it's Tanya you should be asking out."

"Why?"

"She loves you."

"How d'you know?"

"She told me."

"Well, I like Tanya, Jayne, but she's trouble. She's an addict and you just have fantasies."

"Not for long."

"What are you waiting for?"

"Waiting to know."

"Know what?"

"Tell you sometime, later, not now."

While Jayne washed up and looked for her windbreaker I went and stood at the window. It was so dusty it was almost impossible to see out, but on the ledge stood three printed cards, side by side. Picture divided from caption by a thin dotted line: sun, sky, grass. Things we don't see much of around here. They were beautiful and the fact of their existence, the only decor in Jayne's completely functional shop and living space seemed to speak of a longing and vulnerability I never otherwise saw her betray. I felt like I'd uncovered a secret, although it wasn't anything she'd tried to hide. I turned the cards over; on the back was the English word for each picture, and beside it the Chinese ideogram. They were teaching cards, and yet the purpose she had put them to was quite different.

I could have razzed her about it, but didn't; no one wants their shrines desecrated, especially when they only have such thin lonely ones. Let her show me that side of herself when she was ready, if ever.

We went to the last Chinese grocery and bought homemade beer from under the counter, brown bagged it Montreal-style, and wandered the alleyways. There were stars. It was very romantic.

"Hey Jack," she said, "I'll read to you out of this story collection. It's really awesome."

"Oh, right. That again. So read on: the last bit gave me enough to think about for a week."

"I have a new friend now; someone like Jayne, someone like Tanya. A friendship which makes me feel able to complete these stories I abandoned so many years ago for another kind of life. His name is Jack.

"We will squander our youth in the dark nights of the city, counting

stars, like Max and I did that one night. Like holes in space, he said, space itself like the front of the little fifties bar in the booze can we went to: a sheet of metal with holes drilled in it, letting in tiny points of light like starlight from the light bulb behind it.

"The heavens a vast sheet of metal with drilled holes; if we ripped it away we'd find huge fluorescent tubes, or quartz halogen. Anyway a light too bright; it would make everything look white. This is why the holes are so tiny; it's only a small amount of light we can stand. Surely we need a new metaphor for the sky; it's about time we stopped talking about diamonds scattered on black velvet.

"There is a fable about loving too much, but I can't quite remember what it is. My first thought is Narcissus, looking into a still pond surrounded by green stemmed white flowers, delicate and strong.

"And yet was that a story about love or self-obsession? Is that what I'm doing here, writing like this? Perhaps it is a story that needs to be written.

"Up up the dark wooden stairs to the sooty loft apartment where he worked. At a table red candles in old pewter sticks and an open chemistry book.

"Out his back window I looked out at the few mature hardwoods and felt a communion with them, more intensely than I do in the country. Because of the contrast; because there are less of them. Because I haven't been to the country in years. I wonder if it's still there?"

Jayne shut the book, put it in the back pocket of her jeans, and looked at me, ironic and meaningful.

"He was writing about us," I said, "if the author's a he."

"What else is there to write about?" Jayne asked.

"Let's go home." I wanted to go to her place but huffily figured I wouldn't suggest it; she'd upset me with her talk of fantasizing about Max, her nonsense about Tanya loving me.

Was it possible?

On our way we passed her, still sitting under the light. The sandwich I was glad to see was half eaten and neatly wrapped in several layers on the bench beside her, where the bugs couldn't get at it.

Gutter bugs, in summer.

Saturday afternoon. Every day I've brought Tanya a sandwich and water, but only today have I needed to go up the stairs. Max in his visor, working; Lee sitting at the table, smoking, reading a Chinese newspaper I'll never be able to understand, not in my whole life. Unless I ask him. Like Jayne's shop, too, the surface of the table littered with full ashtrays, empty Styrofoam cups, looped brown rings of coffee. Yellow dust coating everything: the lab, the counter tops, the empty take-out food containers. I put my money on the table.

"Don't you guys feel bad?" I asked.

"Feel bad about what, Jack?" Max asked in that convivial way I was always so fond of in college. I'd loved the way he could brighten a day.

Lee looked up from his paper, smiled hello.

"About the newskids, about Sleeptalker?"

"You don't buy from them anymore, Jack," Max said, "how come? You've come straight to the factory every time this month. You better have a good reason; we don't let everyone in here, you know. It's only 'cause we're old pals."

Lee swung his legs, looking decidedly collegiate and un-sinister. Not saying anything.

"It's cheaper," I lied.

"True, true."

Not saying: " . . . because I can't look at your hands anymore. Because I stay away from abattoirs. Because I was afraid of both of you."

Because people died.

Lee got up and went to a shelf, handed me a newly bagged package of Yellow. "It's the first one with a name, not just a number," he said.

"What's it called?"

"Perilous Yellow," he said, as though that was very funny. I wondered how fast I could leave.

"About the other question," Max said.

I was already at the door, wishing I hadn't opened my mouth. "Yeah?"

"There's an answer to that question, but this isn't the day you get it."

I turned back, hesitantly. "When is?"

"The day you stop buying for good."

I left, my boots resounding on the dusty stairs. I could hear them laughing behind me.

The ventilator open as always and yellow dust swirling out, glowing like a cloud of gnats under the streetlight. She sat there, waiting for the Yellow to coat her eyelids, enter her bloodstream through the skin. Like yellow eye shadow.

I heard stapling and turned; Jayne was on the corner of Spadina, putting up her new posters. The stapling sounded angry.

"Jayne, hi."

"I didn't think much at the time, (bang) Jack, but you really got me mad. Who (bang) are you (bang) to talk about what I do? You support the deaths as much as I do, (bang) by supporting the industry. You could just let them live."

"That's what he said."

"Who?"

"Sleeptalker."

"Now you're dreaming about him. That's a beginning, I suppose."

"What do you mean?"

"Listen, I'll read. The book's by Sleeptalker, as you so obviously didn't notice. It's the details that count, Jack, the details. The details will save you."

"I didn't want to check the author's name at the time. I liked the anonymity of someone writing about me, someone I didn't know. But ever since then I've been wondering. I'd walk the street and everyone I saw, I'd wonder. I thought one day I'd find out, one day I'd talk to them about their stories, the ones I'm in."

"Too late. He's dead."

"Speaking still in dreams."

"And in stories he left behind."

"I wonder if he knew he'd die? If he wrote it to leave behind a part of himself?"

"Isn't that why anyone writes?"

"I wonder what he knew, that got him killed?"

"Max, or Lee, or neither? Maybe he killed himself."

"I don't know."

"You should think about it. Listen, though. There's a bit about China-town. I haven't read it yet." Jayne took the book out of her pocket and opened it. I sat on the curb beside her and read over her shoulder. She turned the rough brown pages, always politely asking first to see if I was ready.

"*Before the evacuation when there were more of them, more of us, more people, aside from the young ones who were our friends and made us ginger tea when we had colds, the Chinese were inscrutable as the old cliché goes; divided from us by language and culture, seemingly having no interest in getting to know us better or else just busy with their lives. They said hello when we came into their restaurants, taking great pleasure as always in their food: mu shu pork and garlic eggplant.*

"*I miss them, now that they're gone, miss the stores I loved, the toys, especially the mechanical metal chicken laying eggs, and the picture cards. The strangeness of an alphabet we could never hope to learn, it's form more like painting, like pictures than like words; this seemed to intimate some-thing we did not have and by nearness would hope to absorb through osmosis. Also the imagery, not drawn in a traditional Chinese style at all: moons and dogs and flowers, sun, grass, sky, window; the western-style graphics were simple and beautiful and clear and while ostensibly to teach Chinese children, or adults for that matter, English, to us they had another purpose. We took them home and shuffled them like oracles, laid them out in neat rows on shelves or windowsills: sun, sky, window; their images resonating with one another. Echo, palpation, vibration: they would assume a Delphic aspect; like tarot cards from another planet we would hope to soak up some of the mystery of a different culture and learn about them and also as always, hoping to learn in the mirror of another some-thing about ourselves.*"

As we sat reading the bugs came and began trying to eat the sweat from our sneakers; we moved up the block, to sit protected at Tanya's feet. I noticed someone had been there before us; at her feet lay a bunch of plastic paper-white narcissi, now turned into yellow daffodils, even the stems, the leaves.

Jayne said, "I didn't know anyone else did that?"

"What?"

"The picture cards, as a tarot deck. I thought I was the only one."

"He knew so much about us," I said.

"He was one of us," she said, "how could he not?"

"Who will tell our stories now?"

"Will we stop killing them?" Jayne asked.

"I don't know. We have to see first."

"See what?"

"What happens to Tanya."

"It's all a circle, don't you see?" Jayne asked.

"We're not immune."

"What does it matter—if he killed himself, if he was murdered. Either way it could happen to us. Don't you feel like suiciding, living as we do?"

"No sign of razor marks on Tanya's arms yet. Good-bye Tanya, I'll be by tomorrow." I kissed her on the forehead. Jayne snickered.

We walked. Jayne said, "I never believed the colors were so bad. I believed, secretly, the way you believe things when you're a child, that they were a doorway. The powders would show you a different way to live. It was the contrast that made them suicidal. Coming down they'd see this," she pointed at the sluggish contents of someone's toilet rising from a storm sewer, "and the pain of it, compared to the beauty they'd experienced, was what made them do it."

Jayne in her scraggly brown hair and dirty ink-stained coveralls made me so hot I barely heard what she said but I knew that was unfair and tried hard to concentrate.

"Why does Sleeptalker tell us not to kill them?" I asked, knowing it was important.

"Because it's not our work."

I realized she was leading me toward the dance hall, in the old temple on Cecil.

We went in, while Jayne read:

"I dreamed we moved to the islands in the harbor. I saw a young woman on a houseboat whose top was made of a camper/trailer and something else beneath the sleeper overhang; a small greenhouse perhaps. A young

woman in iridescent blue and purple clothes steered the boat down the lagoon, and suddenly I realized it was Tanya."

At the dance Max was there, and Lee. All our friends; most of the newskids. No Sleeptalker. No Tanya.

I watched how Max and Lee stayed separate, giving the lie to the camaraderie I'd witnessed in the factory. I watched how in their glances people honored one and hated another, and thought: but doesn't everyone know they are one and the same?

Can't they see?

Jayne and I stayed away from the gossip and the rumors, dancing only with one another, resting on the stage to read from Sleeptalker's book. It was as though we had new eyes. I looked out the window at the full moon and worried.

It rained sporadically throughout the night. I worried about Tanya, thought often I should go back and get her, save the one life. But then Jayne stroked my hair and whispered sweet nothings.

As she said, there's no proof. Am I responsible for another's life, even one who seeks her own undoing? I guess a part of me wanted to see. But I still felt bad.

We had a fun night. Jayne's right: Cockroach Culture is better than the one that went before. Except for the cockroaches. The fires. The razor blades. The deaths; among them, rumored or real, one true one, one I called friend.

But that's not much, really, is it? Compared to everything else, I mean.

After the dance, in the bits of sleep arranged like small still ponds in our first sweet night of lovemaking, I dreamed of Sleeptalker again.

His story was in the dream too, and the picture of Tanya it had conjured in my mind. And Sleeptalker spoke again, over my shoulder as I read his words.

This is the woman to ask about how to live.

It's always after a dance they do it, people say; always after it rains, after a full moon, after a new color hits the streets.

We'd had all four.

It was very early morning when I got up, to go to Chinatown, alone.

Tanya wasn't on her bench.

On a hunch I took the ferry to the island. I went to Snake Island first, I don't know why. Maybe because I used to go there when I was young, camp and party with my friends all night long.

On a path I found a bunch of plastic flowers, tied in string, rain washed and white again. I continued walking until I came to a campsite in a clearing. Tanya sat, drying her sneakers on two sticks over a fire. The fire worried me, but she looked quite sane. I tried for the jocular approach.

"You're safe around fires now?"

"Always have been, Jack. It was your fear that prevented you from seeing me."

"These yours?" I offered her the flowers.

"Oh, thanks, I thought I'd lost those."

"Jayne said it was a circle. Sleeptalker's stories, Max, Lee, the bugs. Does he talk in your dreams, too?"

"He talks to me all the time, not just in my dreams. You can do it too; you just have to listen."

"I guess. You know, he gave me a homemade Roman candle once. We set it off together, four in the morning, middle of Spadina."

"I know," Tanya said.

"You do?"

"Yeah. And you said: "Sleeptalker, you're the only one I know who can make the stars bloom.""

"I said that?"

"He told me. He loved you, Jack. A better line than you usually come up with. Like something he might've said. Or written. So why you here, Jack?"

"To bring you your sandwich."

She smiled and took it, went back to toasting her shoes. I noticed she'd finally bathed, and only a few glints of color remained in her blonde hair.

"It'll taste better than those."

She smiled, reluctantly examined the sandwich. "There's meat in it."

"Yes."

She took a bite. "We can never be blame free, no matter how much we do. But we still have to leave."

"To come here?"

"Leave in our heads. Leaving physically is good, too. I won't be able to stay; I was just getting sick of raw sewage. The boat isn't finished yet; we all take time off newsing to come down here and work on it. Sleeptalker says that as long as we kill the bugs we're doing their work. The people who made it this way. Who made the bugs grow, with their poisons. It's not because of the powders that teenagers kills themselves, but because of the world. Why are any of us still alive? Those kids' deaths are just a way to make us feel guilty, immobilize us. The powders are the only thing we have. Too bad it's also a way for them to get us to clean up their mess."

"So?"

"So that's the fable about the people who love too much."

"What?" I took a bite of her sandwich, thinking it really was time to be a vegetarian again, although it tasted good.

"Us. We clean up after them, with our thoughts, with our guilt, with our powders, even our deaths, our deaths most of all. Loving even them, forgiving even them. They'll make us do it forever. Too much love."

"So what should we do?"

"One thing at a time." She led me to a clearing in the trees. Sleeptalker hadn't seen a place like this, for years before he died.

Through the stands of birch I saw a houseboat, parked in the lagoon. It was built entirely out of junk, had a container garden and a satellite dish on the roof.

"Not only that," she said.

"Not only?"

"There's no bugs. We shouldn't kill them, because they're alive like we are, but we shouldn't have to live with them either."

"Then what should we do?"

"Exodus."

"Where to?"

"We'll think of it along the way," Tanya said. "We'll build it along the way. We have his stories, now to show us the way."

"Sometimes I think I'm going crazy."

Tanya laughed, reaching as though across dream space to stroke my cheek with fingers that felt unusually warm. "Does it matter? How can dreams be any less a reliable guide than anything else? Than them? Desire or so called reality; which will you choose?"

"Why couldn't they just do it quietly, jump in front of a subway or something, like a normal person?" Fires and razor blades made me more than squeamish.

"When's the last time you saw a subway, Jack?"

"True. But even still."

"Even still if you're going out why not go out burning?"

"I'd never thought of it that way." She was the first person I'd heard speak with any kind of inner authority for years. It was compelling, but I worried; perhaps all crazy people did that. And yet we heard the same voice, dreamed the same dreams. It filled a longing so old I'd no longer known I'd once had it, until she'd reminded me: beautiful, scary Tanya. "I really do think I love you, Tanya." I did, too. It was almost frightening; she was so weird.

"It's about fuckin' time."

She hugged me and a little color passed from her hair to mine. I waited in vain for the buzz but it was hard to tell, what with standing in a sun-dappled glade with a beautiful, if possibly demented woman, a vision of the future parked in the lagoon.

"Actually," she said, licking my lip, "the powders don't do anything."

"Now what?" I sounded so smart this morning but Tanya didn't seem to mind.

"It's a metaphor."

"Oh, of course."

"It's the last story. You'll understand when you read it."

"Maybe they work on other people, just not on you."

"Not on me, not on Sleeptalker. You're getting warmer, Jack."

I raised my hands up to touch my face, to wonder at skin that had been cold, it seemed, for years. She was right.

ONCE

WAS IT BIOWARE, OR DRUGS? EXPLOSIVES OR MILITARY secrets from the fragmented Soviet Union, peddled to you by disenfranchised scientists, making barely enough money to live on?

You never said much, although once you let me play on the phone, telling me what words to say to a woman in Prague, English words, and yet I didn't understand them. I'd heard you have those conversations too, with strangers in hotel bars where, while you'd talk, you were always wary of the possible hidden mikes, the cochlear implants sitting three tables away. Words like 'come over', 'get across', 'bridgework', 'fragmentation', 'desire', 'disease'. Only to you these words didn't mean what they meant to me but something else, something I never learned. The words could be scrambled to make sentences, their meanings encrypted. On the payphone you told me to ask: "Did desire get over into fragmentation or disease?"

And someone answered, "Afua will do bridgework on Friday, at two p.m."

I told you and you nodded.

I think you were seeing how far I'd go. I think you were thinking of taking me on, as an apprentice. Taking me into The Game, your game, and you had to see. If I'd obey orders without asking questions. If I'd trust you to keep me safe. If I'd say words without knowing what they meant.

You said you'd tell me later, over a drink. But you never did. I guess I didn't pass. It seems odd now; you could've just lied. You could've made something up if you didn't think I was ready. Didn't have it in me.

Sometimes I think you really didn't care whether you died, and sometimes I think you possessed a secret that kept you from harm.

Now, sometimes, I think I could've been shot just for knowing you. For being someone you loved. As a weapon.

Why did I choose to share that life with you, a life I had no understanding of? It was a glimpse into another world, one that worked by different rules. It was the closet anarchist in me I suppose that was attracted; you paid no heed to governments, to laws. You said you did it, not because you believed in any of what you bought and sold particularly, but that you had an intense need to be free. You couldn't live by others' rules.

You paid my air fares, all over the world, for seven years.

A true romantic.

I live in Vancouver now, in a house with a garden in the east end. I have psilocybin mushrooms growing in my backyard, sprouting out of the manure I dig into my delphiniums to inspire them to greater heights. There are peonies too, and foxgloves and rhododendrons. In the mornings I sit in the yard, reading my mail. Mail has been important to me for as long as I can remember—those links made. I still prefer it to e-mail; the feel of paper, the sight of handwriting, the smell. I don't mean perfumed stationery, I mean the smell of my friends. Perhaps my nose has grown more sensitive, or perhaps it's my imagination, but I swear I can smell my friends sometimes, when I open their letters.

Actually I have a secret I don't share often; it was expensive, a frivolity: a few years ago I had my nose done. It was one of the first of the new implants that became available—and popular too. Although why should it be popular—so much less useful, after all, than a new language. Or improved vision. Or hearing.

It was important to people like you, who sometimes needed to be able to smell things. Things in glassine envelopes. Powders. Brown ones, white ones, pink.

In places where no labs were available, for chemical analysis, the nose could do a lot.

Me? I'm a gardener, and I love the smell of flowers, and wanted only to regain what I'd lost by smoking, and perhaps augment the original a little.

If I'd known I would smell my friends on their letters I might not have done it. Memory can be painful—and irresistible. It's hard to find people who will write handwritten letters anymore—even those who use the post mostly write on computers. Handy for typos, the spell-checks and all. No one can spell anymore.

But me? I feel we have hurtled much too quickly into the future. How can it be modern anymore to use e-mail? Of course, there are people only buying their first PCs now. People in the Amazon, in the Andes, or in Bangladesh.

We never thought of these people much, when we were having our information revolution. So intense, so fast.

But now they are saying things. We are hearing their voices at last. All over the net we are hearing their voices now, at so many forums and conferences, so many users' groups.

They are changing the world, with the things they say.

Perceptually.

I on the other hand, feel someone must go the other way. I love books and handwriting. To me, now, this seems the very essence of modernity; to love these things, to use them.

Except for my implant, although I turn it off for weeks at a time. That is my secret. And you.

I eat mushrooms once every two years, in the fall. *Psilocybe cyanescens:* the small blue ones that grow in my yard, beneath the delphiniums. I have a native friend, a Haida artist who says they are very rare, very special. He comes to harvest them too, but we never eat them together, although we are very good friends. In the main, we have different things to see, different spirits whose shelter or intervention we need.

Spirits to catch.

Or to give thanks too.

Although once we did, just once:

It was deep summer and I had mushrooms I'd dried from the previous year. We ate them, sat and drank tea, and talked and at last the house seemed too small around us, too enclosing, tight.

We went outside and walked along the road. We were in the country, at a place of his.

In the swamp alongside the road the bullfrogs sounded like nothing so much as jazz musicians, mournfully practicing scales on their trombones and double basses. In the night sky there were shooting stars, and at our feet, in the bushes along the road, fireflies swarmed. It seemed as though they were a mirror for the shooting stars overhead; it must have been August, the Perseid meteor shower.

Sometimes nature rearranges itself into exquisite metaphors, as though exclusively for one's own benefit.

"As above, so below," I said. I used to practice Wiccan magic, when I was in my twenties, in-between trips with you. It was the first religion I ever came across that meant anything to me. Since then, I have learned that it too is a shell, a husk, though a very beautiful one. Now I do things just with my mind, with my thoughts. Effect change in the world, in those around me.

My sculptor friend and I weren't saying very much, not having need to. It felt as though words would diminish the heightened sensory input, the amount of awe one could possibly contain at one moment, and I think he, like I, wanted to make himself large, be a receiver for just as much wonder as he possibly could. Awe of what? The profound intelligence of nature.

His name was Peter.

I won't give his last name, for obvious reasons.

The sacred plant is still illegal. Although genetic engineering isn't. And nuclear warheads. And the sale of children is practiced daily.

I know this is something else you do, in passing, while you do your other work. Save children about to be bought, or sold. You told me, the first few years, when I still heard from you.

Because, you said, each of them might be your son.

"For every star, a soul," Peter said.

Destiny.

So beautiful one couldn't fairly put it into words.

I think that is the moment when everything changed, when I made a deep internal shift that altered everything, my whole future, and, if mine, possibly also the world's.

We think our choices are not so significant, and by and large we are right; they're not. Because we don't dare.

Perhaps I am only making the choice now; I don't want to give too much import to the plant. I pray that I am making the right choice.

You and I parted ways; I choosing a quieter path, one that allowed more time for reflection, for security. I chose a life where children were possible. Emotional security—you were never short of cash and parlayed it into investments, which, if you nurtured them well, would have bought you the possibility of early retirement. Unlike myself. I live on residuals from a computer game I wrote twenty years ago and regularly update—it proved much more successful than I would have expected.

It was a cross between a treasure hunt and those adventure novels they had for children where you could choose different courses of action, roaming backwards and forwards through the pages of the book as though you were traveling the permutations of time.

The most interesting thing for me, in reading those books of my son's, which in themselves imitated the structure of games, is that I would became aware of the mathematics of probability, of possibility. Of how one small choice, seemingly infinitesimal, could influence much larger outcomes, outcomes that would change lives, countries, worlds.

Chaos theory, I know.

Destiny? What is destiny in the face of that?

Destiny was the name of my game. I called it The Game, too, in memory of you. Destiny, The Game. Perhaps you've heard of it. I played trickster, writing it; it wasn't how many evil aliens you blasted that won or lost you the Earth, but how much you trusted yourself, how you carved your own path through the forest of possibilities.

How you listened for your own destiny, or perhaps, how you smelled it out.

I loved writing it, perhaps more than I loved you. Anyway, it was different.

I thought it would be a little offside, find a cult audience among the artier game players, those who still liked to read literary novels, possibly to garden. Humanities people who had computers because they had to, for work. But not a game for hard core nerds or testosterone driven teenage boys. Nothing against them; I had one myself, and adored him more than, well, you, for starters.

Kids are like that. A deeper, stronger bond. No wonder the men wander: off to wars, into space, across those fluid nightmare borders, into countries whose names are always changing . . . dealing in . . . what?

Strange, but I caught a wave. People loved Destiny. How did I know there were so many others out there who thought like me?

Of course, I didn't know. I did the only thing I could (I have never been much good at anything else). I followed my heart, wrote the game I'd love to play.

I still play it.

In my life, not on the screen.

But who knows what you did? Who indeed, knows anything about you?

I remember Germany, the stairs of a house you had in Berlin, near Käthe Kollwitz Platz. You had something to do, somewhere to go, but at the end of our night in the clubs you lent me your canopy bed in the Persian-lined top floor apartment you kept for yourself—even going so far as to climb the stairs with me, turn the sometimes recalcitrant key in the lock, because you knew the trick. We stroked each other's jackets, giving rise to a feeling that could only be described as painful. As though our lives were so dangerous we might really never see one another again.

As perhaps they were.

That is why I had the implant. Because I have never again lived as intensely as I lived with you. Because smell is the heart and root of memory. Because I have three things of yours. A Japanese money clip, with inlay of bamboo leaves. A Chinese carved ivory bracelet, in the shape of a dragon, biting its tail. It is very old, from before the ban. A shoe. It is the shoe that fell off your foot, the last night we were together, when you had to run. That one took a lot of explaining. You disappeared into the night, as quickly, as soundlessly as a cat, but then, you'd always told me you could do that. At any moment. Of any day. Out of my life. After the first few years, no longer any mail. Maybe that's why I have this mail thing. Sometimes my friends, when they write, ask me about you. But it frightens me, and I only write back to the ones who write in hand-writing, on paper. Because then I can smell who they really are.

I don't touch your things, keep them in a bell jar. Ritually, once a year, I put my implant in; I take them out and I smell them.

And am with you again.

In Germany, that trip, we drank. Once a week, after all your meetings were done, we'd get a bottle and kill it. Of Irish Whisky.

Do you remember the ceremony we always had to make of killing the bottle? Do you remember the time when, the bottle having reached its skeletal state, its life blood having drained into our own, we gave it a funeral? Do you remember how, in order to show our appreciation, we stood it beside the Reichstag and filled it with flowers we'd picked in the garden? It was too dangerous, I think now. You did it for me, for us, so that for one night we could pretend we were living a life of frivolous romance, like all the others.

That was the one summer, of all the summers we spent together, when I felt you were truly in love with me. Or perhaps it was I with you? That was the summer our son was conceived. It was in June, when we still went out alone together. Later, in August, under showers of meteors, there was always Katrina. You worked with her. And perhaps more.

I didn't mind; we'd never owned one another, except now, she was always there and it hurt. It was after I told you I intended to keep the child. You became distant, withdrawn; you told me there was no place for a child in The Game, your game, a game of, above all else, sleight of hand. Or sleight of body: the ability to appear and disappear, to change your name, your passport, even, once, you said, your fingerprints. A child would only attract attention, danger. Of course you were right, but I wanted the child. And so you inducted Katrina into the game, instead of me. Your other lover/apprentice. Sex bought loyalty, the promise of closed lips, you said, and also, you loved us both. It was quite obvious to me you did; it wasn't a lie, it was just by different rules.

And I settled down with my baby and twenty thousand dollars from you, with which I made a down payment on a rather ratty old house, which had, nevertheless, a large yard and an old perennial garden. Twenty thousand—a rather small parting gift, considering. Child support in advance; I knew I'd never see you again. I settled down and wrote computer games to make a living, and eventually, I lucked out with The Game. Which I realize belatedly, I copied from yours.

I too have a secret mission. To save us from rushing too quickly into the future. To remind those working with these new energies (for they are new, and transformative) that they were allowed into being for a reason; to be a mouthpiece for the Earth herself. Why I love games, working with computers; it returns us to a right brained culture, a culture of pleasure and play. It reconnects us to the so-called primitive within ourselves . . . connecting to the Earth in a more direct, immediate way, bordering, at times, on the telepathic. To oversimplify: tribal peoples were right brained; an oral tradition is right brained. We cannot go backwards, and so we go forward into the past—our machines will give us back what we have lost.

Direct connection. As though, internally, in our subconscious, in our bodies, electronic media function less as a technology than print. Language that always distances. Now we tell stories, our own stories, by pushing keys on a keyboard, by reading images.

Paradox.

Information. The metaphor still holds; at bottom it's always information: code, arms, drugs, thoughts. That is all we are selling in the end: the thought-clothes we wear, readable by others as readily as changing fashions, whether we acknowledge it or not. And that is why I'm a witch and you're a renegade.

Witches always loved the Goddess first, the Earth. We had no choice; it has always been she who gave us our power to read minds, to feel the energies of plants and trees and stones.

And most importantly, of people.

You, too, must have known that—how to read a stranger, to know whether she held betrayal or safe passage across the burning border. Which did I hold, for you?

Of course we all have those places inside ourselves. I'm always drawn to them; I've explored my own darkness with the diligence of a fetishist; how could I blame you for doing any less? Who's to say you learned any less about yourself than I did, following Persephone?

That's why I settled down, really: not to no longer be afraid for my life and yours; not to be solvent (you always had more money than me, than I made even after I wrote Destiny), not even to raise our child, quietly and alone, but to have time to dive.

What did you do?

Got your scuba license, one more ticket to add to your list.

Funny haha, or funny peculiar?

As though we were two parts of a binary star, revolving always around one another; one exploring the inner world, one the outer.

Your son looks like you.

I hang my head in shame and cry for what we were not able to do, namely, raise him together.

For many years my children nurtured me as much as I nurtured them, if not more. Schedules and nursing, school lunches and whooping cough all served to cure me of the life of danger I'd lived with you, when I neglected my own life path so persistently it all but disappeared from the forest floor, obscured by scrub.

My daughter, obviously, is not yours. She is Peter's, and is as unlike my son as you are from my sculptor friend. We too, did not manage to carve a life under the same roof although, unlike you, he lives on the same coast as me and spent a great deal of time with his daughter while she was growing up. She is seventeen; my son is twenty-two. She goes home every summer, to Masset, in the Queen Charlottes. She calls it home. She is becoming a carver, not a traditional thing for a woman to do. My son has no such root to ground him; he is restless, and I grow pensive, watching him. Thinking how he takes after you.

I no longer think so much about means, but about ends.

And I think it is how you lived that was more important than what you bought and sold.

Because you lived free. And that is what you sold: the idea of freedom, of self-direction.

I think also you were always careful not to kill anyone. You never forgot that every life was important.

Passwords can be stolen, messages rerouted, handwriting forged. On e-mail, how do I know anyone is who he says he is?

Although, why should I worry? What do I have to say about you?

Gossip, poetry. Your legacy is my game. As though we wrote it together, it's so informed by your life.

But perhaps you were so dangerous that even gossip about you could spread like wildfire, wreaking havoc. Sometimes I hear things on the net. About a man called Helmut. He too, has stopped traveling. Does most of his work on computers now. Of course, that was only one of the many names you used.

Sometimes I leave messages for him, on lists I know he might read, which I'm not supposed to know how to access, but there are a few things I did learn from you. Explosives experts, arms traders, drug manufacturers. Killers. Yes, of course there is a net group for killers. Not that you ever were one. But you knew some.

I tell you about your son, how he loves The Game. He is blonde like you. I wonder, sometimes, if you aren't necessary? If some of what you do doesn't make peace, and not only war? It is a delicate equation, the witch's inner vision versus the outlaw's action. So much now, can be done with viruses. With worms strategically placed to seek out key files in multinationals' systems.

Our son, too, knows his way around the Net . . . he too, has made friends. He found your letters to me, from the old days. He guesses, not that they give much away. He drops your name, Helmut Schnabel. He wants in; I can feel it. There are always those eager to induct new players into The Game, a game where skilled lives are necessary yet expendable. If he will go that way regardless, whether I want him to or not, I want him to have as good a teacher as I would've had. I want him to have you.

And so I leave messages, hinting. But I tell you to write me a letter, pencil on paper. Because I don't want an impostor to answer; I want someone who will care for his life as much as for their own. Someone who will teach him to play as safely as himself. A father.

And because, when the letter comes, I will take out the shoe, its smell strengthened one night by adrenalin. I will turn on my implant, and placing them side by side, I will know.

We are all falling stars.

REPAIR

BEFORE THE WAR, BEFORE THE NEWS ITEMS ABOUT exploding dishwashers killing families of five, before she began traveling, Mandy used to visit her friend Sam. His house was filled with washing machines and televisions and eight-track decks piled six deep against the walls. Coffee-makers, IBM XT clones, toaster ovens, microwaves, DustBusters, waffle-irons, sandwich makers, Beta VCRs, and electric toothbrushes. Sam found the broken appliances on the streets, brought them home, fixed them if he could, resold if there were buyers. Supply always far exceeded demand. That was the thing; Sam didn't know how to say no to a motor. And Mandy didn't know how to say no to Sam; she visited often. It wasn't a romantic thing, but she was fascinated by his obsession; he was the only person she knew who didn't pretend there wasn't a war. She liked being near him, soaking up his fearlessness around electrical cords.

His upstairs bedroom boasted thirteen clock radios and five vintage pole lamps, but at least there was a bed. A real bed, too: not twelve obsolete VCRs pushed together to make the mattress platform. Mandy wouldn't have been surprised. One entire wall of the kitchen was lined with refrigerators. They were all plugged in, too, wreaking havoc with Sam's electric bill. He didn't seem to care, thinking to provide energy for his hapless machines more important than groceries and decent clothing. Sam wore corduroys worn ribless at the knees and cheap sneakers that took on an indeterminate color between grey and beige the third time he wore them, and stayed that way.

He'd be sitting in the kitchen when she came, at a chrome and Formica dinette set, the foam pushing out of rips in the plastic chair coverings. A bottle of rubbing alcohol would be sitting on the table, as well as Q-Tips and oil of wintergreen, for cleaning and restoring the rubber in fan belts and pinch rollers. The innards of a tape recorder would be spread out like the pieces of a jigsaw puzzle, but he'd always push them aside to chat, happy to start up a grinder and a Braun in service of the coffee beans she'd brought. But that was all a long time ago; now Mandy travels, yet she misses him.

Or perhaps it's his house she misses. Sturdily built of red brick, it's the kind of house she grew up in, the kind of house she's never lived in since she left home. It's as though a secure life is something that could only belong to others. She travels; her friends buy houses, eliciting in Mandy a response of both longing and revulsion. Fact is, it's the clutter that frightens her: houses are always filled with closets and basements, walls of cardboard boxes in each. Perhaps that is also why she's drawn to Sam; he dares to be different, just has rooms full of other's people's worn out machines. He's the only person she knows who doesn't have boxes of old clothes and books. For all his junk, Sam is remarkably box free, and this imparts a kind of secret, unassuming genius.

When she's camping, Mandy dreams she does live in a house. She's always so happy to have her own house at last, but then she goes into the living room and sees the boxes. She sits down in the shadowy room, begins to sort. The sun shines through the old-fashioned, too small windows, and she laments, wishing she was outside enjoying it. But the boxes.

Photographs; family trees; unpublished memoirs; ownerships to vehicles that have been sitting on blocks for years, will now, probably never come down off them. Once good cardigans with tiny moth holes eaten at the edges of the pockets; pleated wool skirts; unhappy childhood memories, passed on replete with the discomfort they engendered, never entirely eschewed. In her dreams the boxes are passed on to her by her parents and grandparents. There are tiny yellowed notes taped to the sides: "This one goes to Mandy—good winter things, shoes."

In real life the stuff sits in her father's garage, in her brother's basement. Her brother has a spouse, children, a house. Sometimes she thinks her relatives dare her to get a house, with their endless safekeeping of these objects. No sooner will she have moved in than she'll hear the screech of tires in her driveway, and go outside to see their gleeful legacy to her; a mountain of goddamn cardboard boxes. And so she doesn't.

She lives in tents and apartments, has now, for ten years. In lofts with one whole wall of windows and hardly any stuff. But as she travels, hikes alone along some mountain ridge, she knows the house is inescapable, that somewhere, in some city, there is a two story yellow brick house with an attic and a basement; a covered porch and upstairs bedrooms; a kitchen to organize and cook in and clean every day of her life; a living room with an old floral couch and an out of tune piano. It is a house with her name on it, calling to her, even though she doesn't know where it is.

Once during a trip she comes to a medium-sized city with a river winding through it. There is the clock tower she saw once in a dream; surprisingly, Carl Jung taught her to fly to its peak. She wasn't even in analysis at the time; she was just reading "Memories, Dreams and Reflections." She was good at flying, though; it was only the weight of the cardboard boxes tied to her shoelaces that eventually dragged her down.

She cuts her trip short, saying, "This is where my house must be. This is where the inner world meets the outer." She rents an apartment, waits. Thinks she's ready, walks the leafy residential streets, deep green lawns pegged by mature hardwoods, but instead of finding her house she makes friends and gets a job, counseling troubled teenagers who find their families burdensome. One day she's out walking a friend's dog, and she comes across a house she recognizes. But it's Sam's house, not hers. Sam's house still has the stronger magnetism. It's happened before. She's found his house in other cities where she's settled for a few months or a year. Visited him those times too, yet somehow she forgot—accordioned all his houses into the first house, the Vancouver one. Fact is, it's always been the same house; Sam's house has been moving, following her through her war.

She goes up to his kitchen. He sits there as he always does, shuffling through a pile of yellowed claim chits. She bought a pound of the strongest Columbian dark roast at the gourmet coffee store to take back to her flat, but instead she sets it between them on the table. He's doing the paperwork on stoves and refrigerators today.

"Who do they belong to?" she asks.

He dissembles. "People used to come every day," he says, "to bring me appliances, but no one's come for such a long time." His thin hands caress her paper-wrapped gift; he begins to untie the first of the many careful knots she has left there. The knots are also a gift, to the trigger finger of his memory. She takes one of the seven electric kettles that stand sentinel on the length of the stained counter top, which houses not one, but four built in dishwashers. Mandy wonders why he needs so many, considering how infrequently she's seen him eat. She prepares to fill the kettle, but her hand slips on the smooth surface of the tap. "You could leave," she says. She watches his fingers fold back the paper lips of the package, releasing the rich, secret aroma of the dark powder, a wash of many things long forgotten.

"You always bring such good coffee," he says. She neglects the kettle, the running water. "How could I leave? I wouldn't leave unless they came back for their machines." Water floods over the spout of the kettle that sits forgotten in the sink, forgotten by all but the sink itself. The sink remembers the kettle; stainless steel reflects chrome in a silver colored duet.

"D'you think they'll come back?" she asks.

She knows it hasn't been so very long since he was twenty, sitting in cafés with his friends. He'd only just begun collecting junk; it was before they began to deliver. In those days he still went out. His hands were different then, she remembers, graceful and young looking. Hands innocent of the rough touch of sandpaper, rubbing away at corroded electrical contacts, at the sadness of elements so long in disuse they have forgotten their true purpose: to cook the food and save the time of their patient masters.

"I don't know." Hands wearied by disdain let fall a sheaf of claim chits; they surge to the floor in a yellow surf. "They weren't bad people. They didn't mean to lie. They just forgot."

"Just like we forgot, you and I." But she wonders what it is Sam's forgotten.

Shipments came to his door every day for the duration of the war. He slept through most of the fighting, dreaming long dreams of a soldier's life. While he slept his house grew; it expanded into a hospital for the wounded: the thousands of lonely, discarded household appliances. He has tape recorders people brought him six years before, asked him to repair. They always promised they'd be back in a week, but few ever came. It seems to make him sadder now than it used to.

He drinks his coffee black, but she takes milk, so he opens the refrigerators one by one; the Kenwoods, the General Electrics, the Westinghouses, and her favorites, the squat and jolly fifties Frigidaires. In the last of the Frigidaires he finds a can of condensed milk.

"I think it's still good," he says, peering cautiously into the yellow encrusted opening.

The milk is just a little off, but Mandy doesn't mention it. They sit together at the long counter, sipping their coffees, and Mandy thinks of the Frigidaires of her childhood: plump, happy, well fed Frigidaires, their enamel stomachs full with meat and vegetables, their hunger for human partnership sated by juice, milk, eggs and cheeses. She feels so sorry for these empty refrigerators; she'd like to bring each of them some small thing: a lemon, a jar of seafood sauce, a half empty bottle of soda water left over from a party.

They drink their coffee; Sam shuffles through his decks of file cards. Now and again he pulls one out to show her, as though he felt certain, that of all people, Myrna George would be back for her yellow Maytag washer and drier set. They had been such enthusiastic machines, she had told him, a playful couple, singing through their work like twin canaries. "I've gotten old," he says, looking up at her. "But you're still young. How did it happen?"

Mandy reaches across and smooths the hair out of his eyes. His hand moves, tenuously across the faded Formica, closing around her own. She holds his hand and thinks about the war. Very early on her best girlfriend Shereen was strangled late at night by her vacuum cleaner. That was when Mandy left, on her first trip, to walk through mountains where machines couldn't follow.

"Come live with me, Mandy," Sam says.

"I can't," she says. "I like you Sam, a lot, but I could never live with all this stuff. I wouldn't be able to sleep at night; I'd think they were coming to get me."

"When they've all been reclaimed, then?" he asks hopefully.

Mandy sighs, leafs through a scrapbook Sam has made, full of clippings about the war. "Why are the machines so angry?" Sam will know if anyone does.

"They're being used to do things people should have been doing for themselves."

"I thought that's why we made them, was to help us with the work."

"The purpose of cleaning has always been to order the soul, defrag the community. When people began using machines for cleaning they stopped doing it consciously, with attention. The machines are upset; they don't mind the work but they want people to know they have feelings too." He shows Mandy a photograph of an iron scalding a man's arm, with intent.

"People hoped if they got new ones they'd be nicer, right?"

"It just made things worse." He turns the page. "Here's the one about that woman whose electrical things all short-circuited when she walked in the room. Everything that was on. The last time it happened the house caught fire and burned down. No one got out alive."

"More mutiny. Well, I'm glad someone figured it out."

"You thought I was just killing time, right? And how was your war?"

"Oh, okay. I learned how to fly in my dreams."

"That's nice."

She's suddenly very tired. "I have to go now." It's the weight of the boxes, calling to her to attend to them. They want her to go home and sleep, she knows, and unpack them in her dreams again. Perhaps she could get Carl to teach her how to levitate them, so they aren't so heavy.

Sam gets up and goes into the bathroom. She hears the sound of an electric shaver, followed by a WaterPik. She wonders who they belonged to, before they belonged to Sam. She pokes her head in the door and asks.

"They're Bob Morton's," Sam says cheerfully, reading the ticket. "I'm just borrowing it. They like it when you use them." Sam peers at the tag, reading. "He's coming back for it on Thursday. I can hardly wait. There's a whole box full of fixed toothbrushes waiting for a turn. I worry about the ones I don't get around to using."

She doesn't tell Sam that Mr. Morton won't be back on this or any other Thursday afternoon. She remembers the newspaper article; it must have been one of the few that Sam missed. Robert Morton died in the war, of complications following concussion when his television fell on him. He couldn't take his shaver with him, or his WaterPik, for that matter.

"Tell me if you change your mind," Sam says, as she buttons her coat.

"I might, too," she says, too embarrassed to ask where the stairs are, feeling momentarily lost in his endless upstairs hallways.

In the city there is a café. She talks Sam into going out for coffee the next afternoon. There are plants and afternoon light and the timeless, aimless, congenial feel of bohemian afternoons: drinking cappuccinos, listening to jazz on the radio, reading their horoscopes in the paper. The change of scene seems to be doing Sam good.

"Fuck it," she says, biting into her pita stuffed with avocado, cream cheese, sprouts, tomatoes and black olives; her favorite kind of café food.

"Fuck what?" he asks. He is designing circuit boards on the back of his napkin, quite happily, it seems.

"Fuck the fucking machines. Fuck the appliances. Nobody's ever going to come back for them. They all died in the war."

"The war?" Sam sounds puzzled, as though without his scrapbook, he has forgotten all about the war. Mandy is patient; she knows that during the fighting people began storing even the things they were supposed to remember themselves in machines. It's a kind of electronic amnesia.

"You remember, the war between human beings and household appliances. People using their machines for three years and then abandoning them, not knowing they contained people's memories, their power for self-determination. At least some of them brought their machines to you. They knew you couldn't turn them down. You had the heart they were lacking, the guts, the courage. They were ignorant cowards. But it was better than just taking them to the dump."

Afternoon light diffracted through the glass of a café window, overlooking the river. Water, winding its path through her life, disturbing it just a little, so that the images ripple and she senses the reality behind the dream. But why does her life so often seem like a dream? Why can't she take objective reality at face value, like other people? But no, for her it's always: "Who's that masked man?" Who's that masked reality?

This question of where to be on the outside of her life seems especially important now. It must match her inner reality, her inner needs, in a way she has never found necessary before. Junk into jewels. A big box she opens and is suddenly happy with the contents, instead of feeling burdened by them. That is what she hopes to dream of now. She plans it every night, before she goes to sleep. But no luck yet.

"Just leave them?" Sam asks.

"You heard me."

"But where would I go?"

"On a trip. With me. You could always come back if you changed your mind."

"I haven't traveled in years."

"I know. And I've done very little else. I'd keep going, but every city I end up in, I always find your house, you. It always stops me."

"That's interesting. I don't remember moving."

"You don't. You've still got the same house, right? I think it's following me; it moves in your sleep. You sleep a lot, remember? You slept through the war. You'd wake up every time I visited, 'cause I brought good coffee. But it was always in a different city. It grew, too; surely you noticed that."

"Sure, Mandy. I bet you know what I ate, too."

"Coffee and cigarettes, mostly."

"You really found me every place you went?"

She looks out the window, at the river. "It's not like I wanted to, Sam. It just happened."

The truth is, it's something else she'd like to say. She'd like to say, "Come live in my house with me. It's made of yellow brick. It's different than yours: there's a garden, and a piano. Old perennials in the garden: lupines, phlox, peonies. Daffodils and lilacs in the spring." Except she can't offer it, because she doesn't know where it is.

In her dream she unpacks boxes. Old camping cookware, ugly acrylic sweaters, Corningware dishes, lamp shades, green and white striped plastic tomato hats, five packages of gardening gloves. Then come several extremely heavy boxes; these contain years of Harrowsmith and National Geographics. A lighter box: knitting needles, unused envelopes, spools of thread, yarn. She sets aside the envelopes for herself and the knitting things for a friend who actually knows what purl means, and how to do it. Everything else will be carted off to the Sally Ann, except for one pair of gardening gloves and the camping dishes. Another heavy one; books. Reader's Digest compressions, Robert Ludlum and Danielle Steele go in the out pile; she'll keep the dictionary, the synonym finder and the thesaurus; you can always use an extra one of those.

It's a lot of work, taking days, weeks, years. Funny how years can go by, even in a dream. She looks at her hands; they've aged like Sam's. One box to go; she rips off the first layer of packing tape, taking half the box's lid with it. She sighs; her hands attacking the tape look veined and worn. Life is nasty, brutish and short. You unpack other people's boxes and when you're finally finished and ready to lead your own life you die. Or at least, your hands look like you've worked as a dishwasher for the past twenty years.

The last box contains for once not mismatched bowling shoes but life, a misplaced life when people had their own power, instead of giving it away to machines. Also, surprisingly, it contains a very pleasant life, all her own, a life she shares with Sam. Suddenly she knows everyone must unpack their boxes, down to the very last one; the bottom one is always the one containing the longed for treasure. If only the top boxes in the stack weren't so scary, almost as scary as vacuum cleaners.

She tells Sam, all except the last part. She doesn't want him to think it's destiny; there's got to be his choice, too. He sits there, drawing circuit boards on the backs of napkins.

She has gone to meet him, at the café. On her way she found an open store, and bought a pound of coffee. She watched the long string as it wrapped around and around her parcel: at once protection and imprisonment. For the memories that aren't ready to emerge yet, the boxes still too heavy to unpack, the ranges with too much life left in them to take to the dump. As always, they talk about the war.

"It's not the machines' fault, even though a lot of people would like to make it so. Maximum security for rechargeable flashlights, electric chair for dishwashers."

"The dishwashers are the worst," he says, "really hardened."

"No hope for rehabilitating the dishwashers. But if we'd used them properly they wouldn't have turned against us. Everybody forgot."

"I didn't forget," Sam says.

"I know," she says. "You forgot something else."

"I know. If only I could remember what it was. Are you going to order?"

"I think I'll have the poppy seed cake today. And a cap. Hey look," she puts her parcel down. "I brought you coffee. You can take it home with you. Then you'll still have it in the morning if your house moves again."

"Planning another trip, are you? The jazz show starts in fifteen minutes. Life becomes very real when you've cut through enough shit."

"Gotten rid of enough of other people's garbage."

"You mean boxes, I believe."

"Perhaps in my case," she says. "In your case, we're talking twenty-five obsolete VCRs."

"I'm sorry, Mandy," he says. "I'd like to dump them, but I just can't. My heart would break, and besides, I've been planning to build an editing system out of them for years."

"The VHS," she says, exasperated. "You couldn't do it with the Beta ones."

She walks, her heart heavy with sorrow for her friend and the burden he has chosen to bear, but after a time she forgets. She forgets Sam in his house with the ticking of clocks and the humming of radios, the sighs of sad stoves and dejected dishwashers. He is the custodian of their disrepair; he waits for them all. She knows Sam would like more than anything to dream a new game, but he can't do it alone.

She travels again, comes to another city. She rents an apartment and longs for a house. She thinks she'll find it soon, her yellow brick house, speakers holding the windows open, spilling jazz into the peony garden where she sits talking with her friends, drinking iced tea and eating Pillsbury lemon cake. But she doesn't, and the war is now so escalated she doesn't even find Sam's house. She waits a year to find it, and then she leaves. She's always found his house within a year before.

Years and cities, better counseling jobs and more expensive apartments, Mandy's loss of memory the detritus of a war she inherited but never made.

Her apartments are free of the simplest electrical appliances; her hands begin to resemble her faded dream hands, ever since the dishwasher that came with the flat broke. She never had it repaired; the only person she'd trust to do it properly is Sam, and she's lost her inner compass for his house. She does her wash at the laundromat. The laundromats are crowded now; there's been very few cases of reported machine murder in public coin washes. Still she always hurries, does her folding at home.

Sam sits alone in his house, with all of their throwaway electric hearts, and his own, still human heart grows larger and sadder to accommodate them all. He begins to think humans have lost the war. People who can afford it are replacing their major appliances every six months now. There are no reported cases of assault by an appliance under six months old.

———

On her trip Mandy stops once in a small town, driving in every day from her campground so she can complete a course in small engine repair; it's time she got over it, she figures. It's the only way the war will ever end. And afterwards, her endless dream boxes are easier to unpack.

Sam sees it in his dream, too, and is immensely relieved. His hands look a little younger when he wakes.

Mandy comes again to a city, buys coffee. Walks up the streets, up the hill, as though following other footsteps. Pushes open the door of the big, brick house, which she realizes, has lately gotten a coat of yellow paint, that pale yellow she loves. The interior smells the same. Solder, rotted wiring, chipped enamel paint. Up, up the stairs to the shadowy kitchen where he sits, asleep at the table.

Without waking him up she plugs in the kettle. She makes coffee, and when the aroma of it fills the kitchen Sam sits up and smiles, seeing it is she.

"Coffee's on," she says.

"We did pretty good last time," he says. "Didn't we? Made progress. We even went out a couple of times, somewhere, I forget."

"A café," she says, "with jazz and a view of the water."

"Great food, wasn't it? You know, I'm starved."

"We'll just have one cup here and then we can go out again. So why's your house yellow now?"

"I remembered something while you were on your trip. That I always wanted to live in a yellow house, my whole childhood. It's important to do things as an adult you wanted as a kid, even if you think your wants are different, now you're grown up."

"You painted it?" Mandy smiles secretively, sipping her coffee.

"I had it done."

They walk, hand in hand. She notices their hands look about the same age now. When they get to the waterfront there is indeed a café, and a store front beside it, with a "For Rent" sign.

"Why don't we rent it?" she says. "The war seems to be pretty well over. People will be needing appliances, and this time I bet they'll know the value of old ones, the lost memories they contain. We could sell all of yours. Those other people are never coming back," she tells him, in case he's forgotten again. "They're all dead."

"I think you're right, this time." Instead of going into the café Sam turns down the side street, toward the water. He reaches into his pocket and takes out his stack of yellowed claim chits, fastened together with an elastic band. He takes it off and throws them into the river, where they spread out like a deck of cards.

STONES

FROM A NOTEBOOK, TEN YEARS AGO, A SCRAP OF A STORY: "Tomorrow I will go up to the land. I will bring Fletcher and we will drive. We will go to the old alphabet stones and ask them the way of the world. There is blood on the stones but there is blood everywhere now; there is no piece of earth left, untouched by bloodshed.

"Me and Gypsy Fletch and the alphabet stones, making circles to see which way the world should go. I have not lost Gypsy yet. I will show him the stones where it says our names.

"Gypsy is hurt, and if he is wounded, so must I be."

Time circles back on itself. I opened an old notebook this morning, read it over coffee before I began to work. I don't rely on I Ching or tarot as a daily oracle as some do; instead I open old notebooks. Each time a line, a page springs out to reflect upon my current condition. As it does today.

I'm already in the country, but I am traveling tomorrow to a property in the next county, where an enigmatic ring of stones stands. As though hurled from heaven, it challenges our murky histories, our inability to look into the past and see what was really there. I'd be happy to bring Gypsy, but I can't physically; he isn't real. He's someone I invented, my childhood dream lover. I continued to write about him for years, even

after I married; there was only one like him. I don't even know if Fletch
was really his name. I just made it up; I liked the way it moved in my
mouth when I spoke it. He told me his name was Gypsy. I'm sure it wasn't
really; but the name contained thought-forms that were clues to his identity: wild, handsome, artistic, lawless, and free.

It was like this: I'd forgotten that time, those people, and made a life for
myself. I lived in Vancouver, near Lion's Gate. I was a teacher. I taught
neither the mind nor the body, but the spirit. I had an apartment with
clean blue tablecloths, bowls of fruit, and a view of the water. I was alone,
but I was happy. Then I dreamed. We were playing in the road, my only
sister and I, one of those hot dusty roads up north in Ontario. It was a
game with sticks and snakes. We picked up large branches from a fallen
tree and jousted with them, like the knights in the Arthurian legends we
loved to read above all else when we were children. In my dream we
were older than children, at that slipstream edge of adulthood where
crisis feels like treasure. Why is that?

There were so many snakes on the road; making a path for us to follow
between the stones and dead branches. We didn't, though; we didn't
know how. Still they shimmered there, full of power, offering. My sister
and I threw stones at one another and the stones passed into our bodies,
lodging where they fell like shadows in the flesh. I woke from my dream
saying, "The stone shadows are still there. It's why we are the way we
are."

Not long after the dream I went back east and married a man, a nice
man I had known for years. We had been lovers for a long time, on and
off. It was time. We moved to the country, again that north country in
Ontario, where I had not lived since then.

Then.

Listen how it weights you, the word. How you feel it inside your
mouth, your body. Listen how it heals, the talk at dawn, with your
visiting sister, about *then*.

There is a huge snail in my garden, the size of a rototiller. It walks, making paths. I kill it and crawl into its shell. I shall be that snail. I too shall have a home.

How did I kill it? That game I'd learned, hadn't even known I was learning. Threw a shadow stone at the snail. The snail crawled out of its shell, turned into a man. Something like a man, so strange and familiar both. Why had the snail been in my garden in the first place? It had liked the garden I was making. What was I growing? A different kind of world. Somebody has to, obviously. A few of us are doing it, here and there. Our gardens weave invisible lines of light, creating a web that connects us all, a web of protection. Or perhaps, the tallest plants are radio transmitters.

That was last year. This year the paths are like the paths on a board game, soft and curved. Remember the "Enchanted Forest," with little evergreens for game markers?

In that in-between time, not yet old, breasts only beginning to grow, we lived on a farm, shared by several families, not being farmers. Why is one allowed to do this, to live on farms without farming? What do the farmers do, now, instead of farm? They sit in condominiums in Florida, wondering at their strange new frost-free landscape. Eating citrus fruits by the bowlful; so rare when they were young.

I was young, thirteen. Already I thought I knew how to love. We had games for getting power, I and the other young ones. Everyone knows those games. You have to get someone dangerous to be your friend. I dreamt of a man with tattooed knees, a gypsy and an artist. He had blue hair.

I dreamt of him again last night, my childhood sweetheart. He had a third child, unlike my husband and I, who have two. It made me want another. What does it mean?

When I first dreamed stone shadows I thought they held us, our lives, in certain inescapable patterns. Imprinting. I wanted more than anything to escape those shadows; spent long winter nights dreaming their shapes out of my body like the new stones forced by frost to the surface of the fields each spring. Now I think they were protection—they gave us luck—ensuring we would become who we are now and not deviate, get lost. And yet the shadows are lifting now, willy-nilly out of everyone I know, regardless of our work to pry them out. Sometimes, I can almost hear them: popping and sucking, the skin closes around the places they were, late at night when my friends are over, drinking. You hear it when they laugh, or when they cry. In the mornings we collect empty beer bottles and sweep the new stones out the door, as though clearing the fields at planting time.

Who will protect us now—shall we have to make our own luck? I've had cinnamon buns for breakfast again and my keyboard is sticky as an icy fence in winter. But it's not winter, its summer, when everything changes irrevocably and forever. How do I know this? This summer feels like that first summer I spent with Gypsy, still a child, a year before I lost everything. Time now feels like time then; lost opportunities returning. Not since that summer have I felt so densely this moment when destiny and landscape fuse to form a pattern; the psychic template of a door to life. Last time I didn't have the strength to read it thus; seeing only the loss, and not the chance of liberation.

Notebook:

"It was on one of my walks that I found the alphabet stones. A heap of rocks in a small sparse pasture, its only access a dense mixed wood I struggled through, stubbornly. The clearing straddled the very edge of the property. The grass was long; a place so far afield the wandering cows hadn't found it."

In my garden, a spirit person came out of a snail shell. A fairy, a gnome. I don't know what to call them. Little people. He was indeed, little; about four feet tall. He had a blue bush of hair. He had four arms, two of which were blue. He had a bowl of raw fresh asparagus he held out toward me.

Eat it, he said, it will heal your marriage. Not that there is anything wrong with my marriage; it inflicts only the small sores and bruises of any bond. Perhaps it is a larger, meta-healing he proffers, with his bowl of luminous green asparagus spears. Healing Marriage, with a capital 'M'. It sure could use it.

It is only now, as I write this, that I know who it was. Fletch. Come for me again.

Little people. Stories of them all over the world. I only see them when I'm in that half-awake state just before true sleep comes. They always come to me as the picture, the image to go with something I felt in the early gardening. A lightening, a birth. Always before today it has been women. Not since that first time I dreamed of him have I seen a male.

"It looked like a heap of stones left there when they'd cleared the land and perhaps it was, but there were words there, written out with stones in the grass. I almost missed them—old words left there long ago—by settlers, perhaps. Wedged into the earth, hidden beneath the weeds, trying to regain their old homes there."

All my old lovers are dying. Why is this? I feel it in my flesh when I walk in my gardens in the mornings, picking cabbage moth larvae off the broccoli leaves. Even Gypsy, my favorite, a sweet man whose sweetness I was too young to have use for. I left him and traveled the dark road. I wish now, for his sake, more than for mine, that I could have gone a different way. Of course, we are all dying, very slowly. How much time left?

Did you know you can go backwards and forwards in time? It's what I do with myself now. Other people think I'm gardening, but really I'm time traveling. Fletch taught me, a long time ago. He called it playing cat's cradle with time. He had six arms then; the better to weave time with. That is how I know he is wounded: two arms are missing. Which time did he lose them in?

———

Notebook:

"House, said one, and Horse, Cow and Plough. I didn't know what they meant but I liked their oldness. Someone had made these words, someone no longer living. And they gave me an idea. I gathered stones from the pile and wrote in the earth, making hollow depressions for the stones to nest in. I pulled the grass out with my fingers. It took me the whole long afternoon, writing my name and his: 'July' and 'Fletcher', in two-feet-high letters.

"They embarrassed me when I was done and I tried to cover them with grass and earth, but they made me feel good too, which was worse.

"'There,' I said, as though it was enough that the stones knew."

I sit in a garden in Berkeley, sharing the life we never had together, my childhood sweetheart Gypsy and I. It is strange: I have a real life, a day-to-day life, yet from time to time it is as though part of me slips into this parallel time stream, into this life we would've had together if we hadn't split up, if I hadn't been so young; if he hadn't offended me with his desire for all of me. In my parallel life with Fletch my name is Rebecca; I wear white T-shirts, beige shorts with many pockets, ballet shoes. Life seems easier. I have a dog and an old green Saab. Sometimes I drive north, alone, to the Sierra foothills, an amazement of a place, called French Corral.

That summer, after I first dreamed of Fletch, we did everything together. We walked and drew and painted; we basked in each other's fire; we meditated long before we knew the word. It was during those intermittent years, the ones where you dream of lovers, still too young to have them. Then, suddenly older, my family gone, the farm gone too, I began to travel.

This is how I traveled: I'd get on a plane, a train, a silver bus. I'd meet a man or a woman, and we'd spend a few days together, or a few months, sometimes working, often camping, sometimes being lovers, sometimes that other romance we belittle by calling friendship. And I would learn a place, through their eyes, their lives, their hands caressing my skin, mine theirs. And yet I never stayed. For even though I'd forgotten him, he hadn't forgotten me. My first love, and my truest. It was always his voice, although I didn't know it at the time, that whispered to me to move on, not to stay.

He had other plans for me. He wanted me to share with the world what he knew; he who inhabited another world, and could only interface with mine through me. It was Fletch who urged me to travel, to absorb, to experience. So he could see, feel, learn. Because he had no eyes in this world but mine; no legs to run with.

And in turn, he taught me his world. Strange things he taught me— what made me believe they were true? The truth is, it's because I'd lost everything: my family, my farm, my friends. I'd walked through fire, unscathed, fire which had taken each one of my extended family; only I had been away. We'd had no insurance and I'd had to sell the land to pay off creditors, had only a little left to help pay my rent while I finished high school. I worked, too, in restaurants and cafés, evenings after school.

I had other friends who rallied but I stood on the other side of fire now; it was as though I no longer knew them, so untouched by life seemed they that we no longer had any meeting place. Then I had only Gypsy remaining, only Gypsy to help me find a way out. He, too, must have planned all this so I'd stay with him, and learn. So it was he after all who pointed me on the dark road. He didn't care for me personally, I found out later. He'd tried others, other human women, although it could just as easily have been a man. Fletch wanted someone who knew how to listen, who'd go to school with him, learn things not taught in any university. Things only known to those on the other side.

He taught me that animals talk; you can hear them in your mind. He taught me they'll protect you from danger, if you listen to what they say. Plants, the same, and stones. Always back to the stones.

He taught me to hear the thoughts of others, feel their emotions. Most importantly, he taught me to travel forwards and backwards in time. It's done with the light body, what they used to call the astral body. What is this faint lack we feel, this existential angst that prowls our time like a demon lover? It is the absence of Fletch, of his people. Of the time when they shared this world with us, as we shared theirs. And so I travel through time now, with long strings like spiderwebs of emotion and in the past I retrieve small pieces of the time we need to heal this fraught present. To save our heart, our earth. I re-experience his past, and knowing what it feels like, I can feel it anytime, any place. And so this pool of passed time spills out of me, influencing the time in which I live, healing it. My emotional body is like a copying machine. I travel to other times, make imprints of them, return and print them out.

For years I had many lovers, both men and women, new friends, yet was still alone, trying to teach what Fletch had taught me. To love self and earth before all others, that true love can only come after, not before. And then I dreamed of the stones. It was enough. I wanted a real life, like other people. I said goodbye to Fletch.

But somewhere the choice I didn't make to be with him goes on, and that life informs my life now, when I really am married, have children, and sometimes chafe. Then the sense of freedom and happiness I enjoy in my other life with him bleeds into this one, and I am happy again, or at least, content. Because my marriage to him takes place in some simpler past, when it was less confusing to be married. When you could trust it. Or perhaps this time has never been, yet: perhaps it's in the future.

This other me sits in her garden, full of perennials and self-seeding biennials. Lupines and foxgloves, poppies, phlox. Hollyhocks, hesperis, rudbeckia. I wear little green ballet slippers.

In real life I wonder what would have happened if I'd stayed with Fletch. Wearing angel shoes, drinking lemon tea with women in butterfly-wing cloaks. Garden parties are so important. They are always held in the presence of spirits, of little people. Their invisible influence, felt but not seen. Make sure you plant a garden they like, so they will come. A garden with paths gently curving like streams, like the paths in "The Enchanted Forest," like the stream of time.

A world that no longer exists. A kind of marriage that does not exist yet.

"But the cigarette prices have gone down," my husband's cousin said, at a party two months ago for their ninety-year-old grandmother. Those of us still in our thirties, not yet ready to relinquish our youth, our sense of adventure, sat outside among the first opened bulbs. We talked about cigarette and booze smuggling. "They set the clocks back twenty years," the cousin said, and it was as though it were really true.

I feel the spirit of twenty years ago coming alive in my bloodstream. As though now, I really will be able to live a simpler life, a luckier one, not so full of pain and work. As though, now that the door is open again, I will see it for what it is and step through.

Just now, a woman called Rebecca sits in French Corral, painting watercolors of orange poppies. Drawn here, again and again. She can't get used to it: California poppies really do grow wild in California, are not just something you order from seed catalogues. My alter ego, like me, is from Ontario.

They set the clocks back twenty years. Everything that was taken away shall be returned to us. That is what I want now; the things that were taken away. I want to wear what she wears, talk like she talks, think like she thinks. I no longer want to be one of the damaged, the burned, the ones who walked on water to save the tribe, and were not now (as not then) thanked for it. Then. Listen to the word, how it weights you.

But here is something else, something stranger still. In my childhood, there weren't really any old stones, aside from the so-aptly-named shield rocks. Shielding us every day of our lives. "One reason not to bury nuclear waste in them," Fletch whispers in my ear. "Who will protect you then, when even the alphabet rocks are poisoned?" I invented the story stones as an adult, based on the feelings in the dream, the things I felt on that farm; what I learned by absorbing the land's secrets, those hot dusty melancholy northern summers.

Stones which are very old. Yet now, like so many things I wrote ten or fifteen years ago, they seem to be coming true.

There are so many old stones in this country. Piled into shapes, some with designs on them. Who made these stones? We must listen to the stones, sit down beside them and really hear what they say. They are the mouthpiece of the earth, speaking to us. If ever you should hear stones speak, you must pass on what they say. If you don't, all your old lovers will die.

A man lives near here, with old stones on his property. 'Property'— where did this word come from?

Tomorrow we'll go and see them, my husband and I. Some people think natives made the stones, some think it was the Celts, having traveled further inland than any had believed.

Some even think the stones were erected by two cultures, working together. A somewhat hopeful revision of the past, even if it isn't true. One native man I met says he doesn't care; any made-up histories at all about stones will do, if they help preserve the land, if they make people think there's a reason to keep it free, not build subdivisions.

But I think the rocks have yet another meaning; the circle they make is a door between this world and the other world. Fletch's world. Of course, the true locus of this door is in our hearts, and yet we search the landscape for hopeful reminders, for crisscrossings of light that mirror our desires. And on that stone altar that inhabits the central place, I will make a ritual. It will not be a ritual of sacrifice, but one of healing. I will go there, and I will heal Gypsy, just as he healed me, all those long years ago.

How will I do it? I will give him a place in this world, just as he gave me one in his, back when it made the only possible difference.

RICE LAKE

ALEXIA CALLED HER FRIEND JILL.

"Jill," she said, "I want to come visit for the week-end. Can you come pick me up?"

"Sure," Jill said. "There's a party at Elizabethville. Six o'clock."

"Bye."

Elizabethville, a tiny village near Port Hope. Their friend Raven didn't live there anymore. Moved to the city, gone down to T.O., the Big Smoke, to pursue his career as a freelance programmer. An opposite move to her own; she and Frank were from Toronto, just as Port Hope was Raven's home town.

Winter parties at Elizabethville; Alexia and Frank used to go there when Gerrard was four, the baby Sarah a year or two old, still nursing. They'd stay over, in one of the many upstairs bedrooms, the doors each painted a different primary color. Alexia, seeing them, had thought she wanted to paint her doors like that. Now Raven was gone, and Rita and Andrea lived there. Still had parties in that house that was always, in Alexia's memories, even the summer ones, surrounded by faded brown earth, patched snow, winter trees.

Raven gone. Everything goes. It had been a year of breaking circles; not just her friend leaving for the city but couples Alexia loved splitting up and moving far away from each other, far from her.

One winter her daughter Sarah, then two, had surprised her, picked up an old birthday invitation off the floor, pretended to read, saying: "It says we're invited to a party at Elizabethville on Saturday." And an hour later Raven had called, inviting them.

Alexia had looked at her daughter, astonished. Another Voyager then. Not much she could do about it, either way, although she hadn't been Played herself in years. The Game. Only Jill, of all their old Voyager circle, still had huge circles she'd drawn on the earth in front of her cabin, barely visible under the new grown, unmown grass, in different pastel colors of children's sidewalk chalk. Circles. They'd never faded, even after years of rain. When the grass, unwatered, went bald and dry in mid-July you could still trace their thick outlines. What had Jill used to draw those circles that they'd last like that? Not sidewalk chalk after all, but memory. Her memories of The Game.

Alexia remembered a time she'd been Played with her father. That had been about circles too. Perhaps eleven, she'd gone with him to the snowy school yard across the street from the Toronto house where they lived. Circles they'd drawn in the snow, or perhaps uncovered. The circles had caught fire. She'd never remembered it before that moment, the way she always forgot when she'd been played by The Game. That time, Alexia suddenly understood, had been about gathering strength to survive her mother's coming death, which neither of them knew about. And yet The Game had known; The Game always knew. Why else would it have chosen that moment to Play them, making fire circles in snow?

But there was Jill's VW bus door slamming in the driveway; Alexia grabbed earrings and her green jean jacket, shouted good-bye to Frank and the kids.

The two women poked through the junk. Jill had acres and acres of junk on her farm: fridges, toasters, stoves, nails, screws, ironing boards, doors, windows, shoes, toy tractors, motors, screen doors, window frames, chairs, tables, beds, and skis.

Jill's father collected it all, slowly, over many years, from the dump and out of people's roadside garbage. Now at the height of summer it was almost entirely covered by the carroty foliage of Queen Anne's lace, her white umbeled heads.

Alexia asked Jill why and her friend said: "My father walked barefoot through Russia in the snow. He doesn't want us ever to go without."

Alexia loved the way Jill looked, as if she was a larger version of herself. Tall, slender but broad-shouldered and strong, with large brown doe's eyes, a thick wash of adventurous brown hair. Alexia was tall, but not so tall as Jill, large-eyed, but not as deer-like as Jill, had brown hair she'd taken to cutting short again. Sometimes, hugging Jill, her head reaching Jill's neck, she felt for a moment as though she was hugging her missing mother. Her mother who stayed young in Alexia's memory, the same age as Jill was now when she died.

Jill built a small house out of her father's junk piles, furnished it. Most of the junk was rotting now. Alexia left her friend at the house to walk the beautifully mown paths between the junk piles, where Jill had been sorting. A coffee can for screws, one for nails, a plastic tray of hammers. Alexia could see where Jill had been, as though by trails of glistening snail slime. Each time Jill found another tool she added it to the hammer tray, Alexia surmised, although she hadn't brought it back to the house yet. The screws and nails she had, though; they held her house together.

"We always talk a lot about memory, forgetting," Jill said when Alexia got back, and it suddenly seemed appropriate that her house was built out of other people's forgotten memories.

"What will you do with your life now?" Alexia asked her, just as she did once a year.

Her answer was always the same: "There's enough work here for a lifetime. I'm sorting my father's junk."

Alexia had the sense not to laugh.

In Jill's garden, among piled straw for mulch, rows of scarlet runner beans, beets and cucumbers, the wild mullein was left unpulled, and, manured, it grew taller than the garden fence; huge candlesticks, opening yellow flowered after rain. Alexia's son Gerrard one summer dipped them in melted paraffin, sprinkled them with the same crystals used in fire-logs: torches, they burned green and red and blue. Then, later, Alexia read the settlers did that too, although of course they used beeswax, and didn't have the chemical colors.

Jill had a heavy-duty extension cord that ran up to the main house, supplied her power. Jill and Alexia followed the orange snake through hedgerows, a pile of rusting toy tractors, and an abandoned outdoor seating arrangement made of small cable spools. They were looking for a bottle opener; on the drive down they'd accidentally bought non-twist-off beer.

"My mother won't come up from the city anymore," Jill said. "She hated that there were seven spatulas in the drawer for turning bacon; she could never find the wooden spoon."

"Or the day she wanted one of the seven spatulas there were three corkscrews, twelve salad forks and sixteen paring knives obscuring her view of it," Alexia replied.

"Such perfidy," Jill said. "My father's so rich."

"Makes you wonder why anybody ever buys anything," Alexia said.

"Makes you wonder," Jill replied. "Although some of them are a bit rusty, or bent."

"Or melted," Alexia said, holding up a blackened, spongy green plastic spatula. "So what are you building this year?" she asked, after the bottle-opener was found, because Jill was always building something.

"A fieldstone deck," Jill said, as they made the return journey, past a circle of foxgloves, several screen doors and an oil painting of a child, perched, somewhat precariously, on top of a winding split rail snake fence. "With ramps for Michael." Michael with an angel's name. Alexia didn't think of that with every Michael she knew, but she always did with Jill's son, who rolled through life in a wheelchair. There were ramps she'd built out of dismantled wooden factory pallets, going up and down the sloping hills, through the neglected orchard, to the outhouses full of neatly stacked National Geographics, and, pinned to the wall, the old Peterborough Petroglyphs poster, which they used to hand out free, before the funding cuts. Everyone had that poster pinned to the rotting cedar walls of their outhouses; in fact, Alexia thought, it was the only place you could find them anymore, only the outhouse walls that hadn't forgotten.

So many things gone.

Sometimes Jill walked at night, from town to town, her son rolling along in his wheelchair beside her, his knuckles blackened and calloused from bumping into things. Jill drew then, in a black hard covered notebook like the kind both women used to draw and write in when they were in high school, before their dreams went to sleep, a lake drowning. They didn't know then that those dreams would come easily for such a few short years; that they would have to work hard, the rest of their lives, to keep one scant light of them awake. Jill borrowed her son's oil pastels, drew bright red cornstalks, purple skies. Walked without a flashlight so they could take cover in the scrub alongside the road if needed; hence the psychedelic colors: night visions' delirium. Who am I, Alexia thought, to say you have never seen such a thing, it's never been? I don't walk those roads at night, through to the twilit hours close to dawn, just in time to eat bacon and eggs at the highway truck stop when it opens at six.

"What did we do, after high school?" Jill asked, opening beer for them both, back at the little wraparound porch of her cabin, built, of course, out of junk wood. Basil and pumpkins grew out of old creamers. One of the pumpkin vines had climbed in the front window of the house. "I want to grow indoor pumpkins," Jill added, catching Alexia's bemused stare.

"We went west, separately," Alexia answered.

Went west, lived among trees, learned their mystery. Were still learning, come to think of it. A lifelong task; one of the unsung ones that pays only in deepening joy, greater understanding. Why was it so important? Because of The Game.

In The Game there was A Fountain, a Tree. Your job in The Game, should you wake one morning into its mystery, aside from allowing yourself to be Played like a tiny animated person in a game board big as life, was to care for The Fountain, The Tree. Any tree could be The Tree, any fountain The Fountain, for a few short glimmering moments. Just as any person could likewise be a Player, be Played for seconds, minutes, hours. Few were chosen and of those, fewer still woke to the intensity. And if, for a few moments, they did realize they were being Played, they forgot almost immediately.

It was hard to remember mysteries so much larger than oneself, retain even one note of the song one heard, the song one was. And yet Alexia knew it was only because she and Jill were Voyagers that they still retained any poetry in their lives at all, any shimmering dreams.

Bottles in hand, they went to look at Jill's second garden, in the old cornfield. "I still don't know why you grow more pumpkins than anyone else," Alexia said, and left for the outhouse. She always did her best thinking in bathrooms.

In the outhouse she wondered why there were drawings of snails hidden on rocks beneath the moss that one could pull away like a carpet to look at: snails drawn by time. Once, very young, up north, Alexia had thought how the entire landscape was a clever stage set, a prop built by some master theater designer, her motives unknown, other than her evident, passionate love of beauty. As though one could peel it away like moss too, see the true meaning of things, the writing on the wall, or on the rocks, as it were. A Game thought, she figured, yet that's how the natives preserved their rock carvings before the government built that shiny new white house for them. In the old days the moss covered the images over; people peeled it back only when they went to look at the petroglyphs, savoring them a few times each year. Like the chalk circles under Jill's wildflower meadow of a lawn.

"And we think we know something about preservation," Alexia said quietly, staring at the curled and mildewed poster, reaching for toilet paper. Even when she first moved to the country, approached the petroglyphs on then unkempt wilderness trails, peered through a wire fence, she could still feel them. Now she felt the building. "And that's the whole point of The Game, isn't it," Alexia whispered, "is feeling things. Feeling picture stories."

Alexia picked up the top copy in the ubiquitous stack of bright black and yellow. She was sure National Geographics bred in the closets at her own farm too. There was something in cardboard boxes, in dust and darkness that they required to propagate. She leafed through them, looking for Game clues. What if they could begin to be Played again, as they hadn't in years?

No pictures of fountains, nor of circles, whether drawn by chalk or fire. Nothing that gave her that strong rinsed feeling. Lots of pictures of trees, but none of The Tree. She longed to be Played, to be in a story so real and true it took on its own life, shaped the storyteller, a reverse creation. It's not really me who ever made the stories, she thought, but the stories that made me. And who didn't long to be made anew, as often as possible? She called for The Game, a kind of prayer. Why did they stop being Played? Because so few did. Because they grew up. Because it was hard when no one understood or cared. Much easier to forget, give up, let the flames die. Alexia heard a car pull up, sighed, set aside her reading, her thinking, her searching.

The men had arrived: Jill's new beau Ben and his buddy Milo. They'd only take the one vehicle: Ben's trusty, rusty Chevy Nova, of indeterminate, elderly vintage. The trunk had a cooler full of beer. At the party Jill took Alexia aside, asked what she thought of Ben. "He seems nice," Alexia said, and not: He will go. He's one who goes, not one who stays.

Jill went outside alone to look at the stars, the northern lights, shimmering in green curtains, didn't call them out, so absorbed she forgot to tell them till later. Jill's always seeing things the rest of us don't see, Alexia thought. Drank beer, talked to Andrea and Rita about families, to Ben and Milo about fishing, missed Raven, the way things were before, this house, then.

Raven, her one infidelity. They walked in the woods together at a party, years before, under a moon, the children long asleep, Frank too gone up to bed. Raven's long black hair sweeping over his shoulders, his beaten brown leather jacket. A cabin a mile's hike away, belonging to a friend. She thought she'd feel cheap, sleazy, as though she was breaking things. But she hadn't. Felt only love reborn, love she'd given up hope for, settled for the other thing. It's easy to fall out of love with your husband when you're always tired, up in the night, changing diapers, losing patience, sleep, self-respect. Love runs away to hide under a fossil rock and then you're just going through life together, a day at a time.

And Raven too had made her sad as he talked with smoky eyes of life gone wrong and she'd thought, I can't save him. Why do I always want to? He can only save me; for this one short moment, a moment to take back into life with me. They'd made a fire outside, drunk scotch, talked until five. Still dark then, in winter. He'd walked her back to the house, gone alone to sleep in the cabin, not wanting to be there when Frank woke. Yet he'd been Frank's friend first. And she'd told her husband eventually, how when love's cup is empty you have to find someone to fill it again. Frank had understood, at least enough not to ditch her. She figured she'd do the same for him. Hoped he wouldn't. Who could stand the anger, the pain?

But something else had happened too, that winter night years before. Alexia felt it tugging at her. What? A Game thing. Gone like the electric green curtains flickering in the sky, so impressive just two hours before.

Two in the morning, on the way back to Jill's, they stopped to swim in a pond under an old mill. Scrambled down a bank in utter darkness, obscured from moonlight which fell in yellow wavelets on the pond itself by the mill's shadow; scrabbled in the dark, beer bottles in hand. Tomorrow, Alexia guessed, she'd have the poison ivy to prove it. Alexia didn't swim, watched the others; Jill swam in T-shirt and underwear. She must feel shy with these people, Alexia thought: the Jill she knew skinny-dipped whenever she could.

The only dry one, she sat in the front next to Ben's sidekick. Milo was from Liverpool, in England, and she was enchanted by his Cockney accent, so infrequently heard in southern Ontario. Anything new she craved, bloodthirsty for it. Another side effect of motherhood: starvation for stimulation.

Milo was the designated driver, since he spent the party sleeping on Rita and Andrea's couch, had no opportunity to suck beers like the rest of them. She liked Jill's friends, but they weren't Voyagers, didn't shift out of focus just a little as she looked at them, as though part of them inhabited another space, another plane. But that was okay. Not everyone was. The Game hadn't Played them, all night long. Alexia felt more than a little hollow. But why should it, after all, come back for them when they'd abandoned it so long ago? Along with their hopes, their dreams.

"The Game was our hopes and dreams," she said fiercely. Ben and Milo turned to look at her, curious. Milo was sardonic, but Ben smiled kindly as though he almost understood. It was only Jill who laughed in heartfelt agreement.

Alexia lay in Jill's bedroom, an attic loft full of windows, thinking about families, how she wanted to leave her children unburdened, how it was an impossible task, how, sometimes, burns became later gifts. Picked up a National Geographic from the pile beside the bed, a mattress on the salvaged barn board floor, covered by beautiful ragged old quilts that smelled of Jill. Jill's smell, the enormous light of Jill's rooms. Things not to be done without.

Jill stood on the stairs to pass her food, to set on the floor beside the bed: boiled corn, old and leathery, new potatoes, boiled and dressed in olive oil, salt and pepper, a little opal basil vinegar. Jill's duvet was covered in a homemade case, blue and white striped ticking. Downstairs on the ancient record player, salvaged from a junk pile, Jill and Ben played James Taylor, then Marianne Faithful. "It's like listening to all the years of our lives," Alexia said when she at last came downstairs, feeling social enough to join in coffee, conversation, although Ben was having a breakfast beer. Possibly a good idea, Alexia thought, considering her corrugated cardboard brains.

Jill and Ben drove Alexia home along the south shore of Rice Lake. Alexia thought she saw stories floating there, stories which had only recently been released by the weeds which choked the bottom. Even if she wasn't Played herself, she knew that even this, passing this Game locus, would open out her life in exactly those areas where it felt closed, constricted.

New stories: it made Alexia glad to see them; they seemed glad to be there, morning glories opened after rain. These were stories that had never been heard before. Alexia wanted to stay, rent a houseboat with a slip at Gore's Landing, live on the lake for a month and sit on the deck each morning, pen in hand, transcribing them. She'd have a green Coleman propane pump stove, a yellow enamel teapot, make black tea like her mother for friends who swam out. Like her mother, gone now:

the first to go, the loss all other losses were measured against. The Loss that taught her to treasure her family and friends, while she yet had them. Because they too might go. Like Ben would go.

The Game Played. Alexia saw:

In Rice Lake a drowned woman floated, Ophelia-like. She was drowned but not dead. Bigger than Jill and Alexia, much bigger. Almost as big as the lake. Houseboats went out to look at her, and sometimes their propellers became entangled in the long grey green folds of her dress. Not my mother, Alexia thought, a writer not a painter, drowned like Woolf, yet not Virginia, not suicided like both she and my mother, but waiting, dormant. A temporary drowning. What did she write? The landscape.

Jill, Alexia knew, took creative writing lessons from her. Like Alexia herself, trying always to carve a life out of beauty, a poem.

But they'd already taken the north turn up highway twenty-eight. Alexia enjoyed Ben's swatches of ironic conversation, was briefly sad, feeling again he would go before she ever got to know him properly. If only he'd surrender, let himself be Played. Then he'd stay, Alexia thought, know the beauty and passion he craved were always there, waiting in The Game. Not go running off to look for it somewhere else, in another woman.

A story so intense it shaped the teller.

Mid-July, so hot they decided to stop at the beach at Serpent Mounds on Rice Lake's north shore. Here there were huge submersible mowers which kept the weeds down, in the roped off swimming area. Alexia ducked under the roped rubber buoys which marked the edge, thinking to swim out, touch only the hem of Her dress. But she returned, having encountered a faceful of weeds, and not Her sodden garment hem at all. A drowned woman, Alexia thought, She still dreams stories so beautiful they might yet change the lives of those living on Her shores.

Afterwards she walked the trails, out of the sun, sheltered by trees beside the bog, felt a little history then; feet which walked there hundreds of years before she came. Feet from Before. Wanted to feel what they felt, why they walked there, built their Mounds there. Why? Because it was beautiful.

They made the last leg of the journey to Asphodel Township, where she lived. Stopped at the mill pond near Alexia's house; a stranger in a new four-by-four asked her the name of the river that pooled there, above the dam where the kids caught crayfish, where Alexia first identified swamp milkweed; a milkweed more delicate, more feminine than its fieldborn cousin, with bright lavender pink flowers and fuzzy, slender lanceolate leaves.

"It's the Ouse," Alexia said, thought again of Virginia, her hair spreading behind her like weeds. But those were old stories brought from Europe; the settlers paved the landscape over with old European names. Did Virginia drown herself in England's ooze before or after this river was likewise named? Why were the pioneers unable to think of new names, particular to this continent? Labeling it instead with misspelled, often misplaced native names, or imported names. Unable to read the names which grew here organically, more legible at some times than at others, mushrooms sprouted after rain. Nature's writing, out of rot, compost. Like John Keats: it all comes out of the rag and bone bag, for all writers, nature too.

Alexia's mill pond: was it Lethe or Mnemosyne? Did she come from the city to the country to remember how to be Played, or to forget the pain of her mother's suicide? As if she could, ever, really. Did the ghosts here talk endlessly of the past, or make helpful suggestions about how to live gracefully in the present? Greek legend had it that in the fields of Asphodel, near the gates to Hades, a pink lily of the Allium or garlic family grew, beside Lethe, pool of forgetting; or was it Mnemosyne, pool of memory? What were the ghosts saying? In spring Alexia and her family would go out to the woods to gather wild leeks, a traditional native spring tonic. They boiled them as greens, cut them into salads, even ate them whole, raw, not waiting till they got home. Between Hepatica and Spring Beauty they grew: green, outrageous, smelling like a cancer cure. Not called Asphodels, though, but perhaps Cousins of Asphodels.

Alexia prolonged her swim at the dam, she knew, not only because it was so hot, or to swim off the night's beer, but to postpone going home, to pick up again the reins of everyday life, of meals and laundry and sweeping, of mending children's tears.

When she got home Frank was fixing the truck, asked if she'd help. But she said, "I've already run and emptied the dishwasher twice, done and put away two loads of laundry, put on a soup, swept the floor." She looked at the greasy black engine with some misgivings. "Besides, if women had invented transportation, we wouldn't have cars."

"What would we be doing?" Frank asked, raising a wry eyebrow.

"Teleporting," she said, knowing this wasn't a totally pragmatic answer from Frank's point of view, but it got her out of the repair work, this time; other times she did help. She went inside to get a glass of water, load the dishwasher, put on the wash, do all the things she said she'd already done. If they were as reliable as death and taxes, what was the difference if she put them in the past or future tense? She unwound the plastic vines of flowers from the washer so she could open the lid; the machine was a shrine: the closest she came, in this house, to having The Fountain, caring for it. But why was it so important to have a fountain? She barely remembered. Something to do with needing water for those moments when the fire circles burned too hot, burned away The Tree's new growth and not just the dead branches, legacy of winter storms.

Sitting at her winter window, six months later, Alexia hoped the Rice Lake stories were still there, not destroyed by the storm, their text mixed into a hopeless jumble. Perhaps the stories had been tossed by winter waves onto the shore, whole. Maybe they were even now spreading northwards, toward Alexia's town, cloaking the hills and valleys with new words, more sincerely heartfelt ways of living. And all, Alexia thought, because Jill walked beside me for so long. Sometimes Alexia thought it was she and not Jill who'd endured the deeper burn, although to outsiders she knew it looked otherwise. People wondered how she could choose Jill for a friend; Jill who was so burdened, and gifted with

Michael with an angels' name, the son who never grew up, or at least, not the way her own children did. Grew larger, sweeter, somewhat smarter; at twenty loved to listen to The Wolf, his classic rock station, chat with his friends on the phone; no longer glued, slowly, carefully, his face a mask of concentration, tools and stereos cut out of Home Hardware catalogues onto Bristol board. Alexia had one of his collages, somewhere, kept it safe with Gerry and Sarah's work. But Alexia thought: I always choose the burned as my closest friends; it is they who know how to heal.

She called her friend, got Michael first.

"Hi Michael, it's Alexia. What are you doing?"

"Stereo," Michael answered and squealed by way of punctuation. "Your mum there?" Alexia asked and Michael called out, "Jill! Jill! It's Alexia."

When Jill got on she said that Ben had gone.

"I knew he'd go."

"How did you know?"

"Must be a Game thing."

"The Game is almost lost, from being Played too little."

Had they ever talked about it before? "What was it called?" Alexia asked. "Going West maybe?" Perhaps if they talked about The Game, acknowledged its existence, the giantess wouldn't die.

"Or Broken?" Jill answered, the phone line crackling with winter weather. "There were archetypes, almost like icons that you worked with; the mirror: the fountain, the tree, the circle. There was a whole dictionary of symbolic images; you'd reweave them into endless new patterns, new meanings. Stories."

Excited, Alexia interrupted her friend, rushing on: "The Game was always being played somewhere, an endless Game; you could join in it any place, any time. And you could always tell another Voyager; they shimmered a little. You'd recognize them, walking into a room, although no one else would notice. Or did we call ourselves Explorers? Funny how you forget."

But Jill said, "Funny how much we remember. Maybe it's time."

———

It was early March. Alexia went to a party in Peterborough, ran, unexpectedly, into an old lover from years before. Raven up from the city. Together they went outside into the night. There was a cracked fountain in the center of the back yard. Raven leaned on it, looking in; a crack so deep it couldn't hold water, even now, after rain. "It's The Fountain," she realized with a shock that ran through her like electricity: shockingly. Said, "I'm Being Played again. The Game is still here; I thought it was gone."

She watched Raven to see what he would do.

To be a Voyager one must have a fountain to drink at. The water is full of images, of stories one may live out or only read. The water is clear like any water: only to the drinker do the stories become legible. Like those Japanese paper flowers that bloom when sunk into a glass of water; myths bloom only when imbibed by a Voyager.

Remembered too: she and Raven, the night of their affair, years before in Elizabethville. A Fountain that night too, a stone outcropping shaped like a shallow bowl, full of rain. She'd seen a story there, read it aloud, told him it was his turn. How does one describe that feeling of being Played, a story told in partnership with The Game? She'd waited, hoping, yet every tale he'd tried to tell had been pulled back into the water before it was done. Told with smoky eyes of life gone wrong, his hands glistening and wet with words but no completion.

He'd said even then he was leaving, moving to the city. Unable to be whole, to make a true story, Raven went instead into the world to tell the bright half he knew. Alexia and Jill stayed home on their country farms, telling stories and painting pictures respectively: intricate and self-reflexive, woven, like intertwining vines or the Celtic patterns in the Book Of Kells; their beauty so all encompassing, so complete, so comforting they offered sanctuary. What Voyager who could do that, who could world build beauty so convincingly, would venture far from home, into the world, among the cold starved others who'd never learned the ancient craft? But Raven who'd been Played and lost had gone.

And tonight, again, there was nothing for Raven to drink. His face was illumined, but only half of it, by the moon. The illumined face was happy, but she knew the other, unseen one was not. She watched, knew that soon he would tire of waiting; that with no stories to drink, he would have to leave The Game, just like before. That as he walked away, his snowy footsteps would catch fire. Knew also she would follow, as last time, she had not. Because last time, with the vanity of an Explorer, she guarded her wealth jealously. Because last time her fountain was full and his wasn't.

But this time it was different. This time the Game had nothing to with love, with passion between men and women, if indeed it ever had. Because this time, years later, she knew at last, having half a face was better than none at all. It was the half-faced who made the bridges between the fountain and the world, the pool of remembering and the pool of forgetting. Who stopped the burning. Who cared for the trees, The Tree.

GONE WITH THE SEA

"**W**E GO IN. WE'RE IN ANYWAY. WE GO IN; OUR VIRTUAL bodies eat the virtual fish."

"Yes, but how does that provide nourishment, how does the fish protein enter your meat bag?"

"We don't have meat bags anymore." Snicker.

"Seriously, Jake."

"Seriously, Mum, I can come down and check out your computer tonight."

"Thanks, son. I'll make you dinner. You people still eat dinner, right?"

"Sometimes," Jake said, with just a hint of wistfulness. "But eating is so much trouble. You have to de-gear to eat."

"I know. You live on shrimp pills and Jolt Cola. I'll give you a case of pills to take home with you. I can't afford to pay. For you and your friends. So you don't have to go out, go to the store."

"How come you're so broke?"

"The shrimp are sick. I haven't been able to fill the last two orders. I'm cash-strapped."

"Ship sick shrimp," Jake suggested.

"Ship sick shrimp," she said, "shelling shrimp by the seashore. I know a lot of people do it, Jake, but I just can't."

"Ethical as ever, Ellen. I take it fixing the computer would expedite a medical diagnosis?"

"You got it."

"You should've said they were sick. I'd have come last week."

"Seems to me I did."

"Oh. See you at four then?"

"Thanks. Bye."

"Bye."

OpaeCorp had been built in the last years of the previous century, in approximately the same location as an ancient Hawai'ian fish farm, on the north shore near Haena. Much easier and less expensive to excavate and reline the five hundred year old ponds than to dig new ones; a tribute, Ellen supposed, to ancient aboriginal engineering. Ellen had wanted to expand last year, cut down the mangroves, put in two extra ponds. Her local neighbor Maui had discouraged that, instead talking her into building a small outrigger canoe according to traditional design by hand. "You wouldn't cut them down if you knew them," he'd said, and Ellen had replied they were unknowable. A mangrove forest wasn't the kind of thing you could walk through.

She'd given in mostly because Maui had been so stubborn, and found he'd been right: now she loved the mangroves surrounding her farm. Their fantastic other-worldliness rarely failed to refresh her when she was feeling fraught and burdened, as now. After hanging up on Jake she got her little boat out of the decommissioned outtake canal that was its driveway, sailed it, just for a couple of hours up the coast, through mangroves. All trees, of course, are more or less vertically symmetrical, Ellen thought, it's just that with most we can't see the roots. Not so with mangroves. The roots rise up out of the water, a wickerwork tripod suspending the trunk, the dense, fragrant interwoven branches. The shade, the quiet of the mangrove swamps. It seemed the only peace. And then back to work.

She checked the inlet and the discharge canals, the pump intakes, the sediment traps. While she knew enough to see whether engines were working smoothly, she wasn't happy repairing them. Her mechanic had moved to Alaska the previous winter and she hadn't found a reliable replacement, even though she kept offering Maui the job. And now the pump was coughing. Had it been coughing all week? Was E. coli the cause of her shrimps' illness? She should've checked the pump sooner. She visited the nauplii in their pond, the post larvae in the adjacent one. They were seemingly still healthy, which was a relief, but they didn't solve her business problem. You couldn't ship babies.

The shrimp themselves had been genetically engineered, a hybrid between Penaeus monodon, japonicus, and a freshwater Macrobrachium species that was extremely disease resistant. The ancient Hawai'ians hadn't thought of biotech. Too bad for them. They could've been the ones who made millions, as Ellen's great-grandmother Eileen had, feeding farmed shrimp to a starving world. Of course, they could've made millions too if they'd owned the big resort hotels on the southern beaches. But they hadn't. They'd just worked in them.

It was only biotech that had made it possible to replicate the entire life cycle, from egg to market-sized, in ponds, and that hadn't happened till the millennium. So while Maui had been the one to insist she not raze the remaining mangroves to build more ponds, but rather to plant more to enlarge the final stage filter system, as was traditional, he wasn't really up on modern methods. But he was good with pumps and so she called him, left a message on his voicemail, resisting the temptation to call him Sun God, as she occasionally did, to tease. Did Maui really mean Sun God? Ellen couldn't remember. Did it help him to have a god's name? Probably not. He was very poor. At one time he'd worked as a unionized hotel janitor, but tourism had plummeted, as ozone depletion worsened. No one wanted to lie in the sun anymore, catch cancer. But the world was starving, worse than ever, and bioengineered shrimp culturing methods seemed one of many cures. Those with foresight scrapped their south shore beachfront hotels, razing them to make room for shrimp farms. And so the rainy little volcanic island began to resemble its earlier self, a forested place, the coastal waters farmed. Irony.

Maui often claimed his family had done a little shrimp farming, now and again. They'd practiced the traditional method, allowing juvenile shrimp to be carried by the tides into hand built coastal ponds where they were grown to market size. Otherwise they caught gravid females at sea and allowed them to spawn in ponds. Or so she assumed. Animal husbandry, and not true science.

And here he was already, come to look at her pump. "Where were you?" she asked, stress making her blunt. Or perhaps she'd been blunt for years, just hadn't noticed.

"Bodysurfing," he grinned, already disassembling the motor. "Come with me tomorrow? The weather'll be perfect."

"Bodysurfing is dangerous. I've lost three friends to it."

"I know. They were stoned out of their gourds on mushrooms," he reminded her. "They took stupid risks. They swam in an undertow. The riptides were posted. They were too stoned to read."

"True. You sure you don't want a job?"

"What's wrong with your employees, Ellen?"

"They're doorknobs by and large. Everything they do, I have to check and double-check to make sure they've gotten it right. There isn't that much room for error in shrimp farming."

"You're telling me. But I don't need a job," he said.

"What do you do, now?" she asked. She never had been able to figure. He moved in and out of her life, appearing and disappearing. Alternately friendly and a little distant.

"Huh?" he asked.

"Where d'you work, now?"

"Don't need to work really. My grandmother, she left me a few acres on the coast near Hanalei. I got avocado, mango, banana. I grow a few greens. There's a bit of old terracing there, I repaired it, put in kalo."

"Kalo," she said, trying not to grimace. "That's Hawai'ian for 'taro,' right?" She still thought poi was disgusting, in spite of having grown up in Kalaheo. She'd never been a mainlander. Kama'ainas, the Hawai'ian born whites called themselves. It translated, roughly, as locals. As if.

"You raise a few pigs. You fish," she continued for Maui. "What about money for gas?"

"Oh there's always things. Trade and barter and it's not I don't work. I put in a few weeks each year on one thing or another. What about you, Ellen?"

"I run the farm. Somebody has to or what would the world eat?"

"Is that what you want?"

"It's okay. I'd like to travel, go to the mainland, way up north maybe, Alaska. I've never been to the mainland. A lot of my friends did that."

"I know."

"How d'you know?"

"Kaua'i is a small island. You hear everything."

"True." He was standing there looking pretty well done, like he wanted to leave now.

"Pump okay now?" Ellen asked.

"Pump's fine. I think what you're facing here, Ellen, is a monoculture problem."

"But the wild varieties aren't disease resistant. These are stronger and healthier; you can raise three harvests a year in a much smaller acreage than from traditional methods." She knew she sounded like the OpaeCorp promotional material.

Maui looked uncertain. "Maybe for a few years."

"It's been well over sixty," Ellen laughed.

"That is a few, really, if you think about it. What you figure their problem is today?"

"A new brand of E. coli, resistant to antibiotics."

"What you plan on doing then?"

"Search the web, see if there's a stronger antibiotic I can order," Ellen said.

"You can't eat them if they're all dead."

"But they won't be, you see. And I should've gotten to you sooner about the pump."

"I don't think the pump is the problem, really. Like I said," Maui insisted, stubborn as ever.

"But of course it is. That and the computer. Jake's coming tonight to fix that."

Maui said nothing, crouched down and scooped a handful of wriggling adult shrimp out of the water, examined them closely.

"What d'you know about shrimp?" she asked defensively. "I thought you were a janitor." Now she'd done it. While without a ticket, Maui was the best mechanic she knew. And now he'd never come back, and who could blame him?

"Oh, I've done a little shrimp farming in my day," he reminded her. "Traditional methods, largely."

"So I've heard. That'll never feed a world." Now who was stubborn?

"Maybe. Maybe not. I'm against gene-splicing, if not all the rest of your high tech. You put money ahead of fish, ahead of people, you'll never come out ahead, not in the long run. Nature doesn't care about dollars."

"I always thought so too, actually."

"I'd hope so, or I don't think I'd be standing here talking to you. And on that count I should tell you these fish won't make the week, no matter what new-fangled tetracycline you dose them with. Not a one."

"I've been in this business all my life Maui, don't tell me how to farm."

"Suit yourself, *haole*," he said. With derision. It was amazing how much derision a local could fit into that one little word. Irony-free derision. Watching him leave, she had never felt less a kama'aina. *Haole* meant white, foreigner.

Ellen wanted to travel, but she had to stay because she was the last one who knew how to look after the farm. The old people knew too, of course, in fact had taught her, but were now themselves too old. Most of them lived in Seaview, a seniors' home on a Princeville cliff, overlooking the Pacific. The place had been sold to them for its huge plate glass windowed common room, where they could sit in their recliners, sipping morning coffee and watching whales. But of course, there were very few whales. The humpbacks had moved away, resisting their genetic predisposition to return to this same spot, year after year, and raise their children. There had been too many tourist Zodiacs at the turn of the millennium, frightening them. Their age-old reproductive behavior had been altered. Ellen wondered whether it was a conscious decision to move away from the whale watchers who'd come too close, too often, and too many. If the whales could decide to move north, Ellen thought, alter their instinctive, trans-generational routes and trails through water, as well marked to them as highway maps are to us, then perhaps humans could do the same. As of course they had, in different ways, her own generation and her children's. As with the whales, it was too soon to see what the results would be.

Ellen wondered whether to go to Seaview to ask for advice or wait for Jake. She decided to stay, check the manual systems. It was already two o'clock and she wouldn't have time to make the return trip and prepare food for her son, trial as she knew the dinner conversation would be. She dumped extra tetracycline into the adult ponds, even though, without her computer running properly, she couldn't pinpoint the bacterial problem. But Jake would fix that, hopefully. And it was better than having all the shrimp die overnight.

She'd tried to find an assistant manager to train among the younger people, but they all worked in computers at the industrial park up behind Kapaa. They created virtual shrimp, longing for the day when they'd discover the interface, an alteration in either the cyber-Penaeus or their own bodies which would enable them to eat information shrimp, and no longer need flesh.

Ellen thought they lived in a world of their own making, had been hexed by the cyber-witch, spellbound. It would never happen. They'd depend on her for their fleshly needs, to feed the meat bag which they so abhorred, which, staring at screens for most of their waking hours, they had only a passing intimacy with.

"We're getting closer," Jake said by way of conversation as he rebooted her hard drive, wanting her encouragement as he had as a child. He was still a child, she thought, only nineteen, a cyber-wizard of the highest order yet knowing nothing of life. What had they raised, she and her peers but a generation of little demons? When the ancient silicon based PC she used to monitor the conditions at the farm crashed, as it had now, her son could be depended upon to come down, reboot the OS, reinstall all her applications, check that the IO ports were all working, and the sensors they linked up to still effective. Checking the saline levels, the nitrogen levels, the PH and the E. coli count of the water in the ponds. Yet how to raise the year's shrimp, how to provide optimum breeding conditions, how to cull only so many shrimp for the shipments as well as Kaua'i's winter food supply so that there'd be enough remaining to breed the following year, of all this he knew nothing, and wanted to know nothing, looking a little bemused when she tried to teach him, finding it odd she found it so important.

"The new transistors are all going to be biotech, anyway," he explained earnestly, "living tissue is a much faster transmitter."

"Well, duh," she said. It was only someone from the next generation, the one she'd so foolishly allowed to be raised by computers, who would find this surprising, an unobvious piece of information that required sharing.

She remembered them sitting in the huge blue and green living room, he and his friends, talking about dreams and computer games as though their narratives were interchangeable. They hadn't even noticed they were facing the sea. Prime real estate and what did they care? She should've shipped them all off to some urban ghetto, in the same containers she filled with frozen shrimp. At the time she'd found it fascinating, their exploring, had tried to keep up, even pretending an interest in video games whose narratives she found dull, compared to the life cycle of Penaeus. Encouraging them to learn to program. She wasn't stupid, she too could have learned, she was even yet perhaps not too old, but then what would they all eat?

It was a time sink, this wire head business. Sixteen hours a day; all the shrimp would've died without anyone to look after them. They didn't have children either, not one of them, because of course, they never had anything other than virtual sex, a break in the day's endless code crunching which didn't even require leaving their work stations. Which was perhaps a wise decision in light of the various virulent STD strains, and yet self-chosen infertility was putting an even faster dent in the population than the flu deaths, which had, by the end of the pandemic reached sixteen per cent, never mind having taken both her parents and her husband.

It was like wartime, you couldn't really complain; it had happened to so many. And in spite of her heavy personal loss she'd catch herself thinking the widespread deaths were a good thing. It was because she was a scientist, she knew that. If there's fewer people spewing toxic sludge into the water the oceans will have time to clean themselves, her secret voice would whisper, the fish populations might have a chance to make a comeback. Not that they deserved it, any of them. To have cared so little for the fish meant in the end that they cared equally little for themselves. What was destroying one's own food supply but a form of death wish, a slow suicide?

No wonder her son and his friends were trying to find a way to make digital fish edible. It was a search, however doomed, born of desperation. It wasn't they who'd poisoned the waters but her generation, her parents, grandparents and great-grandparents, right back to the very beginning of the industrial era. Hurtling proudly into the information age, too busy to think about fish populations. And of course, it had taken generations for the effects to show so dramatically, to become something one couldn't ignore. And by then it was too late. By now, Ellen thought, it's really too late. I'm just whistling in the dark, trying year after year to save my family farm. The children have already left, thrown too quickly into a half grown brave new world, not grown enough yet to shelter them. So many of my family, my friends and lovers have died but we'll all be dead before it's over. Of course this was always true, but in those days we didn't care; just like the fish we'd done our job, made grandchildren.

She cried often although no one saw. She cried because she was getting older. She cried because she had no man, no grandchildren and no company. For company she talked with the old people at Seaview. She enjoyed their stories and paid a close and calculated attention to the information they passed on, the tiniest most subtle nuances in the methodology of shrimp farming: a lifetime's experience. It was only a lifetime of attention closely paid that could garner anyone what could truly be called a skill. A skill was worth passing on. The most basic skill of all is my own, husbanding life which is the source of our own life, Ellen thought. Yet her son and his friends didn't want it. It was old fashioned, it made them squeamish; eating cooked fish off a plate made some of them gag, even retch. Jake was one of the few who could still do it.

Strange alien beings. Post-human beings. She'd thought them aliens at twelve, now, at twenty they were beyond flesh, even alien flesh. She missed her friends, but the ones who hadn't died had moved to the melting Arctic.

"Heard from Lucinda?" Jake asked, her machine reliably repaired. She could count on him in that area, at least. This mention of her best friend, on the other hand, was highly unusual. Keeping track of your mother's life, even in the most cursory fashion, asking occasional personal questions had gone the way of thank you notes, and now dinner plates.

Lucinda had moved to the northern mainland, was, in spite of being a GIS programmer, a hippiesque biological Luddite who believed the air and water were cleaner there, that it was necessary to move north for the sake of her family DNA. She'd moved her son Patrick with her.

"She emailed last week," Ellen replied, and added pointedly, "Patrick got married and had children, and the children, so far at least, seem fine. Physically perfect, handsome and clever even."

Jake nodded sympathetically. "It's so rare." A risk not worth taking, he appeared to think but did not say. Up north children still had children. Up north you could be a grandparent. How she longed to go, join Lucinda in her treeline community. Bring Jake. Perhaps he'd still mate, breed. Years of studying marine biology at Hilo, coming back after graduating to take over OpaeCorp, and she was using animal terms to describe human behavior. But what was the difference after all?

"Soon we'll be able to eat them," Jake said, eagerly switching the subject back to his favorite. "Living proteins, strands of DNA now process information; the cyber world, as you know, is no longer exclusively silicon based. Soon we'll be able to eat virtual shrimp and then we won't need you anymore."

He said this as though it should please her, and not entirely as though it was a joke. She cried but he didn't notice. When had she learned to do that, cry in such a way that it was unnoticeable? Probably around the same time she became so blunt.

"But they always did process information," Ellen said bluntly and Jake seemed surprised, not getting it.

"They were just reproducing meat bags, Mum. Now they do something useful."

She listened even though it drove her mad. After all he'd just spent hours debugging her software. And he was still her son, still company; she wanted him just to stay a little longer. They'd go back to the house; she'd fry him real shrimp and make a salad to go with; he'd eat with distaste, mainly to please her; he still needed that. They'd always been close.

He wanted to show her the cyber-fish, the collective pet project they worked on feverishly, in their time off from paid programming. He'd brought his laptop anyway to run the diagnostics on her system because, of course, it had a larger memory than her old machine; he could run more sophisticated debugging software. Jake laughed, calling it her clockwork computer. "It's just wooden gears and spindles in there, isn't it, Mum? Positively medieval; I'll get you a new one."

"I'd have to learn all the systems then," she sighed.

"But you have to someday anyway, or someone does; your machine won't last forever and whoever takes the farm over will have to be younger." Jake looked at her sternly, reminding her of her age as though it was some kind of vice she secretly cultivated just to offend him. "The person you train will be my age; they won't understand your clockwork system any better than you understand my biotech laptop."

"So show me the damn cyber-fish."

It looked like a shrimp of course, swimming around its little aquarium sized screen. That much he'd learned from her, thought it important. The new fish must still look like a fish. Not that it mattered. He could just as easily have wire-framed a swimming potato.

"But how do you eat it?" she persisted. "How does it provide nourishment?"

"The code it's built out of; it's living code. The information is living, it isn't dead. We'll eat the living information."

'Living Information'; it sounded like a new God, or a new nickname for Jake. "That should be your web name," she quipped, "Living Information."

"It is," he replied. "It's from Philip K. Dick."

Whoever that was. With a crazy futurist for a son and an anachronistic aboriginal for a neighbor no wonder she felt stumped. Where had all the normal people gone?

To the mainland. North.

"The same was true when you ate a carrot that grew in dirt," she snapped. Living Information looked completely puzzled then and she had to wonder: had he actually ever done that? She couldn't remember. It was likely he'd only ever eaten hydroponic.

"What I meant is, how do you get the fish out of the machine to put it on your plate and eat it?"

"Oh Mum, we don't bother with plates anymore, you know that. We just use the pills." He looked at her blankly. Not getting it. So smart and so dumb. Cyber-hexed, that's what they were. She cried, she said, "Come north with me."

"I'd like to, Mum," Jake said, seemingly meaning it. "But we're so close, that's what you have to understand. We're so close, it'll pay so well; we're almost there. And once we're there we can close OpaeCorp; you can retire up north, be with your friend, you'll be so old by then you won't be needed anymore anyway. And you'll be rich; I'll make sure of that. Now, I need a month's supply of fish pills to take back to the park with me—are they ready?"

They went to the warehouse; she gave him a box. Laughing, looking at the size of the box, Jake suggested she just email him the shrimp pills, send them as an attachment. She hoped it was a joke but she wasn't sure. She stared at him, said it again: "The material body requires material food; you can't download it, you can't email it, it won't pass through a modem." He suggested she send the chemical composition of the fish pills. "That's the code," she said, "not the actual food."

"There's no nutritional value in code?" he asked, startled. "But that gives me an idea, something to work on." And off he went on his ATV, the carton of fish pills lashed on back, back to the park. He called it the park, as though it was somewhere to play. And perhaps it was.

She watched him lurch up the road, jamming the gears. She was surprised he could still drive. They so rarely left, any of them. They'd chosen to live in dorms at the park; they no longer had homes. They no longer walked on the beach at sunset. They could make better beaches, better sunsets.

Most likely I'll die here, Ellen thought, never get north. And maybe they're right. Maybe they really will make cyber fish with nutritional value, or else they'll remake their bodies so that digital information does provide nourishment.

In spite of heavy doses of antibiotics, the shrimp were dying the next morning, in a pandemic of infectious disease. She'd seen it before, of course. Once yearly a mutated virus or bacterium attacked her shrimp, and she, trying to adjust their environment if not to the original one, for who even knew what that was anymore, then to one which would offset the effects of disease.

And so she rode her dirt bike up the highway to Seaview, to visit Grandfather Frank and his wife Dora. They, of course, wouldn't know how to deal with the new conditions either, but she'd found their wealth of experience more useful than all the fish farming internet forums. She sat and drank tea, prodded their brains, watched for nonexistent hump-backs. She had to listen, yet again, to the history of OpaeCorp, the history of Seaview, their family history going back four generations. The Copelands had apparently hailed from Iowa. Who even cared? Ellen yawned, exhausted, worried. Dora smiled, said, "You're not as old as we are yet."

No. Although she surely felt like it. But in the middle of one of Dora's stories about how Harry Copeland married Eileen Drinkwater the year before he took a loan out to buy the original OpaeCorp property five miles up the coast, Frank interjected and said, "Eileen was the science head; Harry did the money. They started the shrimp farm together, in the beginning the research was government funded. All the mangroves had died, she kept having to dose the nauplii with antibiotics because it seems the mangroves release something into the water which neutralizes the effects of the bacterium in the shrimp habitat. We never did isolate what it was, although we had people work on it for years; we just kept doing it because it worked. They're more adaptive when the intake runs through mangroves."

Dora interrupted, continuing, "And then Eileen had to grow mangroves, not just a fish farm but a mangrove farm, seedlings of it to be planted, she got the boy scouts to help her; Harry said they looked like Chinese planting rice paddies, all forty of them."

And Ellen, who was Eileen's great-granddaughter raised her eyebrows and said, "All our mangroves were grown from seed? You never told me about the damn mangroves before. I learned that from Maui. And he only said the part about them being the best final-stage filter system for effluent, he never mentioned the resistance thing."

"But neither had anyone else," Dora said, excited now, her eyes shining. "There'd been no mangrove on Kaua'i for years and no one had ever mentioned that it was an important part of the shrimps' ecosystem, and Eileen said to her local friend, "But where can I get any mangrove to replant—if they all died we've changed the water so much they wouldn't grow anyhow," and her friend said, "But they've been breeding a naturally resistant variety on Molokai," and so off Eileen flew to Kaunakakai . . . "

And then Dora lost her thread, looking momentarily blank, saying, "Remember Martha's wedding? You were there too, Ellen, only you wouldn't remember, you were two."

"The locals breed things?" Ellen asked, shocked. "But that's science. What was this local guy's name, anyway, Eileen's friend?"

"The cake was six feet tall," Dora murmured.

"Finish the story about the mangroves," Ellen said, leaning over to jab Dora with her elbow. Dora's tea spilled on her lap; it seemed to snap her back.

"Off Eileen went to find the resistant mangrove, gone wild on Molokai, re-establishing itself just enough each year for her to gather an armful of seed, dig up a few boxes of saplings. The locals had been babysitting them for years; it was some little pet project they had going. Eileen replanted it in the shallows of her farm, and now it's spread up and down the coast. But each year there was some new such challenge, and some years Eileen, or now you, Ellen, found a solution and other years . . . "

And other years the old peoples' information was useless and she'd have to wing it, and mostly, Ellen thought, most of all, I miss the friendship of people my own age. At least Eileen still had that. And the shrimp were sick again, and her visit to Frank and Dora was doing no good. We did our bit, their eyes seemed to say. It's your turn now. Her grandfather sighed, as though, behind his memory loss he knew exactly what kind of a failure they were facing this time. He shrugged, he sighed. "More antibiotics, kid, that's all I can think of. Or go ask Maui."

"He's a local," Ellen said derisively.

"All the better," Frank said. "They've been here thousands of years, we've been here a few generations. Information."

"Information fish," Ellen said, getting up to kiss him on the cheek. Thin, thin skin, transparent and dry as paper. And that smell. She wondered whether Akela had them washed every day. "You should have told me sooner," she whispered, feeling terribly sad. She'd lose him, she'd lose the farm. She'd hunkered down under the weight of her previous losses but this was starting to push it, even for someone as blunt and stubborn as she.

"Tell you sooner what?"

"To go to the locals for advice. I thought you thought they were back-wards idiots."

"I thought I thought so too. I'd forgotten they were the ones who'd told Eileen to replant the mangroves. Until Dora told that part of the story."

"And so they're responsible for all our millions," Ellen said.

"In a way. But there was always something new. The mangroves were only a part of the solution."

"How's Harry doing?"

"He's okay. He's older than we are, he forgets more. Why?"

"I want to ask him the name of Eileen's local friend. See if he remem-bers."

"Well, go see him, he's upstairs in 204. He doesn't get out of bed anymore. But he'd love to see you. He might even be having a good day, remember who you are. Just say you're his and Eileen's—"

"Great-granddaughter," Ellen said, running for the elevator.

But Harry was dead. Ellen could tell by the lingering smell, although the bed was empty. Seaview's manager Akela stood at the window, looking at the sea. Ellen had known Akela since kindergarten. They were the same age, but they were no longer friends. "Surf's up," Ellen said, and Akela turned, a vacant look on her face. Ellen couldn't help herself, she rushed forward and took Akela by the shoulders, shaking her. Almost immediately she stepped back, appalled by what she'd done.

"I'm sorry, Akela. But I felt like doing much worse. I wanted to throttle you."

"He was a hundred and two. He did good."

"If you'd kept him alive just three more weeks I would've finished taping him. Put it in the OpaeCorp archives. You don't know what you're letting die here, Akela. It's like destroying crucial survival information."

"So you come work here then, Ellen," Akela snapped.

"But I run the farm," Ellen replied, exasperated.

"The rich bitch. You inherited OpaeCorp, or you will. Your family owns Seaview too. I'm the manager of an old folks' home."

"Jesus Christ, is that what you think?" Ellen sat down heavily in an overstuffed chair overlooking the rising tide. "The money's all in the ponds, the processing plant, the payroll. I take a salary."

"You want to know what I make? And what about that mechanic of yours? I heard you don't pay him a cent. He fixes the pumps for nothing, because you're screwing him."

"Is that what people say? It isn't true, Akela. You have to believe me. We've known each other for thirty-five years, that should count for something. I keep trying to hire him, but he won't condescend to work for me. He's much too superior for that. And we're not sleeping together."

"Why not? He's cute. Or d'you think you're too good for Hawai'ians? You're just like Eileen."

"What?"

"You don't know that story? I can't believe it. Everyone knows that story."

"I don't."

"Well, I won't be the one to tell you. You can ask someone else. If you paid a little more attention to what goes on around you and a little less to the Penaeus life cycle you might even have a life."

"The farm's going down, Akela. My salary won't count for much when I declare bankruptcy."

And Akela sat down beside her in the second chair that matched the first, the one Ellen had meant to sit in while Harry sat in hers, telling her the name of Eileen's local friend.

"I don't actually deserve your forgiveness," Ellen said. She meant it, too. How could she and her forebears have been so blind, and in exactly the same way?

Akela took her hand and said, "I'm sorry, Ellen, and you'll think of something. I know you will. You've faced problems before at OpaeCorp, you've always fixed them. For generations."

"I got a real bad feeling this time, Akela."

"I've always envied you, Ellen. You're so lucky you're a scientist, it's much better than gerontology; you should listen to them go on and on and on, and how they scream when you forget to change their bedpans on time once, just the once."

"I'd scream too," Ellen said, withdrawing her hand. She was annoyed all over again, thinking of Harry, of dirty bedpans, of pathogenic bacteria.

"You only studied marine biology because you knew you had the farm job waiting for you."

"What's it matter, Akela? Any of it. We shouldn't fight, you and me. We're the only ones left from our kindergarten class. The rest have all died or moved away."

"You've still got Jake. I never had children."

"Yes, I have. Although to tell you the truth, sometimes I'm not sure Jake counts."

When she got home it seemed Maui had forgiven her unspeakable rudeness because he was busy touring the farm, checking all her mechanicals. It was thoughtful of him, and he was pretty good about showing up to do it regularly, but she wished she could just put him on the payroll and know he'd be there every day. But that wasn't his way, he always said, and so she was grateful and invited him for dinner.

"How are your shrimp today?" he asked.

"Not well. And how come you're asking me? You're the one who said they wouldn't last the week. You've got me in a panic."

"I'm just a simple mechanic without a license," he said opaquely. "You went up to Seaview today to ask the old people for advice."

"You know everything, don't you?"

He shrugged. "It's not hard." It was funny but she'd never noticed before how cute he was, not until Akela mentioned it. Maybe Akela was right and she hadn't seen his beauty because he was Hawai'ian. Maybe she was horribly racist and had no clue. Maybe all the Copelands were. He was born handsome, and all that bodysurfing seemed to do wonders. There was something to be said for looking after the meat bag, in spite of what Jake thought.

"How's Harry doing?" Maui asked.

"Harry died this morning. Did you know, Maui, that if people don't die of the flu or cancer or industrial accidents, some of them live to a hundred and two?"

"So I've heard," he said ironically. "How old are you, Ellen?" he asked, walking beside her on the path back to the house.

"Forty-two, just like you," she said.

"Rhymes, doesn't it? You gone through menopause yet, Ellen?"

"Is that your business?"

"Not really. I'm just curious. What are you going to feed me, Ellen? Let me guess. It starts with S-H."

It was shrimp, but real shrimp and not pills with the powdered Chitosan included, which the children preferred. Chitosan, basically powdered shrimp shells, worked as a fat absorber, a fiber which collected dietary fat on its way through the body. Being sedentary wire heads, her children's generation shared a propensity toward obesity. Ellen would tell Jake and his friends to exercise. They'd laugh, think her old-fashioned.

And even she found Maui old fashioned. Didn't he eat fruit and vegetables grown in soil? No one else she knew did that. Worse, he opened a Tupperware container of poi to eat beside the shrimp. She gulped it down, not wanting to appear rude. Purple glue. It was their traditional starchy staple, a tuber. If you didn't cook it for seventeen hours until the hard white taro root turned to mauve paste your throat would scratch for weeks. Like eating fiberglass. Ellen knew she was exaggerating, even in her thoughts.

"Tell me about your family," she said. "Did they convert?"

"They converted to Homo Sapiens," Maui said. "My great-grandmother was actually a fish. Or she could turn into one, some full moon nights."

"Really? What kind?"

"Technically not a fish but a dolphin. Bottlenose."

"I see."

"We almost all converted," he went on. "We had to. Some passed on the old ways, though. In secret."

"Kahuna magic?"

"Yes." He looked uncomfortable, as though he wanted to avoid that subject. Was afraid she'd make fun of him. He looked around the room, its muted blues and greens, the acres of picture windows overlooking the sea. "Nice place. I've never been inside."

She felt uncomfortable then. Said, "It needs repairs. The windows leak when it rains, even when there's trade winds. I can't afford to redo them, and it's too big for one person, now that Jake and all his buddies have moved to Kapaa. What's your house like?"

"It's a tin roofed shack on the beach," he said. Ellen looked away. They'd finished eating and she didn't know what to do with her hands. She wished she hadn't given up smoking. "You don't have to apologize," he said. "I like hearing the sea. I can't sleep if I don't hear rain on the roof. I can reach out the window and pick apple bananas for breakfast, and I can sweep all the floors in less than half an hour. This place is spooky, and I don't envy you living here."

"Just asking."

"Just answering."

"So, does it heal?" she asked.

"Does what heal?"

"Kahuna magic?"

"It's science and religion in one. If you want to call that magic, so be it, and maybe it even is. And indeed it does heal, maybe because of that. The methodology of science was never removed from reverence for all life, and its poetry."

"Rain on a tin roof at night?"

"Precisely."

"Women who turn into dolphins at the full moon?"

He raised an eyebrow. "Don't make fun of what you don't understand, fish-killer. I never saw her do it, but my grandmother did, and told me, and I have no reason to disbelieve her. But have you ever noticed the irony?"

"Which irony in particular?"

"You come for wisdom, for spiritual healing, to a culture you set out systematically to destroy. Christianity didn't work out for you or what?"

"But I'm not, Maui. I think you're old-fashioned, not any kind of savior. I'm not a religious person, I'm a scientist. I'm just being nosy."

"That could be part of your problem, did it ever occur to you? No respect for bio-diversity in the science. I'm repeating myself, I know. Although I didn't mean you in particular, Ellen. I was talking about your race's short memory. It's because your grandparents didn't tell you enough stories."

"Seems not. There's hardly any wild shrimp left, in the whole world." It was true. Each year she released a few nauplii and post larvae, hoping to help repopulate the wild, but as the E. coli had gotten stronger, the released fish never survived; they weren't fed antibiotics with their food as the farmed fish were.

"Who's surprised?"

"Although today Frank and Dora told me an interesting story about mangroves. You know anything about that one?"

"Could be."

"You know who Eileen's local friend was, by any chance?"

"Yes, I do. They fell in love. I'm his great-grandnephew. She wouldn't divorce Harry because her lover, my ancestral uncle, was only a local. In spite of having saved the farm during its first big crisis, making her millions."

"I never heard that."

"Like I said, your old people didn't tell you the right stories. The true ones."

"Today Frank said I should ask you for advice."

"Thatso? About a hundred years too late, you ask me. Come body-surfing tomorrow?"

"I would, Maui, but I got a little bacterium problem in my ponds."

"But that's why you should come," he said.

"Bodysurfing. My son and his friends would find you hopelessly out of date. Exercising the meat bag."

"You might yet have grandchildren, you look after your body."

"Jake will never breed."

"You don't know that. But what I meant is you're not too old to start a second set."

Whatever that meant. "You have kids, Maui?"

"Sure. Two girls. They live in Vegas with their mother."

"She local?" It was funny how local meant Hawai'ian, while *kama'aina* ostensibly translated as local but usually referred to whites who'd grown up in the islands. *Haoles.* It didn't really make sense.

"No. She's a *haole*, like you. Seems we never learn."

The next day all the shrimp were dead. Maui phoned, asked her to go bodysurfing. "I got orders to fill," Ellen said, bluntly turning him down. "There's no shrimp to go to the processing plant. I have to pay the workers regardless. It's in their contract."

"Rightly so. It's not their fault you killed the fish."

"A little support might be nice, here."

"Come bodysurfing," Maui repeated. "If your shrimp are dead anyway."

"Maui, this is serious."

"Sounds like."

"Okay. What the hell. I'm coming."

They went every day for a week. He taught her to dive under the waves.

The mainland supermarket chains were suing her. Seventeen messages on her voice mail and another fourteen on email. They all received the same reply: "All shrimp are dead." She'd have to sell OpaeCorp to pay her legal bills, never mind the lawsuits.

"Let it go down," Maui said. "Go down with it. Just as the wave is about to crest you take a deep breath and dive underneath, deep."

She missed it of course, dove too late. The wave caught her and smashed her onto the beach. When it receded her hair was full of grit, her knees bloody. She spat out sand.

"Feels bad, doesn't it?" Maui said, scraping her off the sand.

"Yeah. I'm trying to remember why I came."

"To Earth or with me, today?"

"Both."

"To help feed a starving world, Ellen. You said so yourself. It's the one thing I like about you."

"Well, you can stop liking it 'cause I've failed big time."

"That's the problem with you *haoles*. You never learned to do what feels good. You always go the other way, as though there wasn't a choice, and then you're surprised when your world crashes around you."

"Like the wave?"

He nodded severely. He took this bodysurfing business seriously. He considered it a metaphor. She should've known. She should've stayed in bed. Or shot herself. She had an old hang glider in an equipment shed, she could still gobble three grams of psilocybin mushrooms; jump off the Na Pali cliffs some full moon night, turn into a bat, or a squash. Ought to work.

"Is that Kahuna magic?"

He just looked at her. Derisively. "We'll go out again, next set. When I say dive, dive. Okay? You have to trust me." It didn't sound ironic at all. It scared the shit out of her, his lack of irony. Scarier than her farm going down, scarier than being thrown by the ocean.

She got it the next time, and the time after that missed it but swam under the bone crushing surf, and a little later in the afternoon she caught another short ride.

She went home and cross posted again, without reading her messages:

"All shrimp are dead." She defrosted a pound of frozen shrimp for dinner instead of going to the pond, dipping out a net full of fresh like she usually did. She ate the whole pound. She took the phone off the hook. She went to bed. She was so sore the next morning she wanted to sleep all day but Maui appeared at her bedroom door, take-out coffee and saimin in hand. "Wake up, *wahine*. We got work to do."

A deep cool tunnel propelling her. Across the entire bay. It had its own momentum. Weightless, both supported and propelled by its power. Being picked up by the ocean rather than thrown by it. Its pleasure and its arc were so joyful and required such a similar surrender she couldn't help but think of sex. And she'd thought of it so rarely since Jake's father had died of flu, ten years earlier.

All the shrimp are dead. Who cares?

Trust. She saw him not twenty yards away. What was he? An American, like herself. That's what he'd answer. And: my great-grandmother was a fish.

No kidding.

The wave they were riding was hurtling toward a breakwater made of piled stones, looked to be old, real old. It was funny how much time there was to think in split seconds. Nano seconds, Jake would've corrected her. How old?

Oh, say, five hundred years old.

Jesus Christ, we'll be killed. How could she not have seen it sooner? He meant to kill her, in revenge for all her family's generations of *haole* nastiness, and himself too, except he probably knew some fishy trick to save himself. The wave had carried them so far so fast she hadn't seen the wall coming. Entranced by the ride. Tubular, man.

"Swim like hell," he was yelling. "Follow me." And she did, grateful for her fins. The ancient Hawai'ians, his predecessors, hadn't had those. Or genetically engineered shrimp. It was all fine to engineer them to be resistant to disease but the little problem was the diseases, which had shorter life spans, also grew resistant to the endless antibiotics dumped into the water, mixed into the food. Because the food was spoiling.

Because the water was filthy. Because the shrimp were crowded. Surprising, really, they'd made it this long. That was about the extent of all their big science, really. Not very farsighted, she had to admit. You couldn't beat a bug. Not really, not in the end. They had more grandchildren, and they had them faster, much faster. Grandchildren won.

Simple, really.

She swam like hell, solving her problem as she swam. She'd never swum so hard in her life. She'd never done anything so hard in her life. And then they were in it, a four-foot-wide channel in the piled stone breakwater. Through the channel a clear still pond, many of them linked together.

She treaded water, winded, barely able to breathe. But alive. Unlike her shrimp. It seemed a miracle.

She got home. There was a message from Jake.

"We're experimenting with synthetic stomachs that process digital information," his recorded voice explained earnestly as though the answer was just around the corner and not a hundred years away. "It's not much different from a pacemaker."

"Well," she left a return message, "your implanted cyber stomach, if the body doesn't reject it, might be able to eat a digital data flow but that still doesn't give your cells the proteins they need to keep rebuilding themselves." Just in case he'd overlooked that one little problem. Spending sixteen hours a day plugged in might make you a genius of a programmer but it also had a small tendency, she'd noticed, to impair your sense of reality.

And maybe he'd turn out to be right, one day. Who could blame him for trying? All the wild shrimp were dead after all, and now all the farmed shrimp too. Still, he was her son and she noticed she'd spared him the bad news out of all her correspondents. She hadn't gone far enough, her message should've read: "All food gone". She should've posted it all over the net. No food left. Then maybe they'd wake up. The tribe faces famine. It had been awhile. They'd forgotten what it was like.

It could happen, but not in their lifetime. The children had gone too far ahead, they didn't know the way back; they were visionaries in the worst possible way. They couldn't find their way back now, and in fact they thought back was bad. They wanted nothing to do with their parents' old fashioned notions about the body requiring food. And I never said it's impossible, Ellen thought. But it's too big a leap. They have no idea how far from its realization they are. They don't realize they need grandchildren.

She listened for Maui, hoping he'd come, she hadn't read him wrong. It was funny, she couldn't remember what he drove, a dirt bike or an ATV or a pick-up, couldn't remember the sound of him parking his vehicle, couldn't visualize him walking in the door, a fine coating of Kaua'i's red road dust on his skin.

But he usually came silently she realized, dripping, out of the sea. Having swum around the Haena point. Who could do that but a dolphin or a whale?

"Wild shrimp," he said, carrying a lidded bucket. She could hear it sloshing. "Post larvae. Twelve different species. Nine marine, and three Machrobrachiums. You need to convert one of the ponds for the freshwater. They're important, resistant to certain bacteria the Penaeus aren't. For hybridization."

"I know," she said. "Eileen and Harry did that too."

"And who told them to do it?"

"Let me guess."

He shrugged. "We'll clean out your ponds, restock. They're much stronger, you know. There's much more chance of adaptation, because the gene pool's larger."

"You can swim with buckets?"

"You mean you can't?"

"Is that what you do with yourself," she asked. "Is collect and breed heirloom shrimp species?"

"It's what we do," he said, "for five hundred years."

"But how did you know it was going to be so important?"

He just looked at her, dripping. "*Haoles*," he said, shaking his head. There was a little less derision in it, a little more humor.

"I'm still going broke."

"So take out another loan. Isn't that what you people are good at, is financing? You're a good surfer, Ellen, you just don't know it yet. You can't let your great-grandmother down."

"So what's your big interest, Maui? You got your own little ancestral shrimp farm to look after, round the point, just like I got mine. You showed it to me yesterday, remember? What possible interest you got in saving OpaeCorp from the great white sharks?"

"Yours is bigger. On account of you people being better at money, buying up more of our stolen land. Grow more shrimp, feed more of the starving world. It's not for you Ellen, but for the grandchildren."

"Why didn't you help before?"

"Seems to me I tried, you weren't listening. And you had to let it go down, so you could start over, do it right."

She looked him up and down, assessing the potential of his DNA in the production of grandchildren. He was in great shape, better than she was, and his science seemed to have proved a little better too. Although all the data wasn't in yet.

She touched his arm but he pulled away. "I didn't say our grandchildren," he said. "I said the grandchildren."

"Oh."

He smiled just a little. "Well anyway, we'll just have to see. I've always liked you, Ellen, but we've got to take it slow. One more thing."

"What's that?"

"You got to write me over half your shares."

"I beg your pardon? Half?"

He picked up his bucket of shrimp, headed back toward the sea, to his invisible road. "Remember the mangroves?" he called back. "You people might never learn, but we do, eventually. Think of it as a retroactive share of profits."

Think of Harry and Eileen, of Maui's still nameless ancestral uncle, of the small scary fact, which had just occurred to her, that she and Maui might be a little bit related, on that count. She watched him go, carrying his bucket. Those heirloom shrimp were worth millions, even on a chance. Nobody else had them; if they were hers she really could refinance. She'd do it too, she'd sign over half of her OpaeCorp shares. She didn't care what the old people said. After all, they were old. And they should have told her sooner, about all of it. You can only pretend to forget for so long before it catches up with you.

SEWING FORGETFULNESS

H E HAD RED HAIR. HE SAID: "HERE ARE TWO KEYS." HE gave me a piece of paper with an address. "Go up five flights of stairs. At the top, two doors. Unlock and relock each door."

I felt like the heroine in a spy novel, only I couldn't remember my mission.

People used to say it was the partying that caused the short-term memory loss, but now I think it was the sewing machines. There were two, and I still have them both. My short-term memory still sucks. I'd get rid of them if it wasn't for what Nancy said one night.

In a half empty warehouse, I followed his instructions. At the top of the five flights of stairs, through two doors, a row of lockers and change rooms. Behind an opened door I glimpsed a wall of mirror tile. Perhaps it was a dance company's rehearsal space; there were so many dancers then.

One locker door too stood open; on the bottom shelf I saw a pair of blue shoes. They were a little worn but very nice and they fit. I put them on and ran down the hall past a short-haired woman sitting at a sewing machine.

"But who will get in trouble about the keys?" I thought I heard her call as I ran down the stairs, back out the street door. Within a day I'd forgotten how I'd acquired the shoes.

I spent the week living inside my life, experiencing textures of happiness I'd never previously dared. Everything went well for me; I believed it was my blue shoes. Ariel and I had always been fond acquaintances; suddenly we were close friends.

It began this way; we ran into one another on Spadina twice a week; we'd go for hot and sour soup. It was January and we had our sore throats; ginger helped. Her smile over soup a small gift of brightness, evidence too, I was sure, of the talismanic quality of my blue shoes. She was an artist like everyone else I knew: talented, mostly unpaid. Some were dancers or writers, but really, that's being an artist too.

"The eighties," she said, "are gobbling people up like lunch meat." Someone else had just died, hit by a truck, riding his bicycle home drunk. I vowed to hold Ariel close. If I had fewer acquaintances and more true friends, less people would die, my blue shoes seemed to tell me.

We gossiped and wrote in my notebook, little metaphysical jokes. It was that kind of winter. We were happy. "Manifest toes," I wrote, and turned the book around to face Ariel. She read, smiled, picked up the nice black Pilot Fineliner to write. She turned the book back around to face me.

"Manifest fingers," she'd written.

That January I'd just returned from California, a post break-up vacation. As always I'd bought a new notebook to begin a new chapter of my life, a turquoise Chinese brocade in hardcover, small, with red lined pages and chrysanthemums in the corners of the pages. I lived in an empty loft; endless new space deliciously echoing both inside and outside. The lease was held by an artists' collective, but they were renting a larger warehouse for their winter show, and needed cash toward their original space. During the day I painted and wrote, lived on my savings, threw shoes at cockroaches. The loft has the biggest cockroaches I've ever seen outside of the tropics. I think they must be a hundred years old, to have grown so large. Thankfully, being so old, they're very slow and easy to kill. The kitchen scurries at night with quick small browns but I'm used to those from all of David and my apartments; they don't make me nearly so nervous.

Ariel and I went to a party. I brought a mickey of Johnnie Walker Red; she had just one shot. I'd split up with David just before I'd gone away, thought I wanted a new boy already. Silly, really. Robert leaned against the bathroom door, gave me a smile of such humanity, a knife bright in the dark.

"What's up with you, Robert?" I asked, considering his handsome face, his long dark hair. Robert was a bartender and poet I'd known for years. We'd been friends but never lovers.

He leaned. "Passing through time, like a disease of the senses; in a coffee cup the hours are defiled to a timeless zero as though your eyes had always been here. And always will. Our lives are just the moments that fill in between the coffee cups."

I answered: "Time is a Chinese puzzle, and like a crystal on a string it hypnotizes, but only love can break the spell."

He raised his eyebrows, considering. The look on his face changed, as though someone had thrown a pellet of dark dye into a clear fountain. Not Robert I thought, even if his poetry reverberates, resounds. Not ready for that darkened hunger, a need I suddenly felt would defile me.

Better to run through snowy alleyways with Ariel, duck into basement Vietnamese restaurants with Ariel. In the winter lit afternoons we climbed stairs together, looking for things. A condemned loft building, full of the debris of uprooted lives. Everyone had moved out, left their junk behind. "I like the clear plexi bathtub up on the platform with blue stairs leading up to it," Ariel said. "We could take pictures. Make a little narrative about these unknown departed lives."

We bought film for my Polaroid and went back to that building and photographed things that reminded us of our lost homes.

"How can our homes be lost?" Ariel asked when I suggested this was what we were doing. "We had homes," she said, "we grew up in families."

"The families were broken; we were always ducking plates, knives, fists, groping hands," I said.

"That's what you mean. They were homes but everyone in them was lost. And now we duck an ever-present death that's come to some we know; we try to resist the temptation to die, to not ride our bicycles so drunk we can't see oncoming traffic," she replied.

"Indeed," I said. The thought of Ariel dying frightened me more than a little.

What did we take pictures of? Looking out the smudgy window into an air shaft we saw that a lone tree grew. It was an ailanthus, a tree of heaven. They'll even grow out of concrete; I recognized it by the shape. Someone had tied silk ribbons to the bare winter branches, in gold and green, winter leaves. I was astounded. Ariel stood very still while I focused past the smudgy window. I thought she was as moved as I was.

A sewing machine stood abandoned on a table. Beneath the foot, a beautiful applique underwater scene of fish and brain coral.

"I've always wanted a sewing machine," Ariel said.

"Plug it in, see if it works," I replied. We did, but the power in the building had been turned off.

"We could take it home. It must work because she was still using it," Ariel said.

"Unless she just put the applique there for decoration. A miniature installation piece . . . "

"—inoperative sewing machine sews," Ariel finished my thought for me. "Help me, Veronica; I want this sewing machine."

We carried it down the stairs. That's the thing about living and working in warehouse buildings: there are always stairs, so many breath-stealing stairs. On the wall of the stairwell someone had even sketched stairs in cobalt chalk.

"Where do those stairs go?" Ariel asked, setting the sewing machine down on the landing, pausing for breath. She traced their outline, her finger climbing.

"Up five flights," I said, "through two locked doors. A row of lockers there, a woman at a sewing machine." The image emerged like a lost fragment of dream.

I couldn't remember its source, but Ariel said, "That sounded nice. It's a poetic winter, isn't it?"

"Very." I paused to admire my friend. She wore a midnight blue Russian hat atop her gold curls, a thrift store black borg. She had the kind of lips that are always so red, never need lipstick. Or maybe it was just winter.

She checked me out in return, smiling secretively. When her eyes reached my feet she said, "You never told me where you scored your blue suedes. I've been admiring them for weeks." She lifted up the sewing machine, passed it to me. "It's your turn."

"Okay." I was cheerful. "Let's go for soup after. More than soup, I'm starving. You know, I don't remember where I found the shoes."

"Drunk, maybe, Veronica?" Ariel asked. "So drunk you forgot. Hope you didn't steal them from someone at a party; they had to walk home barefoot in the slush."

"They could have worn mine. Same size, obviously."

"After they figured it out," Ariel said, "four in the morning, upset. But it doesn't sound like you. Even drunk, you're never mean, even inadvertently."

We took turns carrying the sewing machine all the way to Ariel's little rented room on Bathurst Street. She unlocked the door and I, who had taken the last turn, set it heavily down on her table. Ariel made tea, put Nina Hagen on, found bagels and cream cheese in her tiny bar fridge. Her bed was unmade, her floor heaped with clothes. I'd never seen how she lived before. My loft always looked tidy, mostly because it was so large it swallowed my few possessions. Clothes, art supplies, a new futon. A forties ashtray in the shape of a jaguar I'd bought at a junk store in Grass Valley, brought home in my luggage, wrapped in T-shirts. I kept my change and earrings there. The space had come with an iron and an ironing board, a dresser and a mirror. I used the iron; it seemed an incredible luxury, a luxury of order after years of David. He'd sprouted chaos like other people sprout windowsill herbs.

In the piles on Ariel's floor I saw things I'd always loved her in. It made me feel closer to her, as though in her clutter she exposed her vulnerability. Folded neatly in a closet I'd never have seen her beaded shawl spreading in green waves across last week's jeans and sweatshirts. I felt a window opening, of possibility. I mentally asked my blue shoes what it meant, and they seemed to say our relationship was changing. We looked at one other, considering.

I know shoes can't really talk, or send telepathic messages. But feelings accrue to objects, and perhaps even knowledge, for those shoes always seemed to impart a wisdom beyond my own. For some people it's a jade ring, or a painted silk scarf, or a framed photograph of their grandfather. For me that winter, it was the blue suede shoes.

I hugged her goodbye, went home and slept on my giant new futon alone.

Winter continued.

The sewing machine was a nice old black and gold Singer, one of the first electrics, with a big wheel to turn. I'd dropped in on Ariel for tea and bagels, cream cheese and Nina. "These are the very best sewing machines," she said, demonstrating, "they never break down; they're indestructible."

"You were right; it was a good score after all. My savings have run out," I sighed. We'd reached the point where we could discuss our money troubles. I knew Ariel was an exotic dancer.

"You could be one too," she said.

"Maybe," I said. "It's not that I think it's wrong, but it's never really seemed like my kind of thing."

"Me either," she said. "But it pays quite well. You have time to paint, to write, to be with your friends, save money to travel."

"Isn't it icky?"

"We're young for such a short time," she said. "It'll soon enough be over; I can worry about whether it's been icky then. Just come see me at the Silver Dollar tomorrow afternoon, you and Robert. You'll see."

Ariel in apricot satin, appliqued with brain coral, with pipefish, with sea dragons. I supposed she'd pocketed that little underwater scene that day, worked it into her outfit, too good to waste.

"Look," I said to Robert, "she has the sewing machine on stage with her."

She began her set leaning over the old Singer, blonde curls fallen forward, the power cord snaking beneath her feet, across the floor into the little dressing room behind the stage. Her silk satin gown fell open, showing off the curve of her breast. Yet the tableau she'd created was so lusciously intimate; she seemed not an exhibitionist but a beautiful woman alone in her room, sewing. I felt a voyeur all the more.

She sat on a plain white painted wooden kitchen chair, pumped the foot pedal in time to Nina, turned the sturdy black wheel. The machine hissed and snarled, the tension setting gone awry. I realized she had done this on purpose, deftly, as though the machine had foiled her purpose all on its own. How she must have studied and practiced to get that move right, and, I thought that she was sacrificing her machine to this performance, for one can only tangle with a tension setting so often before it breaks down for good. The audience, used to more traditional fare, seemed not quite as taken as Robert and I, with our art school backgrounds, enthralled by her originality.

She stroked the machine, whispered to it to be kind, to be gentle. She lifted one short little leg, bent at the knee over the curve of the engine casing, let it rest there a moment, began to rub it back and forth as though this gesture might coax the recalcitrant machine into performing for her. The other high heeled foot pumped the pedal; her little ringed hand turned the wheel persistently. Her back arched against the chair, head thrown back for a moment, mouth opened; the machine purred into life; sewing her secrets for her. The satin gown slipped askew, off her shoulders.

"It's real satin too, 1940s silk satin and not polyester satin as they make it now. So much more comforting against the skin, so much more real," I whispered to Robert and he laughed.

"Only a woman," he whispered back, "would deconstruct the fabric content of a stripper's costume."

"And her shoes are Capezio tap pumps, not cheap stilettos that damage your feet. It adds to the sensuality, good fabric and shoes. Because she's happier; her sexiness less faked."

"I've always thought Capezios are the sexiest shoes ever, it's true," Robert agreed, ordered us two Black Labels from the passing waiter. "Her legs are a little short," he observed, "fleshy in places where yours, long and bony, are not," but I, the only woman in the audience, was thinking how we were the same as no two others in the room.

"And for all that," I whispered, "it's still her difference that attracts, the ways in which she is not me."

Robert sucked his breath in beside me. It seemed completely out of character for him, distanced and streetwise as he claims to be. But her power over him in that moment intensified my feelings too, and I was drawn equally to Ariel and to Robert's willing surrender: a sharpened breath, breathing desire. Which of them did I want more?

Making love, part of my arousal is self-reflexive; I insert myself into my partner's pleasure in my body: women are so beautiful. I'd never been to see a stripper before, and Ariel surprised me; she seemed so completely transcendent of all the clichés. What if I got up there with her? Climbed the little rickety wooden steps up to the platform, took my clothes off, embraced her, my tongue running down her neck, along her beautiful plump white arm to the hand turning the sewing machine wheel, enclosing it with my own, forcefully making her sew faster and faster so that our lives might be sewn together and not come apart, as David's and mine came apart, as everything and everyone comes apart. But I didn't dare.

Ariel unwrapped her cherubic legs from the machine, lowering them to the floor, ending our view of her hand sewn satin G-string, with craftily attached seashells in decorative places. Fine to dance in but crunchy to sit on, you'd think. She must be careful with it. Real seashells, just like real satin.

For her third song she straddled the sturdy machine, collapsible into its own table, and quite heavy as I'd experienced. I was glad, knowing it would be able to handle her weight. Satin clad crotch tight against the machine's sleek black and gold back she stroked the wheel with her hand, leaning forward, her breasts almost touching the machine, caressing it; a crunching sound accompanied the shedding of broken seashells. Ariel arched backwards in an unlikely bridge, planted her arms behind her; drops of sweat rolled down her neck and onto her breasts; her long gold curls were damp and frizzy, snaking down her well-muscled back. The motor's vibration was her lover, bringing her by the end of this fourth song, to an orgasm which seemed not at all faked. Robert and I stared at one another in astonishment as the last slow tune began, unwinding her like thread from a spool. No wonder, I thought, she isn't as tired as I am on all our endless stairs; she works out at her job every day.

"D'you think she really came?" I asked.

Robert didn't say anything, too moved to speak. I had a sudden urge to climb up on stage with Ariel, bury my face in her satiny crotch, jealous of the sewing machine. Show them, it must be unheard of in a strip club, the second time in one day, real passion and not fake. But the song was over and Ariel climbed down off the machine, slipped on her gown and disappeared into the dancer's change room.

Meanwhile I realized the show wasn't quite over. From inside her dressing-room she unplugged her machine: a mermaid costume slipped out of the machine's teeth to the floor, perfect in every detail, its French seams finished with an exactitude only a master tailor could produce. Her self-love had sewn a peach satin mermaid outfit with tiny delicate zippers everywhere.

"How d'you teach it to do that?" I asked, when she came and sat with us on her break, and sipped desultorily at a Black Label. Robert seemed confused and happy, too nervous to look Ariel in the face.

"You saw it do that?" she asked, wistfully.

"Incredible," I said.

"Not many can see it."

"Why does it make you sad that I can?" I asked her.

"It means things are changing. It means our window is closing. It means we won't have the affair that we've been flirting with having."

This puzzled me. I thought what we had was the romance of friendship, not of possible sexuality. But there had been that moment in her room, where we'd looked into one another's eyes, and something new had entered. And I'd left. Perhaps I was in denial, a supposedly straight woman. Confused, I didn't say anything.

"It means . . . " Ariel persisted, and then gave up, not getting any help from me. "Robert, how did you like my show?"

Robert had seen nothing of the magically sewing sewing machine, only her remarkable act.

"Strippers seem so cynical so often," he said shyly, "but you were different. You're not the best dancer I ever saw but you're very beautiful so it doesn't matter, and to make love to the machine was so original. It was very funny and very sexy all at the same time. And you emanate warmth."

"I try to make them happy. They're so sad. If I'm only going to be on stage for twenty minutes I want to make them happy."

"Admirable," Robert said.

"Will you be able to always do that?" I asked.

"Probably not," Ariel answered.

"Quit when you can't do it anymore," Robert advised.

"Do you get to wear the costumes it makes you?" I asked.

"Oh be quiet," she said, glancing Robert's way. "What did you think, Veronica?"

"It seemed a pleasant bohemian way to spend a darkly overcast afternoon."

We put on our winter bundling and left. "So what's up tonight?" she asked casually, as we walked along the snowing street, lighting cigarettes.

"Party on King Street," Robert said. "Dancers, theater people."

She touched my hand. "You should have stayed."

"Stayed when? Stayed where?"

"Stayed off those stairs."

I knew she meant the five flights, the two locked doors; my prize for having faithfully followed a mysterious stranger's instructions: a pair of blue suedes that seemed to make my life magic. Where had he given me that scribbled address, whoever he was? Even though I'd forgotten all the circumstances, I'd done it anyway, because it seemed so intriguing. Done what, the question remained. It seemed unlikely he could have sent me all that way just for a pair of shoes. What had my mission been, that I'd so carelessly forgotten? Drunk maybe, Veronica? As usual, I kept my fears and my confusion to myself, in spite of being with my supposedly two best friends.

The three of us went out for dinner at a Vietnamese restaurant and headed to the party afterwards. Aladdin was there. He had a bottle of Glenlivet and motioned for me to sit beside him on the decrepit grey couch. Robert and Ariel disappeared onto the dance floor.

"An item?" Aladdin asked. Everyone gossiped so much.

"Them?" I swigged from his bottle, gratefully. "He watched her at work today. I think maybe you're right, that maybe he fell in love."

"Everyone thinks you're a couple," Aladdin said.

"Me and Robert?"

"No. You and Ariel."

"Why would they think that?"

"You're always together since you're back from California. You neck at parties."

"We do?" Then I remembered. We had. Twice this past month. Delicious, delicious, delicious.

Soon half the bottle of scotch was gone and I left Aladdin to exchange pleasantries; in seemingly superficial party chitchat meanings sprouted everywhere.

When I look back on that winter this is what I think still: our lives weren't profligate, wasteful; they were full of meaning. Something in the snow that year, in the hit songs, the soup, the coffee, the parties. When you finally grow up, where does that romance go? And is it even possible to have both, to face one's delusions, one's denials, and to hear bells in the wind that aren't there? Bells at the ends of ribbons, tied to winter trees in airshafts. To search for and find an impossible grace in a dissolute lifestyle; is that so wrong? However fragile and temporary a grace it's doomed to be, however selfish and careless, it still seems to me a better thing than to have never experienced it at all.

A woman with very short red hair rushed at me out of the crowd. "D'you have them on you?" she asked.

"Have what?" She looked vaguely familiar although I wasn't sure where from.

"The keys. He needs the keys back. You were supposed to give them back that day. Remember I yelled at you?"

Oh, so that's who she was.

"I'd rather give them to him myself," I said. Whoever he was.

"Suit yourself," she said. "It was a good opportunity to get it out of the way. Finish with unfinished business."

"The sewing machine sews forgetfulness," I said, fishing for new meanings, for missing pieces.

"But unnecessary things forgotten make room for new, necessary things in your brain," she said. "And things so long forgotten they seem new again."

"Brain coral grows," I said.

"Now you're getting it," she laughed.

"But what color is his hair?" I asked.

"Red like mine. He's my brother. How come you don't know that? I guess it was dark when he gave you the keys." She was wearing a tight, striped tube top with a white cotton oversized man's shirt open over top, black jeans, and the ubiquitous cowboy boots. Hers were red, matching her hair.

"I guess." She headed to the dance floor, motioned for me to come join her, but I smiled in declination, sat back down with Aladdin, his warm bottle. I said, "I guess it's been dark all my life; I've never really been able to see anything."

"How come we all talk like this?" he asked.

"Maybe it's the sewing machines," I drank from his liquid gold.

"Do explain."

"Replacing the brain cells, the memories we lost by drinking too much."

"Replacing them with what?"

"Poetry."

"Of course."

I told him too about Ariel's machine, the abandoned one we'd found in the condemned loft building that afternoon, another drizzly, slushy, overcast one. It was the cold that made us love one another, I think now, that made us run into one another's arms.

"That day changed everything," I said.

"How?"

"I'm not sure yet, but I know. The blue shoes told me."

He looked at my feet, and then at me, questioning.

"They tell me things. They're like a telepathic amulet. I look at them and I have a thought I'd never have had otherwise; I'm sure of it."

"That's how I feel when I look at you, Veronica," he said, but I barely heard him. All the time I thought I was Emma Peel, but I was really just another small-time heart crusher. Aladdin shrugged; I guess he'd learned how by then.

Just then I saw Ariel through a gap in the crowd, still partnered with Robert, dancing so differently: very well but demurely.

"She's an amazing dancer," Aladdin said, watching too.

"Robert and I went to see her work today. She says I should dance; I need a job."

Aladdin said, "I don't think you're the type, 'Rica. It would hurt you."

"What about Ariel?" I asked defensively. "It doesn't hurt her?" Ariel always seemed so soft, so feminine. I was supposed to be the hard edged one.

"She's different," he said.

"Different how?" I asked, feeling dared.

"She's a mermaid. She can always go back in the water from whence she came."

"Maybe that's why she doesn't need to smoke or drink like I do; being so watery she can live unarmored. I'd like to be like that too," I whispered. "Never get hurt."

"It's not that she doesn't get hurt; it's that she can dive in the pool of forgetfulness, wash all her sins away. The pool of Lethe, in the Greek myths."

"Other people's sins," I corrected.

Aladdin raised his eyebrows, considering. "I think maybe you're right."

Presently Aladdin was gone, and I couldn't find Ariel or Robert. I was pissed, or maybe it was the sewing machine sewing stitches on my mind. I hated those moments, the thought of walking out onto King Street alone, hailing a cab, hoping I didn't throw up in it. A red-haired girl called me by name like I was an old friend, said there was another party, just a small one, on the top floor. "The fifth floor," she said. "You still don't remember my name, do you? It's Nancy."

"Okay," I said, thinking I could sober up with them for a while before I went home. "But wait for me, I have to pee."

I peed; when I came back out there was no sign of Nancy, or of Ariel and Robert. I felt surprised by prongs of jealousy, but which way did they prick? I felt I'd be excluded, that our convivial threesome would be over, and I'd be odd woman out. If any of us were going to do it, I suddenly felt sure, it would have to be all three together. That way, if it caused an ending as a sexual aspect often does to what has been a friend-ship, it would be an ending that would include all of us.

The door at the top of the stairs was locked. I remembered the keys in my pocket, the keys I'd taken off the jaguar ashtray and put into the pocket of my black jeans tonight, as though I'd known unconsciously it would be the same building. A slipstream moment, a dropped stitch in time. Short-term memory loss: how come I hadn't recognized the brick facade?

I unlocked the door, walked twenty paces, unlocked the second, sticky in exactly the same way it had been the first time. Very private, these fifth floor people with their locks, very secretive. Maybe they dealt heroin or sewing machines or something.

In the hall I listened vainly for the sound of a party. I called out Nancy's name, but there was no answer. I knocked on all the doors; there were six, and no one came to open any of them. Big factory windows faced an air shaft; dawn light illuminated silk ribbons tied to the bare winter branches of a tree.

"But how could that building be this building? That building had been abandoned," I asked aloud.

Oh, of course, the artist had moved here, or just done it here too. Prob-ably airshafts all over the warehouse district sported beribboned trees.

In the corner under another window looking down onto King Street a dusty sewing machine sat on a table. I looked to see if it was sewing anything. Applique brain coral, mermaid costumes. But it wasn't Ariel's sewing machine; it was mine, and sewed nothing. Ariel had already tapped into her own creativity, so deeply her work was almost magical. I just didn't know it at the time, or chose to overlook it. The beautiful and sexy fill us with need; we think always of what they can do for us, how they and only they can make us feel, forgetting always their need to do for themselves. We become predators, and forget to be friends.

There was a note:

"Veronica: leave the keys here, take the sewing machine."

I placed the keys on the table, carried the machine down the stairs, very, very carefully, because I was so drunk. It was another old Singer, an early electric. The very best sewing machines, Ariel had said. Without electronic memories, but the integrity of a well-made thing. The old machines were truth speakers, the new ones better at unstitching old, worn out ways of being, replacing them with new, happy, surprising endings, totally unforeseen. Perhaps there's one waiting for me out there yet.

I suppose it takes two sewing machines to sew a good life: one old, one new. I suppose I shall just have to be patient, wait for them to sew my dreams together out of these scraps and tatters I've shredded my life into. Soon it will be the nineties; I look forward to them, thinking it's then we'll be able to change, become better people.

I carried it home along King Street to Spadina, slowly in the freezing dawn light. Up more stairs, hacking and wheezing.

"Keep the keys, give back the shoes," I said nonsensically, exhausted. Yet the loft seemed so lonely and I felt a crashing hangover coming so I scraped four dollars in change off the jaguar. Went back out, had a greasy breakfast up at our twenty-four hour Dundas Street spoon. I wanted someone to come in that I knew, a party face with a smile; we could exchange the night's stories.

No one came.

I went home to my enormous new futon to sleep alone.

Before sleep came I obsessed: wondered who did that, with the silk ribbons.

Maybe it wasn't one person, but more than one, like a graffito that passes through many hands. I'd always wanted to do that, write an article about street art. No one I knew had done that yet. There was a new entertainment weekly and I thought I might approach them. It was an excuse, really, to find out.

I didn't see Robert or Ariel that week, and when I heard about Friday's party it was from Nancy, who I ran into on Queen Street. "I'll bring Ariel," I said.

She made a face.

You don't like Ariel, I wanted to say but didn't. Afraid to, I guess. I told her my idea and she said it was a good one. "You would write very well about art, Veronica; you're one of the few people who are knowledgeable enough and also you have a way with words. I've read your stories in Z."

Zed had published two of my stories the year before. I'd been very happy. David and Ariel and I had gone out for Vietnamese food to celebrate.

"It seems so long ago now," I said to Nancy.

"David?" she asked, reading my mind. "You'll get over him. He was cool, but you know, you'll go further faster without him. He held you back. Debts all the time. Bad sewing machine deals."

"So everyone knew," I said.

She shrugged. "Look, here's their card, they're looking for writers; tell them you're a friend of mine," she beamed effusively. I felt honoured. Nancy always seemed so powerful and scary.

I went to the party. Nancy's brother was there, approached me out of the dance floor crowd. I knew it was him because they looked so much alike. "Thanks for the keys back," he said.

"No problem," I said. His face seemed familiar. When I remembered at all it had always been only the instructions, the color of his hair, but not the reason, or the face.

"You found those blue shoes," he said, admiring my feet. "You're the perfect person for them. Why didn't you take the sewing machine the first time?"

"There was a woman working on it." I didn't tell him I'd forgotten, hadn't known the sewing machine was for me. Sometimes it seemed a little frightening, the forgetfulness.

"It was Nancy," he laughed. "No matter how many times you meet her you always forget. She's so offended; she thinks you're snubbing her. I'd told her it was for you but you left before she could give it to you. You did me that favor; the sewing machine was to say thank you."

I didn't ask what favor, clueless as usual. He took my arm. "Come meet the editor at Tabula Rasa."

"Esoteric name," I said.

"Too much, don't you think? I'm going to tell them to change it. Maybe to X," he said.

"Or X-Ray."

"X-Ray is good. Or how about Night Vision?"

"Too poetic," I said.

"But it's that kind of winter. My name's Red, by the way. We never were properly introduced last year, when you and David got us that great deal on sewing machines with built-in memory."

Red introduced me to the publisher\editor, whose name was Evan, raving about me, which is, of course, the only way to be introduced. I told him my idea about the street art, the mysterious silk-ribboned trees.

"But that's a great idea," Evan said, lighting a bootleg Winston. "I don't know much about art. We need an art writer; we'll try you out on this idea. You come so highly recommended."

Red beamed. I suddenly remembered I'd known him after all. He'd had another name last year; it had been Halley.

"When's it due?" I asked.

"Comes out Friday. Typesetting's Thursday; editorial's Wednesday. Can you have it in Wednesday morning?"

"Okay," I said. "If I stay up all Tuesday night doing the final."

"Do it," he said, shook my hand and walked away.

I wrote the piece. Evan and Janice, his partner loved it. I could feel my life changing. I went to that weekend's party, and saw Robert. "I read your article," he said, "it was so great. You're a good interviewer."

"It was a lot more work than the waitressing I've done." I didn't tell him I'd never discovered the identity of the person who ribboned the trees. Somehow it made me ashamed, a secret I wasn't virtuous enough to gain access to. "But I can't cocktail forever, and Evan gave me a check for two hundred dollars."

"That doesn't seem like very much," Robert said.

"I know. But it got my name out, and I've always wanted to get paid to write."

"I lost my bartending job," Robert said. "They fired me," he told me plaintively, "for not cleaning the floor."

"Where's Ariel?" I asked, feeling very badly that I hadn't invited her to last week's party.

"She went on tour in northern Ontario. She's always talked her way out of it before but I guess this time they really needed her. They said they wouldn't give her more town gigs if she didn't go."

"It'll be okay," I said. "She'll be back in three weeks, with tales of Kenora. She'll write postcards."

But she didn't. I never had time to say goodbye; we hadn't broken up, I told myself, because we'd never been together in the first place, not properly.

I was busy with my new job; it seemed I had a knack. Janice and Evan gave me a weekly column; to my surprise and delight I'd turned overnight into an art writer.

I bumped into Robert on the street; he was on welfare. I didn't think much of it either way. I was so caught up in my work I almost forgot Ariel.

Winter discontinued. It was spring. I bought new shoes, black cowboy boots that were a little late in coming but felt like heaven just the same.

I saw Robert on Spadina. Spring winds blew away our previous companionship. We didn't notice. He said, "Ariel fell in love with a man in Thunder Bay, a housing contractor. She's going to stay. She's pregnant. She says she's very happy. She's going to give the room to Nancy as a sublet, but she wants you to have the sewing machine."

"Nancy? I thought Nancy hated her."

"You're so dumb sometimes, Veronica."

"Did you and Ariel ever do it?" I asked, remembering the party I spent talking to Aladdin, neglecting my friends.

Robert just shook his head like I was a moron. "They fought over you. They both had crushes on you. But they were friends first."

"Really?" I asked, but Robert shook and shook his head at me; we parted ways.

I picked up Ariel's sewing machine, from the little Bathurst street room. Nancy and I had coffee together, talked about the magazine. She's in advertising sales at X-Ray; it seems half the city works there now, in one capacity or another. Or at least half of our downtown arty crowd. And everyone who doesn't is envious. Be that as it may: Evan and Janice have done very well for themselves, and for us.

Now I have two sewing machines. I move from one to the other, hoping both will last longer that way, just as I trade my cowboy boots for my blue suedes.

Ariel's sewing machine has done nothing magical. I think now that it never did, that it was a figment of my imagination, or a slipstream moment where I linked minds with Ariel . . . that it was her dream, what she would visualize on stage to keep herself serene while she worked.

She was one of a kind.

It's winter again. David wants me to go back with him, but I won't; he's into heroin. We went to Chinatown for green tea and sweet buns stuffed with bean paste; I said: "Why don't you skip the heroin, just use the sewing machines? Not so addictive. Not illegal. Not painful. No withdrawal symptoms. You only have to learn how to sew memory and forgetfulness, and it's so much easier now, with the new machines, the ones with built in electronic memories. Sewing machines know how to sew the way home. Trust them. They make space so that the poetry has room to enter, which was all you really wanted the heroin for. To scrape away the scabby places where the poetry had been scarred over. Rip out the bad stitches, make new ones."

David grinned and nodded, sincere, heartfelt, agreeing with me. But it was the agreement of an addict. I knew why he'd chosen this particular Chinese bakery; his dealer lived just around the corner. Everyone knew.

He graciously let me pay. He had better things to spend his money on. I offered to give him one of my sewing machines, wondering if perhaps his just wasn't broken, but he said, too cool for words, "I've done sewing machines."

I was afraid to let him go, but I did. They all said the same thing: Ariel, Nancy, Robert; you can't save a junkie, don't even try.

I'm lonely but working hard. Parties don't seem to have the same allure.

Something is different from last winter, when I came back from California after Christmas, something was happier. I have my turquoise notebook to prove it, with lines of beautiful poetry written by Ariel, by Robert: last winter's buddies.

Last week I did go out, to a party with Nancy, Evan, Janice and their crowd; a new different crowd. I left alone, too late as always, drunk, went to the coffee shop. Robert was there. He looked old, grizzled. Dawn crawled slowly up the windows. It struck me he was forty, too old to still be living his kind of life. He said, "You should've kept the keys, not the shoes. Then you could've had both."

"I do have both sewing machines," I said, paying for my bootleg under the counter American soft pack Winstons.

"How many sewing machines does one person need? You have a cool new professional persona but you lost Ariel. I think you'll find it was too high a price. You needed her more than you let yourself know."

"Maybe she's happier now." I said, "it was time for her to quit anyway." And knew it was hot and sour soup with her I missed the most fiercely.

"You could've gotten her a gig at X-Ray," he said. "Writing about dance, street fashion, anything. They were just starting up; it was wide open. And Janice and Evan would do anything you say. You impress the hell out of them."

"What about you?" I asked. "Why don't you write for them? About poetry. You're the most insightful, informed person I know."

"I'm not ambitious that way," he shook his head. "I'll always be a boho bum. Soon to be an old boho bum."

"I'm going to cry," I said, meaning it. His faded eyes.

"Some of us are meant to stay under water, to never surface. I'm one of them. Don't cry for me, Argentina."

"Veronica," I whispered. "My name's Veronica."

"I'll never forget having known you, and I'll forgive you if, when you're famous, you pretend you never knew me."

"Now you're being cruel. I'd never do that."

"Oh, but Argentina," he said, looking out the window and not into my eyes at all. "You will. Just wait and see, you will. Not this year or the next, no. Maybe in five years or ten. I'll be sleeping in a box and you'll step over me. You'll say to your husband, "he looked like a man I used to know," but you won't go back, check to see if it was really me. Then you'd have to take me home, put me on your couch. I'd smell, and the children would be afraid of me. Don't forget that. There are things people do, for the sake of the children, they'd never have considered before."

"Robert, don't talk this way."

"I'll still be a brilliant poet," he whispered viciously under his breath, "scribbling on my box with pencil stubs, muttering. More brilliant than you, to whom success will come."

"Please, Robert."

"Goodbye, Argentina."

I went home. I stood, crying, stroked the peach satin mermaid costume hanging on the wall, believed at that moment everything he'd said would come true. It felt true that morning, a bad dawn and not a good one. A harsh chilly dawn, a dawn that aged us irrevocably.

I'd kept the loft as the artists' collective had moved to a bigger space. They could afford to—I'd written a big feature article on them for X-Ray and it had attracted quite a bit of attention. A lot of people had wanted that cheap Spadina loft with the giant cockroaches, but they'd made sure it had gone to me. For the favor, and so I'd been paid much more than Evan's two hundred dollars after all.

I tried the mermaid on but it didn't fit; Ariel's much smaller than me. Still it hangs on my wall; that woman sure could sew. Or her sewing machine could. For me it only makes lined fringed scarves made from scraps of cloth from Spadina jobbers to give away as Christmas presents. I made one for Robert, keep him warm in the chilly cardboard box he has built around himself. I will send Ariel one, my missing soup partner.

She sent me a picture of herself, holding her new baby. She looks chubby, tired, wistful, unreachably happy. The photograph is double exposed, with winter trees, so she's almost not there. Yellow and green silk ribbons are tied to the bare branches of the winter tree, or maybe her hair, or maybe both. I thought it was a mistake; only lately do I think she double-exposed it on purpose.

I never wrote about her, and now it's too late. She never told me she was a brilliant artist and not just a stripper. The self-esteem; where does it go? Who sewed it over, me or Robert?

Everyone played at being bisexual then; it was a fad, like cowboy boots; all the young bohemians had a same-sex affair to go with their Tony Lamas. But people, unlike boots, have feelings. When the fad is over, you can throw your boots or your blue suede shoes into the street, or into the back of a closet, but where do you put the lover who thought you were sincere, and gave you her heart honestly?

I thought my blue suede shoes were telling me secrets that winter, but really it was Ariel. Careless, careless, careless, she'd have said, if only I'd have listened. We did sleep together, just once. It happened, I remember it now, so very clearly, just before she went up north. I pretended it hadn't happened, or else I immediately forgot; perhaps it's the same difference after all. Why? Because afterwards she looked at me out of huge blue eyes, asked, "Will we be together now?" And I'd known, for the first time that she wasn't just beautiful and sexy, talented and cool, but also frightened, needy, vulnerable. And I hadn't had the time for that, or was it the guts?

LATE FOR DINNER

THE APARTMENT WAS DARK, A BASEMENT AFTER-HOURS club. There were a few chairs, a table, two old couches where people snatched an hour or two of sleep. There was a makeshift bar on one side, a bar I was facing now, across the room, as I listened to my quarters fall inside the cash box, as I gave the long distance operator my father's number. His phone rang and rang. The operator cut in, asked, "D'you want me to let it keep ringing?"

"Sure," I said. What else did I have to do, where else to go? I couldn't leave: my little apartment just blocks away was as impossible to walk to just then as my first home, hundreds of miles away in another country, across a snowy border to the north. A skirmish was taking place outside; I could hear gunfire, smell smoke from burning buildings. I wanted my father to answer so I could tell him I'd done what he'd wanted me to do. It was he who'd first told me about the war, dragging me to a rally when I'd wanted to stay home and watch television: "This country is knee-deep in bones."

I watched the man behind the counter chat with another seated at a stool; he pulled them each a beer. It struck me that they weren't bartender and customer at all, but lieutenants, fighting on the same side and in the same war. Hidden in their party chatter, encoded, even here in their safe house, so that only a careful listener might detect them, were strategy and military logistics. I knew my presence was tolerated only because of the man I slept with; I hung up and left the room, walked into the back, opened a door.

A dark empty room, not even a chair. In the center like a shrine, one astonishing source of illumination: an enormous, lit tank of what seemed like tropical fish; their swimming colors were, on closer examination, not equatorial but truly otherworldly. I'd heard of them, of course; they were on the rebel flag. Like everyone else from my world I'd thought the image was just a symbol. I watched, entranced, thinking about my lover, who was late, and my father.

I know he'd have denied it but I felt as if I'd been sent to live in rebel camps he'd only seen on television, to take the next step. And so when I left the aquarium room and called again, heard at last his anxious hello, hoping it might after all be me, I described the fish. I wanted to explain how their colors were different from ordinary colors, even astonishing ones; only a story would clarify the difference. I chose one about my mother, his wife, dead now for many years. "I remember telling her I dreamed in color, and she was astounded, told me she, and most everyone she'd known or at least asked, dreamt only in monochrome. If she'd seen these fish I know she'd have begun dreaming in color, and because of it she might have lived. Colors we have no names for. Beside the everyday colors of this club, it's as if, like in her dreams, everything but the fish are in black and white."

At least that's what I thought I said. And then by his silence I realized a strange thing: I'd lived among the rebels for so long, for so long away from my own people that even without awareness of it happening I'd gradually forgotten my own language and now could speak only theirs.

He didn't understand a word I said, and said only, "I'm having Petra and Lep and Eileen for dinner on Thursday and they'd love to see you; why don't you take the bus up and I'll drive you back across Sunday night?"

They were activists, those three, like him. As a child growing up, I'd observed how my father had an affinity for the rebels, secretly funded them, helped them plan occasional escape routes across the border to the north. And yet not so very secretly: he was so secure, so established that even in taking a radical position there was little danger of him coming to harm, either professionally or personally. It was I who, growing up in this atmosphere chose to go south.

"I can't leave," I said, "but give them a hug for me." I knew even these words had been spoken in a tongue he couldn't possibly understand.

If he'd known I'd cross over the safety of his threshold and beyond his protection, he might not have been as outspoken and supportive of their cause as he was. He thought I'd do what he did: stay north, lecture and write letters, make donations and telephone calls, walk in largely peaceful demonstrations. Go to law school, perhaps: have both money and a voice to speak for the voiceless.

A sensible choice, yet I knew there was more to the war than that, knew also, for the first time, that in some small way, he approved of my choice; in one way or another I'd done it for him. And my mother. After all, a war is not just a petition but a place.

I knew it had begun centuries before, and, while most liked to pretend it didn't exist, or that it had been over for decades and was a closed piece of history that had no import to their speedy modern world, what I discovered was quite different. There existed people whose families had fought against the state for generations, since they'd first been shipped over as slaves, or first had their land stolen from beneath their feet, their women from their sides.

I said goodbye and hung up, knowing he was falling away from me into a swirling inescapable void of terrifying worry, and that I was falling away, pushed away by an equal and opposite force into the other direction, implacably away from him. Only by going home for dinner on time and speaking his now-forgotten tongue could I soothe his fear, and I knew that was as impossible for me as flying. I crossed the room to buy a beer from the counterman. I rattled the change in my pocket. "I'll take whatever you've got," I said.

"You don't have to pay," the man said. "I know who you are. You've already paid, and you'll pay more before your tour is over."

"Will I pay too much?"

"Only God knows the answer to that," he said, and raised his glass to mine. "But I hope not."

My lover had gone out again shortly after we'd arrived at the club:

business he couldn't take me on. But he'd return, he promised; we'd tell stories and laugh; he'd bring our friends. I knew then he might never return, either to party or to walk me back to my barely heated little railroad flat with its window onto an airshaft.

For the first time I was afraid I might never return to my own country, my old way of life. This is what I'd also wanted to tell my father, but instead described the unbelievably beautiful fish to him. The barman winked as I left again to go back and look at them, carrying my beer. It was as though they swam through panes of glass. I wondered whether they would survive, or whether a stray bullet would one day pierce their tank and they, their water all leaked out, would die, and with them all rebel fire would be lost to the world forever.

I wanted then for my father to come and get me instead, forgetting briefly that his money and power, his prestige, meant nothing here. In the war zone he was no safer than me and perhaps less so, for I now had only the one language remaining to me, one he'd never learned; like extraterrestrial fish it was a myth to him and not a spoken reality: the language of the streets, of this generations-long resistance, of the sweet salt smell of my lover as we lay together at four in the morning, talking.

My lover might never come: powerful as he was, it wasn't real protection for either of us. Caught up in business, jailed, or shot down: all were possible. I wasn't sad, knew it only to be the simple truth, felt lucky to have known him at all, however briefly. What did we speak of, the previous night, he and I, as we lay staring at the ceiling fan, turning and turning as our lives did irrevocably toward one another, beyond reason or will, as if totally beyond our power to control?

This:

"What will people think of our society, a hundred years from now?"

"Depends entirely on which way it goes, I guess."

"I guess. What do you think?"

"I think if there are even people left in a hundred years they'll say it was a time of great darkness."

"Sometimes it seems the worst time of all."

"I know. I feel that too."

It's of no great consequence which words he spoke and which words I spoke. We had reached that point where borders blur, where one becomes the other.

His two trained attack dogs frightened me and his drugs were purer and more powerful than any I'd yet known. They frightened me too: their disorientation was so complex. I know now he thought it was only under their influence I could quickly learn his language, given what little time we had.

What little time had we?

In the morning, before going out to eat and then coming here, he'd said: "We have so much less time left on this earth than we'd planned."

Or perhaps it was I who said it, as we gingerly sidestepped a corpse on the way to our bacon and eggs breakfast special, having been up all night again, planning and making love and talking: I think just as we blurred, so did all these activities.

Of course those words are true for all of us, and at all times. The moment you are born you begin to die.

He turned back. He bent down to the corpse and closed the eyes, saying, "It's terrible to see the dead with open eyes." I was amazed he could touch the dead, said so, and he looked at me and smiled again at my privilege. "You think it's the first time? You live in castles surrounded by moats," he said, "You have no idea how the rest of the world lives, each and every day."

We'd smoked a joint before leaving and once again, as so often happened in his company I warped: whether backwards in time or sideways into a parallel world I wasn't sure: imagining a funeral pyre, sacred rites, I asked, "What will you do with the body?" We were overlooking the river, in a diner we always frequented, and he was glancing at my coffee in some dismay as always; he insisted java, cigarettes and alcohol were all poisons sent by the devil to enslave the people, not just his but mine too.

"But our society runs on them," I pointed out, wondering how people would cope if these props were taken away, not knowing we'd invent new, even more powerful chemical props sanctioned by the state in years to come.

"Precisely," he said; all his drugs were illegal and he thought this no accident. "The cops will come," he said, answering my previous question, "take it to the morgue." And, listening, I could hear faraway sirens approaching, although they could have been heading toward any one of a dozen dead.

"But you said we live in castles. I thought we were time traveling. In this time I've never had a servant."

"No. Just a car and a credit card, a washing machine, a dishwasher, a good school. Those things are more powerful buffers than any moat. Like I said, you have no idea. That's the way it's the same. Remember what Marie said."

"I didn't know you knew anything about the French revolution."

"Figures."

"My middle name's Maria."

"No kidding."

"Why do you love me then?"

"You lost your mother to the war."

"How so?" I watched him spear bacon, wondering why he thought murdered pig was okay and not my second cup, figured we were all allowed a few foibles and inconsistencies.

"She killed herself, you told me. But remember when you showed me the catalogue of her paintings and I said, "Look, there are footsteps. Do you see them?""

"I didn't know what you meant. I thought you were speaking in a language I didn't know. Remember I had no reply?"

"I was. But you know it now, or most of it, which is more than can be said of most who cross over to learn."

"You don't look down on me then, think I'm a child?"

"Not at all. Your seeking is sincere. And I know the price of loss too well. It can be bigger than the original loss itself."

"So what did you mean about the footsteps? She didn't paint footsteps." I had already told him the story: that my mother had been a renowned painter; I'd shown him reproductions of her famous work. And he was able to say something about it that no one else had ever been able to say: not my friends nor the family that remained, and not one of the best art critics, dealers, and curators that my world had to offer.

That's what alien eyes looking through glass from a world as far away as Jupiter will do for you, I guess. For my lover said, astoundingly:

"It was the last painting, the one she never completed. It expressed the darkness that spiraled around her, threatening to extinguish her light. You were the only one in your family who knew how she felt. You didn't know how it would end, but you knew she had gone too far into despair to pull back out. It was as if she was magnetized, could only by then be pulled even further in. And even a few steps further meant out the door, out of her life."

I drank coffee; we ate pig and eggs. Looked out the window at barges crossing under bridges. So many bridges.

"I stood in her painting room, thirteen years old. It was almost as if I could feel it, like a physical force that was smothering her. I tried to reach her, to pull her out but like you said, it was as if she'd gone too far to turn back; she didn't get it, that I could see what was happening to her, holding out my hand. That cloud around her was so thick."

A swirling curtain, thick and cloudy, black and green shot through with yellow. I could still feel its presence, this time around me, as if it had moved from one to the other of us. As if it had some kind of sentience, planned to take us each in turn. We'd lost another to suicide in the previous generation, my grandmother's sister who had the same name as me.

"You tried to tell people too, the danger you felt she was in, but they didn't hear."

"You said I told you all this before?"

"Yes. You were speaking in tongues, in my language before you actually learned it."

"You mean I was stoned out of my gourd and babbling?"

"Shhhh." He looked around.

"What?" I raised my voice, endangering his life as I had before, or at least his freedom. I bet he would've liked to get rid of me then, shake me off like loose dead skin, flush me away like fingernail parings. But no, he took my side; he spoke from his heart whether I deserved it or not.

"The footsteps she painted, invisible on the canvas surface but there just the same, were the path you would take, following her, trying to save her. You were a kid and didn't have the strength, but you didn't know that. You didn't know once she was gone you would follow her too far, trying to bring her back."

"Wow," I said, knowing then that I'd wanted to learn his language not out of voyeurism or childish thrill-seeking or even a misguided, if compassionate altruism, but because only he had ever been able to speak truly to me about my mother's suicide, and only in his own language. What he'd said couldn't be translated, not in all its depth and nuance. I knew then that what my people needed was the thing he'd been born knowing, just as a barren field needs a seed from another land, leaching alien nutrients into the soil, never before introduced.

"But you can't bring people back from the other side," he reminded me. "Or even yourself. That's what I'm here for."

"To save me?"

"Yes."

"Could've fooled me. You're so busy with your war."

"Same war. One saves who one can. If the brightest lights of each generation go down what will we come to? Your mother knew enough to paint the doors and windows to other worlds. Those are the most important doors there are; it's only through them that the terrible darkness of our time can escape, only through them that the fish can swim here. She painted maps for them. If those doors are shut forever, closed to us, we're all lost. And worse than lost."

"And how do you think you'll save me?"

"Like this," he said, and leaned across the table to kiss me.

"Sounds like Eros versus Thanatos all over again."

"Freud was right about some things. You've never been in love like this before, have you?"

"Not exactly," I said, actually meaning: "And I'm afraid to lose it, knowing I'll never have it again; it's only possible once."

"Neither have I and neither will I. We'll part and go on to other lovers. We could never stay together; we're more different than a duck and a goose. It's almost like we're from different planets."

"I've always known you were from Jupiter," I laughed.

"Maybe it's you who's the alien," you said. "I bet you never thought of that. But we'll never forget each other, what we had."

At least the first part is true; I have no way of knowing whether you've forgotten me.

You gave me not a rose, but a year. I thought about you with each waking moment and you were right, it's something I've never done since.

Possibly a good thing. Who could stand such a consumptive love more than once?

I remember one night in your year, one of the nights I stayed with you. You woke suddenly to the dark, crept down the ladder to feed those scary dogs; I guess you'd forgotten earlier. I lay in the loft bed staring at the ceiling only inches away, even after having slept for three hours still too stoned to move. You behaved as though it was all normal and I guess for you it was: you put on Sarah Vaughan and came back to me. We lay there side by side, spiraling up and then down again until blue twilight creased the window onto the air shaft and you said, "You have to go back to your crib. You can't be here when they come unless you stay in here, the door locked. It isn't safe for you to see or hear. Choose which you like; if you go I'll walk you back, there's still time."

"I'll walk alone. It's safe enough this time of day."

Someone knocked on the outer door.

"Too late now."

You closed the door and I heard the lock latch shut, low voices. I was locked in. In time they left and you came back and we made love again.

Sometimes you went out for an hour before dawn, leaving me terrified with those dogs you said would guard me: I couldn't even get out of bed to go past them to use the washroom, and later, when I told you this, you laughed and chained them, indoors, beside the fridge. I know you did this to soothe my fear but I'm afraid it had the opposite effect. Their eyes were too blue, looking into this world from another planet, and not liking what they saw, much. They'd tear it apart, piece by piece I thought, if you ever let them off their chains outside. Your dogs of war, I took to calling them and I think you were a little amused although you chided me once again for my lack of seriousness, my lack of understanding. You didn't come back with coffee after your spooky dawn outing, just more killer joints that sent me to Jupiter and further for so long they gave me food for thought for days. For years: I'm still thinking their thoughts, still think I knew you, still think you held the greater power. Know too your Jovian hell hounds would disagree.

Now I know at last what they knew even then: you were as disoriented by our love as I.

I frightened you as much as you frightened me.

In what way?

You'd never known a woman who could climb so high beside you as if on the same stellar ladder, think the same thoughts in unison, see the same things.

A night fire, a circle of men and women, camouflaged, silent on cat feet. Another time, and yet this same time we inhabited together, wearing different clothes.

You were afraid that in my foolish youthful altruism, full of ignorance, I'd come to harm, and I terrified you because you hadn't planned on caring so, and to keep me out of harm's way, to look out for me, put a big dent in your game.

You might misfire, and you'd always been so sure.

I've only just gotten home, just now, at this very moment. Seated across from my father at his antique wooden kitchen table we drink black tea out of my mother's chipped brown stoneware pot, the only one that survived her death; the others jumped off the counter two weeks after she left, unable to live without her, trying to follow her just as I tried, unsuccessfully, to do.

My father lights one of my cigarettes, says, "What did you learn?"

"I learned despair. When Mother died I'd thought I'd known what despair was but I had not."

"What is despair?" my father asked.

"Despair is this: your daughter sells herself to enemy soldiers so that she might have the money to feed her own child. She got pregnant from an enemy rape, yet she still loves her baby and holds it more dear than her own fragile and defiled life. Despair is that you don't know her name or what she looks like, because her mother and you separated before she was born. It's like you were torn apart by the war."

My father stared at me.

"Despair," I continued brazenly, "is that you walk the street at night, your gun in your pocket, knowing those young girls, their sullen, stupid faces masking their beauty, their intelligence, their own rebel fire, with needle marks in their arms and bruises on their cheeks imperfectly masked with makeup might be your daughter. And you are powerless to protect her from the badly paying and disease-ridden enemy soldiers, because you don't know which of them she is. Impossibly dressed as they are, in the colors of fish which might only be legends: green and pale blue vinyl jackets, shimmering wet red boots, cut to the thigh."

My father sighed and put the kettle on for more tea, afraid where this was leading.

"Despair is this: This has been happening for generations."

You never told me what despair was; I only felt it seeping through your skin, marveled at what a great comfort I could be, not knowing what you kept hidden within until we walked past that line of girls one night on the way to a film party and as I made a disparaging remark you dug your fingers into my arm more fiercely than you needed to, and said, "You don't know what you're talking about. Any one of them could be my child."

I began, very slowly and in spite of my upbringing, to learn your way of life.

What had attracted me to you in the first place?

Your beauty, your mystery, your power. Your excellent drugs, perhaps even, a little, the glamor of your gun. At least to me it was a little glamorous; I'll admit that now. To you it was just more. More what?

More despair. Generations long despair. A blanket of despair thick and all-encompassing as snow.

My father and I talked all afternoon. We sipped scotch from a mickey of Johnny Walker Black I'd inadvertently smuggled across the border in my jacket's second waterproof pocket. He made me dinner, ratatouille over rice: my father's first and best dish. We talked all night. At dawn we were out of cigarettes and drove out to breakfast at an all-night greasy spoon and he bought more even though he'd never smoked till I came home.

Despair is this: you must make your lover understand. But she is from the enemy side, although at least ostensibly from a prominent liberal family which yet favors the rebels. You have only one hope: that you are able to make her see what it's really like, what it's been like for your family for hundreds of years. She is your only hope. If she understands, and if she tells, the world will perhaps open an eye to your pain at last, and lend a hand. Not fucking likely though, for she is foolish and very young. Intelligent, she seeks the mystery, and doesn't, cannot, understand the despair.

Unless, perhaps she lives it herself.

And so you do what you don't want to do; you cut the strings of language that tie her to her own community, to make her truly one of yourselves, so that she might learn.

You turn her out. Or more properly you say nothing as she takes to the streets herself, taking her place beside your mother, your sister, your daughter, silently handing you the money later that you might use it for ammunition.

Just as they do.

She learns this: these women love each other, love their mothers and daughters, and in one another's company even laugh a little.

Are afraid even more of their men will die. Just as some will die themselves, too young, of disease and violence. War casualties like her mother.

You hope she will survive, knowing it's quite possible she won't, but will instead get shot, either accidentally or on purpose, by a rebel or an enemy soldier: stateless and homeless as she now is, it could yet be either.

And yet, far away from you, on her own at three a.m. in an after-hours club she won't be able to leave for days, she walks into a room where there are fish. The rebels' secret: a life of beauty so profound it melts all despair, at least in their presence. Their secret wellspring: magic is real, and if magic is, then so too, and perhaps and probably only then, can a true democracy, and true gender equality, be invoked. She crosses the room, slips her hand into the tank, folds a fish into her hand, pockets it. Her fear is not that it will die in the water-filled pocket of her orange vinyl jacket, but that, when and if she ever gets it home, she will not be able to create the right conditions for it to flourish.

When I described fish on the phone that night, so many years ago now, to my father, fish he'd never seen or known in all his waking life, had only heard rumors of: mythical, magical fish so beautiful they could only live among rebels whose culture was as foreign to ours as a Jovian one might possibly be, I think I gave him both hope, and the first notion that I might yet die.

Perhaps rebels have always known the price of hope is death among their numbers, and so with this knowledge I made my father truly one of us and not just a pretender to the throne.

She waits for you and you don't come. She makes her way home slowly, although it takes many years. She crosses the border at dawn, riding with a friend in a stranger's car. Waiting for a ride they'd walked along a railroad embankment, an orange moon larger than harvest painted in the sky above their heads. And gone down into the coffee shop when it opened at six to beg a lift and drink the devil's coffee. The second girl knew you too and they both wondered if they'd ever see you again.

One did and one didn't.

It doesn't matter much which. There are thousands of girls like them after all, gone down to rebel fire, their hearts caught in the crosshairs of a gun.

Her father had old friends for dinner. When at last she arrived and they asked her, "What did you learn?" she said, only the faintest stain of needle marks and bruises still visible on her skin: "I brought a fish through the door, across the border," and watched the indescribable looks on Petra, Eileen and Lep's faces as she removed it from her pocket and unfolded it on the table where it began to swim in slow lazy circles. She knew then that all her training, and all her defilement were to this one end, to be a translator, to propagate miracle fish, fish smuggled across the border from another dimension, another world, in her own community.

HOLY MACKERELS

O N HER WALKS, SHELAGH PREFERRED ALLEYS TO MAIN streets: they seemed always to lead to water, as though the city's unknown builders loved what she loved: alleyways and waterfronts, and arranged the city to link these two pleasures. The waterfront was actually an industrial wasteland on the banks of a wide slow moving river. Shelagh stood smoking as two huge barges moved slowly by. Where were they going? What were they carrying? No one ever seemed to know.

Could a city really have been designed with her, and only her innermost desires in mind? And if so, how was this possible? She felt exquisitely captured, as she did each morning, by this small moment by the river. It was as if, back home in Montreal, someone had come into her little apartment on Guy and asked her to design a perfect walk full of images, exercise, and sound; a mix of nature and human industrialism. And, having designed exactly this moody, poetic walk in her mind she woke to it one day, woke to this city. Did everyone here feel this way, she wondered or only she?

Shelagh walked the city, she thought the city; the city thought her, or so it felt. A child's secret garden, painstakingly fascinating, ruthlessly entrancing. Her secret child's garden, dreamed of but never attained. She'd never felt this at thirteen when she'd needed it most. Now twenty-three, she'd given up, had learned to cope, to get through a day, like all the others. What a dangerous thing. Hope reawakened.

She looked for fish. There weren't any. They'd all been killed, perhaps by oil leaks from the barges. It didn't hurt her. Even this brought joy, here in this city, or perhaps here her joy was unimpeachable, impervious even, to the shuddering sadness of dirty water. Water for life, killing its own denizens; what could be more unspeakable? She thought of the St. Lawrence belugas at home: tumorous, their reproductive DNA irreparably damaged, so people could have tin cans. Yet she didn't weep over this river, though she'd never once seen a live fish in it, only dead ones, floating belly up: silvery slivers in the dark water, opaque as her old life was becoming.

It came back to her like slivers of dream: getting up at noon, showering and going to a cafe for breakfast, going home to get dressed for her job waitressing in a nightclub. Her boyfriend picking her up after work; they'd go to an after hours club on The Main, drink and dance till sunrise; go back to her tiny apartment where they'd make love on the unwashed sheets and pass out. And the next day the same.

Yet here the memories grew steadily fainter: now she had to work hard to remember she hadn't always lived here, that she didn't wake to this city each and every morning of her life. It was the solitude she loved most, she had to admit; perhaps she'd never really enjoyed the crowds perpetually surrounding her, perhaps her boyfriend had grated on her nerves more than a little. For here she treasured her days; days upon days of not knowing anyone. No one visited; no one called, no one disturbed her. All she had to do was walk, think and write. She wrote on the walls of her apartment: columns of text, a journal of her empty thought filled days onto the peeling plaster. Anywhere else she would've been afraid she was crazy, that her euphoria had a dark flip side, was a mania that might soon cycle downwards into crushing obliterating depression. Swoon into darkness, not light. But not here.

She watched the barges; she smoked, shortening her own life a little to give to another. On the spiralling plume of tobacco smoke, a prayer for fish. That they might come back, feel what she felt.

She took a new route home to her large crumbling apartment, and came upon a tiny square, one she'd never seen before. A square in an alley, with little pots of geraniums and herbs; here too someone had tried to make a garden, perhaps for a child. Basil and oregano, lavender and chives masked the smell of rotting garbage, a little. She'd never once seen a garbage truck.

They winged in from a second alley, crosswise to the one she entered from; there were six or eight or maybe more, perhaps thirteen, she thought, now that the stragglers had floated in too. Their long white robes, apparently pieced together out of bed sheets, flapped and swirled about their ankles. They mumbled and their hands made fluttering gestures in the air, not like birds but like fish. Flying fish. Each one, Shelagh noticed, wore a segmented silver fish on a chain. The fish thumped on their breastbones as they leapt.

She turned around, looked down blocks of alley at last to the slice of river where just then a barge was passing, pumping clouds of purple black smoke into the air. She looked from one view, the fish dancers, to the other, a barge on the river. Connected by a long brown alley, children's white undershirts and little red socks fluttered like pennants on a clothesline strung between fire escapes. Whose clothes, Shelagh wondered, realizing for the first time she hadn't seen a single child, not since she woke here one morning, a year ago today, judging by the marks she'd made on her walls.

She turned to the fish dancers and asked, "What's it mean?" They didn't explain, as though the meaning couldn't be had in words but only through gesture or jewellery.

She didn't understand. Why this particular city, seemingly a mirror of her innermost desires? Why was she here? Where was here? And why was even its polluted rotting ugliness such careless beauty to her? All she knew was that it answered something she'd forgotten she'd ever asked. What was the purpose of life? She'd been thirteen, she remembered. An adolescent's question, made virtually inaudible to her parents, her relatives, her teachers, by its seriousness, compromised as adults were.

And the answer was so breathtakingly simple: to feel like she felt, exactly as fulfilled, as free, as answered. Maybe I'm mad, she thought, this happy dream an invented reality painted so thickly on the insides of my eyelids it obscures real life. Pondering this possibility, Shelagh wasn't sure she cared. If only the mad were so happy, why not let them stay that way? It was more than most people got.

One of the dancers, genial, a little shy, neither threatening nor frightening in any way, came to her out of the ever moving group. She listened to his white robes clinking, and guessed he had a pocket full of fish.

"What's it mean?" she asked. He smiled and took a fish out of that big, big pocket, opened the chain into a circle. Reached forward and upward, for she was much taller than he, to put it around her neck, but she intercepted him, took the necklace and put it back in his hand.

"No," she said. "Thank you but no."

He smiled quizzically, shrugged, like a mummer not speaking.

"Thank you so much for trying to include me. It's very beautiful but I can't accept it. I can't wear it if I don't know what it means."

He shrugged. OK. Turned and joined the others, waving before he surrendered to the dance again. She was relieved he was neither offended nor hostile, and continued down the alley, which brought her, after a few wrong turns, back to the main street. Comprised of four lanes instead of two, it passed between four-storey row houses built of now crumbling brick, their street levels used for commercial purposes. Rusty one speed bicycles, their bells constantly clanging, raced past one another and past her. At last four small old trucks rolled by, their engines rebuilt, she knew, to run on ethanol. Purple smoke bellowed out of their exhaust pipes. One was an ambulance, she also knew, although not so marked, one a police car marked with a five-pointed sheriff's star. She stepped into a bakery, and bought a fresh hot pizza bun for lunch. Seventy-nine cents and she wouldn't be hungry till dinner.

At the pub six doors down she paid a two dollar cover; the city's Poet Laureate was to read that afternoon. Peeling posters on hydro poles had announced it; put up six months early they were today so rain washed, peeled away and plastered over with more current playbills that almost everyone had forgotten.

He hadn't bathed in days. He smelled of rancid sweat, old cheese, stale beer and cigarettes. He wasn't reciting poetry; he was yelling at the walls, and while she could make out a word here and there, there seemed no connecting thread at all. He didn't see his audience, or if he did, he mistook them for people who had betrayed him years before, a bitter fun house mirror, its transformation instanced by bile. His audience seemed to have come just to laugh, to sneer. Yet when he grew especially vituperative, they backed away, giving him room. Afraid of upturned chairs. Of broken bottles. At last he screeched a sentence: "Each dead fish equals one drowned child. Bring them back to life."

Shelagh was shocked. It was as if he was talking about her morning, describing her thoughts, her secret prayer. Maybe she should've taken a fish. What if she never found the dancers again? What if a child drowned because of it?

With her remaining ten dollar bill she got a pint of dark ale, pocketed her change and settled into a booth alone, in the back near the washrooms, under a speaker and a peeling poster. She couldn't hear the performance anymore, but the Poet Laureate, after his one clear sentence, had reversed into unintelligible gibberish. But, done yelling, he came to sit with her anyway. He smashed his bottle on the table, gave her a fishy stare, and cut his cheek with it. The few patrons and the bartender came to watch, as though this was how he shaved, but Shelagh whistled, shocked. "Holy Mackerel," she said, and everyone seemed to find this funny.

"Because of the child," the Poet Laureate said mildly, as if this made sense, not looking at her anymore, seemingly mollified now that the blood flowed unstaunched from his cheek, as though all his bitterness and violence was flowing out with it.

"No broken chairs today, thank stars," the bartender said. "A good thing. I can't find any more. There's a chair shortage of some sort."

"He broke most of them last week, remember?" someone whispered.

"I'm sorry now I didn't take a fish," Shelagh told him apologetically, sure she needn't explain further, that he'd know exactly what she meant.

"That way's not for you," the poet replied. "But you're quite right. You should be helping the dancers bring the fish back to life."

"Which way is my way then?" she asked him, thinking perhaps she'd at last met the person who could answer all her questions about her mysterious life here, charmed as it was.

"We banned the use of toxic chemicals after all the fish died," he said, staring from one to the other of his audience, as if daring them to disbelieve he was able to make more than three complete sentences in a day.

"What do the barges run on then?" Shelagh asked, truly curious.

"It's their ethanol mix. Smells and looks terrible but breaks down very fast, actually," the bartender said, watching the old poet carefully.

"Same stuff as in the little trucks," an onlooker added.

"Lotta good that'll do ya," the poet said.

"What?" another customer asked.

"Banning the chemicals after all the fish are dead," the poet replied. "It's a sequential error." He picked green glass shards off the table, examined them as if they were secrets. Quietly weeping now, he traced his nicotine stained fingers through the wet rings left by his bottle. "I'm sorry I broke it," he whispered. "Could I have another?" His fingers traced between shards and slivers. Shelagh was terrified he'd nick himself; they were so long and thin and razor edged. His fingers were scarred, as though he'd been this route before.

The bartender's hands reached in quietly, scurrying to retrieve the slivers, slices of green light, sharp so very sharp. He seemed afraid of the poet, Shelagh thought, yet still needed to protect him, as if the old man's necessary wisdom might drain out with his blood. Afraid too that his violence might erupt again. The old man's face dripped onto the table, and no one did a thing.

"You can only get one more, Holy Mackerel," the bartender said gently, "The pay for your reading went against your tab and you had two over, and that was one there."

"Start me a new tab."

"Not until May. It's the fiscal year for tabs."

Shelagh couldn't stand it. She looked for paper napkins but there weren't any. She tore the cuff from her old shirt, so wash softened it ripped easily. Clean that morning, she folded it into a square, and reaching forward she raised the old poet's chin with her finger and pressed the cloth against his still dripping cheek.

He raised his head to look at her: quizzical, amazed, broken-hearted. Like all old drunken Poet Laureates, Shelagh suspected he yet hoped she might take him home to bed.

The bartender shrugged, wiped up the tables' blood, remaining shards, and the puddle of dark ale with a dirty rag, now dirtier by far.

"Don't rinse it out," Shelagh advised, "throw it away, burn it; his blood might carry."

"Carry what?" the bartender asked.

"The disease of genius," the poet said.

Shelagh nodded; this was exactly what she'd meant. She took her cuff away from his cheek, unfolded it, looked: a perfectly symmetrical red butterfly fluttered.

"Throw the rag in the river," the poet said. "The fish need that virus. It'll bring them back to life."

"Really?" Shelagh asked.

"You're given your heart's desire here not to hoard it but to share it with another," he said, speaking directly to her. "Your drowned child. Only by giving your joy away will you be allowed to keep it. A paradox. A duty."

"You only had to recite for an hour," the bartender said softly, looking at his watch. "An hour against a whole year's tab."

"My words must be worth a lot," the poet said. "But I think I'll go over today. A few free words of wisdom for you all. Maybe you'll remember it one day when I smell especially bad and you don't want to let me in." He turned to Shelagh, gestured at the cuff. "Keep it forever," he said, "a blood stain from an old poet. Carry it in your pocket and when you leave this place to go home you'll be a genius writer forever. Infected."

"No one's ever talked to me about home before. Do you know the way back? Although I've been so very happy here, but you seem to think that's cheating in some way."

"A fork; it's a fork, not a spoon. You must choose. Words. Words that heal, words that kill, words that write the city. If you choose to go home, as you can now, they'll all be yours."

"How do I go?"

"Just by choosing. How d'you think you got here in the first place?"

"Because I chose? That's all?"

"Yup. Got a beer for an old man?"

She dug in her pocket, found her handful of coins; it was just enough. "We'll share one." She nodded at the bartender. "Bring a bottle, two glasses, and then leave us alone." The other patrons were drifting away, although some had planted themselves at tables within earshot. The Poet Laureate having a conversation with someone other than his demons. It hadn't happened in years.

Shelagh was suddenly in tears. She wasn't sure why; maybe it was the thought of leaving. "It's very thoughtful of you to share a little of your genius, to let me take some home with me so I can be your pale reflection."

"Yes," he agreed, "You'll become very famous, and very rich when you go home, with just a drop of my blood. Unlike myself," he harrumphed, but didn't seem to begrudge her. "So why are you crying, darling?"

"Yes," she nodded through her tears, "that's what I thought you meant, "but you don't understand. I've never been happy before, not really, not before I came here. It's as though this place was made especially for me; it feels so perfect, every single day of it."

"Then stay. Find your child. Share your happiness with her. If you do that, you can stay."

"But I don't have a child. I lost her," Shelagh cried, knowing it suddenly to be more true, more sad than anything in her short unaccomplished life. "Because I forgot I ever even had her."

"No matter," he said, "Everyone else forgot theirs too."

They shared their beer and wept, each for their own reasons.

The next morning when Shelagh walked to the river alone, expecting to see black water, a sooty sky and dead fish she saw instead a child sitting on the breakwater, her little white legs and her fishing line hanging over the side. Perhaps seven or eight years old, she wore a white night gown. Beside her was a bucket full of water, the water full of living, wriggling fish.

"The earth fish will be alive now too, because these fish will," the girl said, barely glancing up, continuing to fish, so very solemnly.

"The earth fish?" Shelagh asked, not understanding, a little frightened of her child. Soil fish? What could be meant?

"The fish on Earth. You know, where you come from. The big white ones in the big river, the ones you liked so much. Not fish really, but . . . "

"Whales?"

"Yes, that must be it. Whales," the girl said firmly, as though she'd just learned a new word.

"Well, that's very good news." Shelagh sat down beside the girl, looked down the embankment into the river. It was cleaner than she'd ever seen it, and full of swimming little silver fish. "They must be Holy Mackerels," Shelagh said, "but why?"

"You did it, mummy. Because you were nice to papa. Most people are so mean to him. It's not his fault he's old and drunk and smelly."

"Very smelly," Shelagh said, and asked, perplexed, "Why do you call him papa? I've never slept with him."

"But you must have," Shelagh's daughter said, with the clinical detachment over reproductive matters of the pre-sexual. "For else how could you have given birth to me?"

Shelagh began to cry again.

"What's the matter, mummy?"

"I have too many gifts today. I have the poet's blood; the fish are alive and well again, not just here but on Earth; I have you. It's too much for one person; I'm just overflowing is all. Don't worry; I'll be fine in a moment."

The child smiled brightly. "But that's what I'm here for, to help you carry your gifts. Don't forget the fish; we'll cook them for dinner. Let's go home," she said.

"Does papa live with us?" Shelagh asked, a little worried.

"No, he likes to sleep in the streets. We'll bring him some fresh fried fish tonight. I know where his mattress is."

"Yes, I suppose you would," Shelagh said, still a little intimidated by this child she loved more than her own life. And how to execute her duty, of sharing her boundless joy, when it was a joy that came of solitude? And wasn't happiness in any case a child's department? Shelagh thought back, remembering. Perhaps not.

They walked hand in hand until they got to her own fire escape, where, to Shelagh's amazement, for she couldn't remember washing them or even having them, little white socks, undershirts, pants and dresses flopped noisily on the line stretched across the alley. But maybe there were many things about happiness she'd forgotten, that she would have to learn as if for the first time, like a baby learning to walk. For instance there was this terrible, unfamiliar joy she felt at being with her daughter.

"I'm so happy today," the child said, climbing the last step to the little landing.

"And why is that?" Shelagh asked.

"Because I've been drowned in your forgetting for so very long, and you finally remembered me. I'm always so happy when I'm with you."

"I see." Perhaps it wouldn't be so difficult after all, if the child's loving intensity would mirror her own. There was a faint smell of urine on the fire escape landing, and Shelagh said, "I guess the tom cats must have been fighting here again."

"No," the girl said, "That's just papa. Sometimes he comes and sleeps on the fire escape, because he likes to be near us. But he doesn't come in," she giggled. "He knows he smells. Let's take the washing in."

Shelagh felt both guilty and relieved, and suddenly remembered she'd always felt just so when the girl's father left. Perhaps it wasn't her old life in Montreal she'd forgotten, but her life here. How to be happy. They began to unpeg socks and shirts, fold them into the laundry basket beneath the line. Shelagh put a little shirt to her nose; even washed and line dried, it smelled sweetly, just a little, of her girl. There was no better smell in all the world.

"It's a trick," her daughter said.

"What is?" Shelagh asked, terrified this alarming, all consuming new love could yet be whisked away. But the child answered, giggling: "If you choose the right fork you get the spoon too."

"What?" Shelagh asked. The girl took after her father that was for sure. What could she mean?

"You get the whole mouthful, everything in one bite. Because you chose me, and not the words. Let's go inside now."

"Oh, I think I understand. Because I chose you and not the disease of genius I actually get both?" Shelagh asked, pushing the window up.

"Both me and the words."

"Words that kill, words that heal, words that write the city," Shelagh said, knowing she'd be saying it for the rest of her life.

"You'll be Poet Laureate after him," her daughter explained. "Not that I know what that is. But you don't have to go home, because you are home, mummy. I'll hold the curtain out of the way so you can put the bucket in."

Shelagh knew what this place was, for the first time. Home is where the child is.

A RIVER GARDEN

I'D GROWN UP HAVING A SUMMER GARDEN AND KNEW I'D
miss the homegrown flavour of organic vine-ripened tomatoes. I
knew River Garden, who lived not far away, had seven acres so I
drove over one Saturday morning in early May to see if he'd let me plant
at his place. River had inherited his little white frame bungalow from an
aunt when he was just nineteen, and had lived there ever since.

"Go ahead and plant, Mel," he said, "I couldn't grow a garden if I tried."

"Why's that?" I asked, because from what I knew River's family was
good at everything they laid a hand to.

"It's stuck in my hand," he said, "I can't get it out."

I left that alone. Both River and his mother Gifted spoke cryptically
on occasion, a kind of metaphoric Life Poetry. Sometimes I knew what
they meant; sometimes I didn't; sometimes I felt stupid for not knowing
and sometimes I was irritated.

"Whatever," I said and River started the tiller and motioned for me to
get to work so I did.

The machine was hard to control as are so many tillers but what didn't
help was I'd incurred a bad cut the winter before and my hand wasn't
quite back to normal. River told me to get a beer out of his cooler for my
break; he was busy under his truck. I told him about my accident and
asked if he could help me till the last few rows.

"No," he said, "other people's gardens make me too sad."

I didn't know what that meant either and I didn't want to say something dumb so I finished my beer and got on with the work. At last I was done and could plant my seeds; I put in a little of all the usual: beans, corn, tomatoes, lettuce, peas, beets and carrots, cucumbers, cabbages; I had lots of cabbage seeds. At sunset I thanked him for the beer and the use of his land; he grunted "You're welcome," from underneath his GMC half ton and I drove home.

Everything grew even though I didn't get up there much. River told me so when I passed him on the road coming home from work; we'd both stop, roll our windows down and have a little chat. I was teaching a pottery class in town for children, and what with one thing and another there hardly ever seemed the time to get to River's even to gather greens for salad. I told River to eat what he wanted and he said he would.

By the time I set aside a full day to weed it was already the beginning of August: tomatoes turning orange before red. We'd had a lot of June and July rain, which was unusual but the only thing that had saved my garden from neglect; the cabbages were huge, Findhornian. River pulled a carrot, brushed the dirt off and began munching. They're never sweeter than when you have them that way. He was staring moodily at my faerie cabbages, as though they meant something other than good soil, lots of rain, and his three black hens having the run of the garden, picking the cabbage butterfly larvae off.

But between the cabbages the weeds grew even taller: pigweed, lamb's quarters, mallow, purslane. Actually the purslane wasn't tall but it was rugged, a dense succulent rug. Of course you can eat all those too but it's a little pointless when they're crowding out the things you actually planted.

There I was, weeding, when River came out of the house to chat. "Why don't you have a garden at your dad's instead of here?" he asked, watching me. "Peter's tiller is big and new; the soil's got years of compost you've been adding. It's closer and you'll get to it."

My father had hundreds of acres of land, but I didn't live there anymore. "He doesn't want me gardening there, now I've left," I said, "and where I live they don't want me to plant either." I didn't add that I'd never grown giant pumpkin sized cabbages at my father's house.

"Where do you live?" River asked.

"I thought everyone knew by now. I squat in that house in the county forest."

"Oh, I know that house; it's cool," River said.

"I love it," I agreed, "except the floorboards are rotting out. I know I shouldn't but at night I worry rabid skunks or rats will scramble through the holes and bite my feet while I'm asleep."

River smiled indulgently. "That's a pretty house, though," he said. "Tell you what, let's drive over and I'll help you fix the floor."

"That's nice of you but I haven't got any wood."

"I've got lots; I've been collecting planks other people have been throwing away for years," River said. We went around to his shed, filled up the back of his pick-up with floorboards, a saw, a bag of screws, a hammer and nails and a drill; I made sure he brought a cordless as we didn't have hydro.

He was following me in the truck; I was in my little red Mazda with rust in the floor I'm always hoping the cops won't notice. He stuck his head out the window when he pulled up beside me at the intersection and we talked about how wonderful summer was in our part of the country, made up as it was of fishing, swimming, road trips, playing with turtles, watching herons and eating out of the garden.

"Still, everything's not quite right," I said.

"So what's the matter?" River asked.

"The matter is I'm having accidents," I said.

"What kind of accidents?"

"I cut an artery in my hand," I said. "I was sorting cans for recycling, believe it or not."

"I guess I did hear that. So how'd you fix it?" he asked and I rattled off the list: ambulance, emergency ward, Demerol, anaesthesia, and microsurgery. But the sadness and terror my accident had left me with still hadn't faded, and I told River how I felt; he somehow made me feel I could.

We drove, our windows still rolled down, still pulling up side by side at intersections. It was nice to be getting to know him better, in a different way from him being that guy three lines over it seemed I'd always known. He rolled two smokes and passed me one, explaining it was tobacco he'd grown and cured himself. Lighting up, River said, "I can't grow a garden at all, except for the tobacco."

I said, "So you keep saying, River, but why not? I mean with a last name like Garden? By the way, I've always wondered what your first name was before you decided to call yourself River."

River said: "My mother gave me this name. You should know; we've known each other forever."

"What does she do now? Software?" I said snidely. The truth was, people often said unkind things about River's mother. She lived alone, had lovers, and was more than a little eccentric.

"She lives in the woods," River said mildly, ignoring my insult. "She homeschooled me. You're a bit of a dryad yourself, why I like you I suppose."

"I did go to school but it was the Waldorf; it hardly counts, although I learned enough pottery to get a job teaching it, straight away after graduating."

"Beats working behind the counter at KFC, like most kids your age," River said.

"I wouldn't know," I replied. "But you must have gone to school eventually?"

"Homeschooled, like I said, and by the time I left home I knew how to study on my own."

"You've turned out quite well," I said, thinking what a wit I was, "considering you were raised by a nut case."

"Look who's talking," River said amiably, nonetheless giving me a level stare so I'd know I'd crossed the line. It was true my father was known as a little on the prickly side. Peter The Porcupine, people called him behind his back and sometimes in front, not without reason; I'd run into his prickles more than a few times. Probably it was where I got my famous sarcasm. "But you're right," he added, to make me feel better for having put my foot in my mouth, "Gifted is a nut case."

"What's she do?" I asked again.

"Grows a garden, goes deer hunting in November, sells a few pigs in the fall and eggs throughout the year."

"I mean aside from that," I said, "She must have one little job or another, if only to pay for gas and repairs on her van."

"She tells people when their cats have been taken over by aliens," River replied, totally deadpan.

I snickered. It sounded exactly as fruity as I'd always heard. "She gets paid for this?" But with the Gardens you just never knew; anything was possible. Maybe exorcising cats actually was software; maybe his mother was one of those back woods types who was always building new neural pathways, had no fear or mental blocks whatsoever about learning. It was quite possible she'd taught herself graphics and programming at the age of forty-two, had a dedicated work station running on solar panels with a satellite linkup. Or maybe she had hydro after all; maybe I was the only one who didn't. Maybe "Alien Felines" was a computer game written by a nut case for other nut cases, cashing in on the current media generated fad for fringe kookiness and River's mother was actually a Gatesian billionaire.

Stranger things had happened, and, I figured, would again, maybe very soon.

"No," River said, "but people give her stuff to make her go away."

"Yeah—stuff like what?"

"Oh, usually the stuff she wants. She'll come and hang around for a couple of days and harp on about their cats and the aliens and then she'll finger their best Guatemalan shawl or their beautiful handblown glass bowl with the fish designs in it and they'll say, "Here's a present for you, a trade for exorcising my cats," and she'll take it away."

I wasn't sure if he was pulling my leg or not, feeding into all those rumors. Perhaps he was defensive about having a kook for a mother, just as I was sensitive about having a porcupine for a father.

"Gifted?" I said snidely, as though I'd never heard that was her name before. "What was she called before that? Sandy?" It's been said before that sarcasm is harder than cigarettes to kick and it sure seemed true for me that day and dumb to boot, considering how cute and companionable I was finding River.

"No; Gifted Dreamer is what her mother called her," he said, still maddeningly, stubbornly sincere, still ignoring my mean streak.

"Wow," I said, still unable to help myself, "You're a third generation squatter nut case." It occurred to me he was so sexy and nice it made me nervous and my acerbic wit leapt up as an instinctive smokenscreen. Worse yet, he could probably see right through me.

"As you know I don't squat, I own," he said, and then added, just to prove he wasn't completely bereft of snideness himself: "You're the one who squats, Melneeda."

Melneeda, that's my name. Sorry, but it's the unfortunate truth.

River went on, "Hard cases. We're not nut cases exactly but hard cases. Hard seeds. You need to soak 'em to make 'em grow."

Hard seed cases? It was a gardening metaphor too dense for me, and I was tempted to make another prickly aside but figured even River might have a limit to his tolerance, so I let it go.

My place is where the river crosses under a bridge. When we pulled up the owner was standing there with a crabby look on her face. She started screaming at me, having suddenly decided I owed her four months rent even though she'd said several times it was okay for me to stay there, and what with the house's condition she couldn't have charged a normal tenant anyway. It didn't seem fair but what could I say? I didn't have it on paper. But River strode forward and gave her six hundred dollars in cash, crisp fifties pulled off a roll, said, "I think that's quite enough for four months at this place."

"Three hundred a month," she growled, looking wonderingly at all that hard currency.

"For three-fifty you can still get a rundown farmhouse with hydro, flush toilets indoors. Who'd pay three for this place?"

She growled some more. River started to reach for his money then, asking politely whether she needed any exorcism on her cats. Looking just a tad alarmed, she put the money away, got in her van and left in a hurry.

I looked at him in stunned awe, meaning to thank him profusely, instead saying, "Seems like all those rumors about Gifted stand you in good stead."

"What rumors are those?" he asked archly.

I sighed; he was on to me in too many ways.

"Well, I'll pay you back," I said.

"Of course you will."

"So who's your dad? For some reason I don't know." It occurred to me belatedly I sounded like I was prying.

"Stuart Garden," River replied. "A good guy; they're still friends, even though he lives in Nova Scotia now. We talk on the phone a lot, him and me."

"So that's where you got your last name," I said.

"Well, Gifted had a dream when she was pregnant that my true name was River and she thought River Garden sounded better than River Dreamer."

"River Dreamer's nice too, though."

"Yes, but perhaps a bit too drownable," he said.

Not knowing what he meant like half the time I just ignored it, asked "What about my floor?"

"Okay, let's get to it."

We worked: high speed, butt-busting work till I hammered my thumb in August's last light. In any case the drill was out of power; we'd traded it in for hand tools an hour before. I thought I had a couple of boxes of Kraft Dinner in the pantry and offered to cook River supper on my little yellow Finlay cook stove but he said he had plans.

Still, I wanted to make sure I saw him again, a wee bit more formally than watering the garden or passing on the road. I was working hard on an excuse but what came out of my mouth was: "I think my cat is invaded by aliens; think you could drop by with your mum for a visit?"

"It's not your cat," he said, "it's you that's invaded by aliens." He looked at me sternly as though I should've been able to figure this out for myself. This was news to me but somehow I felt a great relief that someone was taking an interest in my ennui, my feeling of unwellness, my healing, and so I said, "Can she do people too?"

"Of course," he said, "We'll go see her. Saturday, 'kay?"

"'Kay." Saturday I worked but I thought I'd get my friend Hannah to fill in for me; this was too important.

When I saw Hannah at work the next day she said, "Don't go, Melneeda; everyone knows Gifted is crazy." She swung her wings of dark
hair at me, ominously, I thought.

"You're usually a reliable purveyor of information, Hannah, but I'm
going anyway."

"It's your funeral," she said, shaking and shaking that hair at me. I'd
grow my own that long and learn to work it like she did; people would
have more respect for me.

"Thanks for covering for me."

Hannah sighed and walked away.

Saturday morning I followed the scribbled map, not even noticing
how I didn't get lost once. When I arrived Gifted was having a yard sale;
she had three tables set up and every single item for sale was gorgeously,
stunningly beautiful. She was wearing a long paisley skirt and a green
velvet jacket; her hair was long and grey. When I noticed her smoking
she said, "I have to; it's a smoking jacket, isn't it?" I laughed politely, not
knowing what to say but Gifted took my hand and shook it firmly. "You
must be Melneeda, River's friend," she said.

"I've known him forever."

"More or less true," River said, coming out of the house to join us.

"But I don't think you and I have ever met," I said.

"Oh, we have," Gifted said, "but you were just a baby. Your mother
and I were friends. But after she died, you know, Peter and I never got
along that well."

"Sounds familiar," I said and Gifted laughed, a cross between grateful
and gracious.

"Nice stuff," I commented, looking at her sale tables.

"I'm selling the stuff people have bartered me for my alien exorcisms,"
she giggled, as if it was all a big lark. "This is my third weekend and I've
made thirteen hundred dollars. Don't need that much myself, I only
needed to pay for repairs on my van. I put half of it in your account,"
Gifted explained to River. "Figured you could use a little mad money."

"I noticed," he said. "Thanks." He didn't tell her he'd just paid my rent
with it and was back to broke as usual. I was relieved that in some ways
she was still just a mum and he just her son.

"Your mother's generous," I said. "My father's relatively rich compared to most people but he won't even let me grow a garden on his land since I left."

"It was a good thing, maybe," River said. "Have you driven by there? The corn's still short, thin and spindly even though it's rained twice a week since April."

I nodded. "I used to hear there were barrels of PCBs buried under the cornfields; truth is it sure felt like that."

"I heard that too," River said.

"No one talked about it much."

"I guess not," he said.

"Now," Gifted turned to me. "River tells me you're here on business," and she led us inside. We walked through a kitchen crowded with beautiful objects both old and new and into a hallway where a torn green curtain was strung up in front of an alcove. There was a big rip in the middle she hadn't bothered to mend, and a Queen Anne chair upholstered in blue velvet facing it. "Sit down, my dear," she said. "This is where it all happens."

River played assistant, brought me a mug of steaming herb tea and I thought to ask whether it might make me hallucinate but stopped myself, on account of possibly seeming rude. I knew I was just being influenced by all those rumors again. I sipped the tea; it wasn't too hot, and fragrant and delicious as if made from a blend of a hundred flowers that grow on a much happier planet than this one. I drained it all in a big series of gulps. I guess I'd been thirsty and the tea had a strong and immediate effect; it made me cry. I cried so much and for so long that at last even River and Gifted asked me if that might not be enough.

I cried because my dad and I had fought so much before I'd left, because I'd injured my till then supposedly impermeable body so very badly, because my landlady had screamed at me, because I owed River six hundred dollars which at my present rate of pay would take me as many years to pay back, and because my mother had died when I'd turned fourteen. I'd cried about that before, of course, but a little extra releasing never hurt, I guessed. I also cried most of my famous sarcasm out, but I wasn't aware of that part.

"That's Teary Tea for you," Gifted told me when I'd subsided a bit, "doing its job just like it's supposed to. You can't heal if you don't vent first; no one can. Now listen up, child. Are you ready to listen?" I nodded, afraid I'd cry some more if I spoke. "The aliens are on the other side of the curtain," Gifted said, completely without apology. "In the alcove. All the aliens I've exorcised from people's cats, and from the people themselves, are behind the curtain."

Maybe it was the Teary Tea but I took her at face value, or if not that exactly, at least felt I wanted to go along with her story, see where it led. I already felt better than I had in a year, just from all the crying. "You already put your hand through," Gifted said, and I looked at her in horror as though the alcove behind the curtain really was populated by skittering, hostile, utterly alien beings. I was afraid then, like a child woken from nightmare, wanted only for Gifted to take the aliens that were in me out and stuff them in that hole where she stuffed the others, because she could, because she was the only one who wasn't afraid. I didn't know what she planned to do with them later, didn't really care. I figured if Gifted could exorcise aliens she could deal with them too.

"Alienation," Gifted said, "it's a common problem."

"I'm in love with your son," I told her hopefully, startling even myself, relieved he was back in the kitchen washing his mother's morning dishes. I'd had no clue those words were about to pop out of my mouth. It occurred to me later that was part of her healing; to make me a person brave enough to speak her heart's truth instead of always hiding it behind sarcasm.

Gifted looked at my untidy hair, ripped jeans, holey boots, and winsome smile as though I just might do. "Full of foolish bravado, you stuck your hand through the curtain and they cut you, that's all," she repeated implacably.

"You're talking about my accident?" I guessed, as I'd never been to her house before, and had never once stuck my hand through the curtain. I wasn't about to do it now, either, considering the spooky visions she'd just implanted in my impressionable, tear-soaked mind.

"Yes. The important question is, what did you bring back through? They're hoarding the good stuff over there, the stuff that makes us feel better, not so alienated anymore. I hope you realize my little set-up here is symbolic." She glared at me, as though suddenly suspicious I'd run off and tell Hannah and everyone she was even crazier than everyone said she was. "All this mass hysteria about aliens abducting or invading people is missing the point," she added emphatically, "even if it does turn me a tidy profit." She lit a cigarette, continued. "If we can't be happy, how can we learn to grow, love one another? Even my son. I tried my best to raise him right but the world's too cold, too alienated by far. In spite of all my hard work he's never been able to grow his own garden."

We all went back outside and Gifted resumed her work of rearranging beautiful objects on her yard sale tables. I went into a dream, or perhaps it was a continuation of the same dream I'd inhabited with River since the day I'd planted a garden at his house. I didn't know we were about to make a fair trade, that momentarily he'd be planting one at mine.

I thanked Gifted, not really understanding any of it. I remembered then how I'd seen her in town once, only a few years before, had guessed who she was. I'd turned my head away when a bunch of kids had thrown rocks at her van, cracking the wind shield, screaming that she was a witch, a bitch, all the usual and crazy whore to boot. I'd been eleven, old enough to know better. Worse still, River had saved me from the corner bullies more than once when I'd been buying my drugstore candy.

I sucked on guilt; meanwhile she went on in her busy, competent, let's-get-this-job-over-with voice, as though it was all tea and cookies from where she stood, no harder than slaughtering chickens, which, admittedly wasn't easy but all in a day's work. "You're just a little scared is all, because you've so recently left your father's house. You're a good camper, a good traveler and that's the main point. But I still want to know, and you need to know too, what treasure you brought back from the other side, stole back from the aliens hoarding it, keeping most of us miserable all our lives. Hoarding our joy, our desire, our magic."

She seemed almost normal then, just a middle aged lady who had a firm grip on life and knew a lot of stuff and I said, "I'll figure it out eventually, Gifted. I'm sure I will."

"Okay," she agreed as she thought this was good enough for now.

"Thanks," I said, "and what do I owe you?"

Gifted just waved her hand, said, "Take care of my son." I nodded cheerily even though I was a little concerned by how she might mean that. It would be a major disappointment to me if she had it in mind I should start doing his dishes and laundry.

River would drive me home, he said, because my carburetor had fainted the minute I'd arrived. He'd come back and take a look, he promised. But even his usually reliable truck stalled on the way and in spite of our best efforts to get it going again, nothing worked. We were still six miles from my place but River took his canoe off the back and made me help him carry it through the woods to the water. We paddled home down the river, stopping just this side of the bridge. I thought we'd get out and portage up the steep bank and across the road but River said, "Let's canoe under," and we did even though we had to keep our heads down, the bridge was so low. I liked it though; it was a cool, froggy, echoey minute. Hauled the canoe out, set it on my bleached, parched lawn of quack grass.

He stood, looking at the river, at the brown grass, while I mentally struggled for the umpteenth time this summer, with how I'd ever pay him back for all he'd done. "River," he said inexplicably, out of the blue, as though his mother's healing had made him feel dreamy too, "my name is River Garden."

"So why don't you garden then?" I asked yet again; I really was curious. I felt so much better at speaking my heart since I'd met his mother, yet I knew I'd have to make it a daily practice, a habit, or I'd lose it again.

"Because my garden isn't like other people's: it's a garden existing only in the palm of my hand, invisible, and I've never figured out how to get it out of my hand and plant it, grow it up, normal sized; right now it's microscopic."

"Not seeds?"

"Hard seeds. Hard cases." River looked like he was going to cry.

I thought of how he'd let me plant at his house, paid my rent, helped me fix my floor and taken me to meet his mother, who'd cured my existential angst, exorcised the metaphorical aliens possessing me; he'd driven me home and most importantly been good company, good conversation at every stop sign and every red light over the summer, not staring out the window as though what was on his mind couldn't be shared, like so many men I knew. I thought of how so many good turns must deserve at least one in return, and if he didn't want to be my boyfriend, ever, I'd just have to let it go. I put my hand on his; it was my left hand, the hurt hand, although only a scar remained, a bit of numbness in the cold. I kept it there for a long time, felt gradually a charge building up, a kind of pressure which then began to flow from my hand into his. It was the life force, I knew, the green force, the force that had been stuck, unused, hoarded by my own alienation on the other side of the torn curtain.

"How long do I keep my hand there, d'you know?" I asked.

"Till it stops flowing," River said, looking into my eyes; his were very large and brown indeed.

"I've never done this before," I said. "I don't even know what I'm doing."

"It sure feels like you do. Just keep doing it, whatever it is. I think maybe you're soaking my seeds."

"What?"

"If I'm right, Melneeda, you'll see in a minute. It'll be a surprise. But that's what happened, why you tore your hand. You were supposed to be using it and you weren't. You cut your hand so the healing force could come through. The dam would be opened, the clog unobstructed."

"But I almost lost my hand."

"Use it or lose it," River said.

"But I'm only seventeen," I said.

"Age has nothing to do with it. It's because you've prayed all your life. Most people don't, you know. I could see it in you when you were just a kid. Remember how you used to spend the fall sitting up in the apple trees, eating yellow apples, writing, reading, and drawing?" he asked, with something like entreaty in his eyes. I'd always thought he was so self-contained, moving through the world; not needing anything from anyone, always having something to give. "Your force was clogged and how could it not be growing up on a toxic waste dump?" he added. "You know the former owners made a shady deal when they closed the old General Electric plant. They made a fortune burying that stuff."

"I kind of heard that, but it's such a big farm," I said guiltily.

"It doesn't matter how much, it matters how clean."

"Peter got it cheap."

"No kidding, Melneeda."

"They didn't tell him."

"Of course not," River said. "But he just pretended not to know; everyone knew."

"He said I needed a lot of land to grow up on, after mum died. For the mother you've lost I'll give you a big piece of land to mother you; woods and fields and ponds. He said he did it for me."

"He was just greedy. I've never had more than a few acres. It's enough. Neither has Gifted."

I thought our conversation was quite possibly the most interesting one I'd ever had, seeming to explain so many things I'd always puzzled about in my life. The flowing had stopped; suddenly drained, I got up and walked toward the house. In front of the window a small bed of scraggly cosmos bloomed. In it sat my morning coffee, half drunk and abandoned there. I picked it up and drank. It was a pale blue cup, my favorite although already cracked, a house warming present from my town buddy Hannah.

"Those cabbages I grew at your place are weird," I said, offering the cup to River. I thought we needed coffee to restart our brains, lost to his mother's soggy healing rituals, and cold abandoned cosmic java seemed better at that moment than me leaving him alone to go inside and make new. I felt fragile as I knew he did; our fragility linked us.

"Gifted knows how to make sauerkraut," River said. "We'll get her recipe. But more importantly, they're how I knew about you."

When I turned back River had placed his garden hand on the ground beside the river; the seeds had loosened and fallen in that scratchy gravelly hardpan, barely good enough for chickens and a few leggy cosmos that had been self-seeding for years. But to River's seeds it was darkest loam.

Already you could see the seeds germinating, sprouting, growing at hyper speed like time lapse photography. Foxgloves, lupins, old single hollyhocks in every shade; tomatoes, beans, squash, corn, peas, sunflowers, chamomile, bergamot, cabbages, broccoli. Also a little patch with a beautiful white bellflower I didn't know, an orange milkweed of all things, and several grasses I'd never seen before.

"What's that stuff, the plants you invented?" I asked.

"No, it's my regeneration project. Eastern prairie; indigenous to Ontario. Like the Eastern bison, it's been mostly wiped out by settlers and lawns and parks and all that. We're supposed to start it up again, so this is my contribution."

"Very pretty," I said admiringly, "But it's a shame it's here and not on land any of us own," I said.

River was leaning over, watching his tiny garden grow. It was as big as his hand now.

As my hand.

"Maybe it's better this way. If someone's driving by hungry they can collect some food, or dig up a bit of their favorite shade of peony to transplant; that's all I ever wanted my garden to do."

As it grew we could make out more and more varieties of food, flowers, herbs, teas. You name it; River grew it.

We sat there the whole afternoon watching his garden grow, felt the tickling of creeping thyme emerging under our behinds by way of purple fuzzy pillows.

"What about after I move? Who will look after your garden?"

"This garden will be here, self-seeding forever; you tore it through from the other side of the curtain where the aliens were hoarding it. Now d'you think your injury was worth it?"

"Only a little numbness in the cold," I said, looking at the scar, and River took my scarred hand in his now empty garden hand and kissed it. As we went inside together the last of the tingling faded away.

IN DREAMS WE REMEMBER

I HAVE DREAMS ABOUT A SCHOOL. THE CLASSES WERE ALL girls, and taught by women. They were outside. We'd follow the teacher along country paths, usually passing the villages, sometimes stopping at the inn. Most nights we slept under the stars. That's when astronomy class was held; at night, after we'd made our fire and cooked our dinner. When the sun fell behind the green hills we'd unroll our bedding and lie down, staring up at the canopy of stars and our teacher would name them. So many stars. Later we were also taught astrology, or predestination, and one night, alone, much later, I saw how one woman's fate was spelled out in stars. She could no more have changed it than I could turn into a swan: now, here, in this world. She comes to me in dreams, white faced, raven-haired. I have never seen a face so proud or haughty, so fierce and womanly at once.

This is a new world, and women no longer turn into swans, and don't hold their heads so high anymore, as high as she did, my proud and lonely queen. In this world we aren't taught the right things: to revere trees and wells and art and wisdom and transformation of many kinds. In this world we make do. And we pine for another way of being, and sometimes, in dreams we remember.

I began to read, trying to discover where and when my lovely school had been, if it had even existed, who the woman had been, my beautiful queen, her face so haunting in my dreams.

And I began to try and expand my dreaming, to see more of that place and time. To my surprise, it was as if I already knew how, as if there were techniques I'd once learned, which slowly came back to me.

I left something back there, something back then. Something important. Was it my sisters' hands in mine, sitting by the stream, braiding daisies into one another's hair and reciting love poems to the salmon?

Could I really have had the ability to turn into a swan?

From my expanded dreaming I learned many things: that we students enjoyed each other's company immensely, women and girls of all ages. We carried sticks with bells on them. They rang as we walked. We wore white. We carried crystal eggs in the big pockets of our robes in beautiful colors: translucent red, green, and blue. We talked as we walked, sometimes just joking and gossiping but more often studying, memorizing verses, thousands upon thousands.

We'd stop at the holy wells, make sun-wise ritual to Brigit, to Macha, to Eire.

I learned that when we became older and had studied long enough we were called upon to adjudicate disputes in the villages. We were looked upon as wise and learned and our judgements were generally followed, for it was known they were not given lightly, nor taken lightly. We took our work seriously, yet so much of it was pure pleasure: to learn the stars, to chant poetry that encompassed all of Eire's history, all of her legends. When we grew up we had many opportunities for employment. We could teach or practice law or medicine, all things we'd learned in those countless verses committed to memory. We could guard a sacred well, priestess to the goddess. Our job then was to make sure the kings who stopped there always took the land into account, her voice, her needs, her pleasures. In times still older than ours only a king who did so had the right of kingship; it was the land herself which bestowed it upon him. And if he strayed, well, we were there to gently remind him.

Or so I thought when I was still young, in that other life I miss so much, but even then, the world was already changing, our power slipping though our hands like water from a shattered cup.

We eventually raised a building, a more permanent home to study in, at least in the winters. It's the school I miss the most, this time around. The school stood for centuries, on Brigid's Hill. Later it became a convent. That part I read in a history book. Queen Maeve visited us there, for I discovered it was indeed she I dreamed of, over and over and over. I was still a child, perhaps ten or eleven, and Maeve took me aside from the other girls and gave me a pin: the Celtic triple spiral emblazoned in silver: three for the Goddess who is tripartite, now as then. She had such fondness for me, she said, giving me the pin.

Of course, they burned the academy to the ground, but that was hundreds of years later; I read about it in the same book. It's true I too have been raped, just like so many girls of this time, but not with the murderous violence bestowed upon those poor girls then, and sometimes, waking at midnight, melancholy, filled with rage and sorrow, I think perhaps some of my despair might rightly be theirs. For I have enough, in this world. I have many pairs of shoes and a roof and a car and a computer and a hair dryer, things not one of us had then, not one. Except Maeve.

She had many pairs of shoes and a choice of roofs to shelter her at night, but then, she was Queen of Connaught.

I eat. My family was good. How can I complain of my life?

Sometimes we accompanied the kings to war. Oh, there were so many kings then. Kings and kings and kings, kings upon kings. It was hard at times to tell them all apart, which could of course be embarrassing, for we too were expected to pay homage to the kings and their sons, kings again.

Maeve stood out all the more for it.

I went to war once, but not for a king. I went for my queen. I did not want to go, but better a druidess along on a war than not, I thought. Perhaps I could have some small influence on events, point toward a harmonious outcome. I could mitigate, search for harmony, weave a new piece out of the bloody shredded tapestry of battle. I went with her in the end, because she begged me to; although in spite of all my druid magic I could no more change the course of events than the course of the stars.

I thought I could be a swan, then, a peacekeeper or maker and perhaps if I'd been older and stronger I could have or perhaps war just turns all it touches into ravens, ravening birds of prey.

Like them, those two men; they didn't turn into swans or owls, but into birds of prey. And that is what they were; that was the bird their spirits most resembled, bloody clawed carrion crows. They pulled all they touched into war, into bloodshed, including me. Shape-shifters too, trained in the same techniques as I, yet far more powerful, they used their power to create adversity. Not one noble along on that still famous cattle raid knew who they were except the druids, but Maeve and Fergus and Ailill, Conchobor and Cuchullain didn't listen when we told them. Oh, they probably believed us; kings and queens believed their druids. They just didn't see it as a reason to stop the game.

It's been said you become what you hate. Perhaps I shouldn't have hated them so much, those two men, taking us all into bloodshed with them, for the sake of their huge folly, their childish competition. People even today, who know her story, will tell you it was Maeve who was childish and competitive, taking so many thousands to die in battle for the capture of a bull. It is true they all loved a game, all those Celtic kings and soldiers and their haughty gold bedecked women: a sport above all else, but never forget it was their contest, those two wizardly pig-keepers, which was far the greater, and she was an unwitting pawn in their cosmic game.

We could marry. We could have children. We were not cloistered, but learned women of the world. There were men among our ranks too, of course, but the school I went to was for girls.

We could own property; it did not go over to our husbands at the marriage ceremony, and that was true of all women then, legally and in regards to our rights as females: we were no more privileged than a milk-maid or a baker's assistant. Our knowledge didn't earn us privilege, but duty.

We were not afraid of death. We knew we would return. This was part of our practice, our learning: to study techniques by which we might remember previous lives, when we came again, so that all our twenty years of studying might not all be for naught, to illuminate only one brief candle's flicker of a life. The candle, blown out, might be relit and remember its past burnings.

That was the highest teaching at our disposal and the most difficult. I was one who was successful in learning it. But only in part.

A druidess, I crossed Maeve's path, and she asked me to go to war with her, to be her Seer, help her plan. An October path it was, just before Samhain. I was on my way home from Alba where I'd been studying for a turn of the year. Yellow leaves on the forest paths, sorrow at the sacred well. She never let a living soul see her cry except the little goddess of the well. She'd creep out of her war tent at dawn to weep there. Proud and mighty queen, fierce and fearless, for whom did you weep? Did you weep for Cuchullain who might yet have died in your raid had not the Morrigan herself, goddess of war, come to heal him?

Eel, raven, she-wolf, hornless red heifer: she was the original shape-shifter, her origin divine. Mortals could learn from her but never make more than the palest copy. Not even the two druidic pig keepers, who, after generations of battling in one fantastic creature's skin or another, turned in the end into two bulls, the most powerful two in all Ireland. Settled in two provinces, so many transmigrations later all was forgotten; no one living remembered they'd once been men, and plotted mischief still, as men do. When Maeve woke one day to banter with Ailill, her kind husband, to compare and contest over who owned more, did she know it was a wizardly man and not a beast she hankered after, when Ailill's property turned out to exceed hers by a bull?

She didn't know. She went to Ulster to capture the other, so she and her husband could be equals. They believed in equality, she and Ailill, as much as possible for a royal couple who kept servants, something not well looked upon in my time now, and for good reason. She sent her forces, in single combat against Cuchullain, sole defender of Ulster, of the Brown Bull of Cuailnge. She could have sent thousands and over-whelmed him, but they wanted to play fair, she and Fergus and Ailill. It is Cuchullain's story of course, that is told in our time and not Maeve's, less even mine. I met him and could add another word or two to his legends but to what purpose?

His exploits have been well documented. For my own part, it's not the battles at all I miss but the school: I long for that life among the trees, green beings both worshipped and worshipping. I long for the company of my sister students, their eyes alight with the fire of learning. How proud we were of our quick and subtle minds, the difficulties of our course of study.

Sometimes now, I long for that look so, I spend whole afternoons walking this city's streets, watching for one with that light in her eyes. But I never see it. I think too, there might be another girl here from then who remembers, and she might be the one to carry that light in its little cage, guarding it forever. Yet, when I look in the mirror before I leave for work in the mornings, rearranging my scarf and retouching my lipstick, my eyes are much duller than they ever were then. They used to say I had triple irises, and I thought I was lucky to be born so pretty and with such eyes but looking back I think I earned them; my remarkable eyes reflected my hard working soul. So few opportunities for a soul to do her work in this world, in this life. If I was to cross paths with a fellow student on a dusty gritty street today, as I crossed Maeve's path in the shadowy Irish forest two thousand years ago, would we even recognize one another, our eyes and spirits so dulled as they are?

"Fedelm," she asked me that October morning, "Have you the Imbas Forasnai, the Light Of Foresight?"

"I have," I replied.

"Then tell me what you see," she said.

"I see crimson. I see red," I answered, yet my prophesy of bloodshed wasn't enough to make her turn back.

"All wars shed blood," she said, sounding rather like the Morrigan herself, "it's what they do best."

Later on during the march, tired and hungry and enervated, my light began to recede and Maeve cut down a forest, thinking it would clear my mind, improve my vision. I cried that day. To cut trees down for a druid is to poison water so we might drink it.

Still, it's funny how, in this new world it's still Maeve I miss the most, her strength and cunning and fierceness, her glad heart and her generous charm. It is her hand I would like to hold, sitting beside a slow moving river. But she I will not see, and if I did, we wouldn't know one another, for she went to the famous Scathac's school for warriors while I took the gentler path, and went to my beloved academy. And they no more taught warriors how to remember countless incarnations than they taught druidesses how to take an army into battle.

Perhaps they made a mistake, and I should've gone to her school for a turn or two and she to mine.

A queen alone on a windswept hill. She traveled with an army of fifty-four thousand, was never alone, and yet I remember her as being alone. She carried the fate of her men in her hands. It was a heavy burden and not even her husband could share it with her, though he went beside her to war, he too thinking she had a right to the famous brown bull. They had separate tents, but visited often, many times each day. They loved each other very much, she and Ailill; that I know for certain. You could see it by the way they looked into each other's eyes.

She stood alone on the windswept hill, looking out at the herds of cattle, knowing what she must do. Caught in the terrible inevitability of her time, that moment where she stood, before the Ulstermen awoke from Macha's curse, the last battle ensued.

A queen caught in a cosmic snare, so large she couldn't see it for what it was, know she was caught, that if she yet saw she was trapped, there might be a way out. I tried to tell her, but she was too proud to listen, even then, in days when the druid spoke thrice, even before the king.

She could not change the tale, only live it out. She was a warrior, confined not just by armor but by blood. How often seeing her just as the first light began on her hill overlooking Murtheimne Plain, I longed to ask her to leave her way, to join us, be a druidess and not a queen and I did ask her once and she laughed at me, and slapped my thigh, roughly, as if she were a man. Maeve's deep throaty laugh, so rich; there is none other.

"But Fedelm," she said, "I'm a bear and you're a kitten, if a very wise kitten who remembers all her nine lives. You, like the Maureen, might be able to change shape but I could no more take on your still quiet form than I could be subservient to anyone, man or woman. I'm made for war. I serve Macha, goddess of war; only she may hold her head higher than I."

Yet, what if she'd come with me, spent the rest of her life beside me, wandering the forest paths, teaching and learning hand in hand as they are best, looking into still salmon pools to laugh at her own reflection broken suddenly by the nose of a magic fish? Would they have fought without her leading them, I often wondered? Let them, I felt. Or perhaps they'd go home to their thatched huts, their decidedly ordinary wells, their women and babies, their calves and ewes, their mare and their little ploughed field.

The goddess is stern. So much better to lead an everyday life. What do we know of the gods' ways in the end? When the raid was at last over, the bull brought home to Connaught, thousands upon thousands dead, I too longed to be ordinary, to grow potatoes and have babies of my own. But by then I already knew too much, and knowledge exacts its own price. I felt I'd seen too many horrors to ever enjoy an ordinary life; I'd wake my husband with nightmares, screaming, "Death, death, death," just like the raven. In the end I no longer felt my way was better than Maeve's, my gentle wooded path. We were equally stained.

Those damn bulls were a curse. And they had the last laugh. What did they become when they died the last time, died out of their bullish selves? What secret plot are they yet hatching to lead gentlemen and proud women astray? They were men once, and they had the last laugh.

Oh yes, they most certainly did, summoning Macha, staining all those people's hands and yes, my own. What might I have said to Maeve, if I'd known then what I know now? The eternal regret of age for its misspent youth, my young life two millennia ago?

"Mother, you can capture as many bulls as you like, just stay a few seasons at the druidic school, learn a trick or two, so that, reborn in this time we might yet arrange to be together. We'd both be single, but have lovers. We'd share an apartment and give dinner parties. Standing at the door together, putting on our lipstick as we left to go to work at different jobs, we'd look into one another's eyes and laugh. See for a moment the salmon pool, the salmon of knowledge swimming there, the knowledge of who we were never far from the surface."

I never told you she was my mother, did I? That is the thing of it; Maeve was my mother.

And I could stand this darkened time where the birds no longer sing in great multitudes as they did then, darkening the skies, I could even enjoy it, if she was there beside me, sharing it with me, as she was then.

It was all written.

I saw it in the stars, as irrevocable as the turn of the seasons.

I will tell you all of her story but first let us make merry, we'll do the spiral dance one last time as we used to do it at the castle of the same name. Beltane fire festival at Spiral Castle; bonfires on all the high sacred hills of Eire, including Brigid's, mother of us all. We danced like this, inwards to the center of the spiral galaxy.

BLACK LACE

NO ONE IN THE VILLAGE KNEW HOW THE KEEPER DID what she did; many knew nothing, having never met the elves. These people thought Issa was just an old eccentric living in a cabin in the woods beyond the village boundary, and they were right, in their way. Yet she had practiced her work every day since she'd come, even when she didn't light the fire; mending, after a time with thought alone, the torn curtains of reality so there might yet be peace. The water clear, the animals and plants strong. The people free.

She burned sage on a plate in front of the outdoor hearth, laid it carefully with old papers and odd bits of lumber. Peace had to be maintained, it did not stay all by itself, it needed help and work. It was as if pain leaked out of people and was attracted to her, attaching itself like burrs. As time passed the work became a little easier, although Issa still had to remind herself, on days when the despair was fiercest, that when she burned sage and drank elvish tea and made herself as still as peace, it would all flood out of her again: all the gathered shame, sorrow and fear, and she would use it for fuel, to keep the peace light burning. But she had to feel it, on its way in or on its way out, or it couldn't burn.

Even though she often felt tired, her hands and feet performed with little conscious bidding, and Issa wondered whether what felt like exhaustion was perhaps only stillness, an ever deeper peace. She couldn't ask the other keepers: each kept their own fire, was tied to place. Striking the flint, Issa had a premonition it would be the last fire. It scared her, a little; ritual and ritual maker had over time become one to the extent that Issa couldn't imagine doing anything else.

She could go back to Taylor, but not to Black Lace.

The berries were fatal but the distillate was mildly psychoactive. Drinking it, she and Taylor could still work, learn their lines, write new plays, layer cleverness on cleverness, outwitting one another and their audiences, the Black Lace always inspiring them to do more. They'd traveled from town to town performing shows in the crumbling community centers, telling themselves that one day they'd be rich and famous.

There was a critic who lived in a tower in the city, an old man with an enormous and terrible reputation, a final arbiter of taste. Careers hung on his words; everyone admired and feared him. He had a goatee and a good suit and a cane; he lived in a big clean apartment with handsome young office staff. Issa kept sending him invitations to their shows, which went unanswered. A scholar, he'd written books upon books about theater, poetry and music and the nature of the creative mind. Issa had a few of them still, on a bookshelf inside her little elvish house. A beeswax candle shaped like a toadstool burned there at night so Issa could read—about theater, about writing and art, although it had been years since she'd seen a play, never mind writing or performing in one.

The elves had given her the funny candle; their gifts often exemplified the silliest clichés of elvish lore, from the time before their return. Issa had seen her elves wear red conical hats with white polka dots so they could imitate Amanita Muscaria, take these hats off and hurl them into the air, laughing. In spite of their silliness, they were never other than dignified, even when they made fun of her, or of themselves. She did not see them often, but when they visited they always brought her the wild tea she drank as she lit the ritual fire; the elves told her it could open memory boxes. Memories of the future, of other lives, other worlds, worlds one had made and then locked away for fear of looking at what one had created. The tea never had this effect on Issa, so far as she knew, although sometimes, after a pot, she recalled having gathered it by moonlight. The tea was a shade-loving plant and thrived, like memories, in underbrush, best gathered at night, at full pungency.

At last the critic said he would come. Too much depended upon his review for Taylor and Issa to behave as though they cared, so they offered him Black Lace and taunted him when he turned it down. Still they put on their best show: Taylor singing, Issa speaking, he playing the harp, she the lute, drinking Black Lace all the while; they thought it improved their performance. Taylor had been so handsome, although Issa imagined he didn't look as good anymore. Toward the end, their life together was already starting to show on his face and bony frame. Issa, shallow in her youth, and drawn largely to his looks, could not discard Taylor even then. Not like the young men before him, whom she flirted with, then spilled wine into their laps—a lot of them, before Taylor came with the Lace he drank any chance he got. Had her lover been Taylor or Black Lace? Had he known from the first that the way to keep her was to offer her Lace repeatedly, till she couldn't turn it down, nor him either?

Still, she had left him when she found the heart tree, a gate to the elf world. And with her training had come something unexpected: a better drug by far. No keeper would do the dangerous work without recompense: Issa's reward was a regularly scheduled blast of bliss. She didn't know if it was a result of the work, an endorphin flood released by all that meditation, some kind of chemical effect in her brain or just more elvish trickery. Anything that could be experienced through drugs could be arrived at another way; had to be, or the receptors wouldn't be there. Elves. They were her new pushers, supplying her with a better bliss than in all her years of addiction. Had she found peace, or replaced one addiction with another?

Damn elves.

She and Taylor threw cats at the critic and laughed. Young black tomcats, on Black Lace—they had sunk that low.

The critic had called them juvenile, yes, preposterous, ill-mannered, uncivilized, drunken, squalid, reviewing not only their work but their stained broken teeth, their broken black-painted fingernails, their scratched and muddy feet; not a pair of decent shoes between them.

Things no amount of Black Lace could alter, although Issa remembered for a time she'd had red boots. Who had given her those?

Then they were gone; she must have lost them, drunk or stoned, or traded them for a tiny vial of Lace.

After their show, she and Taylor were given a room in the village hotel if they had performed there; more often it was an old community center. Issa and Taylor would unfurl their old quilts and duvets and sleeping bags in a corner of a store room, or under the bleachers, to sleep. Sit outside in a weedy yard making tea in the mornings over campfires. Going without shoes, without dentistry, so they could drown themselves in that deep cherry ooze.

The critic said Issa was a genius, Taylor merely acceptable.

Oh, he couldn't have found a better way to destroy them.

Maybe, she told Taylor, he'd always wished to be an artist himself, had been sad to find his well empty of inspiration, talent. He'd had a great mind, a powerful light of a mind that had read and studied and taught, and those things paid much better than scrabbling shows together in drafty stairwells. Drunk and drugged, hoping their beautiful shiny black hair, excessively enlarged pupils, pale skin, could save the night. They were clever and darkly romantic, pretty to look at and slightly scandalous. So people came, paid them. While creating, they felt absolutely brilliant, but the muse tells that to all her servants. Keeps them working, serves her purposes: like the elves paying Issa for her peacekeeping in drops of bliss.

They could play several instruments between themselves, write a catchy tune or a sad one, threading their songs through a story. She and Taylor were so good looking that people were happy to watch them, especially if Issa kept several buttons of her black lace shirt undone and bit Taylor at timely moments, till the blood ran.

Taylor, she figured, must have a lot of scars.

The blood always looked good running down his chest.

Had she bit him till he bled in every show? Who could bite so hard? Had she filed razor tips on her canines, incisors? Had she used a tiny knife, pretending to bite, veiling the act under whirling skirts of black hair—hair dyed using the black liqueur itself? Wastefully, for there were no chemical dyes now, and of the organic dyes, only Lace gave that wonderful deep almost black red.

If she found the critic and killed him, would it bring Taylor back?

He hadn't listened when she said everyone knew the critic had lied. Instead, he had told her to go on to a brilliant solo career. "You'll be rich, you can go to a good spa to kick. You can live in an apartment in a city looking over a lake, you can have sexy office staff and lots of good clothes and nice dinner parties."

But Issa liked Taylor too much. In spite of promising themselves it was wealth and fame they wanted, Issa liked their cats and shabby clothes and wondering where they'd get the next fix. Liked waking in damp bedding beside a cold fire, liked rehearsing in draughty holes. Even liked the time a tomato hit her full in the face. She wouldn't have liked a rotten one so much, but she stuck to their road, stuck to Taylor.

The elves came, made heart trees everywhere they went. You didn't apply for a job as a keeper, it just happened.

Six months after the critic's verdict, not a jot of Black Lace between them, penniless, they finally booked a job and didn't get paid. The hall owner insisted she had no coin, but did have some young toughs equipped with old saw blades attached to axe handles. Issa and Taylor ran, hungry and cold, to the woods. Took shelter under a tree; cuddled up in damp bedding, tried to sleep. Told themselves they weren't feeling bad because they were facing withdrawal but because they were hung over, hadn't eaten, were cold, damp and broke. They sucked on one another's hair, pretending the toothsome love of it cheered them, but really, sucking the Black Lace dye kept the beasts of withdrawal at bay.

In the morning she noticed the carving in the tree.

It spoke to her of lost magic, a beauty of far greater power than anything art or drugs had offered. She hadn't noticed the house the night before. "We'll stay a day," she told Taylor. "It's beautiful. I know we'll be safe here. She wouldn't have sent her thugs after us. We'll sleep one more night. Inside."

But he would not come in.

"I'll sleep outside, in case they come back."

Next morning when she got out of bed, she picked up a mirror from the table. She'd lost weight, was alarmingly thin. Looked older, but her skin had cleared. No more dark circles under her eyes. Her fingernails and feet had healed. Her hair was brown, not cherry black.

She went outside.

No Taylor.

Had he left or been killed by thugs?

She began her work, preparing the ritual for lighting her first peace fire. Assembling the world's pain into manageable burnable packets. Burning the sage. Drinking the tea: there'd been a jar of it. Sweeping the hearth. She sat beside the first fire meditating. It was absorbing work, difficult but not impossible. She knew when it was finished. She put the fire out. She went into the cabin and slept, wondering how long she'd sleep this time. She was hungry but there was no food. The moon rose.

In the morning she woke to a knock at the door. It was a girl from the village, carrying a big bag of what smelled like food. Issa hoped it was for her. The girl smiled and gave her a packet of money. Issa wondered how much Lace it would buy; she could lure Taylor back. But she didn't want Lace. She had kicked it as she slept.

"Thank you for volunteering," said the girl. "This tree gate has been empty since it was built."

Issa nodded. She had learned it as she slept.

"The young men were forming gangs. There were two rapes, a murder. My mother said someone had to take the job but she couldn't, even though she could speak with elves."

Issa asked her in. The girl unpacked bread and cheese, milk and apples and a marinated vegetable salad. She found plates on a shelf, set them out.

"These elves," Issa asked, because she had learned the work, but nothing of actual elves, "why don't they do the peace work?"

"It has to be a human. To prove our good intent, welcoming them back."

"I see. Damn elves." It was the first time Issa said it. She looked over the young woman's shoulder, out the opened door, as if Taylor might appear.

He did not.

She heaped her plate with food and ate, famished after years of sleep. I'm just a drug addicted scenery-chewing actor. Don't make so much of me. Issa didn't say it. "Will your mother come? She sounds interesting."

"She moved away. She always wanted to act. When we were all grown up she could finally leave, go to theater school in the city. We're all very glad she finally got to do what she wanted. She raised the money for you before she left. Is it enough?"

Issa nodded. "What about the food? You can't bring food every day."

"The village is two miles, by the path I came. There's stores and a weekly market there. Will you stay?"

"I don't know." But Issa knew she would, that she was the work; that not doing the work would be like not breathing. The moment she'd entered the heart tree, everything had changed. Was the house really inside the tree? Maybe. They weren't called misty woods for nothing, after all. "I used to work in theater, self-taught. There weren't many schools then, and they were expensive." Wanting to be hospitable but with little to offer, Issa poured two cups of cold elvish tea.

"That's why he started one," the girl said. "He knew a good theater school was needed. Where people could teach and learn."

"Wh—?"

"The man you came with."

"How do you know?" Issa asked.

"He stopped in the village on his way out. He stayed here for days, then left for our village, to see if he could find someone who knew what was happening to you. My mother told him you were training to be a keeper, which was why you couldn't wake up. He didn't believe her at first. Who would? Then the elves came and said the same thing and he had to believe them because, well, they were elves. You can't help but believe elves."

"Why?" Issa asked.

"Because they're impossible magical beings," the girl said, "and if you go so far as to believe what you see is magic, you might as well believe what it says."

"Couldn't magic lie?" Issa asked.

"I don't think so," the girl said. "I don't think it can."

"When do I get to meet these elves?"

"I have no idea. I only spoke to them the once, with Taylor and mother. My mother spoke to them more often but she left. Will you leave your work to go find him?" the girl asked.

"I don't think I can," Issa said. "Just like—"

"Elves can't lie?"

"Exactly," Issa agreed. She remembered Taylor never had any confidence in his work after the critic's article. He needed more Black Lace than before, just to get on stage. Issa was loyal. She didn't pity him. She didn't stay with him to be merciful. She loved him and kept hoping he might recover. It was hard to get as much Black Lace as they needed. They became poorer, and they got older. That made it harder; it wasn't the same game at thirty as at twenty. And then, traveling through the woods from one village to another, they had come upon the heart tree.

"We were Black Lace addicts," she admitted after all.

"Black Lace, that's the worst," the girl said. "Taylor had dreadful scars. They looked like bite marks. It was so sad. I didn't know he was an addict. Is that what addicts do when they've run out—bite themselves?"

Issa caught her lip, hating the woman she'd been. "Will you fire me, now you know who I am?"

The girl shook her head. "Even the elves can't do that. You don't finish the training unless you can make a good job of things. Otherwise you wake up halfway and wander back to your old life. You just end up with more interesting dreams than most people."

"Well, I shouldn't keep you," Issa said. "Say hello to Taylor if you visit your mother in the city."

"I will." The girl took the empty food basket and bowed. Issa had been bowed to before, but this was different.

"When do I get to meet these elves?" Issa asked.

"I don't know. They're elves. You can't run their lives."

Issa watched her take the same path Taylor had left on. "I wonder if he's happy. I wonder if he misses me. I wonder if he kicked. I wonder if he kicked the critic—I mean killed him. I have no way of knowing," Issa said. "But I know I'll be good at my job."

The elves came a week later. They laughed a lot. Sometimes they were very short, and then stretched to become taller than Issa herself. They wore baggy green clothes and gave her an enormous heap of them, as well as a pair of excellent boots. The toes curled. Issa had to laugh. The elves spoke English although they explained it only sounded like English to her. They made her smoke with them out of a water pipe, some smelly mixture they explained would keep her sane and gleeful as they, even if it did smell of horse manure. "You can drink it as a tea, smoke it in a pipe, use it as a smudge, flavor your muffins with it, anything!" They said they would teach her to gather it by moonlight, following her nose.

They gave her candles shaped like yonis and penises and toadstools, as if they were the funniest things ever. Slapping their thighs and making lewd remarks. She missed Taylor's hands, his penis.

"I never slept with anyone but Taylor. And he either."

The elves stared. "How do you know?"

"Oh, I had lots of boyfriends but no sex till Taylor and none since. Stop with the dumb jokes already, you stupid elves, or I'll cry," and she pushed them out the door with her broom. They made themselves small again; it was like sweeping out live dust bunnies or mice. Risky, sweeping shrunken elves: disrespectful. They were elves after all, and quietly, slowly, healing Earth and all her people of all the harm done over the millennia, and if one day, the elves chose to stop because some stupid man or woman had insulted them, well, it would all go to wrack and ruin, like that time long ago, of which evidence remained. Buckled highways, ruined cities, dumps people spent their lives excavating.

Awful, the elves remarked when they next visited, having resumed a height like Issa's own, forgiving her manic housekeeping. Once, they told her, an even longer time ago, the Earth and the elves' world had been one; the two races lived in relative harmony. But as people became greedy, stupid, warlike, the two worlds divided like amoebas. The elf world shimmered away, its vibrations too gossamer to coexist with what on Earth, had become magnetically leaden. Humans had fallen from grace. Some missed the magic; some were glad it was gone, had, in fact, tortured its practitioners, gleefully, every chance they got when there were still living denizens of Earth who could pull it off. In time no one believed it had been real. Now the two worlds were inching together.

Most of the nastiness had left Earth at the great Change. But the elves took no chances, and built gates with elvish metaphysics, like the heart carved into the tree, set with stones.

Issa put the last fire out, drank down her tea. She had a memory then, of Taylor sleeping with the critic in exchange for Black Lace when they had no money. She remembered he'd done it often; the critic fell in love with him, asked him to leave Issa. Taylor could share the apartment hung with banners in the airy tower; every night they'd dine on the best food and wine. The critic would take him to the most expensive spas. If Taylor tired of theater he could learn to be a critic. She watched the story unfold, as if for the first time. Taylor had said no and the critic was furious; no one said no to him. He vowed to destroy them. And he couldn't have picked a cleverer way. Because even though Taylor knew the critic was being vengeful, he was still The Critic.

Had Taylor told her the truth, and she'd been too drugged to hear? Or had she learned the story in training, and it had only come to light now? Maybe the elvish tea had at last opened that memory box, a black suitcase she'd hidden in the bottom of her heart. In the end, did it make any difference at all how she'd come by the knowledge? The elves were comfortable with the concept and the reality of the multi-verse, could live no other way. They'd once said they built realities, then pocketed them for future need, under a bush or in a drawer.

Taylor had always looked noncommittal when she'd written out yet another invitation. Who had she thought their supplier was? Taylor had always come home with the stuff, reliable yet mysterious, sometimes after being away for days. She saw it then: Taylor's mouth open, the critic spooning Lace in with a little silver spoon. The critic had gotten Taylor addicted long before Issa's time. So ugly and so old; maybe beautiful young Taylor would love him back a little if he saw a little less, pleasure masking the revulsion.

"Go," the elf spoke from behind her. "Find your lover." Issa turned; it was the tall thin one who always did most of the talking, a man. He wore a conical spotted cap. He giggled a lot, but spoke seriously.

So much to regret. "I will not be able to face his scars."

"No. But you will be able to heal them. What is the point of learning how to heal the world if you cannot heal your own past?"

"But which story is true?" she asked.

"What did the tea tell you?"

"Today it told me, it told me—that Taylor and the critic were the same, except that in my case I loved Taylor back, and he could never love the critic. But is it true, or just something I saw?"

"All of your performances: were they true, or just something people saw?"

Issa looked at him, not understanding.

"Think of what you saw as a story written by the tea plant. Like all stories it is a gift, and free."

"The Lace was never free," Issa said, "although made from a plant just like the tea."

"What's the difference?" The elf took off his red spotted cone hat and turned it over in his hands, thoughtfully, waiting for an answer.

"One's an addiction, the other not."

He looked at his feet; so did Issa. The toes on his boots curled, as did her own. "The critic only lusted after Taylor, but Taylor loved you, though he sought to hold you by less than perfect means."

"But isn't that what you did with me?" Issa asked.

"It was your choice to come through the gate. Lace offers no choice, only compulsion."

"Is that what I did, go through the gate?"

"Where do you think you've been all this time, if not in our world? Such peace is not possible in yours. Although it's beginning to be, because of you, and others like you."

They'd find a replacement, they told her. Not to worry. She'd done her time. Issa said goodbye to the disappearing elves, left for the city, cat in bag. She never traveled without her cat, not even to the village. His name was still Black Lace, although he must have been the sixth or seventh cat of that name. She would not throw this one in a critic's face.

ISOLDE, SHEA, AND THE DONKEY BREA

THE RIVERS WERE NO LONGER POLLUTED WITH BLOOD. Once again it was possible to grow more than oats and spelt. The invading army had left, leaving behind only the so-called peacekeepers. There had been little resistance. We were an easily subjugated population, too afraid for our daughters to be anything else. My friend Shea and I had lost almost everyone and everything; we had huddled in our village for years. More than anything, we wanted to see something other than our own fields, our own woods, the faces of our own townsfolk again. We set out: myself, Shea, and the donkey Brea, to look for the secret library.

On the winter trail I dressed as a man and learned to lower my voice. I had been wearing men's clothes for years anyhow; they were comfortable and convenient. Even way back when my daughter was a small girl she told me the neighborhood children teased her, saying I walked like a man. Shea wore skirts; she said she was so old and ugly no soldier would bother her. For our small meals we would try and find a copse of trees in the lee of a hill, out of the wind. Here I would study Shea's profile as we ate. She had aged well, I thought, and was still extremely beautiful, no matter what she said.

I touched her shoulder beneath its felt cape. "Have you finished your dinner?"

Shea nodded and looked at the sky but she didn't answer. I patted her knee. I liked touching Shea. She was fifty-five and not forty-five as I was.

We had been looking for the library for almost a year. I knew the winter trail was wearing her down; she had recently talked of turning back. The library was a mirage, or we'd have found it by now. "Just let me sit a little longer," she said at last. I allowed myself to agree. "The wind beyond that rise is fierce. I can hear it howling. In a little while it'll die down and then we'll go on. At sunset the wind falls, almost always."

She offered me half her oatcake.

"I'm not hungry," I lied. "Give some to Brea. Look how cold she is. If she eats a little she'll be stronger." The little donkey was indeed shivering, and seemed sad.

Shea didn't know all my secrets, in spite of being the only person I had left from my life before the invasion. A patrol had killed my husband, early on. He'd been fool enough to argue with them over the life of a neighbor's son. Alone now, I was afraid even Shea would leave me if I told her the truth, and then I'd have only Brea. Spring was late. Our rations were running low; the stores at the inns were as well. If I went on without Shea, the donkey and I would have more to eat. But I didn't think I could. If I told Shea what I'd done maybe she wouldn't judge me. Maybe she'd stay instead.

At last Shea and the donkey rose. Twilight painted the sky and I thought how it was the one thing that in all the years of the occupation had remained reliably beautiful. An army, no matter what else it destroys, cannot also touch the sky. Unlike our daughters, it would always remain out of reach.

After dark the wind did indeed fall, and a plume of wood smoke became visible. We walked, and as we breached the rise we saw the source: in the hollow beyond, a small inn sat nestled amongst the rowans.

The innkeeper gave us a room with one large bed instead of two small ones and I knew my impersonation was complete; they took me for Shea's younger husband. I asked for a ground floor room so the donkey Brea could sleep with us. If they said no I'd tell Shea to stay in the room, and I would sleep on the stable floor with Brea. I'd miss Shea, but I couldn't leave Brea alone.

We sat in our room. There was a fire so we were warm enough. There was wine but no water. We didn't want to go to the common room; three peacekeepers were staying at the inn as well. After a time there was a knock at the door. The donkey brayed. Shea got up, let in a young woman carrying a tureen of lentil soup and a loaf of spelt bread. There was even a little butter for the bread, a ham bone in the soup, and a few dried greens from summer. She introduced herself as the innkeeper's daughter. Tears welled in my eyes to see a beautiful young woman. She looked at Shea and me and smiled.

"I think you are right not to come to the dining room. Your disguise is almost perfect yet I noticed. I can switch you to a room with two beds instead of one if you prefer."

"We do not prefer," Shea said. Calmly, I thought, given how peculiar we must seem.

The young woman continued to look at us. "There's something about you," she said.

"Something about you, too. Best soup I've had since before we left," I quipped. "Why is it no one knows how to cook anymore?"

"Because they have nothing to cook with, mostly," the girl said, which of course I'd already known to be true.

Shea raised her eyebrows. "Something other than two women traveling together, one pretending she is a man?"

The girl hesitated, and then said, "They poisoned our well at the beginning of the occupation."

I shook my head. I'd turned my back on all that.

But Shea nodded. "We're willing to see what we can do. We can't promise but we can try."

"I'll come at midnight. I'll take you around the stable. It's too cold for the soldiers to venture into the yard, even drunk as they'll be by then." She petted the donkey. "Sweet little thing. Are you sure she wouldn't rather sleep in the barn?"

"No. Brea stays here with us."

Wherever we went, people found it strange how inordinately attached I was to Brea. I didn't like letting her out of my sight for more than a moment. People were still poor; the orchards had not yet grown back but it was once again fairly safe to travel; the most dangerous thing on the road was not, as we were often told, small bands of thieves but the peacekeepers, and I knew even a donkey might be stolen. In the lean winters after the occupation began and there was not enough to eat for any of us my neighbors complained of me sharing my meager store of oats with Brea but I did, winter upon winter. It has been five. I have had Brea for five years now; my husband has been dead for six. I do not worry about disguising Brea. Even the invaders, callous vermin that they are, mostly wouldn't stoop to rape a little donkey.

"Very well," the innkeeper's daughter said. "I'll bring you straw for the floor so she can have a bed."

"Thank you."

"Thank you for coming. We haven't seen any wise women for years. My father and I have been hoping someone might come who could clear the well."

She seemed safe. "We're on our way to the library," I dared. "We heard we're not far."

Rumors of the library lingered on throughout the war years. Some said it was a legend only. Others said it did indeed exist, but that once people got home and unpacked the spells they'd painstakingly copied they found instead a pouch of dust or a handful of old apple cores.

The girl nodded. "I haven't been there, and neither has anyone else I've ever met, but the stories do persist, and many do say it's in this area."

The tale was told thusly: our best spells had been placed in the secret library for safekeeping lest the invaders find our scrolls and turn them to ill means for ill gain. The library was housed in a small hidden fortress on an island past the mountains, its location well protected, so that none of ill intent might find it. The most powerful magicians had all written their invocations down, even and especially those they knew only by memory, so that should they and their apprentices be killed, these magics would still exist somewhere. In this way, when the time came the invaders departed for new lands to pillage, or were by some miracle defeated, we could go to the library and relearn what had been forgotten.

The turning of sweet water into wine, or if the wine is of poor quality, the other way around. Teleportation of both people and objects. Shape-shifting, either of oneself or another.

"Or they do now," Shea said. "Perhaps it's been moved."

At the outset we'd always heard conflicting reports. And had, because of it, wandered in ever widening circles for a year. First we'd been pointed east from our village, and then south, and then west, and finally north. For some months everyone we'd asked had said north, and I, at least, was heartened.

The girl said, "It would be good if it was found." She turned and left. And came back in. Stared at Brea.

"What is it?" Shea asked. "Did you change your mind about us?" Perhaps the thought of two middle-aged women sharing one of her father's beds disturbed the girl after all.

"It isn't that," she hesitated.

"Then what is it?" I asked. Still she stared, not at us but at Brea. Finally she spoke.

"I think the donkey isn't really a donkey, just as you are not really a man." It was my turn to look at her, considering. I too looked a long time before opening my mouth. Perhaps the innkeeper's daughter knew exactly where the library was kept, and was hiding her secrets just as I was hiding mine. Perhaps we could make a trade.

"You're right," I said at last. "The donkey is actually my fifteen-year-old daughter Bree. A sorcerer turned my pretty girl into a beast. That is why we're looking for the library. We need to find the spell that can change her back."

Both Shea and the girl looked astounded, although for different reasons. "I thought they made those stories up," the girl said.

"So did I," I said, "until I saw it with my own eyes." Satisfied, the girl nodded, and left again.

Shea glared at me. I hung my head. She had a right to be angry. "I thought we'd come to know everything there is to know about one another," she said.

"We have, dear Shea," I said, reaching for her knee again. She withdrew, still miffed. "All except that."

"How come she could see it and I couldn't?" Shea asked.

"Some people were just good at telling about shape-shifting, even before," I said. Which, at least, was true.

At midnight the girl came back for us. It was hard to wait up till then; we, and especially Shea, were so very tired. I'd have let Shea sleep but the work is more powerful with two. The girl led us through a back passage to a side door and out into the yard. We passed the door to the common room; the soldiers were still awake, singing about the empire. Stupid empire. How I'd come to regret the word, a place I'd never see but that had nonetheless taken almost everything I'd ever had. We snuck into the yard. Flakes of snow drifted through the sky.

"Can I watch?" the girl asked, looking around to make sure we were alone. Her father, she'd explained, would stay inside entertaining the guests. Which really meant, he'd try and prevent them from breaking every glass in the house. They'd never had many to start with.

"I need water from the well," I said. The girl obediently lowered a tin bucket. Shea scooped out a handful of water and grimaced. We held hands and prayed.

Shea twitched and broke the circle, said, "We need a third. The poison was too strong."

"I have no power," the girl said, "it won't help."

I took one of her hands, Shea another. We closed the circle again. Everyone has power, girl. Most have just forgotten, or hidden it away. She prayed with us, standing out in the snowy yard. I worried about Brea. Had we locked the door to the room? It broke my focus and we had to begin the prayer anew. When we were finished Shea and I in turn placed our hands in the bucket of spoiled water. "You too," Shea ordered, and the girl did as she was told. At last Shea lowered the bucket back down into the well. Again we joined in a circle and prayed. A crash came from indoors. I raised my eyebrows.

"They always turn over the furniture," the girl said. "Sometimes they even break it. Then they complain we barely have any. My mother hated it. I wish," she added sadly, "she could see me now."

I didn't ask the question. For some it's their mother, for others their daughter. For me it was both. Either way, the line is broken, the result the same. The heart is broken, power abandoned. Power doesn't want to be abandoned. "Let the bucket up again," Shea said. The girl brought the bucket up. Shea cupped her hands a second time, offered the girl water. "Drink," she said.

"I'll die."

"You will not," Shea said. "The water is pure again. I can feel it. Believe me."

"If, in the morning," I said, "you wake as a spirit then you'll know we lied." Still the girl hesitated. I felt better when she laughed a little, acknowledging my attempt at a joke. It was my nerves, what with my daughter alone in our room, so close to the soldiers. I wanted the thing finished, now. I stepped forward and drank from Shea's beautiful hands. Seeing this, at last the girl drank too, and then finally it was Shea's turn.

We went back. The donkey Brea snuffled happily in her sleep, sensing our return. I wanted to fling my arms around her, cover her with wet kisses. I always felt that way, even when we'd been separated for only a few short moments.

"Don't," Shea said. "If she wakes up and brays, it'll attract attention." I knew she was right. We went to bed in our clothes, so we could save time on dressing in the morning. I threw an arm around Shea, although I knew we were both too exhausted to do anything more than sleep. Well clearing is tiring work, my mother had always complained. Still, it was a comfort to have Shea there beside me, and my daughter wheezing gently on the straw at our feet. "At least I know why you do that now," Shea said tenderly, forgiving me at last. I'd heard well clearing will have that effect; one feels affection afterwards for those with whom the work was made. Perhaps it is the gratitude of the little water spirits, infecting even human relationships, bringing us small joy even in wartime. That thought made me pause. Perhaps we ought to do more of the work, Shea and me. It would help keep us cheerful enough to go on, would help the farmers and innkeepers we met along our way. We'd never tried it before, hadn't known whether or not we'd succeed. I felt proud, and kissed Shea's silver hair. But I still didn't know what she'd meant.

"Do what?" I asked.

"Treat that donkey like a person, Isolde. Better than me almost," she grumped, kneeing me sharply, which I liked.

In the morning the girl woke us before dawn. "If your work at the well is discovered you're sure to be killed or at least imprisoned."

I nodded. It was true we were in danger. I didn't mind so much that I'd risked my life, but I felt very bad about having risked my daughter's and Shea's. The girl packed our bag with food, including, proudly, a corked flagon of sweet water. We watered Brea. She had eaten only snow for so long.

The girl didn't charge us for our room. At the door she gave us each a kiss, first on our cheeks, and then, mischievously, on the lips. Shea laughed and stroked her glossy black hair, and the girl let her.

"One question?" she begged, unlocking the back door. Dawn swirled along the horizon, or perhaps it was just more snow. She pointed out where the trampled trail exited her yard. It was visible even in the dark, between the lingering moon and the bright, bright snow. The donkey huffed little clouds. "Sweet child," the girl said, ruffling her ears. "May you find all you seek, and all you deserve."

"Of course," I said. I wanted to please the innkeeper's daughter. We were leaving after all, and I guessed we were better company than drunken soldiers, who, even if they did nothing more, probably asked her to sit on their knee while they drank and sang. Poor thing.

"Why," she asked, "did you not use your magic against them when they first came?"

"It was our magic they came to destroy," I said. "They had none themselves, hence they hated it in us." We hadn't enough magic to turn all their spears into flowers, although we tried. We hadn't enough magic to turn all their stone hearts to sweet water, although we tried. Sometimes we were successful. Just not enough. There were so many of them, and so few of us. How quickly even magic vanishes. Already many said we never had been able to do those things, which was what the invaders told us. To make us weak, they mocked our now lost or hidden skills.

When the sun rose we sat down to breakfast, first spreading out a blanket to keep our clothes dry. The girl had even wrapped a jar of hot tea in a cloth to keep it so. It was almost heaven, or at least, the best morning we'd had since long before we'd left. A good dinner, a successful well clearing, hope. Tea with breakfast. Unless you've gone without as long as we had, you can have no idea what a difference hot tea makes. Shea. I always arranged myself so I could gaze at her astonishing profile while we rested.

And then my beautiful Shea had to spoil it all by saying, "Perhaps it was never true."

"Then I'd be a fool for having shared my best oats for the last five winters when we had nothing to eat, the three of us, except for moldy spelt flour and wormy carrots," I replied, trying to make a joke of her disbelief, which wounded me.

"We could be having dried apples right now if they hadn't burned the orchards," Shea said.

"They wanted us to starve."

"Why?" she asked. "What use are we to them, starved?"

"That is the use," I said. "Our suffering is like food to them, more delicious than rabbit stewed in apples and honey."

"Please don't talk about food that good."

"I wouldn't except the girl's soup was so tasty I feel I can begin to imagine again. We best be going, Shea."

Again Shea said, "It's so beautiful just now. Look, the sky is pink."

It was, and so were Shea's cheeks, and then the insides of my daughter's furry ears. Such a color, pink.

"The snow will begin to melt if it keeps warming up," Shea went on. "Just let me sit a moment more. My knees are stiff." Even Brea began to paw the snow aside, as if she smelled the grass seedlings just below the surface, waiting to break out anew. Shea watched my donkey intently, and I began to feel my companion wasn't procrastinating at all, but drawing energy right out of the earth, storing it away, just as leaves store the energy of the sun.

It was a beautiful moment, but the occupation had taught me to be careful of too much joy. I was afraid if I relaxed too much I'd let my guard down. One must remain practical. "They're sure to come after us when they find out," I reminded Shea. "It's best we're well on our way before they wake."

"They all drank themselves stupid, didn't you hear? They'll sleep till noon. We're safe, Isolde." Shea offered me another oatcake. I took it, but I gave it to my daughter.

Shea was right; it was turning into a sunny and not another snowy morning. Soon spring would really come, and the donkey Brea would be able to graze again. Our rations would go further. Shea would stop asking to turn back. I was glad. I wanted Shea to stay with me for company but also so that Brea, when she changed back, might have someone other than me she recognized. Shea had been our small family's closest friend.

"Perhaps this donkey has always been a donkey," Shea said with unexpected bitterness, perhaps because once again, I'd prodded her out of her beloved rest. "In spite of what both you and the innkeeper's daughter say. Perhaps in your grief you saw what you wanted to see, rather than what really happened."

I stared at her, shocked. "What do you mean, Shea?"

"Perhaps they took her, and you just pretended she'd been changed into a donkey. A lesser evil."

Shea was telling me I'd gone mad with grief. And I couldn't judge her for it. "An evil sorcerer turned her into a donkey, Shea. I saw it," I insisted, which wasn't exactly true, and perhaps this was what Shea sensed when she questioned me. I gathered up our cups and remaining bread and packed them away. Walked away down the trail, my daughter trotting faithfully beside me. Hoped upon hope Shea would follow, but I was too hurt to turn and look.

I knew a woman who had killed both her daughters when the invaders were still in the next town. She had not even seen what could happen, unlike me, who had. But to her the stories were so dreadful that she thought perhaps death was a kinder fate for her girls than what would happen to them at the hands of the soldiers. I couldn't judge my neighbor, not really. In wartime one learns not to judge, never sure what one might oneself do one day. Yet I'd thought I had a better idea, a thing that like our well clearing I'd never done at the time but was willing to try.

Spring came two weeks later, and then in a year it came again. That entire year we kept traveling north, passing after a time through towns we'd never even heard the names of. We continued clearing wells and streams wherever we went. There were more fish, hence less starvation. People had sometimes heard of us now, even before we arrived. We were well fed, slowly putting back the weight we'd lost in the first years of the occupation. Even my poor daughter's ribs filled in; her coat reclaimed its glossy shine. Even a hardy little donkey wants apples and carrots sometimes, can live on moldy hay and hardened oatcakes only so long before she begins to wither.

"Remember the girl at the inn?" Shea asked me one day while we walked, "How she believed in us, Isolde?"

"She didn't believe in us at all," I reminded Shea. "She thought we were old and crazy and that we were poisoning her, but that it was worth a try. What had she to lose?"

"Only her life," Shea said.

"I drank first," I reminded her.

"Still, even that bit of belief she gave us helped to change not just her, and her water, but us. I hadn't known it would work, even though almost everyone knows those spells. Bring me flowers, Isolde, and your donkey."

She held the donkey's face. Brea, sensing something, held still as a stone in Shea's long fingered hands. Shea closed her eyes and prayed. I sensed her life draining dangerously but I also knew I wouldn't ask her to stop. She gave Brea the donkey all she'd ever had, including all the energy she'd drawn out of the earth while meditating, her eyes closed, all those mornings and evenings I'd resented her for slowing us down. Now I wondered why I'd been in such a hurry. We'd still never found the library.

Before my eyes the donkey Brea began to change. It was a slippery thing to watch, and made me feel, I must admit, a little ill. The energies swirling about the beast were so powerful they upset not just my mind but my stomach. It was like being in a storm at sea. I longed for land, and even more I longed for the turbulence to last, so that the work could complete. In spite of her stiff knees Shea crouched on the ground beneath the rowan, her eyes closed, her hand on my donkey's neck. Pea green and ice blue swirled. I vomited, again and again. Blessedly, Shea ignored me, and my donkey didn't move from beneath her magic touch.

"Should I help?" I asked when I could, remembering all the wells, but Shea, eyes still closed in concentration, shook her head almost imperceptibly. I felt bad for interrupting yet again, draining her focus. Perhaps this was a work that could only be done alone. Or else I was too ill to help. I feared for Shea. We'd had good years, in spite of everything. She'd worked hard to help me forget the grief of losing my beloved husband. But I couldn't ask her to stop, not now that little feet had appeared beneath the same green dress I'd last seen six years before.

And then my Bree stood suddenly before me, shaking her head, shaking the mist out of her eyes. I was surprised to see she was in her early twenties, and no longer fifteen, although seemingly, the dress still fit. Had she worn nothing else these past six years? It seemed in good repair. Where had my daughter passed her time, I wondered, examining her face for clues. Even when she was little, my Bree had been able to see and hear things invisible and inaudible to others. Gazing at her, my first impression was that these abilities had, if anything, intensified. She looked wiser even than before, but more importantly, quite happy. I was grateful. Sometimes the wise are burdened by sadness at all they see which others do not. I was also relieved. Who, after all, has any idea where people's souls go when they turn into cats or donkeys? My mother might've known, and a few others like her, but most of those so wise had been killed at the start, and those few who survived had taken their knowledge to the secret library and never returned. I hoped that in my mother's case it was the second, for one day she'd simply disappeared and no one could tell me where she'd gone. Still, my Bree might've returned as a madwoman, or evil, or both. It was something I knew a little about, how quickly one can change, become in one act a person unrecognizable even to oneself. Bree hugged me and I thought I might die from happiness. She laughed again, turned to my spent companion.

I felt badly; drinking Bree in like a woman who's been dying of thirst, I'd overlooked to check how poor Shea was faring.

"Greetings, Shea," Bree said. She sat down on the warm earth at Shea's side and arranged the flowers I'd picked into her silver mane, and it was only then I noticed Bree's left hand was still a hoof. "Still as beautiful as ever," she told Shea.

"I'm old and ugly, you mean. It's you who's beautiful, Bree," Shea said. "And more importantly, safe. Don't blame your mother for what she did." I sighed in new relief. Shea didn't judge me after all. But what did she mean? Don't blame me for turning Bree into a donkey without knowing how to turn her back, or don't blame me for letting Shea waste herself in this work?

I watched the hoof. It stayed a hoof. "Where have you been?" I asked Bree, politely ignoring the hoof as best I could.

"Well, part of me was a donkey, grumbling because you didn't give me enough to eat. I liked it when you scratched my ears, wished you'd done that more. It was nice sleeping in stables, all three of us, surrounded by the comforting smells of the other animals. I liked that better than when you and Shea slept in the beds and I was given the floor. Even when I had straw, the fire always went out before dawn. That's when it's coldest and I'd shiver."

"I'm sorry, Bree," I said. I stared and stared at her. Still I couldn't get enough, thought my heart might burst.

"But another part of me went to the most beautiful place," Bree continued. "I hadn't a body there, for my body was a donkey, but I still had my mind and my soul. The people there could sense me. Some could even see me, a little. They were welcoming."

At last Shea and I looked at one another. Shea had always looked young for her age, but she had suddenly turned into an old woman. A happy old woman though, immensely proud of herself.

"What a witch you turned out to be," I said.

"No regrets, Isolde," she said, and I feared again. "Promise me you'll have no regrets." She patted the ground beside Bree and I too sat beside her and buried my face in her silver hair and smelled it so I'd never forget my Shea.

"What kind of place, dearest child?" Shea asked.

Bree took one of Shea's hands and held it. I took the other. Three women making a circle. "There was an island," my daughter said, "and a castle, and in the castle the most beautiful scrolls."

"Why did you go there," I asked. "How did you find it?"

"I could feel how much you wanted it," Bree said, "and how good it would be for everyone if I went. Following this thought is how I came upon it. And also, my grandmother felt me searching, and met me halfway."

"We could have searched these mountains our whole lives and never found it," I sighed. "But that doesn't mean it doesn't exist."

"It does exist," said Bree, "for I've been studying there. But," and she waved her hand as if parting a curtain, "I think it exists there, and not here."

"It was fearsomely clever of them to do that," Shea said, "hide it there, and not here."

"I think so, beautiful Shea," Bree agreed. "I read the scrolls there one after another, for years and years, committing them all to memory."

"You good and beautiful girl," Shea said, and then she died. Bree and I sat with Shea a long time, still holding those astonishing long-fingered hands. A breeze sprang up, and rowan blossoms fell into her upturned face. It was my daughter who closed her eyes for her, for I could not; my own were too filled with tears, of both gratitude and sorrow. Shea had told me not to feel regret, but still I did, I did. For all of it.

BORDER CROSSINGS

H<small>IS KITCHEN WENT ON AND ON, THE BETTER TO HOUSE</small> endless rows of old toasters and kettles and waffle irons.

"What a long kitchen you have," she said.

"It's all done with mirrors." He cracked a small smile.

Above his head there hung a framed hand-tinted photograph of a dog. The dog was a mongrel.

"I don't remember that hanging there."

"In my worse moments I tell people it's a self-portrait," he said, fishing.

"A nice looking dog," she said.

"But still a dog."

She didn't react. Melanie didn't know she knew him when he was a dog. Or did she?

So hard to tell. Even for him.

Between the toasters ovens, the irons and waffle makers, their pale fifties hues bleaker than a city sunset fading like a badly preserved photograph, she found an electric can opener. She held it up. "Only one. That's unusual."

"It came this morning," he said. "I haven't screwed it to the wall yet."

"It looks very dangerous."

It didn't, not particularly. Still, he nodded. "It depends on how you look at it. Anyways, you only need one."

"Only need one for what?"

"For opening things."

She looked at him. It was possible that in one way she wasn't even really here. Perhaps, for instance, she was at home in her bedroom, sleeping, dreaming this moment. It was day, her curtains pulled against the glare. The television was on, although the sound was turned off. It was an old black and white, dyeing her room blue. When she woke up, would he disappear?

Or would she disappear, and his life here go on without her?

He had to keep her here, seemingly real.

"Did you bring me anything?" he asked.

"Coffee." She took a can out of her cloth bag.

"That's what the can opener is for," he said, watching her face.

She was definitely afraid of the can opener. And she didn't know why. But some part of her must know, or she wouldn't have cringed.

"Is it the coffee that wakes you up, or the can opener?" he asked.

He wished she had more guts. But she was all he had to work with. The only one who got through. Just like the other time.

He struggled with his desire to tell her everything at once. That they knew each other in another time as well, one in which he was a dog, and she a woman. Or perhaps that was also now, just somewhere else. Or perhaps it was still in the future of this same time and place in which they were both now living. In the future someone would turn him into a dog. He would be caged, tortured. Who would do it?

"Whose side are you on?" he asked, unsure, afraid he was making a terrible mistake letting her in on his secrets, bit by bit.

Except they were her secrets too. She just didn't remember. But what if she did know, and it was exactly in this way that she trapped him, by pretending she didn't know?

"There are infinite sides," she said at last. "Not only two. That makes the morality of it all a tricky question, yes?"

He knew what she said was true. Only nodded.

"I'm sorry," she said guiltily. "I'll miss my return ferry." Hastily she got up, slinging her purse over her shoulder, smoothing out the folds in her checkered skirt.

He unplugged the kettle. No coffee today. He mustn't rush her.

Somewhere, she woke up. And he fell asleep.

The blue multifaceted crystal, its infinite sides reflecting into one another forever and ever amen.

She would wake up from . . .

Was the body she fed him her real body, or a body she had only in dreams? The dream etched on her mind, irreplaceable but always changing.

The television's glare enveloping the room, its blue light interfering with her love of peace, of forgetfulness. Her love of life and rain.

The pulled curtains. She sighed and drew them back and looked into the alley. It was night. She thought about heating up yesterday's coffee on the hotplate.

She was afraid. What if it wasn't coffee at all, but something else, blue and strange and fearful? She took a test sip, wiped it hurriedly from her mouth where it clung in small soapy bubbles. That should have been the end of it but the spoons on the counter were all reflecting blue light as if the mirrored hallway had sent the television's glare all the way to the kitchen where she now stood, but how did she come to be here alone in the first place?

She wandered through the apartment looking for her bed, for the radio, for time, for her own sentience and sensibility. She needed them, their cold real gaze.

It was always like this when she woke from dreams of him, just a feeling, the same feeling she'd had as a child lying awake in bed at night, staring at the ceiling, seeing colors she was absolutely certain had never until that moment been seen by human eyes, except for the times she'd seen them with him. The colors were connected to him. She'd known it even as a child.

Tangerine. Say it.

Except it wasn't tangerine at all. That was why she looked for him every night, in the worlds between dreams.

———

The surface of his desk was patterned by looped brown rings, reminders of the last time Melanie had come. Doing his accounts he would look out into the yard, seeing little beyond the grafittied layers of exhaust left on the glass by the trucks whose engines idled outside early every morning. He never spoke to the drivers; they left his shipping sheets in a bag looped over the doorknob. The roaring of their big engines backfiring across the lawn always woke him. He'd rush to the door, wanting to leave too, take the long road out to another place and time.

He was always too late, and it didn't work that way. The trucks didn't go where he needed to go. They couldn't cross the borders between worlds.

Only Melanie could do that. And while she could come in, even she couldn't take him back out.

In his life as a dog she came more often. It was almost preferable.

He stretched out on the cot he still found room for in his overpopulated kitchen, his hand clasped around the red pencil he used to do his accounts.

Dear Melanie, he wrote, *Please come soon. I need coffee. I'm having a lot of trouble staying awake.*

He began some version of this letter every day but never finished it. He lay the blue ledger down on the tile floor beside the cot, thinking he would rest for just a few moments.

And afterwards this sensory disorientation lasted for too many long minutes.

Of course it was only coffee. She'd just let it boil over. The electric can opener screwed to the wall above the hotplate briefly terrified her before she continued rationalizing as she always did, had to, really: the room was just blue:

in the blue TV screen light.
I drew a map of Canada,
With your face sketched on it twice.

Except it wasn't Canada, where he lived. Not even remotely.

"What do you want?" she asked the dream she'd already, as always, mostly forgotten.

"Throw the seeds over the wall."

She nodded. She knew the seeds were coffee beans.

But what if she didn't need him anymore? Perhaps now she could, as she had as a child, learn to see the colors again on her own. He hadn't been there, had he, when she'd seen them on the ceiling? Her mother opening the door. "You're not asleep yet?" Even when the lights were turned off.

Maybe her mother had seen those colors too. Maybe they were visible, but not to anyone else, and their presence on her bedroom ceiling was how her mother knew she was awake. Leaking out over the doorsill into the hallways.

Tangerine. Say it.

Except it wasn't tangerine at all. Not Canada, and not tangerine.

If I meet you over and over in dreams does that mean you are somehow real? 'Cept she hadn't, or hadn't yet. Or she had, but promptly forgot. Willfully, she bet. But she missed him. She missed him as she always had. Maybe her mother had known him too. Maybe they were both the certain kind of woman that he liked. The special kind. The brave kind that could learn.

It was time to leave for work. She went to the closet and fished about for the night's costumes. The parochial school girl. The fan dancer, and her favorite, the mermaid.

This time the coffee was high quality beans in a paper bag. He was pleased, but had to find some other excuse for her to use the portal opening device. "Is it the coffee that wakes you up, or the can opener?" he asked. Looking through the smeared glass front of the pantry he saw an unopened can of condensed milk.

"Canned milk," he said, "and the opener's wall mounted now." He looked up, gaging her reaction. This time she didn't blink. "Would you mind?"

"I was hoping you'd ask." She placed the milk into the can opener, had a sudden feeling of disorientation, so strong she felt she might throw up. "Oh, boy." But she tried to be brave and turned it on.

He was kept in a large cage and threatened with torture if he didn't talk, which was difficult to do, being a dog. On the first Wednesday of every month Melanie came to visit him. She would bring him something to eat. He looked forward to first Wednesdays and groveled when she arrived.

"What is it?" he asked, in his rasping dog's voice he despised himself for, when she reached into her purse for his present. It came out half garbled, but Melanie had known him long enough to make out the words.

"My left hand," she said, unwrapping the bloody parcel.

"Thank you thank you thank you for this gift." He gobbled the meat voraciously and stared at her, his large yellow eyes luminous with greed. "Anything else?"

"Wait till next month."

And he waited. As the time passed between meals it became harder and harder to sleep. The cool blonde women walked up and down the hall, their heels clicking every day. They weren't dark like Melanie, their blondeness made him feel ill and weak. They spoke to one another about him in the third person, as if he weren't there.

"He'll give in."

"Of course he will. He'll weaken."

"He'll talk."

He chewed at his paws and stared at them with his yellow dog eyes till their hearts dropped out and fell to the cold concrete floors, quivering like fish out of water.

Except of course, they didn't really. That was just his fantasy. Like Melanie stealing the key and unlocking his cage. They'd run away, be free together, somewhere where there was a lot of grass and it smelled clean, not like puppies in formaldehyde. Were any of them his puppies?

If they did that then he could eat all of her.

"I want you to know how it feels," he told the blonde women.

"What?"

"Did you say something, pooch?"

They laughed.

First Wednesday fell next on the full moon. Melanie was distracted, never giving him her full attention, the one thing he desired. He grew impatient and snapped at her.

"When?"

She was cool then. Cool as the blonde women, ready to turn and go without even scratching him behind the ears.

He apologized, hiding his teeth and looking humble until she softened and sat down on the concrete beside his cage, getting her pretty flowered dress all dirty. She patted his nose and told him a story.

"In his dusty little office behind the loading dock he would make out and file the shipping sheets in their pale blue cloth bound ledgers. He lit his only cigarette of the day and longed for coffee."

The blonde women came by before Melanie got to the best part.

"Visiting hours are over in fifteen minutes."

What was that part?

The part where she arrived, bringing coffee.

Was that the best part?

No, the best part was the same as the best part would be now: leaving together, perhaps on one of the delivery trucks. To a grassier place that still smelled of the sea.

No, you hairy smelly fool, that's not what she's for. You could run off with any woman, or at least, any woman who would have you.

What, then?

"We have to follow the program."

"Regulations are all we have to keep the whole thing from falling apart."

You're supposed to get her to open the can.

I did. But why?

So she can see, remember.

See, remember what?

This.

And then what?

Then maybe the worlds can join. That would be the real freedom. Otherwise you'll always be running, both of you.

He was a pretty smart dog, if he said so himself. He wished his English were good enough to tell Melanie everything he was figuring out. But he had to eat before she left, or he'd die. Even the blonde women knew. They hastily clicked down the hallway, not wanting to see what they knew happened next.

"Well?"

His smallest dog voice was almost soft; it was the most polite, the most human voice he could manage.

"Well what?" She was coy.

He pretended to bite for fleas. "Oh, nothing."

"I bet you I know what it is you want."

She reached into her bag and removed a wad of balled up bloody cotton. "Would we like to unwrap it ourselves? Would we? Would we?"

Unable to contain himself, he let his huge tail crash against the bars until they were covered with a sticky mass of his hair. The bars rattled, resounding up and down the corridor.

When they had stopped vibrating she threw the parcel in. He held it with one awkward clumsy dog paw, nosing it, nibbling at it, trying to restrain himself from swallowing it whole, summoning all his self-control so that he could unwrap it and see what it was, it was, an ear?

He chewed it lovingly, his tongue curling 'round the delicate lobes, licking at the fresh red wetness of it. And then he swallowed it and was enormously happy, bouncing from the bars of his cage, bruising his dog bones in pleasure.

The lights switched off and on. Soon they'd come and usher her out. He had to hurry.

"I'm really a man," he said.

"You poor old mutt, you." She reached between the bars to scratch him.

The following month, his insomnia worsened.

After she brought a toe, he slept for a night, but only one. The next time it was her knee, and he was a little better again.

It was a bad year. They were checking papers at every station, and

Melanie didn't have security clearance. They didn't let her through, however hard she tried to disguise herself. When she wore sunglasses and loose clothing her hair gave her away. When she wore a scarf it was too turbulent a shade of violet. She was afraid and her fear made her cunning. Nothing could be proven either way and in December she had a stroke of luck. They apprehended someone at a junction, someone very much like Melanie. The suspect young woman was forced to undergo the most rigorous cross examination. They wanted to know why she was smuggling coffee.

"For my friend."

"Why?"

"He has narcolepsy. Trouble staying awake."

"Okay. We have to be careful."

"Why?"

"People sneak back and forth across the borders at night, trying to find the missing parts of themselves."

"Maybe that's what I'm doing too, only I forgot."

"There's only one way to tell."

"What's that?"

"Are you awake or dreaming?"

"How about dreaming awake?"

"Now yer gettin' smart. Too smart."

She turned out to be an informer, a double agent. As further luck would have it the same thing happened again before New Year's. The real Melanie, on the first Wednesday in January, tried again, and by then the guard was as she had hoped, relaxed and almost conspiratorial. He went so far as to wink, making oblique remarks about her good work.

And so she was through.

She caught a ride on a truck bringing old stereos to his house, the only one near the ferry dock on the bay. They kept the long sandy river road graded just for the trucks. She could see the smoke stacks and towers of the city poking little needles above the horizon. She used to live there, and work as a dancer. Not anymore.

On the way she worried.

"Why?" the driver asked, sharing his water. It was so hot and the AC was broken so he had the windows rolled down. Sand blew into her eyes. She tied the violet scarf around her hair, to stop it from matting. She was glad for her nice white sunglasses with the big frames. She felt glamorous, like the female lead in an old spy movie.

"What if it was me, that girl they caught? What if I'm actually a bad person, and really do work for their side, only even I don't know it?"

"Maybe you only think you're bad."

"Please explain."

"Maybe you forget for the same reason you make a copy of your body for him to eat, so that you can both survive."

"I haven't remembered that yet."

"So forget I said it. What I mean is, maybe you're right, and they caught a part you split off from yourself, but maybe you did it so that, if you were tortured, you wouldn't give anything away. Because the part you split off didn't know anything. And you did it to make a decoy, so that when the real you crossed, they'd think you were the double agent, and let you pass."

"What if they caught the real me, and I'm the split, the double agent?"

"Even if you're one of the split parts, you can still be good."

"How is that possible?"

"The good one is the one that wants to join with the others. It isn't always the original."

They'd arrived. She climbed out and ran round to the door while the driver parked and unloaded. She knew her lover's narcolepsy would keep him from waking till the truck was leaving. It was always the same.

She'd made it! A little disheveled, wild and fraying, the way he loved her best and this time she'd brought him . . .

Oh! It was too much to ask, it was, it was . . .

He fainted and she had to wake him. She fed him gently through the bars of the cage, morsel by superlative unimagined morsel, her left breast, and he cried. When she had gone he was even able to catch up on his sleep.

He didn't have to hear a single malicious word spoken by the horrid blonde things, and during the entire month before she returned he dreamed one long continuous dream. In his dream he was a man and lived in a house with a long slender kitchen, and Melanie would, just as in his life now, come to visit once a month. She brought him coffee and they would sit together in his kitchen and talk.

He woke only when his sensitive dog ears heard her footfalls along the corridors, wet and moody footfalls, footfalls so unlike the chilly white footfalls of the blonde women, so unlike them as to be their antithesis, dark and bloody.

She'd brought him a photograph. He was angry.

"What's this? I can't eat it." He snapped at her fingers. The blood that fell from them was the blood of a real woman, and not that of a copy. It tasted different.

"It's a photograph of the moon." With dripping fingers she tied the photograph to one of the inner bars of his cage with a strip of bandage. "I couldn't find the body," she explained. "And there's not much left."

"Then we have to hurry."

"Hurry at what?" she asked.

"What we're trying to do."

"Do you know what that is?"

They looked at one another, each afraid to say what they knew.

What if the other was a spy?

She didn't come for a long time after that and when he was sad he looked at the photograph of the moon and remembered how to howl. He thought he saw her face there, in the face of the moon.

He noticed that the white women were very angry when he howled. And he gleefully howled all the more, loudest when the moon was full. They asked him how he could know the moon was full. But he had always known when the moon was full, even if he couldn't see it, tucked away as he was on a corridor of dog cages, long and thin as his kitchen in another life.

Just as he had always known how to talk.

They laughed at him, telling him he would, like all the others, talk under torture, and then he also knew they were right, that he had been talking under torture all along, on the first Wednesday of every month.

It wasn't Melanie's fault. She didn't know the cages were all wired for sound. She didn't know that the purpose of his imprisonment was to record what he said to her. The dogs only spoke when their cross border visitors came. That was the only reason the visitors were allowed. Eventually, the dogs would give all their secrets away to their visitors. All their plans for escape, and after escape, insurrection.

And he'd thought he was such a clever, cunning dog.

As if they heard his thoughts, all the other imprisoned dogs howled.

The blue multifaceted crystal, its infinite sides reflecting into one another forever and ever amen.

She would wake up from the dream etched on her mind, irreplaceable but always changing. The drifts of sand in the kitchen were higher each time. Now she had to walk in, and it took days. The trucks no longer ran, and the ferry only made the return trip.

The drivers had always been kind to her.

She'd brought coffee each time, she didn't know why.

After half a dozen visits, she had to admit the truth to herself.

He'd been captured, and turned into a dog. They'd made him talk under torture and he had told them about this place. Then they'd crossed the border and captured him here too, and also made him talk. What would he have talked about, under interrogation?

Do it to Julia.

They'd find her, no matter which world she hid in.

She went to the pier to wait for the ferry. She'd wear the mermaid outfit to work tonight.

It was a kind of orange color.

Tangerine. Say it.

AIRPORT SHOES

IRPORTS ARE ABOUT COMING AND GOING; THEY ARE
never about being anywhere, except perhaps the bar. I paid out
a lot more cash to bartenders and ticket agents than I ever did
on rent that summer; mostly I stayed with people. When I wasn't waiting
for a flight, my yellow shoes keeping time to the Muzak, I was drinking
in other people's kitchens, or taking baths in their tubs. I chose my friends
that summer for the size of their tubs and their taste in magazines.

It's possible *friends* isn't the right word.

I'd get home and slip my shoes off, but it didn't help. Like a music box,
they played the same dance number again and again, a tune that's always
on the play list of the radio station you're listening to in a car at night;
crossing a border far away from home.

Home. I've said it twice now. I must have had one. Except I didn't. I
shared an apartment with you, but by then you scared me so bad I didn't
want to be there much. There were times I walked in the door and you'd
tell me about some flight you had to catch, someone you had to see, so
maybe you felt the same way.

But our shoes still liked the music they made together. Sometimes
they danced us to highways instead of airports.

At Niagara an orange moon hung above the river, tenuously. I thought
of men who crossed Niagara on tightrope wires, and that those men were
perhaps a little like ourselves, who had so few homes then. We had,
instead, when we weren't living in high heels and airports, a plethora of

kitchens and bathrooms, none of which were our own. At least once there were stone lions on the terraces outside, who grew white coats of snow in the moments between seagulls' house calls.

My yellow shoes were happiest flying, but they didn't really care about the method, so long as they kept moving. For instance, I took the streetcar across town the first time I visited Gregory in his High Park room at the top of the stairs.

He made me tea in the kitchen he shared with his sister. We drank it together. It was good. His evenings hung between us, empty.

"There they are," he said.

I got up from where I'd been seated on the edge of the bed to take a look. They stood, lined up in ranks on top of the second dresser. There were perhaps thirty. The mirror behind them made it appear as though there were many more.

"Can we make them go?"

"I suppose so." He seemed dubious, but his big hands moved slowly to the dresser and took the robots down, one by one. Lovingly he brushed the dust from the shiny metal bodies.

Gregory folded his big body into an uncomfortable crouch on the floor. It was a nice floor, clean and made of wood. There was a big mirror leaning up against the wall on the opposite side of the room. He pushed the 'On' buttons of the battery operated ones. He wound the keys of the windup ones. Hesitantly, the robots began their march toward the mirror. They were startled by their reflections, which they had not seen in years, and had trouble remembering their moves. Seeing the forgotten light in Gregory's eyes, they tried harder.

Don't see you, don't even write to you anymore. Was it you who encouraged me to give you my apartment? Did you do it so that, when I needed more than an acquaintance's bathtub to sleep in, it was you I'd call?

As with God or the Devil, everyone faces their customs agent entirely alone.

Unless they have robots.

I still have my first.

He only works half-days now. Robots have shorter life spans than human beings; a lack of flesh and blood causes them to tire easily at an earlier age than we do. Removing him from the shelf where he lives in happy retirement with his cohorts I, like Gregory that day, wipe the dust off his forehead and from underneath his armpits. I wind up his arms to give him a spin. He wavers; he putters; stutters, stops. I'm not half as peripatetic anymore as I was that summer, either.

He looks like a mechanical Humpty Dumpty. Egg-shaped, he wears red plastic pants to hide his knobby wheels. He is three inches high, including the revolving radar screen which protrudes from his head. His expression is disgruntled on his good days. On his bad days he personifies Doctor Doom.

I bought the little guy in an airport gift shop for $2.49. He almost made me miss my plane, but nevertheless I noticed a marked improvement in my life following the purchase. At customs desks they suddenly ignored my suspicious luggage, instead yelling, "Hey Eddie, ya gotta take a look at this!" That would never fly under the new rules.

My little guy spun and waved his arms for them, just like the Tasmanian Devil, and I was waved through instead of taken aside for questioning. I wasn't smuggling anything, but both friends and officials often wondered. "Let them wonder," I'd tell you when I saw you next, and we'd laugh.

It is almost always useful to amuse the enemy.

That sounds like something you might've said, and not an original line of mine at all.

Even if I wrote and asked, you're no more likely to remember than me. Anyway, good lines were a collaborative project, something we swapped and augmented, like good lies, like our airport shoes. Remember the ones we spray-painted gold?

Of course I went out and bought more robots.

I wore my airport shoes to visit Gregory. They were four-inch espadrilles, the straw covering the platforms in colored bands: red, orange, yellow. The leather sandal straps were yellow. When I wasn't calling them my airport shoes, I called them my sunrise shoes; I saw a lot of those that summer too. They were the most expensive thing I'd ever bought with my own money. Oddly enough, they're a style that's in fashion this summer too.

They were never all that comfortable. Maybe I drank so much to mask the pain.

I used to hide them under my pillows like an alarm clock. I didn't always want to hear that song. If I stuffed them into some alley trashcan, would I be able to stay in one place for more than a few days? Still, knowing that song is probably why I visited Gregory. It's not a thing I could do today, when both my mouth and my shoes are much smaller. But in certain parts of airports, only a big mouth and big shoes will do.

That summer we had telephones instead of addresses, and one of our homes was the long distance wires. To illustrate, when I leaf through my notebooks from then, I see they consist almost entirely of telephone numbers. Of the things I was good at, telephone numbers came second only to airports. I had almost everyone's number that summer, including yours.

And I had Gregory's. A girl who worked at Mr. Gameway's Ark on Yonge Street gave it to me when I went in looking for companions for my little friend. He'd left it, hoping to meet other robot aficionados. "He seems like a really nice guy," the girl implored.

Yonge Street. It was like a fever. I'd grown up not far away, and I was about to live there again, in sight of the clock tower. But I didn't know that yet.

Once every year or so I find myself standing outside my old apartment, searching my pocket for keys which are oddly still there. I unlock the street door and climb those stairs as though I had never left.

Gregory's room was very neat. He had a bed, a dresser, and a window with a tree. His bus driver's uniform hung from the wardrobe. On the dresser was a framed photograph of his two sons. He and his wife had been separated some years earlier. I wondered whether he had bought the first robots for his boys.

Some of Gregory's robots wouldn't go at all. Out came the oil can and the screwdriver, and Gregory worked his magic with them. I watched, suspended somewhere in the vicinity of robot heaven.

It's not a bad place to be.

Tape reels have been replaced by silicon chips, but they made better robots in the old days. They paint the gears and rivets now; in the forties they were real. Some of Gregory's robots were older than me. We got about twenty-three of them going on what little space was available between the wardrobe and his bed. Some actually shot torpedoes. Some had eyes that flashed. Some had little pretend tape reels that wound and buzzed ominously, recording, I felt, our very thoughts.

What were mine?

Where would I live?

Were you good or bad for me?

Were our shoes dancing a beautiful pas de deux or just a folie à deux? A little of each.

And Gregory's? I don't know. I was so used to men, even middle-aged men, asking me whether I was available, but Gregory did not. He seemed also, terrified that I might. He asked nothing at all about me, only whether I wanted to go shopping for robots with him at Christmas time at Mr. Gameway's. I left, promising I'd return.

Flew back to my other city.

Dawn was often coming as the club closed; once a guy from the Third Street Crew offered me a ride home on his Harley. He was a young blond kid and seemed nice enough, but, I figured when you were talking Hell's Angels, discretion was the better part of valor. Hence I declined that story, even though it would've been a good one to share with you. I asked him for his number, though.

The checker cabs were my favorites, room enough to stretch out on the vinyl for a snooze during that long haul downtown. I'd get out at Second and Seventh as the streets turned from darkness to a monochrome of greys. I wasn't twenty yet. I still enjoyed staying up all night. Sometimes I'd skip breakfast, walk alone through Alphabet City to watch the sun rise on the East River. It was a bit frightening so I didn't often go alone.

In the East Side Deli I would spread out my newspapers, scanning the headlines, the horoscope, the funnies. Dick Tracy was up to more of the same, but Gaylord's grandfather had seen the light. I would watch the sky change color, a transient blue, last night's edition of the *Times* fluttering in drainpipe eddies outside the window. I read the *Post* and the *Voice*, but mostly whatever was there. I would chat with the waitresses, the locals, the cab drivers. One of them bought me breakfast one morning, cream cheese and lox arranged on the plate in a circle, slices of red tomato and see-through cucumbers arranged in patterns that splintered behind my eyes. It tasted even better. I remember wondering why he'd bought me breakfast, and thinking that I frightened him, a little.

One morning a strange young man came in, wearing an aviator's helmet. He was slight and olive-skinned, the tatty leather jacket engulfing him like a cocoon, or a straitjacket. I watched, my eyes following him over the rim of my coffee cup. He sat down at a table diagonal to my own, muttering to himself, a long refrain, a litany of up all night. Opening his battered suitcase, he ran off a monotone inventory of the contents. I think whoever was working thought he might go off any second, but I found him interesting. His act struck me as performance rather than craziness.

His sharp black eyes moved to meet mine. "It's been a long night."

"It's morning now."

"Not quite." He paid for my coffee, introducing himself as Donny. We began walking. Bits of broken glass and bottle caps gleamed on the asphalt carpet like jewels. We decided that, together, we were brave enough to go into one of the abandoned buildings on East Sixth. From his suitcase he procured a telescoping walking stick. He poked about in the dim lobby, where a single light bulb still burned, high in the green-painted gloom.

"A flashlight would be good."

He had one, of course. It even worked. Curved staircases ran off to either side, a shadow of Busby Berkeley gone by. I could almost see the chorus lines of junkies come dancing down. This was before crack.

"Are you afraid?"

"I have my stick." He shook it violently. I laughed; the chorus line missed its cue.

We peered in the window of an inhabited dwelling, saw a kettle puffing on the stove. The porch was freshly painted in bright reds and blues, cosmos overflowing a sagging picket fence. The house was a tiny one-storied affair, yet obviously loved and looked after. And on either side the dark holes of windows, the garbage, the ashes, the grey. I wondered who could live amongst the burnt out abandoned low-rise tenements, exactly as if normal life had never ended. The little house belonged to an alien, obviously.

He was a Gypsy, he said. His mother lived on Long Island. He stayed there sometimes. He lived two streets over in an abandoned tenement, with his friend. They had fixed it up quite nicely, furniture and everything.

Poking in a heap of rubble, he bent to pick something out. A white plastic rose. Removing one of the pins that held his jacket together, he pinned it to my collar. "There," he said, "an American Beauty for an American Beauty."

"I'm Canadian."

"I tell you, it's magic."

"I know, I know," I said. "You don't have to tell me."

Everything was magic.

I bent to pick up a card that lay face down in the gutter. "Look," I said, "it's the three of hearts. You know what card that is?"

If he was really a Gypsy, I thought he ought to know tarot and be able to transpose from one deck to another. Although, for all I knew, Roma didn't tell fortunes from tarot at all, as my aunt and I did, but from regular playing cards.

He nodded. "You keep it. I've got lots."

"Okay." I thought of me and you and your friend Joan, all together as we'd so rarely been. Three women dancing, wine cups held aloft. The three Graces, and, I would learn later, the triple Goddess. It's Joan and I, of the three of us, who remained friends. At the time I was jealous of her, wanted you all to myself.

At the river, the sun was already high in the sky. We leaned on the breakwater together.

"Well, I guess we missed the sunrise," Donny said.

"It doesn't matter," I said. "It's still magic."

Donny the Gypsy, the river wind blowing his hair. I'd put an emoticon here if this was email, so you'd know I'm being tongue-in-cheek, a little.

We watched the greased water swell and recede. Seagulls dove for dead minnows. Across the water, the smokestacks puked purple. It was a morning made in heaven. "Now what shall we do?" he asked. I noticed his eyes were green.

"I have to go home and sleep," I said. "I've been working all night."

"Where do you work?"

"I'm a dancer in a club off Forty-Second street."

He opened his suitcase and laughed. "Let's throw it all overboard!"

"You don't want it?"

"I don't need any of it anymore," Donny said, setting his walking stick aside and surreptitiously tucking the flashlight into his jacket pocket. The first to go was a moth-eaten feather boa. It struggled like a duck in an oil slick. In went the bottles of Evening in Paris. "You don't want them?" he asked me.

"God, no." In they went. Plchunk splutter gurgle sunk.

Next came the decks of cards, blowing like leaves on a fall day, black and red. The polyester shirts went gratefully, glad to be back in their own petroleum element. The combs hopped like skipping stones. The semi-clad ladies on the covers of paperback thrillers smirked crazily into the sun. Single torn pages blew up the river like kites.

"Upward mobility," Donny said.

"Yes," I agreed.

"Have you ever gone?"

"Where?"

"Into the back room?"

"Once. I went with a beautiful young Brazilian guy. When the waitress opened the curtains of the booth to bring our champagne, she grinned like I was the luckiest girl in the world, giving my Brazilian the once-over. It was kind of sweet."

"Everyone's had sex with people they don't really like. Take someone home from a party when you're lonely and bored. Why is it worse if you get paid?"

"We didn't do anything. We drank and talked."

The last to go was the suitcase itself. It made a firecracker crash and listed down toward the harbor, the wreck of a pirate's galleon. We laughed and laughed.

"When you take money you're crossing a line," Donny suggested. "You end up burying a lot of rage."

"How do you know?"

"I just do. You sure you have to go sleep?"

I looked at him. "Yeah."

"Okay," he said. "I'll go visit my mother."

"Don't you turn here?" I asked as we passed Tenth Street, on our way back to civilization.

"I'm going to the train station."

"Oh. Do excuse me for having forgotten already." I took him for a bit of a bullshitter, and was ribbing him for it in a friendly sort of way. But maybe it was all true: living in a squat, being Roma, visiting his mom on Long Island. What I didn't say was that it was one of the best spontaneous dates I'd ever been on. It was a kind of game I played semi-regularly, but most didn't understand the rules. Donny implicitly got the whole point, which was to create a fairytale, to write a short story by living it. You follow the woods path to a clearing, you meet a stranger there, you wander together, battling dragons and finding mysterious objects of magical power. Who were the monsters, though?

I guess we were surrounded by them. The young always are.

"That's all right. When will I see you again?"

"You will."

"But what if?"

"Listen, it's inevitable."

We parted ways, kissing one another on the cheek.

I went home and slept and didn't quite forget him. I ran into him once more, at a party in the West Village a couple of months later, so I ended up being right about that part. We didn't exchange contact info that time either, and after that I really never saw him again. I've wondered, at times, why I didn't look for him.

Why do I still wonder? As though I could still touch that time. Touch him, as I didn't, beyond our goodbye kiss. But perhaps it is best to let some of the magic ones slip off. As it was, I got to keep that odd, lovely morning forever, something held back in my pocket for rainy days.

Spring turned to summer. On my flight north I went through my book, looking for Gregory's number.

Some of Gregory's robots had screens as breastplates. As the big robots marched across the Martian terrains of their imaginations, alien space-craft fled across their chests, somewhere south of Jupiter. These were Gregory's prized Video Robots, he explained, although of course it wasn't real video at all.

"How do the screens work?"

"I never thought about that."

I had to figure it out. Whipping out my notebook, I made little diagrams of drums on which were pasted Buck Rogers-type space war scenarios. The drums revolved behind lenses. They had to be lenses, I explained, because the space craft shrank and distorted as they neared the perimeters of the screens.

Gregory nodded politely. I got the feeling he couldn't have cared less. "How many robots do you have?"

I was ashamed to tell him I had only half a dozen, all new, made in Hong Kong. He didn't seem to mind. I told him his robots ought to be exhibited, photographed. I could make a short documentary film about Gregory and his robots. A cup of tea. Pictures of the wife and kids, or maybe just the kids. His TTC uniform hanging on the hook behind his door. Forget film and do it on a Portapak. Here was a man whose mind and collection stretched the span between Buck Rogers and *Star Wars*, between Robbie The Robot and R2-D2, with Apollo Eleven somewhere in-between.

Another polite nod, noncommittal.

We couldn't do the moon shots now, I read recently. The guys at NASA who knew how have all retired, and they didn't pass the information on. It's all stored on obsolete hard drives, in languages no one understands anymore.

"Why don't we form a club together?" Gregory asked.

I pictured me and Gregory sitting in his apartment, placing ads in collector's magazines, dialing their phone numbers. And once we had our club, then what? Would we take minutes?

"I'm out of town a lot," I said, looking at my yellow shoes, thinking of airports, you. Maybe the tea had been more weak than good after all.

"You're going away?"

"I live in New York, sort of."

Gregory looked worried for me.

"But you should do it, Gregory, you really should. The club idea."

"Um."

"You have the most wonderful robot collection I've ever seen."

"Next time you come, I'll have the other ones working."

Gregory accompanied me down the stairs, and at the door we shook hands gravely, thanking one another yet again.

On the street the summer sun fell through the leaves. A plane screamed toward Malton. That was before they changed the name to Pearson International. I wondered if it were mine.

I knew this time I'd stayed so long I'd missed my plane back to the big Apple, to you.

New York, New York. So nice you've got to say it twice.

CBGB. The Grassroots on St. Mark's place. Patti Smith at The Village Gate in a neck brace from her fall. Reading, not playing, although incanting is a better word. I got too drunk too fast and had to leave before her show was over.

Those were some of the good parts.

After leaving Gregory's I took the streetcar back downtown, ran into my friend Al in The Black Bull. He told me he was leaving his cheap, excellently located Yonge Street apartment, I could have it. I told him about Gregory. It was a good story, Al said. I felt a little bad about that, as if I'd collected Gregory as a tale to earn me free beer, without any intention of giving him anything in return.

But I didn't know that yet.

I didn't know I wouldn't buy any more robots, ever. Didn't know I was daunted, had caught a glimpse of how many years and dollars it would take to build up a collection that would never equal his.

"I travel in my mind," Al said, in response to my telling him what I'd been up to.

How many years did Al have left? Five? Ten?

When I had the apartment, Gregory called me a few times, but I never called him back. We never went shopping for robots at Christmas, even though by then I lived across the street from Mr. Gameway's. Maybe that was all I'd really wanted. It must have been a great place, or I wouldn't keep going back there, my pockets jingling with keys I've kept for decades, keys that still turn in those locks.

We used to travel to the moon in our minds, like Al. Then, for a brief period of time, we were able to cart our bodies along. Now we're back to the old methods.

I see the clock tower first, then the railway bridge. I unlock the street door and climb those stairs as though I had never left. Sometimes there's people living there. They look at me oddly, but they don't say anything. Maybe they don't really see me, as I'm only visiting in dreams.

Is it only my dreams I'm visiting in, or theirs too? I have little worries on these dream trips. Do I owe years of back rent? Whose bedroom do I get? Where will they sleep instead?

Am I going back to get something I left behind, or to bring something to the me who lived there, finally moving permanently back from New York? Or are both of these questions actually the same question?

I used to find those fruitful lines of thought, but now I don't.

We don't know how to go to the moon anymore, but I know how to get to my old apartment. That's what counts. I think I left a filing cabinet there, with good stories still in it, like this one.

I want them back now.

The other day at a garage sale I saw a *Battlestar Galactica* torpedo launcher. I thought of Gregory for the first time in years and smiled, bought the toy for fifteen cents. Gregory. His robots kept me so entranced I stayed in town, ran into Al, didn't go back to the wicked city.

Thanks for the apartment, Gregory. I still have the keys, even though they only work in dreams anymore. I keep them on a shelf in a locked room, beside a white plastic rose, the three of hearts, a little wind-up robot, and a pair of yellow platforms.

This is the year I took the shoes out, blew the dust off them. Wound the keys in their backs, tried them on.

They still fit and they still play a traveling song about luck and love and magic.

As to you? Maybe I'll solicit your email on the grapevine, send you the link to this story.

Vaya con dios, sister.

THE THINGS IN THE BOX

H<small>E HAD ENORMOUS BLACK LEATHER BOOTS, WHICH HE'D</small> procured out of the Salvation Army box on Adelaide Street when no one was watching. He talked her into coming along one night. She did, but she worried, looking up and down the street, hoping no one she knew would see them. He fished out a satin quilt, handmade, each vertical stripe a different shining hue. It was very well sewn and had only one tiny coffee stain. She refused it at first, for she knew what agreeing to take it home would mean. She could never again complain about the growing stack of stereo receivers, now on the sidewalk beside the box, in the morning due to arrive at the store belonging to his friend Grey who knew exactly where Fred got these things, and, like Fred, thought it perfectly acceptable. Fred was not his name. That was the Anglicized version he chose. His real name no one could pronounce, let alone spell.

"The things in the Salvation Army box ought to go to the Salvation Army, where they'll be sold to fund dinner programs for winos," she said.

"I don't care about those people." This was possibly more honest than she could stomach, even if it obviously reflected most people's feelings about the old men.

"Fred!"

"What I took was a drop in the bucket." Objectively speaking, this was also true. "It isn't theft. The things in the box don't belong to anyone, not really. They did once, and they will again, but not quite yet."

The quilt would be warm. It was beautiful. She dropped it off at the dry cleaner's in the morning on the way to work, resenting him for being able to sleep in when they'd spent the entire night sitting in a speakeasy or making mad love or dashes back and forth from his room to the big red Salvation Army drop-off bin, staggering under the weight of tuners and amplifiers. She'd been the work shirking traveling sort herself once, but more recently she'd been buckling down as a graphic designer. Her boss and his friends were smug sorts, driving around in leased BMWs, talking on the phone all day. They were half brain dead from too much coke, but they had, for a little while at least, enough money to make sure no one noticed. No wonder she liked Fred. She was at heart a romantic idealistic sort.

It began late one afternoon in Grey's store. All three were seated in comfortable Victorian parlor chairs, drinking tea from a flowered porcelain service, the price tag hanging from the teapot's handle. Fred passed Grey a watch he'd procured from the Salvation Army box. It was a nineteenth century pocket watch, real silver and not plate. Grey passed it from one hand to the other, as if weighing it. He liked to touch the things he bought and sold. He named a price and Fred said it was too low. She was grateful; the watch, it was suddenly obvious, was her soul. It was so obvious, in fact, that she wondered how she'd missed it up until now.

Suddenly, and without prior notification, she also knew Grey was the devil. His face altered, seeming to reveal his true features which waited just beneath. The utter wickedness of these heretofore hidden features was, in fact, sickening. She stared, unable to remove her gaze, her heart pounding. Told herself her imagination was overheating in reaction to too many deadline filled days at work following sleepless nights at the speakeasy.

Just as quickly Grey was thankfully only Grey again, winking as if now they shared a secret of some magnitude. Why had he done that? She wished terribly that he hadn't. Fred and Grey continued to bicker over the price of the watch. Name too low a price and she'd belong to the devil, which was, given the wickedness that had once again smirkingly revealed itself, quite an alarming thought. She looked at the watch, she looked at Grey, she looked at Fred, whose face, as she looked, rearranged itself into one of shocking, shining beauty. Was he God? Was he Jesus? What did that make her? Being a woman, it stood to reason she must be Mary, but if so, which one? She continued to examine Jesus and the Devil's faces, as well as the face of the watch itself, where the seconds sped by with terrifying rapidity. She hoped desperately that, on one or more of these faces, she might find a clue as to how the transaction might turn out, to which of these two men she'd belong. What happened next surprised her. Jesus was staring at her. "Get up," he said, standing up himself. When Jesus asks you to stand up, you stand. Relief flooded through her. Surely he'd won. She watched carefully. The devil had not given her soul back. Which meant he still had it.

"Give the watch back," she said.

"Why?" the devil asked, a little too maliciously, she thought.

"He won."

"Won what?" Everyone knew Jesus had saved Mary Magdalene, the Mary she in all likelihood was. She opened her mouth, ready to explain, but Jesus took her by the elbow, tugged her, almost roughly, out the street door. He seemed angry.

"I'll come by tomorrow," he told the devil meaningfully. It wasn't over, not at all. She sickened. It was night and snowing outside.

"What's going on?" she asked.

"I was going to ask you that."

"Why?"

"You were acting so strange in there, the look on your face."

"I thought you were Jesus and Grey was the devil." Telling Fred this, she had to admit it sounded a little ludicrous.

"You did?" He stared at her. "Seriously?"

"Yes." He seemed quite alarmed. They were crossing the street. She was glad he still had her elbow, because of the traffic. She didn't have the judgment for traffic right now, she knew that.

"You're crazy," he said.

"I am?"

"If you really thought that," he said, as if waiting for her to admit it was some kind of bizarre joke. But it wasn't, she didn't. And now she was even more scared than she'd been before. If she'd really thought what she'd thought, seen what she'd seen, then she was crazy, exactly as Fred had said. She wasn't sure just then of which she ought to be more terrified; the devil coming into permanent possession of her soul, or being schizophrenic. Which was a worse verdict? She knew that as a choice, it sucked. She watched Fred carefully. What if he, like the devil before him, had just resumed his human cover? She thought of the loony bin, where she'd visited a friend in the past. It had been full of shufflers and mumblers, every one of them sad, decked on pharmaceuticals and madness. A lot of them had talked about Jesus and the Devil. By sheer force of will, she made a third choice. They were almost at her door. She opened it with a key. She could manage that. They walked up the two flights of dirty stairs, Fred in the rear, as if afraid she'd make a run for it. In her big front room, a combination of studio and living room, Fred closed the curtains against the streetlight's glare, the whirling snow. He put on a record of old folk songs and went down the hall to make more tea. In his absence the song's lyrics seemed momentous, portentous.

Oh, Jack was every inch a sailor, Five and twenty years a whaler; Jack was every inch a sailor, he was born upon the bright blue sea.

Songs and stories with water in them scared her. The people in them often came to bad ends. She was afraid the song would turn out to be about someone she knew, possibly even her own drownable self. Fred came back and took her by the arms. "Stop it," he said. She was able to. He read aloud to her, from "The Big Mirror," by Mohammed Mrabet. This time it was she who asked him to stop. The Moroccan story was so creepy she was almost convinced it was about what was happening to the two of them. Blood and hair and mirrors. Of course. It was all so obvious.

"A drink might help," she said.

"You have those seasick eyes again," Fred said. "We'll go to the speakeasy."

"I can't go out. And if you went, you'd be gone too long. Knock on Samantha's door, downstairs. She always has scotch."

"She'll want to visit."

"Tell her she can't, I'll explain later."

He came back with half a bottle of Johnnie Walker Red. They drank and listened to old records. Even the record player was from the box. Eventually they went to sleep.

She went to work the next day. She worked hard and left early, took the streetcar back to their neighborhood. Went to Fred's room. He came downstairs; they walked the block back to her place, which was a whole apartment, and not just a mousy room above a hardware store. Around four in the afternoon it began again.

"We were taught that black was bad and white was good, but that isn't the case," he said, looking up from his reading which today was "Beyond Good and Evil," by Jean-Paul Sartre. What he said made so much sense it was enough to cause her to slip easily back across the divide. This time he wasn't Jesus. This time there was a black place across the iron curtain where he was from.

Across the iron curtain there was a piece of glass
when Mary went to sit down
She hurt her little—
Ask me no more questions
I'll tell you no more lies . . .

Mary again. In a place where white shed light on black and black shed dark on light there were shadows that had a life of their own. They would detach themselves from their owners and float away and do whatever they wanted to do. Their owners would run after them and try to catch them and reattach them but it didn't work. The shadows were too strong. They'd pull themselves away and run off laughing. You knew they were laughing because of the sound. A world that was as dark again as black is to white. Can you imagine such a dark? And from that world, only their laughter reached her. Or a white smile.

"I just want to sit with scissors and cut out the moon. I want to paint the moon, and I don't mean painting a picture of it, but painting the actual moon the way you might a room. The moon is smiling. I want to glue the moon down," she told Fred. He nodded, smiling too. He approved of art, all it was capable of, both for the maker and the viewer.

Brought her, alongside tea and scotch: paper, scissors, glue, the moon. This time she'd keep it to herself, not tell him she knew. She'd learn more by pretending not to notice. But she couldn't help herself. After an hour of cutting and gluing, she broke their silence.

"Your country terrifies me because it has no name." Even in real life his passport said he was stateless. He'd explained why, once. She couldn't quite remember, or he hadn't told her the entire story. Maybe he'd done something bad in Europe. He nodded and smiled, went back to his reading. Later he made an enormous pot of real goulash with mounds of sweet paprika. Meat. Blood. Hair. Mirrors. She ate it anyway.

Before they went to sleep under the astonishingly beautiful striped quilt he turned to her and said, "You will go to the black side two more times." She was shocked, but hopeful. Usually he pretended there was nothing strange going on, other than her being a little nuts.

"I'm always afraid I won't be able to get back," she said.

"I've got white tickets." You got back from the black place to the white place with a white ticket. Of course.

"Why didn't you give me a white ticket before? I could've used one at Grey's store."

"I made you leave with me. Once you were outside you knew who I was, who you were. What was that if not a white ticket?"

"Give me one now."

"I'll sell it to you," he snickered. She was angry because he loved her, or so he said. He should've given her a ticket, not sold it, because of that. He reached under the covers and into the pocket of his shirt which he'd worn to bed because of the cold that swept through the single paned windows in defiance of the quilt.

"Will it be permanent?" she asked, watching his hand carefully, which she hoped would open to reveal her ticket back to sanity. It was the silver watch.

"That is up to you," he said firmly, giving and not selling it to her after all. She felt ill, but she knew it was true. Make the third choice and only viable one, where all is real in its own way. Learn to step from one to the other, when it's called for. They went to sleep.

In the morning she went to work at the design place. She tried hard not to fuck up, and she didn't. Her boss took her out for lunch to a nice restaurant. He liked her, she knew, more than a little. He didn't understand why she was with Fred. How could a deadbeat compare to sole meunière and goblets of white wine and free coke? She hated coke, but her boss didn't know that. "He reads books from Black Sparrow Press," she said. It was the best she could do. The rest of it would just get her incarcerated, she knew that now. Better not to tell. She was fine during the day, then when she got home it would start again, a little after Fred arrived.

When Jack grew up to be a man he went to the Labrador,
he fished in Indian Harbor
where his father fished before;
On his returning in the fog he met a heavy gale,
And Jack was swept into the sea and swallowed by a whale.

Perhaps that was her problem too. Was Fred a whale? The scissors and papers and glue helped. They gave her something to do with her hands while it was happening. So did the tea and the scotch and the old folk songs on vinyl and the goulash, which ran out after three days. Grey's store wasn't doing much business and so he wasn't buying many of the things Fred found in the box, hence Fred was broke. He hated asking her for money; he knew she worked hard. Instead, he walked up to Kensington Market and came home with an entire flat of eggs for two dollars. The eggs had feathers and dirt on them.

"There's nothing wrong with feathers and dirt," he said a little contemptuously when she pointed this out. Probably his mother had kept chickens. Probably every egg of his childhood had been embellished by feathers and dirt. Probably to Fred, that was just the way eggs came.

Feathers to fly on, dirt to eat. Really, it was worthy of Mrabet. They ate eggs every night for a week. Fred was good at eggs. He made them a lot of different ways.

Oh, the whale went straight for Baffin Bay, 'bout ninety knots an hour,
And every time he'd blow a spray he'd send it in a shower;
Oh, now, says Jack unto himself, I must see what he's about,
He caught the whale all by the tail and turned him inside out.

Indeed. Maybe it wasn't Fred who was the whale, but she.

———————

A month later it had finally stopped. Without it, she no longer found Fred interesting. He wanted them to discuss the Bowleses and Jean-Paul Sartre in speakeasies at four in the morning, but she didn't like the people he wanted them to be friends with; some of them used needles, which she didn't like, whether or not they read literature. Fred even began remarking about her nondescript, comfortable wardrobe, asking her to wear short black things from the Salvation Army box instead. A black leather mini-coat and a white opera scarf. Not only did it seem a little obvious, the black and white part reminded her too much of the tickets.

He could tell she was bored. If it wasn't going to work out he would leave, Fred said, for a trip around the world. She agreed this would be best. Still, she began to wonder whether maybe it had only happened to her, and not to him. Before he left she asked Fred and he sighed. "It's better for you this way," he said.

Fred called from Japan, three months later. She was still working at the graphic design company, but she'd enrolled in a night class in English at the university, where she could ace her assignments even in her sleep. She'd already read everything they wanted her to read, some of it twice. Her life made more pragmatic sense but felt dull compared to how it had been with them. Sometimes, she had to admit, she wanted only to sit with those terrifying things he'd shown her and play with them forever. Paper. Glue. Scissors. String. Paint. Moons. Tickets to hell. White return tickets if she was lucky. But he was right, it was better this way. Quieter.

"The only place worth falling is in love, and that at least we did do," he said. Briefly. Strangely. She nodded, knowing he couldn't hear that. "What I remember is how our knees were always wet," he said. She thought: *Don't forget the buckets. Awash in sea foam, sperm, kelp. Green and brown things, fecund, rotten. Smelling of salt and elopement. How we ran away together, you and I. We ran and we ran and we ran and we ran, buckets sloshing. There were little phosphorescent sea creatures in the buckets. As they sloshed. This is how we found our way. At the party they'd make fun of us, ask why our knees were wet. Or maybe they envied us.*

"What are you doing?" she asked at last. She didn't think he could hear her thoughts, or, if so, only a little.

"I have a young Japanese girlfriend. She's from a wealthy family. Very spoiled. Next month I'll go to Java. Also, I'm reading the most amazing books." Amazing books she was always interested in.

"What?"

"Black Sparrow Press. I bought them all. "The Big Mirror" by Mohammed Mrabet. You have to read it."

"But we read that to each other."

"We did?" Maybe it had happened to him too, just in a different way. "Did you ever get a new passport?"

"No." Still stateless. She knew she'd never hear from him again. She still has letters and poems from him in a box. It's not the original box, though, wherein she found the rainbowed quilt she still sleeps beneath. Before he hung up, he said, "The things in the box don't belong to anyone, not really. They did once, and they will again, but for a brief moment, they're just there." *And we found them. Of all the luck.* She keeps her soul on her wrist now, where it belongs. She is more careful of it than she was before she knew him.

EVEN THE MIRROR

ONCE AGAIN, I HAD DREAMED WE WERE THERE together. I spent a month, walking the streets of Montmartre, missing you as always. But the next time you made a dream appearance it was in New York; we met on the steps of the Museum of Modern Art. Together we looked at Rousseau's Sleeping Gypsy.

I crossed the big pond. I waited on the museum steps for a very long time. Eventually I went inside and looked at the painting alone.

Fall is a beautiful time to be in New York, to look at all those famous works by Matisse, Derain, Cezanne, Picasso, Klimt. No matter how often we see them reproduced, to stand before them in the flesh is another thing altogether. It inspires an awe of the sublime that's sometimes physical. I know a painting speaks to me if the fine hairs on my arms rise. Because of the dream, this time when it happened I thought it was because you were near. I ran back to the Rousseau. I waited for you to appear in the flesh, which as ever you did not.

Perhaps, in your dream, it had been a different painting.

In my next dream you were in San Francisco. It only came back to me as I visited with the gatekeeper lions of the library and later, as I rifled through the treasures at the Strand Bookshop. The first snow in New York is so beautiful but I've always preferred Christmas in California. I booked a flight.

The same day of my arrival I hurried up the steps of Coit Tower but before I arrived at the top you'd already disappeared, taking some other path only you knew down to the street. Or you'd never been there at all. I went inside and looked at the murals as we had done together in the dream.

I had crossed the Atlantic but even as I followed my dreams of us together from city to city I remained in the north. All those cold northern cities, the darkness around them like hands to a throat. They are always the same in their way, the summers so brief one is never without fear of the cold.

The dreams in which you and I were together were slowly being replaced by ones in which I watched you and Tullis walk hand in hand along the Berlin canals. I did not know her name in the dreams; I only watched, always on the other side of a busy roadway, and even when I was able to get close, neither of you seemed to see me. Or maybe you did, but it didn't matter that I was there.

The years and cities and transatlantic flights; they all passed. I inherited money I hadn't been expecting and bought an ancient little house in Berlin but rented it out, only keeping a tiny attic room for myself. Mainly it was filled with books I'd never found the time to read. When I passed through I'd pick them up, wonderingly. Most of them I couldn't remember ever even having bought.

I met Tullis on the subway once. When I think of this, it seems almost impossible.

I'd seen her face in dreams so often, yet she was no one I'd ever met. I'd never met you either. It seems very strange for there to be two people in my life I only know from dreams, but so it is.

Was it on the Paris Metro or was it in New York that I met Tullis? Why do I forget such a thing? Too many cities and years, too many underground trains, but such a momentous meeting; you'd think I'd remember.

Maybe I didn't want to remember.

I'd dreamed her so often I recognized her at once. She had pale red hair and pale eyes. She was maybe thirty, a few years younger than you and me.

"Any luck?" I asked.

"I'm Tullis," she said, and shook her head. "No, no luck yet. Will you keep looking?" she asked.

"Years ago I bought a house we lived in together once. In Berlin."
She blinked when I said Berlin, but she didn't say anything.
"I travel too much to spend much time there," I continued.
Tullis shook my hand. Her gloves were leather, and green.
Her train came.

Maybe she had found you, but didn't want to tell me. Why else would you continue to appear together in my dreams?

I must have appeared in her dreams too, for us even to have had our conversation. If she'd taken my hand and shaken it, she must have recognized me. But what if she just thought I was a once-liked co-worker, a distant, almost forgotten cousin? Our talk was so short I may yet have misinterpreted its meaning.

Why, of the two of you, should it be she I met in the flesh?

I continued to dream of you together. So often on subways. In New York, in London, Toronto, Paris. Nowadays I can tell the subways of cities apart, even in dreams.

It is her blink I follow now, like the truth I belatedly recognize it for being. I should have done it years ago. I bought that Berlin house for a reason. There was a time when the dreams of us together there followed one upon the other like light emitting dominoes. I should never have left, following years of your dream appearances back and forth across the water.

I would go to Berlin. I would tell my tenants it was time to leave and I would stay. This time it would be I who was the magnet, and not you. Surely this was what you had wanted from the very beginning, had only been waiting half our lifetimes for me to understand the obvious. Yes, you have aged in my dreams.

I met Tullis a week after my arrival in Germany, again on the subway. I reached my hand out and she took it immediately, shaking it firmly, a warm smile on her face.

"Coffee?" I asked.

"Cognac," she replied.

We went to Schwartzes Café, on Kantstrasse. Every time I return to Berlin, I go there almost immediately, just to see if it is still there. In these days of the internet it would be easy to find out in advance, but I never do. Sometimes I liked to pretend I live in a world where such things don't exist. They make things too easy, and in another way, too hard. They make it too hard to access the other kind of magic. The real kind. They erase it.

I must not allow this to happen. If it is erased, I might lose you, and we've never even met.

"Do you know him?" I asked once our drinks had arrived.

"Of course I know him," she said. "Just as you do. But—" She shook her head. She didn't smile. "Not in this life."

"Do you look for him?" I asked.

"I used to," she said. "But now I think if it's meant to be, we'd cross paths. If he is alive in this time, and he wanted to, he'd know how to find me. He of all people. What do you do?"

I repeated what I'd told her the first time we'd met. "Years ago I bought a very old house here we lived in together once, or so my dreams told me. I recognized it immediately, just as today and that other time years ago, I recognized you."

"I remember it very well," she said. "It was in New York. You showed me a book you'd bought at The Strand."

"Funny, I don't remember that part at all. What was the book?"

She waved her gloved hand dismissively, as if that was of no consequence. "For years I too dreamt we were in Berlin together," she told me, "so I came here as often as work and family allowed. But—"

"Not anymore?" I asked.

"The dreams stopped," she said. "But I still come." She shrugged. "I can't really help it."

"Do you ever dream of me?" I asked.

"Of course."

We finished our drinks. I tried to order another but she said she had to go. I walked her back to the subway, descended the stairs with her to wait on the platform. I didn't want to let her go. She was the closest I'd ever come.

I wanted to know if she ever dreamt of me alone with you, but I didn't ask.

Tullis shook my hand. This time her leather gloves were blue. Or was it purple? Why can't I remember? Maybe if it really was important the Color would come to me, and I weigh an irrelevance with meaning it doesn't actually contain.

"Best of luck," she said again. I wondered if she remembered that was what she'd said by way of goodbye years before.

Again I wondered why I thought it important.

Her train came. I've never seen her since.

There is a tarot card for this feeling or an esoteric diagram. Or maybe just a memory of a note scribbled on the back of an envelope full of dried flowers, found in an old occult text, purchased on a whim at the Strand. Taken to Berlin on a flight and left unopened in an attic. The handwritten note, by an anonymous author, contains much more in the way of useful information than the entire worm eaten tome.

Alas, the note is lost.

The one that explains which of the countless dreams and signs have true importance, and which do not. Without the note we wander dreams and cities and years, always still lost to one another.

I wash the curtains. Years of neglectful tenants have left them yellow.

How often have I come to Berlin, searching room after room of this old house for you? Glimpsing you on a train, only to have you skimmer away, an apparition, a fragment of dream held by the waking eye. Was it real? Were you there?

One opens the door to a passageway in one's heart and closes another. Sometimes I don't think I can stand another minute of it, this fear of losing you, you whom I have not ever even found, never really even begun to. Sometimes I glimpse your face in the moment before I enter a room and my own appears in the mirror frame. That may be the only reason I bought this house, so I could spend an entire life visiting it, to glance at your face on a few scant occasions.

We are always the same age, growing up together, feeling a bond that surpasses any in waking life. Why is this richness only available in dreams? Why can it not be transposed to waking life? And, obsessed with you as I am, have I forgotten there might yet be another in this life who could make me feel as you do?

Even the mirror loves you so much it cannot let you go.

You always look the same. I, too, must wear always this same face in your dreams, the one that looks out at me from the mirror.

I left Rome where I had gone to search for you and went back to Paris.

HARVESTING THE MOON

USUALLY SHE WOULD WAIT UP FOR ME AND GIVE ME FIRST a washcloth for my scarlet face and bloody knees and then mullein tea and a bowl of lentil squash soup. Before we went to bed my mother would always ask, "Did you remember to share?"

"Yes," I'd say, but I was often lying. I usually skipped offering any of my moonberry harvest to my mirror friend when I passed her on my way into the house at first light. I remember well its happy little smile the few times I did.

"Just one berry, maybe two," my mother implored.

"I'm so tired," I said. "Could you do it?"

"It will eat from my hand but it metabolizes more of its food if it eats from yours."

"So tired."

My mother took a small handful of berries from my pail leaking on the kitchen floor.

"Put them back!" I shrieked.

She'd tried to be so quiet but nevertheless I'd turned and seen her on my way to the stairs that wound from the kitchen to the upper bedrooms. The truth is I was saving money from the sale of my berry harvests to go away to teacher's college, and wanted the saving to go more quickly than it was. My mother hadn't enough to send me, although she too squirreled away some of what little she made in those days toward my tuition. I intended to train as a teacher so I could help in her old age, which as far

as I could see was just around the corner. I never told her that was why I
was hoarding my harvest.

It's my mother's hands I remember when I think of her, scarred and
knotty from carving rudders out of young heaven trees all her adult life.
Maybe she carved so much because she didn't have a woman friend to
spend time with. The other mothers didn't let their children harvest the
moon, and especially not their daughters. The rain barrels by their doors
were mainly empty. I think she was hated for that sometimes. It seemed
like most people preferred to forget their families too had once had little
spirits living by their doors.

"When I was growing up everyone had a rain barrel in which they
could check for their reflection as they went in and out. We should never
mistreat our mirror spirits," my mother told me. Often when she spoke
she stroked her hands as if to stroke away the scars where her carving
knife had slipped. "They love us and they love their work. If we mistreat
them it will break their hearts and they wouldn't be able to give any
more, and would return to the rivers rather than die."

I remember my brother saying, "My friend's family says the spirits
aren't real. They say people have the rain barrels just as decoration. It's
just a story, like Santa Claus."

It's funny how clearly he speaks in my memory.

"In one way you're just a story, like Santa Claus. That doesn't make
you any less real," my mother told him. She always had an unusual way
with words, our mother. She'd say something so strange you'd puzzle it
over for days wondering what she'd actually meant. When I think back I
understand that listening to her is part of what made my brother such a
good poet.

And so we went on, tolerated if considered a little odd by the neighbors. They'd look away when they came over to return a tool if our yellow
spirits were on the surface of the barrel that day, somersaulting through
the water, using their flat beaver-like tails as launchers. Our friends
would pretend the little spirits were invisible, and maybe they were right.

"Without getting to know their mirrors, the elders used to say, children would grow up weak," my mother would explain for the hundredth
time. "Without this skill, they said, we might even make war on a neigh-

boring village, not knowing that all their animosity was in fact but a reflection of a part of ourselves."

My brother and I rolled our eyes at her for keeping to the mainly abandoned old ways but secretly we liked it that we still had not just a rain barrel by our door but little fat spirits playing in them when so few other people did.

My brother's mirror spirit was a gentle soul. Sometimes it gave him a new poem, passing it up out of the water like a scrap of blue soggy paper. It never minded if he signed his name and so while still a child he already had some renown, and much was made of the poet he would one day become. But my mirror friend told me I would find my joy if I climbed the cliffs at midnight and so I climbed, my knees ragged by morning, my face equally red from the moonberries I'd compulsively munched.

My mother worried. She knew if she told me not to go I'd just sneak out the window once she lost the battle with her exhaustion. She also knew how much I needed my wild rambles. That wasn't really the part that had her so fretful.

She went out to the rain barrel. All three of our friends were up on the surface, playing catch-my-tail. Frisky as baby otters, they were so caught up they barely noticed her. It had rained the night before. There is nothing like fresh rain in their barrels to bring the elusive little spirits up from the bottom where they like to lurk, playing with our secrets as though they were a deck of cards, in a game only they know the rules to.

At last she took her friend by the tail, making it squeal. It blinked its eyes at her in consternation. She handed it a little piece of cheese. Mirror spirits will eat just about anything, but it must be offered by its human friend. This was how she knew I'd been neglecting mine: both her spirit and my brother's were round and jolly, but mine was shriveling and pale, barely yellow at all anymore. It tended to be the loser at catch-my-tail because of this, which it disliked. Luckily for me, or unluckily if you think of it another way, this was on most days unnoticeable, as the three sat together at the bottom concocting fates and destinies for us which they altered as quickly as they'd invented them.

"One day your Fates will fix for good," my mother said. Interminably, I might add.

"How do we make sure the right Fate adheres?" my brother often asked.

It was me she usually glared at. "Feeding your spirit now and again helps more than a little."

I wonder now why neither of us ever asked her whether her Fate had adhered yet, and if so, whether she felt it was the right one. I suppose it's because we were self-involved as young people often are, and need to be, for their own sakes, at least a little.

After the cheese my mother's spirit focused on her. It bobbed up and down, its little yellow hands spread out, palms up, offering its services.

"What should I do?" my mother asked plaintively. "My daughter doesn't feed her friend from the berry harvest, and yet I know I cannot keep her home on full moon nights, and it is her mirror friend who asks her to go, so I know it's important, terribly so. When she doesn't feed her spirit I concoct punishments to which she acquiesces without complaint. She has no wish for clothes or pretty things or to go out to the dances. She minds neither cooking nor cleaning."

When she had finished my mother's mirror friend thought for awhile before it said, "So few know us anymore, and when the last friendship is broken, the world will come to an end." It slapped its bright yellow tail for emphasis. "We will share our food with your daughter's spirit as long as we can."

And then all three caught one another's tails in their mouths all at once and plummeted to the bottom to retrieve their deck of metaphysical cards and play a few more rounds of Fate.

Of course the cards were notional. Or perhaps they were laminated. I've always wanted to see the images but the spirits are fiercely protective of them. Mirror friends offer advice and useful reflections of us but they guard their card hoard jealously. Perhaps they fear that if we saw a hand they played, one of our many possible Fates, we might become hypnotized, magnetized, adhere to a Fate which was not after all the one we were supposed to fix to, the one which would benefit us and our communities the most.

Based on her friend's advice which indeed confirmed her own intuition my mother always let me go. Of course she felt terribly guilty when

I didn't feed my ailing little spirit upon my return, saving every last berry beyond the ones I'd eaten for strength and night-vision on the descending trail to sell in the Saturday markets. Of course it wasn't her fault she earned so little. No one bought her rudders, even though they were so good. They didn't buy her rudders because she let me climb the cliffs alone at midnight, and because only I of all the village still harvested the berries, which properly prepared are a cure for most any ailment. They bought my berries even while they scorned her. A study of how envy can destroy has been very useful to me in the intervening years.

She is an elder now. I missed the ceremony, traveling. I know if I get home, her bare feet will still smell like summer. I know in spite of her wisdom my mother feared change, and that it was I who taught her change must be embraced. I wonder whether she will ever forgive me. She writes that her new rudders never go off course no matter how fierce the storm, and that their price has risen accordingly. Is it only when we have learned to forgive ourselves, she asks, that our work can be recognized for what it is? The truth is, she tells me, her rudders are much the same as ever. I remember well how she was pitied and ignored in the most ramshackle corner of the Saturday market, while my berry booth was always right in the center, along the main aisle from the entrance. Among other things, her letter made me wonder what my work will even be.

My brother wasn't a man yet when I left with a circus. They were happy to have me because of my nimbleness that before them, only he and the sea cliffs knew. I lived and trained and traveled with them until I tired of them, or they of me, and since then I have lived mainly on one farm or another, trading my labor for room and board. When I tell people I used to harvest moonberries they mainly don't believe me, for gatherers are rare and becoming more so and mainly well to do because of it. The berries are still the best cure for the scarier things. Medicine has advanced largely to compensate for their growing scarcity.

Given enough time, wounds can heal or at least scar over, as my mother's hands attest. Now it is my skin that is covered with storms instead of my soul. I have tattoos of lightning, tsunamis, hurricanes, floods and storm clouds. One day, I tell myself, I will earn a tattoo of a peaceful lake, or of the sun glancing down on a field of flowers.

"Better strong pictures than no reflections at all," my mother used to say. She said that's what would've happened if the mirror friends had died of their love for us, floating belly up in rain barrels by our front steps, shaded by sweet cicely and Syrian rue and comfrey grown tall and leggy from all the spillover. So depleted they couldn't even make it back to the rivers and the sea. At least, she wrote me once, this was not my spirit's fate. I wondered whether that meant she had forgiven me, and then remembered what she'd said about self-forgiveness being the more powerful tonic.

It was a stormy moon. I'd begged to go in spite of the rising winds. My mother asked my brother to go with me. I'd be giddy with the combination of my monthly risking of the sea cliffs, the pull of the full moon, the glutinous feast of berries which ripen only beneath its light. It is also true that I always managed astonishing nimbleness in spite of these things. Yes, I'd return home with gashes on my ankles, but I'd always return, and with my berry bucket unspilled.

I told them it wasn't necessary and that he was an uncoordinated poetic sort but she begged him with her eyes and so he agreed but not before telling me calmly that I was nuts.

"Did I already say I was saving money to go away to school?" I replied. "Reverence doesn't pay rent."

"Reverence?" he asked, lacing his boots tightly beneath the window. The moon was so bright my mother had turned the lamps down to save on the electricity that we, like most people, made at home when the cliff streams ran past as now, it being late summer, they did not. We were all waiting for the first storm so we could have lights again and also wished it would not be tonight.

"I had hoped I wouldn't have to point out that poets are generally penniless if revered for their eloquence," I said, tying my hat firmly beneath my stubborn little chin.

Moon shadows dancing in triplicate, the mother goats screaming for their wild children to come home and take shelter, the out of nowhere storm whipping branches against one another and the sea below against its rocks and me and my brother on our knees, but he grasped the slender trunk of heaven with one hand and mine with the other while I held fast to my skidding bucket, setting it aright just before it tipped. After that we clambered to the west side of the trunk, wrapping our legs around it for stability while we waited for the next gust and the one after, and after that the respite I knew would come, having done this often, in which we could begin our way back down.

I leaned my head against the tree to gather wits and breath. The tree whispered to me that my mother would like it, could use it. Almost but not quite a hundred years old, it was only barely young enough, but it could still keep someone safe if she and not a lesser craftsman carved it.

It had just kept me safe, hadn't it?

I didn't answer, the tree so much like my brother.

Some days now it occurs to me that my mother's rudders weren't so incredible because of her craftsmanship, which was only a little better than average, but caused by something her hands leaked out when they carved, something that leaked from her hands into the fine cured wood of heaven. Of course it takes two to create a rudder that never goes off course, no matter how fierce the storm: the tree is no less important than the carver. Just as to cure a dreadful illness requires not just a moonberry but a gatherer.

I ate three berries to regain my strength, just three, that was all it took. I sucked blood from my knees to wash it down.

I forgot to share.

He did not mean to fall.

And neither did I.

We let go of our protective tree and began the return journey. Was it the moon or the wind or my angry mirror spirit who let loose a stone that precipitated a rockslide, small enough to be sure, but perilous in the by now lathering rain and the still whipping wind which tugged at the tree now too far behind us to offer hope? I saw there was a second a scant arm's reach ahead, although lightning split and now dead.

My brother threw himself below me on the dry stream's rapidly filling wash where I'd lost my footing; his body stopped mine long enough for me to grab the splintered root and regain my ground but he lost his grip on loosening stones below me. Watching him tumble I understood my mother was right, that even then or perhaps then most of all, he was a story telling itself in the most beautiful possible way. I also had the ridiculous thought that now at last the water wheels would turn again, and that she would be so pleased to have the electricity she'd missed the whole long dry summer.

Why are heaven trees called heaven trees? They are small, partly because wind whipped on a nightly basis, but so strongly and deeply rooted even on the stony footing of the trail that their reach to heaven is more powerful because of it.

What goes down must also come up.

He did not perish, no. At least not like that.

If there was a spirit in the rain barrel, or a stream close by the house where I'd planned to stay, I'd travel on, no matter how much farther the next tavern, how cold the storm. It wasn't enough I no longer knew my own mirror; I couldn't bear to be near anyone else who knew theirs either. It seems so long ago now. That young girl, that family, that mirror friend I left behind. What have my years taught me, if anything?

Cold steel at the throat, both given and received. An ocean of spirits, the bottled kind. An ice land of waiting, and one of remorse. Beneath it, still hiding, the pain of a child, gone too young and too long gone. If I'd looked into water I might have seen not my spirit but my memory of its yellow smile and so I didn't. I wouldn't ever even look into my tea mug or my tavern wine goblet.

Always and always and always away from you.

"It is good to know them," my mother always said, "good they still show us ourselves, even if sometimes the picture is too strong and it drowns. It happens so rarely it is barely worth troubling over."

But sometimes, instead, it drowns someone we love.

No, not like that.

No rocks pierced his skull or shattered his bones, no riptides pulled him beyond the surf so far out to sea he could never return.

Our mother says the strange things she says, but I say, "What is love but another mirror of all we are?"

He fell for me.

I fell from grace.

My mother is too old for the cliff trail. And even when she was younger, she was never as sure footed as me. My mother was only good at things to do with the sea. Carving rudders. Playing with her mirror spirit. Sea witch! Sea bitch! How they reviled her for that.

Now they know better. It is her mirror spirit, after all, who taught her how to make the best rudders. Now the others wish they too had trained as long as she. For what is playing with one's mirror friend but training for all that is?

It's the berry gathering I miss the most, if I'm truthful. The raging profundity of it.

My mother wrote me that the price of berries has gone up as the skill is further lost. The few who gather now might still go on the full moon, but they go in daylight, afraid of the windy night trail. If there are elders in the market, the gatherers sell their harvest shamefacedly, but sell it they still can, for none after me dared what I used to dare. If I went home and resumed my childhood trade I could easily sell the berries for an exorbitant price. I could buy a fine coat and a finer horse. I could buy a proper house in town to replace my mother's seaside shack and one in a country far away for me. I picture a tower far from the sea, in a country where the rain barrels were all halved long ago and planted with white geraniums and purple petunias, side by each. I could buy rich gifts for a lover who promises me love eternal. I could believe her when she does, at least for a while.

My mother and I still write. My brother, she says, waves from beneath the surf below the cliff while my mirror friend plays with storm petrels. It tries to teach my brother how. It left its rain barrel that night and followed us but kept to the swimming trail at the foot of the cliffs and not the trail for two and four-footed high above. I've often wondered, as I drank either alone or amongst strangers, why I didn't sense it following us that night. Perhaps it disguised its presence, both hungry and angry as it was.

Angry and hungry it still knew my brother and me better than we knew ourselves. It even knew my mother better than she knew herself.

My mirror spirit caught him. It saved his life and then it stole him. They still live in the sea below that trail to the north. He misses the sandpipers in the delta. He misses poetry. And his friend? Always a quiet sort, she doesn't say much.

Now the rain barrel by the door at home houses only my mother's and my brother's spirits. They no longer smile when my mother goes in and out. They don't even surface and make a little wave. Instead they lie at the bottom, eyes closed, curled tightly around one another.

Or so she writes. She isn't angry, she says. Just tired. Just telling me how things are. She knows she was overprotective and everything happened because of that, partly.

I remember praying as one knee after the other lost its skin, that the sky clear, the wind die, that we make it back down, even without my bucket of berries.

But I always made it home with my bucket unspilled, even that last time I returned alone.

My mother refused to sell that harvest, and refused to let me either, until I told her I'd use it to buy a horse and go away. Even added to my savings it would not be enough for teacher's school.

"Why not a boat?" she asked, still my mother in spite of everything. "I'll make you a rudder."

"You can't go up the trail for wood. Heaven trees grow only on the trail, as you know."

"At least the decent ones," she agreed. "But your brother will go as he always did to cut me a tree. In daylight when the moon is new." She gave me a glance of some scorn as if it were after all my fault that my mirror friend was so wild she sent me berrying for magic up the moonlight trail.

I looked at her. Had she gone mad? Maybe she thought my spirit would let him go in a day or two and that our lives could go on as before.

But I knew my mirror friend better than my mother did. Nothing if not tenacious.

"You know he can't do that anymore."

She lowered her eyes in shame.

"And anyways, even if you made me your best rudder ever, I wouldn't go in a boat."

"You could carry the rudder in your saddlebags," she joked.

I didn't laugh. "I'll never travel by water again, even though no rocks pierced his skull or shattered his bones. My mirror friend prevented all these things from happening. It saved his life and then it took him below. As you know."

Now the berries are worth more than salt or silver ever were. I could return to my village and gather again, throw the entire bucket over the cliff at full moon, at high tide.

My mirror friend has always been good at catching things.

It would gorge, mashing the berries into its mouth, spilling them wastefully into the froth. At last satiated, the second half it would feed my brother, one after another.

In one way they'd be the same berries I should've fed him that night. The ones I should've fed my friend all along. At moonfull not just their monetary but their medicinal value is at its peak. Form follows function. With each berry chewed and swallowed he'd grow lighter, able after years to breathe air again. And with the last, he'd reach the shore, feet planted firmly on the ground.

My mirror friend would miss his kindness, but still she'd let my brother go so he could yet grow up to be the poet he was fated to be. She'd do it for me.

I hear the circus I traveled west with is heading east again. If I practiced with them nightly, and performed along the way, my nimbleness might yet be good enough even for the trail which I fear I shall be too old for after one last climb and one last tattoo. I have been away even longer than I think, and I think it's been very, very long. As to my mother: her rudders now sell for a price as high as any of my un-spilled berry buckets ever did or will and her retirement is no concern of anyone's, least of all mine, for she says she will happily carve till the day she dies, and that she prefers her sea shack to something fancier, although a new generator would be nice. It is strange how I sometimes feel I have become older than she. Perhaps if I too become a mother I can grow younger again, younger and older all at once. Perhaps I will ask my mirror if it is so. For what in the end is love but another mirror of all we are?

ACKNOWLEDGEMENTS

The author gratefully wishes to acknowledge the support of The Canada Council for the Arts and the Ontario Arts Council during the writing of some of these stories.

She wishes to thank the editors of the publications in which these stories previously appeared, including but perhaps not limited to: John Clute, Peter Crowther, John Cullen, C.J. Dorsey, Nick Gevers, Gavin J. Grant, Susan Marie Groppie, Jed Hartman, D.F. Lewis, Kelly Link, Susan MacGregor, Sally McBride, Maryanne Mohanraj, Steve Mohn, Derryl Murphy, Cat Rambo, Jena Snyder, Dale Sproule, Paul Tremblay, Gerry Truscott, Jeff VanderMeer, Sean Wallace and Diane Walton. Folks who have read and commented on various drafts include, where memory permits, Doug Back, Anita Buerhle, Sherry Entus, Jan Thornhill, Alister Sutherland and the late Norbert Fortener.

The author also wishes to thank her publishers Peter and Nicky Crowther, and her editor, Nick Gevers, for their interest and enthusiasm. She wishes to thank cover artist Francois Thisdale for his lyrical evocative work, and Candas Jane Dorsey for her fabulous eloquent introduction.

The stories in the volume have previous appeared in the following publications:

"The Water Man" in *Tesseracts* 3, ed. Candas Jane Dorsey and Gerry Truscott, 1990; "Version City" in *Senary* 1, ed. Derryl Murphy, 1992; "Telepathic Fish" in *Leviathan 1: Into the Grey*, ed. Jeff VanderMeer, 1996; "Bugtown" in *Transversions*, Volume 2, # 2, Winter 1996/97. Illustrated by the author; "Once" in *On Spec*, 1997; "Repair" in *On Spec*, 1997; "Stones", in *Divine Realms*, ed. Susan MacGregor, 1998; "Rice Lake" in *Tesseracts 8*, ed. Candas Jane Dorsey and John Clute, 1999; "Gone With the Sea" in *Tesseracts 8*, ed. Candas Jane Dorsey and John Clute, 1999; "Sewing Forgetfulness" in *Clean Sheets*, Winter 1999/2000; "Late for Dinner" in *Strange Horizons*, January 2001; "Holy Mackerels" in *Deep Outside SFFH*, February 2002; "A River Garden" in *Land/Space*, ed. Candas Jane Dorsey and Judy McCroskey, 2003; "In Dreams We Remember" in *Lady Churchill's Rosebud Wristlet* #12, June 2003; "Black Lace" in *On Spec*, Fall 2004; "Isolde, Shea, and the Donkey Brea" in *Strange Horizons*, December 2006; "Border Crossings" in *Bandersnatch*, ed. Sean Wallace and Paul Tremblay, 2007; "Airport Shoes" in *Strange Horizons*, December 2007; "The Things in the Box" in *Fantasy Magazine*, August 2008; "Even the Mirror" in *Nemonymous Ten: Null Immortalis*, ed. D.F. Lewis, 2010; "Harvesting the Moon" in *The Company He Keeps: Postscripts* 22/23, ed. Peter Crowther and Nick Gevers, 2010.